Brendan Behan:

"Rabbi Cohen is a man of ideals, having the idiotic notion that he should speak out against injustice wherever he sees it ... the whole book is the battle of David Cohen with the forces of darkness, both in and out of the Air Force ... a funny book ... wonderful"

George Burns:

"All I can tell you is I read the book, I loved every paragraph of it and I think it's great."

Taylor Caldwell:

"Delightful, touching and charming! Thank you!"

"Every once in a while a novelist comes along who can make you laugh loudly or think seriously. Herbert Tarr is one. . . . He has written a novel which is at once a sensitive, compelling human drama and a light, almost rollicking narrative ... has 'best seller' written all over it"

Buffalo Courier-Express

AVON BOOKS
A division of
The Hearst Corporation
959 Eighth Avenue
New York, N. Y. 10019

Copyright © 1963 by Herbert Tarr

Published by arrangement with
Bernard Geis Associates.

Printed in U.S.A.

Avon Edition
First printing, April, 1964
Sixth printing, April, 1965

FOR MY PARENTS

who wanted their son to be a doctor

THE
CONVERSION
OF
CHAPLAIN COHEN

Chapter : 1

DAVID COHEN, who had lived all his life in New York City, was so provincial that when, after an hour of milling around with some two hundred other unclothed males undergoing a physical examination for the Army, his eyes told him that he was the only Jew in the huge room, all of a sudden he *felt* naked. And all he held in his hand was a three-by-five-inch index card.

David's hand sprang to the hat on his head which he had been unable to check with the rest of his clothing. Reason reigned, however, and the hand dropped, empty, to his side as he shifted uncomfortably from one foot to the other, cleared his throat, shrugged his bare appurtenances, and turned sideways. Yet wherever he looked among the smorgasbord of males—tall ones, short ones, skinny ones, round ones, muscular ones, flabby ones, dark ones, light ones—he could see only further corroboration of his singularity. Lifting his eyes upward, he fiddled self-consciously with his navel as he glanced around the drafty room.

Many of the goose-fleshed men there—from the Little Italy section of New York, it appeared from the looks of them—had darker hair and deeper-set eyes than David's, swarthier complexions, fuller lips, more prominent noses; some even wore glasses, which he did not. Yet it seemed to him now that only he possessed the maximum combination of facial features which people usually labeled as Jewish. His hair was charcoal brown and curly; his eyes chestnut and deep-set in olive drab skin under heavy black brows; his nose prominent enough to have impelled him once to fall in love with a high school classmate simply because her name was Roxanne; his lips full and usually poised upon a smile.

But today no smile lurked behind David's lips, for he had found himself in a surprising circumstance. This was the first time in his life that it had been borne home to him in so graphic a fashion that he was indeed a member of a minority group.

During his seventeen years of religious education, time and again his study of Jewish history had impressed upon him the fact that the Jews were the tiniest of minorities—less than three per cent of a nation of one hundred and eighty million Americans, a scant .004 per cent of the world's population of three billion. But this realization had always been an intellectual one. For in school and outside, on many of the streets of Brooklyn, on the buses and subways, most of the people David saw, certainly nearly all the people he knew, were Jews. Sabbaths and holidays could not have been observed more scrupulously in Israel than they were in his neighborhood, whose nickname was Little Jerusalem. In fact, even the anti-Semites that he knew were Jewish.

Yet here now in 39 Whitehall Street David stood out as unique and alone—*so* unique that he alone was aware *how* unique. If only the card were eight by ten . . . *halvai!*

David could not help smiling. Now he was beginning to think like his Tante Dvorah who punctuated most of her remarks with a blessing, a prayer, or a *halvai*. "If only you're 4-F!" she had exclaimed that morning as he was leaving their apartment behind the fruit store. *"Halvai!* Of course, I don't mean the doctors should find anything fatal with you, God forbid."

Uncle Asher had entered a dissenting opinion. "Dvorah, you're crazy."

"I'm crazy?" Tante Dvorah had inquired.

Uncle Asher had responded tolerantly, "Of course, you're crazy."

"Nu, so I'm crazy."

"The best thing in the world would be for Duvid to go into the Army right now."

10

"Why? Tell me," Tante Dvorah had demanded.

Why, David himself had wanted to know.

"Because the Army will take Duvid out of Brooklyn, and the Army will also take him away from you—a double-header—that's why."

Tante Dvorah, pouring her husband his morning glass of coffee, had sniffed, "Fifteen cents on the subway can do the same thing. And the subway doesn't take two years either."

David had intervened. "There are a good many posts outside of New York, Uncle Asher. I don't have to stay here in Brooklyn."

Placing a lump of sugar on his tongue, Uncle Asher had sighed. "Duvid, I'm just afraid that going from Brooklyn and your Tante Dvorah to the outside world so all of a sudden, you might come up with a bad case of the bends. Two years in the Army will be a good—how do you call it?—decompression chamber."

"The bends?" Tante Dvorah had interjected. "Do you think they would give Duvid a 4-F if he came down with some of them?"

David himself sympathized with the viewpoints of *both* his foster parents. For loving his country as much as all other patriotic Americans, he also assumed it was one of his inalienable American rights to escape Selective Service. Sadly, his only legitimate chance of doing so, failing his physical exam, was a frail one; he had reached adulthood hale and healthy, with nary a bodily scar, a fractured bone or even, despite Roxanne, a cleft heart. Repeated nasal hemorrhages were his sole medical affliction. But they could not have been too serious, unfortunately, because he had continued both to bleed and to flourish at the same time. Still, when those nasal blood vessels hemorrhaged, all that gushing bright red blood might yet influence some impressionable young doctor to brand David unkosher for the Army—at least that had been one of Tante Dvorah's *halvais* for the day.

"So remember, Duvid, when you get to the nose doctor," she had coached him that morning, "*bleed*. Bleed all over him till he hollers 4-F."

"Dvorah," Uncle Asher had said between sips of coffee and sucks of sugar, "you're a regular momism."

Tante Dvorah had bridled. "So if Duvid's nose which bleeds all the time anyway forgets to bleed today at Whitehall, what's wrong with him giving maybe a little scratch? Your father and my father did worse things in the Old Country to get out of going to the Army. Why do you think they left Russia in the first place if it wasn't to rescue you and Duvid's father and my brothers from the Army?"

"Dvorah, I've got a great big surprise for you," Uncle Asher had replied. "Are you ready for a shock? Well, here it is: Believe it or not, things are different now. This is America."

"So what am I, a subversive or something, just because I don't want our Duvid to go into the Army? I can tell you stories how plenty other mothers dodged their sons out of the Draft."

"Mothers," Uncle Asher had remarked. "I think all mothers should leave home when their children turn eighteen."

"Tell me you feel different than me about Duvid. Go ahead, tell me."

"Dvorah, America is Duvid's country as well as our own. Isn't it only right that—"

"So who's talking about right?" Tante Dvorah had turned her broad, sweatered back on her husband and, raising her moon face toward the cracked ceiling, had addressed heaven. "I'm talking about what I feel in my heart, and he starts singing me the Star-Spangled Banner. Next thing, he'll be drinking his coffee out of a *cup!*" She had turned back then to score a point. "Besides, how can Duvid find himself a nice Jewish girl in the Army? Tell me that, Mr. America. The Army'll take him and stick him some place in Kalamazoo where there's no Jews. So how's he going to get married then? You expect maybe to parcel post him a Jewish girl, like a

12

salami? Am I a Communist just because I want to see a little *nachus* from Duvid already?"

Uncle Asher had taken Tante Dvorah's chapped hands in his own chapped ones. "There's another good reason for Duvid to go into the service. It's a selfish reason, Dvorah, so maybe it'll appeal to you. In the Army, at long last, Duvid will get to see the *world*."

Tante Dvorah had pulled her hands free, the better to punctuate her indignant exclamation. "So where's Duvid been living all these years—on the *moon?*" And she had pointed an outraged thumb at the sun shining in through the kitchen window.

"Maybe not the moon, but not the world either. Brooklyn." Uncle Asher had shrugged his wiry frame. "And Brooklyn is Brooklyn. Here all the time all he sees is the same old things he sees all the time anyway —the same old people, the same old neighborhood, the same old ideas, our same old fruit store, even the same old fruit flies. He might as well be living in a little *shtetl* back in Russia. *Or* on the moon. Or in a *suburb*. Why, the best thing in the world for Duvid right now would be to . . ."

"Turn your head sideways and cough."

David, his thoughts arrested by feeling strange fingers digging into his groin, jumped back, startled. "I beg your pardon!"

The fingers followed after him. "I asked you to cough." The portly examining doctor looked up and took David's card. "Say, aren't you—"

David, left with nothing to hide behind, interrupted. "Yes, I'm Jewish," he said self-consciously, then forced a cough. "Now can I have my card back?"

"Sure, your name is Cohen," said the doctor as he returned the card to David who didn't quite know what to do with it because it was too small. "I wasn't sure at first, but didn't you go to college with my son Dick— Dick Anders? You were the class valedictorian, I remember."

David stopped fiddling with his card. "That's right."

13

"I *thought* I recognized you," said the doctor, "but without clothes—"

"And how is Dick doing?" David asked.

The doctor's thick features lit up with *nachus*. "Oh, fine, fine. Dick's got a good job as a chemist. He's married now with a baby on the way and the Army *out* of the way. He finished his two years last June. That's why at first I didn't think you were Dick's classmate. You must be as old as Dick—twenty-four. And you're just going into the Army now?"

David emitted a sigh which set his torso quivering from his sternum to his coccyx. "Yes."

"How come it took the Draft Board so long to get you?"

David shifted from one foot to the other. "Well, you see, I'm not being drafted now. I'm enlisting, you see."

"Enlisting? Did you say enlisting?"

David grunted with embarrassment, for to him enlisting in the Army was comparable to trying to break into jail.

"Say, Doc," called someone on line behind David, "are you going to play with your friend here all day long?"

"I'd better move along," David said, and moved ahead. "My regards to Dick," he called back. Then, as he waited for the next doctor to burrow into another part of his anatomical landscape, he remembered that he knew no Dick Anders. If only he could have lived out his days as ignorant of 39 Whitehall Street and its parade of humans, like livestock at a show—*halvai!*

Yet here he was shuffling through the military maw that gobbled up civilians and spit out servicemen. How, as Dr. Anders had put it, come?

The answer lay in the fact that David was not exactly volunteering; he was *being* volunteered. There was a difference.

"Of course, Rabbi Cohen," Dr. Greenberg, the Chairman of the Chaplaincy Committee of the Rabbinical Group and a former instructor of David's in homiletics at Rabbinical Seminary, had said to him, "if you don't care to go into the Army, you needn't."

"I don't have to?"

"No, my son."

"*Wonderful!*"

"You can enlist in the Navy."

"Oh."

Dr. Greenberg looked pensive. "Although on second thought, the Navy quota for Jewish chaplains may be just about filled for now." He brightened. "But then, you can become a *real* sky pilot, my son. Would you like that?"

"Sky pilot?"

"That's slang for a clergyman. Sky pilot—you know, a sort of heavenly guide. And I was thinking—what branch of the service would be more appropriate for a sky pilot than the Air Force?"

"*Air Force!*"

"Does the idea appeal to you?"

David shuddered—he had a horrifying fear of flying —but he forced a smile. "And what if *none* of the services appeal to me?" he asked lightly, as if in jest.

Dr. Greenberg smiled too, as if he indeed thought that David was only joking. "Of course, no one can force a rabbi to enlist. All clergymen who have congregations are exempt from the Draft, of course. However, since the Rabbinical Group believes so strongly that all rabbis with no previous military experience should serve as chaplains, we don't feel that we'd be able to recommend a shirker for any pulpit. And, according to the present Draft Law, all clergymen who do not have pulpits are subject to the Draft, like anyone else."

It was then that David confided his decision to enlist in the Army chaplaincy after all.

Dr. Greenberg could not have been more enthusiastic had he been Billy Graham and David had just made a decision for Christ. "That's the spirit, my son!" He passed him a dozen blank forms. "Just fill these out and mail them back to me by the end of the week. And it's a

15

wise choice you've just made, my son. Believe me, the chaplaincy will be an experience for you."

"That's what everyone who's not in service keeps telling me," David remarked. "Only what *kind* of experience will it be?"

Dr. Greenberg shrugged the shoulders of his expensively tailored suit. "What's the difference? An experience is an experience." Dryly he added, "Now, there's a good title for a sermon, my son: When Is an Experience an Experience? Don't you think so?"

David grunted noncommittally at the gibe. For once when he had stated his belief in class that sermon titles should state their topics with precision, Dr. Greenberg had labeled him a visionary, warning that when people knew exactly what to expect in a sermon they usually did not come to hear it unless, of course, it dealt with psychiatry or sex or, preferably, both. The only course, Dr. Greenberg had advised, was to tantalize the congregation, entice them into the synagogue with vague yet evocative titles. "You mean, beat the movies to their own game?" David had impulsively inquired, thereby incurring the rabbi's eternal hostility.

Dr. Greenberg stood up then to indicate that it was time for David to cease taking up his time. "Well, good luck, my son."

A thin-lipped, wide-hipped doctor in front of David was saying, "Spread your cheeks."

He turned around, complied, dropping his hat, and by the time he had retrieved it, the doctor had grunted his satisfaction. David straightened up and moved on, deliberating now how best to start his nose hemorrhaging, then whether or not to stand there in a pool of his own blood manfully shrugging off all offers of medical aid until he was awarded a 4-F. For two years is a long time in a man's life, he reflected, especially when one has trained an additional four years after college to become a rabbi. Why should he have to go into service now where there would be so few Jews to be a rabbi of? And those few, all stationed near cities containing an in-

16

evitable synagogue, did not really need him as much as did the civilian communities who were complaining about the shortage of available rabbis.

Then too, didn't the new Russo-American conferences now being held at Geneva, with all the benevolence of the yearly interfaith meetings of Brotherhood Week, augur a lessening of friction between East and West which, in turn, would lead to a reduction of armed forces soon, possibly even to disarmament, and consequently to a surplus of chaplains, especially Jewish ones?

A third possibility occurred to David: He was rationalizing again.

Possible, that's possible, he grudgingly conceded. But there was good reason for it, of course. Ignoring his own "Really now, isn't there always?" he called to mind not the ancient religious tradition of his family but its historical position of Anti-Draft. If his mind were being dredged by a psychiatrist at that moment, he would have explained, "You see, it all started with my great-grandfather . . ."

"*Great-grandfather!*" the psychiatrist would have said. "Isn't that going back a bit far?"

"Not at all. You see, some one hundred years ago my great-grandfather lived in Russia under the reign of Nicholas the First, who got a novel idea for solving what's called 'the Jewish problem.' His plan, which the Soviet Union is copying today, was simply to de-Judaize all the Jews in Russia."

"Oh? And how did Nicholas propose to do that?"

"For one thing, by drafting Jews into the Russian Army at the age of ten and keeping them there for twenty-five years. By the time these draftees got out of the Army, most of them couldn't tell the difference between Communion and a *minyan*." Noting the Jewish psychiatrist's blank look, he would have paused to explain: "A *minyan* is a quorum of ten Jewish men." He would have continued: "Well, my great-grandfather was among those who had been drafted at the age of ten.

17

But within two weeks he managed to get out of the Army."

"And how did he manage that?"

"By jumping from high places and lifting heavy objects from low places."

"I see."

"So did the Russians, after hernias reached epidemic proportions among the populace."

"What did the authorities do then?"

"Well, instead of automatically exempting or discharging ruptured men from the Army, they operated on the hernias."

"A hundred years ago? Wasn't the mortality rate high?"

"It wasn't high; it was total. That's why the hernia epidemic cleared up so quickly. It was then that Jewish boys began chopping off their trigger fingers accidentally."

"Is that how your grandfather escaped the Russian Draft?"

"No. What Zeide and his brother Shloime did instead, once they were drafted, was to eat nothing but salted herring. And it worked: The diet wasted the men away. Inside of a month, both men were discharged from the Army—Zeide because he was sick and Uncle Shloime because he was dead. But Uncle Shloime had died a devout Jew, so he would not have minded his death. At any rate, that's what Zeide always told everyone, and Uncle Shloime was never heard to contradict him. And that's what made up Zeide's mind to come to America after the first world war. Not for wealth, you understand—Zeide left a lucrative lumber business and nearly all of his money in Russia when he chose to emigrate. Nor for comfort. 'If man were created for the sole purpose of making himself comfortable on this earth,' Zeide would often say, 'he'd never have been created in the first place.' No, his only reason was that his sons, my father and my Uncle Asher, might evade the Russian Draft and worship as they pleased."

The psychiatrist, if he were at all discerning, would

have interrupted then to ask, "Are you implying that you object to entering the American Army because you're afraid it will interfere with your freedom of worship?"

"Oh, did I imply that?"

"Why did you waste all this time telling me why and how and when your great-grandfather, grandfather, and father dodged the Russian Draft? Does any of this have any bearing upon your subconscious desire to dodge the American Draft here and now?"

David would have squirmed. "Well, no . . . not really . . . I just thought it was interesting, didn't you?"

"*Why* are you so reluctant to go into the Army?"

"I just don't feel like it, that's why. Do I have to have a valid reason?"

"Yes." The psychiatrist would have persisted: "Why, Rabbi Cohen, why are you so intent on dodging the Draft?"

"*Why!*" David would have bounded off the lumpy couch. "Do *I* ask *you* embarrassing questions?"

"Wider! Wider! Wider!"

Happily David abandoned his imaginary session with the realistically obnoxious psychiatrist and turned around.

The wide-hipped, thin-lipped doctor, whose specialty it was to peer between cheeks, was berating a slight, frightened, doubled-over Puerto Rican youngster. "*Wider!*"

"*Ancho, más ancho,*" translated another Puerto Rican nearby, and the frightened boy complied.

But his efforts did not satisfy Thin Lips, who said mockingly, "What's the matter? Don't you understand *any* English? I said *wider.*"

No one, not even the other doctors in the room, said a word as their butterfish-shaped colleague continued to shout at the terrified Puerto Rican, now striving to split himself up the back. "*Wider,*" Thin Lips yelled, getting up on his toes like a ballerina reaching for the spotlight. "Don't they teach you *anything* in that stupid country you come from?"

"You're certainly no advertisement for America, Doctor."

The doctor slumped to his original height as everyone turned in surprise to see who had spoken out. The only one in the room who did not turn was David because, though no less surprised than the others, he knew the identity of the challenger.

The Puerto Rican was forgotten as Thin Lips searched for his new target. *"Who said that!"*

It was perhaps the Biblical prophets who were more responsible than David for his impulsive outburst. Ever since their teachings and trials had been introduced to him in parochial elementary school, the prophets, who always spoke out for Righteousness and Compassion and Justice even in the face of personal danger, had been his ideal—so much so that while his playmates had spoken of becoming doctors, lawyers or gangsters, David had yearned to grow up to be a prophet. It was only later, when some of the would-be doctors settled for dentistry and some of the would-be lawyers went into business instead and some of the would-be gangsters turned to accountancy, that he realized that for a Jewish boy the rabbinate was a more practical line of endeavor than prophecy.

"Who *was* that?" the thin-lipped doctor repeated, anger honing his voice to the sharpness of a scalpel.

Tentatively David raised his hand behind his ear, hoping the others might think he was only scratching himself. But immediately the men around him drew back, whispering, and he was left exposed in every way.

"Did you say something?" Thin Lips asked in the tone of voice of the judge who asks for the prisoner's last words before pronouncing sentence. All the men in the room fell silent as befitted a public execution, which seemed to be the general expectation.

David, dropping his hand and fiddling with his navel, nodded.

"And what was it that you said?"

"I—I—I said—" Oh, *why* did he have to stammer at a time like this, especially when he was in the right! "I said that—that I thought you had finished examining the boy and he could move on."

Thin Lips, taking David's change of words for a retreat, pushed forward for a complete rout. "There was something *else* that you said, wasn't there?"

"Y—Yes," David said, and now he was blushing. In his lifetime he had been engaged in several heated exchanges, but usually while wearing more than a hat. He felt all 180 pounds, seventy-three inches of him turn red as the index card beat out a syncopated tattoo against his thigh.

"And what was it that you said? Do you perhaps remember?"

David faltered. "Not exactly."

A smile of triumph darkened Thin Lips' face. "I was sure you wouldn't." He turned back to the terrorized Puerto Rican and dismissed him contemptuously. "All right, you can go now, you ignoramus. Do you understand *that* much English?"

Impulsively David blurted out: *"Horshoim kayom nigrosh ki hashkeit lo yuchol, vayigr'shu meimov refesh votit."*

Thin Lips turned on David. "What was that again?"

David swallowed. "Hebrew."

"Hebrew!" Thin Lips snorted. "Doesn't *anyone* here speak English!"

"English translation," David burst out: " 'The wicked are like the troubled sea for it can never rest, but its waters cast up muck and garbage.' Isaiah, 57:20."

The quiet room suddenly reverberated with laughter. "Garbage and guck!" chortled one boy. "Isaiah!" hooted another.

"WHAT'S YOUR NAME?"

"Tell him you're Jimmy Durante," suggested the fellow in front of David.

"Say you're a Chinaman," advised the boy behind him, "and your name is Scroo Yoo."

David hesitated for a moment as the fellows nearby

21

cast their ballots between Jimmy Durante and Scroo Yoo, then gave his legal name.

The thin-lipped doctor took out a prescription pad and made an elaborate show of writing down David's name, dotting the one *i* in his name three times and crossing two imaginary *t*'s. Then, through lips that were now so constricted there seemed to be no lips there at all, he snarled: "For *your* sake, Cohen, I hope you're 4-F!"

"Amen!" David whispered under his breath as No Lips turned his back on him and reverted to his original line on cheeks.

As David stepped back into line, several fellows patted him on the back, nudged him in the ribs, or slapped other portions of his anatomy, adding as they did so, "Nice going!" or "We certainly told *him!*" or, simply, "What a bastard!"

He stirred uncomfortably. Before he had only *felt* conspicuous; now he *was* conspicuous. And it would take more than an index card at this point to shield him from his newly acquired notoriety. He hurried through the remainder of the physical exam as quickly as he could, muttering an embarrassed "Forget it" to the young Puerto Rican who came up to thank him, grunting to the others who spoke to him, and silently following instructions. And when the exam finally ended, he rushed out of the examining room.

Outside in the corridor someone grabbed his hand and pumped it. "Hey, congratulate me! Congratulate me!" a freckle-bodied fellow shouted as he shook every limb in sight, like a Jewish boy at a nudist *bar mitzvah*. "Congratulate me! I'm 4-F!"

"*Mazel tov*," David said, and only then did he remember his own flickering hope. The disturbing incident with Thin Lips and his subsequent embarrassment had made him forget to tell the nose doctor about his hemorrhages. Furious with himself for the oversight, he rushed back to the sergeant who had taken his records from him. "About my physical—"

22

"Sympathies and condolences, brother," the sergeant said with a grin. "It's 1-A all the way."

David clapped a hand to his forehead. *"Shlemazel,"* he labeled himself.

Suddenly a red spot dotted his other hand. Swiftly it was joined by other red spots, larger ones this time, then by a shower of them. David bent his head backward and put a hand to his nose, which was bleeding rapidly now.

Now it was bleeding!

"Damn!" he exclaimed softly. "Damn, damn, *damn!*"

Chapter : 2

THREE months passed, and David was still waiting to hear further word about his enlistment. Meanwhile, six of his fellow classmates had entered Army Chaplain Training School and two, more fortunate ones, had been rejected. ("One had very bad eyes, and the other had a very good psychiatrist," he explained to his foster parents.) But no notification whatsoever came to David.

"Maybe they've forgotten all about you, *halvai!*" Tante Dvorah suggested hopefully. "Or maybe your bloody nose in Whitehall made a good impression on somebody there, *halvai!*"

Uncle Asher shook his head hopelessly. "Dvorah, maybe you'll stop already with your *halvais. Halvai!*"

When still another month passed with no word from Washington, David called Dr. Greenberg to inquire about the delay. "Why don't you come over to my office next Tuesday?" Dr. Greenberg said. "I have an empty half hour at two o'clock."

David arrived late for the appointment, well aware of the subconscious reason for his tardiness: He disliked Dr. Greenberg. For with his highly polished manner, assiduously cultivated speech, mellifluously intimate voice, supremely humble self-assurance, manipulative approach and sanctimonious mien, Dr. Greenberg looked to David like a confidence man who had made good. He even sported the confidence man's title of "Doctor," the product of a degree conferred on him by some post office box number in New Mexico. David recalled one of Dr. Greenberg's most impassioned exhortations to his class: "Get your doctorates as soon as you can, boys. You have to impress your congregants—that's the most important thing. So get those Ph.D.'s—it doesn't matter from where or in what, just so long as you have that title." Idly David had remarked, "I've always been interested in animal husbandry." "Good, then get your degree in that," Dr. Greenberg had swiftly replied.

David disliked Dr. Greenberg's office even more than its occupant because it suggested that in his youth the rabbi had taken a vow of prosperity. The carpet on the floor was much too thick, the furniture too plush, and the drapes too heavy to let resound from the room anything but an "Amen." The luxuriant fabrics in the room muffled sounds so much that one felt he had to shout to be heard. And, according to David's way of thinking, that was one of the major functions of a clergyman: to shout, to protest, to disagree. What kind of religious leader was content to be a mere echo of his people, a nonhabit-forming tranquilizer, or a congregational pacifier?

Seating himself in a chair so comfortable that it felt as if its arms were loving him, he noted that Dr. Greenberg was smiling even more than usual. Uh-oh, David thought, he has bad news for me.

"I have good news for you," Dr. Greenberg began.

I was right, David concluded.

"I just spoke to Washington yesterday, and you'll be able to go into service next month. Your class begins on the fourth of December."

David relaxed. "That *is* good news. Because being ripe to go into service as I am, no congregation wanted to take me."

"I assumed you'd think that way. That's what I told the Chief's Office at Headquarters USAF."

"The Chief's Office? Yoosaf? What's that?"

"The Chief is the Chief of Chaplains, and USAF is the United States Air Force. You should learn that much terminology before you enter—"

"The Air Force? What has the Air Force Chief of Chaplains to do with Army chaplains like myself?"

"That's why I wanted to see you, my son—to explain—" Dr. Greenberg paused just long enough for David to say, "Uh-oh." "The quota for Army chaplains is filled. So is the Navy's. That leaves—"

"The Air Force!"

"It would seem to be the Lord's will," said Dr. Greenberg, accepting David's fate with no difficulty at all.

"Impossible!" Surely the Lord knew, even if Dr. Greenberg did not, that David was scared to death of flying.

Dr. Greenberg shrugged. "Let's just say then that it is the *Army's* will. It seems—now this is confidential, please understand—it seems that Army authorities received an uncomplimentary letter about you from some doctor, and—"

"Oh!" Thin Lips! "I can explain that—"

Dr. Greenberg held up his manicured hands. "There's no need, my son. The Army has already filled the slot that was intended for you, and now they're not taking any more Jewish chaplains for another eight months."

"But I *have* to explain." And he hurried on to tell of the incident involving Thin Lips and the Puerto Rican youngster.

When he finished, Dr. Greenberg commented, "So?"
"So!"

Dr. Greenberg heaved a sigh. "So you did right, my son. Good for you. But surely by now you must have realized that if you're going to insist on telling people the truth, you'll have to learn to take the consequences. For example, at Rabbinical Seminary you couldn't have expected the faculty there to embrace you after they selected you, as the most promising student, to speak at

Founder's Day Exercises, when important contributors and people from all over the country were in attendance, and you chose to preach on What's Wrong with Our Rabbinical Seminary. Or take the time when Rabbi Kasdan exclaimed how fair and impartial he was in placing student rabbis in pulpits; for once you did not speak out, and that was good. But you sat there looking at him as if he had just announced that the moon was made of gefüllte fish, and that was worse. Is it any wonder then that you were assigned a congregation with nineteen families in it five hours from New York? Rabbi Kasdan may not be impartial, but he does have very sensitive feelings, you know. Now we have this doctor at Whitehall Street. His action in blackballing you is deplorable, of course, but it is understandable. And when I say that, I hope you don't think I'm biased against you merely because you happened to criticize my last demonstration sermon as being Norman Vincent Peale with a skullcap."

What was the use of trying for debater's points now? David figured; so, instead of defending himself, he asked, "What about the Marines?" They were rough and tough but at least they were rough and tough on the ground. "Surely the Marines need Jewish chaplains, too."

"The Marines get all their chaplains from the Navy."

"Oh. And when will the Navy be taking on new chaplains?"

"It's hard to tell. The Navy uses only a third of the Jewish chaplains that the Army or the Air Force does. You may have to wait until June."

"But that's nine months from now!" In that time David could complete almost half of his military commitment.

"My son, if you're worried about being the only Jewish chaplain at the Air Force Chaplain School, you needn't. There will be another rabbi—from Yeshiva—in the next class with you."

"Oh, that doesn't bother me so much as—" David checked himself.

"Yes? Yes? Are you perhaps afraid of flying?"

David cleared his throat. "Afraid?"

Dr. Greenberg probed again. "*Are* you afraid to fly? Is that it?" David hesitated. "You can tell me, my son."

Yes, I'm *deathly* afraid of flying; David was not ashamed to admit it to himself. "Of course, I'm not afraid to fly," he lied. He, so proud of his rationality, *was* ashamed to admit his phobia to others.

Worse still, he could not even console himself with the thought that the phobia was the product of some forgotten childhood trauma, because he remembered acquiring it only three years before on his first flight or, rather, near flight. At that time he had received an offer from a summer camp in California to be the camp rabbi. Tante Dvorah, ever cautious, insisted that David take the train to California. Uncle Asher, the adventurer who had once gone up on Coney Island's Parachute Jump all by himself (which was more than David had ever done), urged him to fly.

Tante Dvorah declared that if it weren't for planes David would never have been orphaned at seven, since his parents—they should be resting in peace—had been driving to the airport when they had been killed. Uncle Asher said what did that have to do with the price of tea in Moscow. Still, Tante Dvorah implored David to go by train and he, loath to worry her, said that he would leave for California from Grand Central Station, which is what he did—technically.

Tante Dvorah and Uncle Asher took David to the station. There he kissed them both good-bye on the platform, entered the train, walked through three cars, and got off the train just before it pulled out of the station. He would not do anything to worry his beloved Tante Dvorah, but he refused to be infected by an elderly woman's absurdly irrational fears.

Across the street from Grand Central Station, David took the limousine to Idlewild Airport accompanied by several other passengers and no more trepidation than is normal for a person about to embark upon his maiden flight who could not figure out what it was that kept planes from falling down after they had gotten all the way up into the thin air. Once aboard the plane, he settled back in his seat with Dramamine pills, a few Bonamines, a magazine, and his insurance policies, still trying to figure out why planes shouldn't fall down. He didn't have long to wonder about it, however, for soon his plane was streaking down the runway, and a few hours later David awoke in a hospital.

The nurse explained that his plane had cracked up slightly on take-off, and later the stewardess came in, entirely unbruised and still smiling her stitched smile, to say how sorry everyone was about the whole thing. As for the cause of the mishap, David was never very interested. Who cared whether the plane had crashed because of the stick jamming, or the wheels locking, or the pilot bailing out? He *still* had an assortment of contusions, abrasions, and a concussion.

He also had a phobia, but that he did not know until he left the hospital a few days later and tried to board two successive flights to Los Angeles only to land puking each time in Idlewild's men's room. Finally, after faking a long distance call home to lie about his pleasant train trip, he took the train to California.

At times it disturbed David that he had succumbed to an irrational fear. However, since there was no actual necessity for him ever to fly, he did not concern himself unduly with his phobia. As long as the phobia did not extend to riding New York's subways, he did not think that he had much of a problem. Yet now . . . Now . . . !

"What's bothering you if it isn't the flying?" Evidently David's denial had not satisfied Dr. Greenberg. "Why do you seem so disturbed at the prospect of entering the Air Force?"

David, pressed for an answer, talked as he tried to think of something to say. "I just don't care for the Air Force, that's all. Last week I saw a reissue of that old movie *Strategic Air Command*, with James Stewart and June Allyson, and I just didn't care for it."

"Because if you *are* worried about the flying, let me

28

assure you that you will never have to fly in the Air Force."

David pounced on the rabbi's words. "I won't?"

Dr. Greenberg smiled his most reassuring smile. "Of course not. A chaplain is never on flying status. In regard to flying—and in most other respects too—it makes no difference which branch of the service you're a chaplain in."

"Well . . . !" David allowed himself the luxury of sinking back into the plush arm chair. Aloud he reflected, "After all, it was only a *movie* . . ."

"Splendid! Splendid, my son!" Dr. Greenberg effervesced. "The Air Force will be—what can I tell you?—an *experience*. Good luck, my son."

"Thank you," David said, and he could not resist adding, "Dad."

The next morning David went to McGuire Air Force Base near Trenton, volunteered, and underwent another physical exam. There, despite remembering this time to confide to the nose doctor that his nose never hemorrhaged more than once a day, he passed the exam.

Tante Dvorah took the news stoically. "Duvid, there are all kinds of new diseases going around between now and December. Who knows? Maybe you'll be lucky yet."

"Your tante," Uncle Asher noted, "has low hopes."

Within four weeks, David was awarded his commission and sworn into the Air Force at a familiar place, 39 Whitehall Street. And three weeks later he was ordered to report to Chaplain Training School at Landers Air Force Base, Texas, on December 4th.

Tante Dvorah and Uncle Asher took David to the train at Pennsylvania Station. There Uncle Asher continued to express his disappointment over David's refusal to fly. "A chaplain in the Air Force yet traveling by train—it's blasphemous!"

"And if I were a Navy chaplain," David said lightly, "would you expect me to report to duty by submarine?"

Uncle Asher refused to be confused. "From New York

to San Antonio is less than six hours by plane. You could stay with us two more days. But by train—"

Tante Dvorah interrupted. "Leave Duvid alone. Let him make up his own mind, Asher," she said, always open-minded whenever anyone's decision coincided with her own. "Duvid prefers to go by train, so let him. Would I think of trying to change his mind if he wanted to go by plane?" The answer to that question was so obvious that no one bothered to answer it. "Besides, being alone on the train for three days will be good for Duvid. It will give him plenty of time to think about getting married already."

David smiled. "Tante, you're playing our song again." Even before he had known the difference between boys and girls, his aunt had indoctrinated him with the difference between a bachelor and a husband. The former was, to put it baldly, "a bummer," while the latter was "a absolute necessity."

"After all, Duvid, you're twenty-four years old now. It's time already."

"Tante, I'm twenty-three."

"In China you're twenty-four," she corrected him, drawing upon a fund of knowledge expanded from religiously reading "Believe It or Not" before wrapping soup-greens in it.

"All right, you win. So I'm twenty-four."

"So it's time already you settled down. You're not getting any younger, you know. You owe it to your unborn children that they shouldn't be getting an old decrepit for a father."

David chuckled. "How my unborn children must hate me for depriving them of a mother up until now!"

"Exactly," Tante Dvorah said in earnest. "Duvid, it's time already you picked a wife, settled down, raised a family, had aggravation like everyone else, and gave us a little *nachus*."

Nachus! Translated, that pregnant Yiddish word meant some nebulous pleasure that a person could never keep or even acquire for himself but which he was forever obliged always to give away to those who loved

him. Specifically, *nachus* usually meant a wife; para-
doxically, it wasn't the newlyweds who enjoyed the
most *nachus* then but their respective parents, families and friends. Even more specifically, *nachus* meant
children, on whom one could finally exact revenge by de-
manding *nachus* from them even as it had been demanded from him.

Tante Dvorah continued: "Duvid, next time we'll be
seeing you, God willing, you should only be returning
from Texas with a fine Jewish girl in one hand and a
baby in the other. Such *nachus!*"

Uncle Asher remonstrated, "But, Dvorah, he'll only be
in Texas for not even three months."

"That's all right. It only took God six days to create
the world."

"Finding the right wife isn't as easy as creating a
world," Uncle Asher said. "Look how long it took *me*
to find *you*."

"Finding me you did in a minute." She shook a callused finger at him. "Making up your mind to marry
me—that's what took so long."

"I couldn't believe my good luck, that was all," Uncle
Asher said. "It took two years for me to convince
myself I was worthy of you."

Tante Dvorah beamed. "Isn't your uncle a wonderful
man? He lies so beautifully! That's what you need,
Duvid. Someone to lie to you. And *with* you—that's
all right too. Duvid, are you listening?"

"Am I listening?" David laughed. "I'm already up to
the part where you tell me that while a bachelor bummer ages arithmetically, his libido multiplies geometrically until, poor thing, he either runs amuck or passes
the point of no return."

"Such a wonderful vocabulary our Duvid has!" Tante
Dvorah gloated. "Sometimes I can't understand a word
he says."

The conductor called, "All visitors off the train!"

"Oh, Duvid . . ." She hugged him to her bosom which
smelled of fruits and vegetables and a mother's love.
"Take care of him." These last words were addressed not

31

to Uncle Asher nor even to the conductor, but to God. Tante Dvorah spoke to Him freely and often, for the Lord, to her way of thinking, was a person-sitter to whom loved ones were safely to be entrusted, as well as her senior partner in the business of living, always accessible and invariably amenable to petitions of love.

David looked at his aunt and uncle—she, with hands chapped and hard from selling fruit and vegetables outdoors in all kinds of weather, the face ruddy and round and invariably smiling, the heavy body more accustomed to half a dozen sweaters at one time than a single coat, the hair the color of moonlight now, but the dark eyes still bright; he, with his slight wiry body strong and bent from lifting too many fruit and vegetable crates for too many years, the wind-burned skin, the swarthy face impassive except for the wry mouth— the childless couple who had taken the orphaned David into their home, rearing him since the age of seven yet refusing to be called "Mama" and "Papa" for fear that he would forget his real parents.

David grabbed their rough peddlers' hands in his smooth student ones. "How can I ever begin to repay you two for what you've done for me!"

Uncle Asher spoke gently: "Duvid, there's a saying: 'The love of parents goes to their children, but the love of these children goes to *their* children.'"

"That's not so!" David protested. "I'll always be trying to—"

Tante Dvorah interrupted. "Duvid, what your Uncle Asher means is that a parent's love isn't to be paid back; it can only be passed on. That's how ignorant people like your uncle and myself, who don't even speak good English yet, can become the teachers of future brilliant generations—through love that's passed on. That's how your real parents—may their memory be a blessing!—still live on like those stars I read about in Mr. Ripley. They're no longer there—they became extinguished millions of years ago, believe it or not—but their light still shines on us."

"*Nu, nu*," commented Uncle Asher. "Ever since you've

32

become a rabbi, Duvid, your Tante goes around with sermons. It's a good thing you're leaving alro Who could live in a house with *two* rabbis? Tha would be enough to drive *any* man to sin."

The conductor announced, "Last call! All visitors off the train!"

Tante Dvorah pulled herself away from David and forced a smile. "Good-bye, Duvid. Be good."

David forced a smile too. "Be good? What a thing to tell a rabbi!"

"Imagine!" Tante Dvorah exclaimed, and there was wonder as well as pride in her voice. "Out of our fruit store—a rabbi!"

"Good-bye, Duvid," said Uncle Asher quietly, thumping his nephew on the shoulder. "God lead you in the right path."

They left him then. "See, Asher? I *told* you I wouldn't cry," David heard Tante Dvorah saying as she stepped off the train. "So where's your handkerchief?"

A few minutes later the train began to move. Sitting down in his seat, David closed his eyes. He began to pray.

Chapter : 3

THE train trip to San Antonio proved to be uneventful, dull, tedious and monotonous. Yet to David it still possessed one great virtue: In three days the train never once took to the air and flew.

He utilized the time to study the military, its men, their behavior and way of thinking. This he did by reviewing *The Naked and the Dead, A Soldier's Story, From Here to Eternity, Crusade in Europe, Mister Roberts,* and *The Authoritarian Personality.*

He also carefully observed the servicemen on the train but none of them, it seemed, were reading any of the books that he was. Instead, their reading matter consisted chiefly of a magazine whose Christmas cover featured the names of several prominent writers interspersed among a color cut-out of a pink, full-bodied girl wearing a white Santa Claus beard, a green pompon, a red-lipped smile, and that was about all. In the interests of researching the literary pursuits of servicemen—he convinced himself—David bought a copy of the magazine when he changed trains in St. Louis.

Back on the train he leafed through the publication and was taken aback to discover that it was little more than a bound collection of what he had always imagined French post cards to look like. The nude photographs could not be accused of being suggestive, however, since they were so altogether explicit. Embarrassed by the profusion of bare bosoms and barer buttocks, guiltily he could almost hear Tante Dvorah exclaiming, "*Nu?* So wasn't I right? You see what happens when you're not married? You get itchy eyes."), he hid the magazine among his chopped-liver sandwiches.

It wasn't until the following afternoon that the train arrived in San Antonio and David was able surreptitiously to dispose of the magazine whose nudes the chicken fat from his chopped-liver sandwiches had made even more naked by rendering them translucent. This accomplished, he carried his two suitcases to a nearby bus whose destination, proclaimed by foot-high lettering on its sides, was Landers Air Force Base. There he was soon surrounded by a crowd of nervous teen-aged enlistees who, to the native of Brooklyn, looked strangely out of place without a candy store behind them or a poolroom around them.

"Howdy, fellas!"

Descending from the bus was a tall, heavy-set sergeant with a face like a well-worn saddle and a voice like spurs. Amiably he chatted with the boys, joking with them about their home towns, their way of dress, their girls. Genially he offered the youngsters cigarettes which were accepted by all the ones who did not look old enough to smoke. Playfully the sergeant shoved the boys into the bus as they joked back at him, enjoying the friendly banter and the brotherly attitude of the sergeant which continued all the way to Landers and until the very moment when they all stepped off the bus.

There the sergeant underwent a startling transformation: The American big brother suddenly became George Orwell's Big Brother. "Atten-hun!" he demanded, and only a fool or a civilian would have thought that he was still joking. The cigarettes of those who did not come to immediate attention were yanked out of their adolescent mouths and ground under the sergeant's heel. "What the hell do you think this is—a kindergarten!"

"But, Sarge," one boy complained, "I didn't finish my smoke."

From the sergeant's mouth belched forth an obscene roar. The words themselves were unintelligible, but their import was unmistakable. And delivered from the proximity of two inches from the offender's nose, the sergeant's message got through quite clearly—so clearly that the boy, a guileless civilian just a moment before, was transformed in an instant into a docile recruit crying, "Yessir! Yessir! Yessir!"

Even more surprising to David was the fact that he found he too was standing rigidly at attention with his head and shoulders thrown back, it seemed, a city block behind the rest of him—and trying to think where in San Antonio he might be able to get his teeth into a barrel of salted herring.

But you're a first lieutenant, he suddenly remembered, and that outranks even a sergeant. He thanked God and relaxed, stooping over to pick up his luggage.

Suddenly, just behind his left ear, a verbal depth charge exploded, scattering obscenities in every direction but focusing on David. Recoiling, he looked up to see the sergeant's tongue working him over like a blunt instrument, as he questioned David's legitimacy, humanity, and even what he did with himself in his spare time.

David mustered his most surprised tone of voice. "Is something the matter, Sergeant?" he asked. "I'm Chaplain Cohen reporting in to Chaplain Training School."

"Oh!" The tongue slunk away to hide behind gritted teeth.

Several boys began to snicker. The snickers died stillborn, however, when the sergeant turned the full force of a malevolent eye upon their perpetrators even as he somehow managed to signal the bus driver with his other eye. "Hey, take this here new chaplain here to the Chaplains' Barracks, will ya?"

"Sure thing, Sergeant," the bus driver responded.

David returned to the bus.

"Chaplain!" David turned around, and a smooth-cheeked youngster with a high blond pompadour cried, *"Don't leave us!"*

Hastily the sergeant interposed. "Of course, I don't like to see you go either, sir," he said, and motioned to the driver to be on his way. Then, as the bus started off, the sergeant turned on the group and roared, "All right, who was the freak who called out while standing in formation?"

"Welcome to the Air Force," the driver said.

"Thank you," David said, uncertainly.

He took a seat and surveyed the base as the bus proceeded along. With its hundreds of identical off-white two-story wooden barracks identically framed by identical lawns whose grass was of identical height, Landers looked like a typical suburban development, caricatured. For, in addition to suburbanlike shopping centers of tailor shops, laundry and dry cleaning establishments, cafeterias, refreshment stands, chapels, movie theaters, swimming pools, tennis courts and clubs, the base even had no sidewalks.

But more important, David realized, was what the other chaplains and the rest of the Air Force personnel would be like. They might yet turn out to be as identical to one another as the Landers barracks, but surely they would differ radically from him, an urban Jewish reluctant first-generation serviceman, probably the first one in his family to serve voluntarily in the armed forces since the Maccabees.

"What do you think of the base?" the driver was asking.

"Looks fine," said David, "but isn't something missing?" He recalled the imposing sign at the Landers gate: *Welcome to the U.S. Air Force—Air Power Begins Here.* "Where are the planes?"

"There's one." The driver pointed to a fighter plane beached on a barracks lawn. "There are others, too, sprinkled all around the base."

"Only sprinkled?"

"This here is a training base, you know. A cockeyed school is all it is. No planes really except for those exhibits there. Only books here, and obstacle courses, and sergeants' dirty looks. But if you're really hot to do some flying while you're here, Kelly and Randolph Air Force Bases aren't too far away. And you being a chaplain, you can get yourself a flight real easy."

"I think I'll be able to control my passion for flying," said David, "until I leave Landers."

Inside the Chaplains' Barracks, some thirty men in civilian dress were congregated in small groups in a large dayroom, chatting with one another with the politeness of people trapped together at the bottom of an elevator shaft. Only one of them, David suddenly recalled, was Jewish, but—*now* he remembered—he had forgotten to ask Dr. Greenberg for the other rabbi's name. Placing his suitcases in a corner, he looked from face to face as he tried to ferret out the Jew from amongst all the Christians. Surely, he told himself, he should be able to recognize a fellow Jew even when fully clothed.

One man—probably not the other Jew, David felt certain, or else he would not have appeared so relaxed —came forward graciously to greet him and introduce him to some of the other chaplains, all of whom were pleasant, cordial and decidedly Christian-looking.

Ill-at-ease (for some strange reason David felt as if he were caught up in a pacific pogrom), he acknowledged each introduction even as he forgot everyone's name while it was being pronounced. But he was not so nervous that he did not perceive that some of the others were also nervous. They'd have had to be nervous, or else why would they be grinning like headwaiters at such statements as, "I was supposed to be in the previous class, but I had to have my gallstones removed," or "To my way of thinking, Paul Tillich is the greatest theologian of our times," or "I almost got killed in an auto wreck on my way down here"?

Only once did one of the nervous smilers, a priest, stop smiling for a moment, and that happened when someone remarked that as a child he had always believed that only nuns were allowed to give birth to priests. Could that someone be the other rabbi? David wondered. But then the non-Catholic added, "I certainly hope you priests didn't believe that only the Devil could give birth to Protestants."

There were six Catholic priests present, all looking from five to ten years older than the others. They were grouped together in one corner of the dayroom, and David envied them. At least they could recognize one another by means of their clerical garb.

In quest of his fellow Jew, he circulated around the room, introducing himself to the others and striking up conversations with them during which he would surreptitiously drop words like Torah, Tu B'shvat, chopped liver; and when these would elicit no discernible reaction, he would move on to another chaplain. He terminated this practice, however, when one man cordially informed him that they had met at least twice before, and wasn't David the one who kept referring to a friend of his named Blintzes?

David was embarrassed. "I'm sorry! But I haven't seen so many new faces all at once since the last time I went to the Brooklyn Paramount."

The other chaplain reacted with amazement. "You mean you come from Brooklyn? Really?"

"Yes," David said. "Why?"

"But you don't talk like you come from Brooklyn!"

Uncertain whether to feel flattered or insulted, David asked, "Oh, do you live in Brooklyn too?"

"Oh, no, I've never lived east of Virginia City," the man replied. "But I've been to so many movies."

Other chaplains nearby began commenting on David's lack of what they considered to be a Brooklyn accent, making him so self-conscious about his speech that he soon found himself talking with a Yiddish Cockney intonation. It was then that he resolved to mention his birthplace as New York City.

"Oh, so you're a New Yorker," the next chaplain said coolly.

"A Noo Yawkuh, eh?" echoed another, a Southerner, with unconcealed suspicion.

"My home," David added, testing for effect, "is in Brooklyn, really."

"Did yew say Brooooklyn?" The man was positively astounded, also amused. "But yew don tawk lak yew cum frum Brooooklyn!"

A redheaded muscular minister, with a friendly freckled face, detached himself from a nearby group and approached. "Did I hear right? Is your name David Cohen?" David nodded. "That's wonderful! My best friend in the Navy was named Dave Cohen. I guess it was just predestined that I meet Dave Cohen again." He grinned. "And from that remark, I imagine you can tell I'm a Presbyterian. Oh, my name's Paul Smith."

Suddenly David could not remember why it had seemed so important to him only a few minutes before to find the other Jew there. He had found a congenial spirit, Christian yet kindred. Though not *altogether* kindred. "Did you say you were in the Navy?" David could not conceal his surprise. "That means you didn't *have* to enlist in the chaplaincy now, did you?"

"No, I didn't have to enlist. Why? Did you?"

David hesitated. "No, I didn't *have* to." Technically that was the truth. As Dr. Greenberg had conceded, the Armed Services could not draft clergymen or make them enlist; it was only that the Rabbinical Group had the power to make one *wish* he had volunteered. "Why did you enlist?" he asked, then immediately regretted doing so for fear he would be asked the same question.

39

"I think the Navy made up my mind for me," Paul replied. "During my two-year hitch, I saw how the men lived, what they lived by, what they lived for. It wasn't very much. So I became convinced a minister could do a great deal to raise the sights of servicemen, lift their aims in life. Especially if he had been an enlisted man before. Why did *you* enlist, Dave?"

"Well . . ." David began.

Fortunately, a new arrival was brought over just then. An intense, gaunt fellow with a pinched face and a protruding vein running upward like a thunderbolt from a threatening bushy left eyebrow into his black hairline, he was introduced as Clifford Fowler.

David, happy for the interruption, clasped the chaplain's hand warmly. "Very glad to meet you—"

"You!" Clifford Fowler jerked his hand away. "I remember *you*. You were reading *Playboy* on the train!"

David flushed.

"And you're a *chaplain?"*

Embarrassed, David retorted: "I remember you too. You were peeking over my shoulder, all the way from St. Louis."

The vein in Clifford Fowler's forehead came to throbbing life, swelling and reddening. *"Oh!"* He spun around on his heel and strode away, but not before he had called upon the Lord to try to find it in His heart to forgive all the liars in the world, provided they first repented of their priapic prurience.

The chaplain who had attended so many movies nudged a colleague. "What's prurience?"

"That's easy," was the reply. "But what's priapic?"

David turned to Paul Smith. "I wasn't *really* reading that magazine. I only bought it to see why all the servicemen on the train were reading it and—"

"A likely story," Paul said gravely, then burst into laughter as David continued to protest his innocence. "What a scene! It was the prophet Nathan confronting King David with his adultery all over again. You remember: 'Thou art the man!' Chaplain Cohen, thou wert toying with *Playboy!* But don't worry, Dave. I'll persuade everyone here to take a Christian attitude toward you."

Relieved, David laughed too, then checked himself. "What does *that* mean?"

"Hating the sin, but loving the sinner . . ."

"But I'm *not* a sinner!"

"Why, then you must be a saint, Dave," Paul commented.

David smiled. Then, looking across the room at Clifford Fowler who was loudly explaining to another chaplain what was the matter with naked women, he confessed, "I do wish I were saint enough to know how to control my tongue."

"It's easier to curb the tongue when the cheek is turned," Paul suggested.

David looked inquiringly at Paul. "Was that a commercial?" he asked and Paul laughed.

"Would you brethren knock it off for a minute?" twanged a voice which reverberated through the room like a guitar, all steel and all Texan.

David and Paul turned, as did the other chaplains, toward the doorway. There loomed a burly chaplain, a lieutenant-colonel who looked like a clean-shaven Santa Claus with a cauliflower ear. About fifty years of age, he had snow-white hair, round bright blue eyes, a rounder red face, a beer-barrel belly, and the shoulders and stance of a heavyweight boxer.

"The name's Radcliff, and I'm Director of this here Chaplain Training School. Welcome, fellas!" he said. "I reckon the first thing I should do is tell you all what we aim to do with you here beside chew you out regularly. Fair enough?"

The chaplains smiled. "Fair enough," one of them responded.

The Director squared his shoulders as if he were about to take on all the men there. "Well, first off, let me say that we are *not* here to make you clergymen, fellas. That you have already been trained to do by your church. What we *are* here to do is to introduce you to the Air Force, teach you its ways and organizations, and help you adjust to a new way of life and fit in. For you're entering a foreign country now—as far as you're concerned, Landers might just as well be Mars—and you must learn its customs and ceremonies to belong. You can't behave now as you did in civilian life.

"I might add parenthetically that we have found that the Roman Catholic men, because of their training, fit into our disciplined way of living more easily than the others. But with the three-month training period provided here, we hope all of you will learn to get on in the military and adapt yourselves to its necessary disciplines. If you don't, Lord help you!"

Was it only his imagination, David wondered, or was the Director looking now accusingly at him?

"You have a mighty important trust now, fellas. I'm not one to wave the flag, but I want you to bear in mind that one million Americans enter and leave the service each year. And no one has as much influence on them as do their chaplains—for good or for bad. These one million souls enter the military as boys: seventeen-, eighteen-, nineteen-year-olds; and even our R.O.T.C. fellows are no older than twenty-two. But when these million souls leave—whether it's when they retire at the end of twenty or thirty years, or whether it's four years later when their tour ends—they leave as men. For better or for worse. The chaplain, of all people, can help make that for better, by instilling in them the proper values and attitudes and guidance upon which *all* our religions are based."

Against his will David found himself very much impressed by Chaplain Radcliff's words. "It's all a plot cooked up by Paul Smith and Chaplain Radcliff," he warned himself. "I'm being brainwashed." Yet he moved forward so that he might not miss a word of Chaplain Radcliff's remarks.

"Think of it, fellas!" the Director exclaimed, and his stomach swelled with pride. "One million souls will be passing through your hands every year on their way back to civilian life where they will raise families and

lead lives colored by your teachings and your efforts—
or lack of them. I know of no greater responsibility."

He held up a mimeographed sheet of paper. "Now,
fellas, I'll read off your room assignments," he said,
then paused to explain that the chaplains were being
assigned alphabetically, two to a room, in order to en-
sure the maximum mixing of the various religions and
denominations. In this way the Chaplain School sought
to have the chaplains fraternize closely with one another, which they possibly might not do if left to choose
their own roommates.

David looked at the six Catholic priests still grouped
together, then thought of his own desire to find the
other rabbi, and conceded the truth of the Director's
assumption.

After the list of last names and room assignments
was read (David, listening for Jewish-sounding names,
detected five), the men went to look for their rooms.
David found his at the beginning of the corridor on
either side of which were identical medium-sized
rooms, each with two beds, two desks, two closets, two
windows and one wastepaper basket.

Noting a priest across the hall from his room, David
paused there in the doorway to introduce himself and
say hello. On the priest's desk was a portrait of a lovely
little blonde girl of about two years with an Irishly
angelic face, and David commented, "She's a beautiful
child. Your niece?"

"Oh, no," said the priest, Jim Mackey from Minne-
apolis, as he removed his black jacket and Roman collar, "she's mine. Her name is Ann."

"*Yours?*"

"My daughter. She *is* a beauty, isn't she. I'm not at
all ashamed to boast."

David was surprised. "I didn't know you were able
to adopt children."

Now Jim was surprised. "What makes you think she's
adopted?" he said, as he took off his black clerical
dickey. "Perhaps it's selfish of me not to adopt some

needy child, but since God has enabled me to have my own children—I guess if you could get married, you'd understand."

"You mean you entered Divinity School after your daughter was born?"

"Oh, no. We had Ann during my first year in school," Jim said, taking out a picture of a pretty blonde girl and placing it on the desk beside the other picture. "And this is Ann's mother, Greta. Ann looks just like her, doesn't she?" David nodded, aghast. "But that's not exactly fair of me. Perhaps I shouldn't be flaunting pictures of the women in my life before someone like you who can't get married."

"What do you mean—*I* can't get married?"

"Well, you're a rabbi, aren't you? I mean, I assumed from your name and all—"

"Yes, I'm a rabbi, but rabbis marry. They're *encouraged* to marry. It's not like being a priest like you who's never even supposed to so much as—I mean—"

"Priest?" Jim regarded him quizzically. "You don't think I'm a priest, do you!"

David pointed to Jim's clerical attire. *"Aren't* you?"

Jim looked at his clerical garb, then at the two pictures on his desk, and burst out laughing. "I'm Lutheran, not Catholic. Just ask my wife and baby; they'll tell you."

David turned red with embarrassment. "I thought only priests dressed like that."

"And I thought rabbis had to be celibate," Jim smiled.

A voice broke in. "Is this 14-A?" A stocky, dark man of about thirty-three was standing at the door. Jim nodded. "Then this is home, I guess," the swarthy man grinned and held out his hand. "Dan Miller. I'm from New York."

At last—the other rabbi, David swiftly concluded. Dan had a swarthy complexion, a slightly hooked nose, he looked intelligent or at least his eyeglasses made him look so, and he was wearing a bright red sport shirt under a plaid sport jacket. As if in corroboration, when David mentioned his name and origin, Dan Miller grinned, "Say, we have a lot in common, don't we?"

Before David could reply, however, a priest came in and called Dan to the phone. At any rate, the priest was dressed like a priest—or like a Lutheran pastor.

David then went to his room, and spent some time speculating about whom he had drawn for a roommate, wondering whether it would be better to room with a Protestant or with a Catholic, hoping the roommate would be as congenial as Paul Smith or Jim Mackey or his fellow rabbi, Dan Miller, praying that it would not be someone like Clifford Fowler.

Finally the roommate arrived. He was about thirty years of age, with the build and limber walk of an athlete. His coloring was pastel: his straight hair pale yellow, his skin an off-white, and his eyes a faded blue.

"I was informed that this was my room," he said rather formally and with a definite German accent which, to David's mind, completed the picture of a typical Aryan.

Interested in seeing the other's reaction to his obviously Jewish name, David swiftly introduced himself. "Cohen's the name."

"Yes," the other said.

The German did not even have the decency to introduce himself, David noted angrily. He was probably a Nazi; he certainly looked like one.

Yet he must not jump to conclusions, David cautioned himself. "My friends call me David," he said, trying to sound pleasant.

"Please call me Albert," the other man said in a reserved tone of voice, without even mentioning his first name. He looked around the room as if it were a manor and he its lord. "I think I had better begin to unpack now."

"Yes," David said shortly, and both men began to unpack in silence without looking at one another.

"Hi!" A dark, lithe fellow popped into the room waving a printed form. A young paraphrase of Cary Grant with a cleft in his nose as well as his chin, as if originally he had been intended to be twins, his jaunty manner and crew-cut good looks lent an air of dashing elegance to the faded blue-jeans and Yale sweat shirt he was wearing. "Got any extra hangers?" he asked.

David pointed to his closet. "Help yourself."

"I have extra ones too," Albert said.

"Thanks a lot." The newcomer ambled from one closet to the other, collecting hangers. "Did you get this instruction sheet yet? How To Make Mountains out of Molehills, I think it's called. We're ordered herein to put our shirts on separate hangers spaced exactly one and a half inches from each other and all turned in the same direction. Any shirt caught fraternizing with another one will be shot. Sorry! I forgot my manners. My name's Bentley Lane. I know it sounds like a street, but that's my name. And to listen to the other high-minded characters here talk, I have still another distinction: I'm the only one here to whom enlisting in the chaplaincy was neither a sacrifice nor a challenge. With me it was sheer necessity; no civilian church would have me."

David smiled, yet he chafed too. Now why couldn't he have drawn someone like Bentley Lane for a roommate? He was brash, perhaps even cynical, but at least he was human and non-Aryan.

"By the way, I'm a Congregationalist," Bentley added. "What churches do you two belong to?"

It was the most natural question in the world to ask in a chaplains' barracks, except that David had been conditioned on several occasions while in high school to the fact that when someone asked him his religion, it was only to refuse him a job. "My name is David Cohen," he said, "and I'm——"

Albert drowned him out with a Germanic laugh.

David turned on him angrily. "What's so funny!"

Albert's face was now pink from laughter. "Then before you were telling me *your* name——"

Bentley smiled uneasily. "Say, what's going on here?"

"Suppose you explain yourself to Chaplain Lane," David said coolly, "so that he too can know exactly what you are."

46

Still chuckling, Albert said, "Well, David, my name is Cohen too—*Albert* Cohen." David gaped. "And with a name like that I don't suppose I have to tell anyone my religion, do I?"

Bentley looked from one Cohen to the other in amazement. "You mean you two have spent all this time unpacking together without knowing you both were Jewish? Why, I always thought Jews had some kind of sixth sense for recognizing one another, like radar."

David shook his head dumbly. Jim Mackey wasn't a priest, Dan Miller wasn't a rabbi, Albert Cohen wasn't a Nazi, and he, David Cohen, was a *schlemiel*.

Chapter : 4

DAVID's favorite psalm was the 139th:

> *A psalm of David . . .*
> *Whither shall I go from Thy spirit?*
> *Or whither shall I flee from Thy presence?*
> *If I ascend up into heaven, Thou art there;*
> *If I make my bed in the nether-world, behold,*
> *   Thou art there.*
> *If I take the wings of the morning,*
> *And dwell in the uttermost parts of the sea,*
> *Even there would Thy hand lead me,*
> *And Thy right hand would hold me . . .*

And Texas, he felt, was one place that put this psalm to the test. For the state seemed Godforsaken, as far removed from his idea of civilization as heaven and the uttermost parts of the sea—and considerably more spread out. Back home one fifteen-cent token would take him to the ocean, the hills of Central Park, the theater, museums, lakes, the Metropolitan Opera, the Fifth

47

Avenue Library, Broadway, Greenwich Village, a thousand different synagogues, Coney Island. At Landers, however, one had to go on a safari just to get to a kosher delicatessen.

Surrounding the base was an infinite desert, lying in wait, which made David appreciate for the first time the Israelites' forty years of wandering in the wilderness. He had never before seen anything so vast, so barren, so uninhabited, unless it was Ebbets Field in Brooklyn after the Dodgers had deserted.

The weather did nothing to lift his spirits. For Texas was the only state in the Union where a person could get pneumonia in the morning and sunstroke in the afternoon. Frost greeted every dawn and a freezing, clawing wind kept it company for an hour or two. To keep warm in the morning one had to wear his entire wardrobe, including pajamas underneath. And then, as the day wore on, the divestiture would start; men would be discarding pieces of clothing one by one, as if in one gigantic game of strip poker, until by afternoon, after the end of classes, when the temperature frequently hit ninety degrees, some of the sweating men were down to the hair on their chests. And this was the month of December! Strange country, this Texas.

That David was now indeed a subject of a foreign country he realized the day he and the other chaplains purchased their blue Air Force uniforms at the Base Exchange, and he put on his and stepped outside the BX where he paused to tie a shoelace, resting his foot on the bumper of a shiny new Oldsmobile whose license plate sported a star.

The reflection in the car's simonized hood was a stranger's: a tall, swarthy, broad-shouldered fellow in an unfaded postman's outfit with a silver bar on each shoulder, like twin mezuzas. Only the Jewish chaplain's insignia—the Tablets of the Law affixed to a Star of David, pinned above his left breast pocket—reassured him that he had not been snatched away from Brooklyn by gypsies and imprisoned in some enormous Texas post office.

48

"Lieutenant!"

David looked up to see a colonel standing beside him. "Yes—Colonel?" (Still a civilian at heart, despite the Air Force uniform covering it, he could not bring himself to sir anyone.)

"That's General Price's car!" said the grim-looking colonel.

"Oh." Vaguely David recalled that General Price was the name of the base commander. "Thanks for telling me, Colonel." Having finished tying his shoelace, he had no further use for the General's car anyway. He turned to go.

"Lieutenant!"

David paused. Why did the colonel insist on punctuating all his words with exclamation marks? "Yes—Colonel?"

"You forgot to salute the General's car!"

David chuckled, envying the colonel his ability to keep a straight face while satirizing military discipline. "Salute a car!" David laughed. "Say, that's a good one!"

The colonel's face twisted into a maze of lowered eyebrows, narrowing eyes, flaring nostrils, and constricting lips. *"Lieutenant!"*

The colonel was, incredible as it seemed, *serious!* He actually was ordering David to salute a *car*—and an *empty* car at that. "If you insist," David muttered, flushing. He threw General Price's car a grudging salute while he restrained himself from inquiring, "Am I supposed to hold my salute now, Colonel, until the Oldsmobile returns it?"

"That's better!" the colonel exclaimed and stalked away.

"David, you mustn't feel so foolish."

Feeling foolish indeed, David turned around to see Roger Allerton (his new roommate after the Director of the Chaplain School had decided that the alphabet should not thwart his wish to have all the chaplains fraternize) separate himself from the group and come

49

up to him. "No? And why not? Saluting medium-priced cars!"

"Just look at it this way," said Roger. "Jews have the Star of David, we Christians have the Cross, and Landers has General Price's Oldsmobile."

David smiled and fell into step beside the shy 6' 5" chaplain with the posture of a question mark, as the others followed behind. "I guess so."

"But then, all is not Oldsmobiles here, David. After all, if it weren't for Landers, we'd never have gotten to know one another, would we? And I'd never have gotten this wonderful opportunity to learn all about the Jewish religion from a rabbi."

The two of them came upon a new flaming red Cadillac near the BX, and David stopped short. This time he did not even hesitate; swiftly he threw the automobile a salute. Immediately Roger threw back his round shoulders and saluted too, and several dozen other men around them, including all the chaplains, followed suit as a master sergeant approached the Cadillac and helped his wife and two small children into it.

Paul Smith expressed everyone's bewilderment when the sergeant drove off leaving some fifty puzzled men in his wake: "But why do we also have to salute that Cadillac?"

"Don't you know?" David replied soberly. "Cadillacs outrank Oldsmobiles."

Bentley Lane, the chaplain who looked least like a train conductor in his new uniform, hooted with laughter while the others groaned or grinned. "Cadillacs outrank Oldsmobiles—that *sounds* like a reg!"

Roger clapped a hand to his forehead. "And without even thinking, I saluted too!"

David smiled. "Roger, you're in the Air Force now!"

Clifford Fowler stepped up to David. "So are you," he said coldly. "Or have you already forgotten?" And he walked away before David could reply.

In their first school session, Chaplain Radcliff informed

the men that they were being assigned twenty-two courses.

"Why, that's more subjects than I have fingers and toes," Bentley Lane remarked.

"Oh, stop being so modest," said Chaplain Radcliff and the class laughed, but no louder than the Director himself.

Chaplain Radcliff went on to say: "Now, fellas, it is my job to teach you history, the history of the chaplaincy, and I will teach it, as I do all things, with a bias —the bias of a Baptist. I can't help it. I am a Baptist and I see all things through the eyes of my religion. Now I wouldn't for the life of me offend any of you, but I do have two fervent wishes: I wish all Christians were Baptists, and they're not. And I wish all Baptists were Christians, and *they're* not. And what a pity that is! For I know a lot of people who could be good Christians with a third the effort it takes me to keep out of jail." His red face crinkled into a Santa Claus smile.

"But to get down to our subject—the history of the chaplaincy can be traced all the way back to the ancient Egyptian Pharaohs who took their holy men with them into battle. Men have always had chaplains accompany them to war. Why? Because it is utterly impossible for a man to be nonreligious. Especially in one of his supreme experiences: war.

"The Children of Israel were never without a chaplain during their wandering in the desert. Moses was their chaplain then, and afterwards Joshua was commissioned. 'I've given you the whole land,' God said to Joshua. 'All you have to do is take Jericho. Just follow my directions now.' And Joshua said, 'You've really given it to me, Boy, haven't you? You've put me in a *box.*'"

Clifford Fowler sucked in his breath sharply.

The Director paused. "One thing I'm glad of is that this job was not given to the Baptist Church. Because you can't get all the Baptists to do anything at once without *someone* raising an objection. And don't smirk now because I don't think any of *your* denominations can either!"

All the chaplains chuckled, except Clifford.

"Now, fellas, if you'll take my hand, we'll skip a few thousand years to the American Revolution. The Continental Congress allowed their soldiers freedom of worship. Sounds wonderful, doesn't it? Only it wasn't. Because each brigade voted what type of chaplain to have, and the majority ruled. So what happened? Only Protestant chaplains were elected. There were no Catholic or Jewish chaplains. Then during the Mexican War, we reaped the results of our folly. One of our battalions was composed entirely of Irish Catholics. They were stationed across the Rio Grande from the Mexicans, who started circulating letters promising every man who would desert fifty acres of land in Mexico, also money. Only a few deserted, however. Then the Mexicans tried *muchachas* —come over to Mexico, get land, money, *and* a voluptuous *muchacha*—and these *muchachas* would parade in front of the battalion every morning. But nothing doing. Finally, the Mexicans played their trump card. They had their Catholic priests appeal to the Catholic battalion to abandon an imperialistic war and come over and join the God-loving Mexicans.

"And so, just as soon as the whole blamed battalion deserted, the President of the United States ordered the Army to get Catholic chaplains also. Later, in 1862, Congress opened the chaplaincy to rabbis as well. This was done at the personal request of President Lincoln."

When Chaplain Radcliff had departed after the end of the session, Clifford Fowler's comment on the lecture was louder than all the rest. "Disgusting!" he exclaimed, silencing the others with his vehemence. "Imagine—referring to the Lord as if he were a fellow barfly! Such disrespect!"

"Familiarity is not necessarily disrespectful," David said, then regretted it for he had no wish to engage in any further altercations with Clifford. But he did feel compelled to defend Chaplain Radcliff against an unjustified attack, and so he continued: "For example, you remem-

52

ber from the Bible how Abraham bargained with God, like a man with his friend, for the lives of the people of Sodom and Gomorrah. And then there's the poignant *Kaddish* prayer of Rabbi Levi Yitzchok of Berditchev that goes like this: 'Good morning to You, Lord of the Universe. I, Levi Yitzchok, son of Sarah of Berditchev, have come to You in a lawsuit on behalf of your people, Israel. What have You against your people, Israel? Why do You oppress your people, Israel? An end there must be to this. This persecution, suffering—it must all stop. Do You hear me, God? It must stop! *Yisgadal, V'yiskadash.* Hallowed and magnified be the name of God.' "

"Lovely!" Bentley Lane exclaimed softly. "Lovely!"

But Clifford said, "Well, that just proves my point: Chaplain Cohen agrees with Chaplain Radcliff."

David reddened.

Bentley Lane, Albert Cohen, Roger Allerton, Paul Smith and Dan Miller all began speaking at once in David's defense, but the next instructor appeared and called the class to order. The men quieted down as the instructor then delivered himself of a boring lecture on pay and allowances to which all the chaplains, except David who was still smarting from Clifford's words and Dan who had taken a vow of poverty, listened with rapt attention. After that, a full forty minutes was devoted to the salute.

First, the philosophy of the salute: It is a way of greeting a superior officer, like saying "How do you do?" You are not saluting the man, but the rank. Like the use of "sir," this is not a sign of servitude or subservience but of recognition and respect. Do you understand?

David was uncertain.

Now, the mechanics: Hold right hand straight out at side, turn the palm upward, move arm to forty-five degree angle from body. Turn lower arm upward, making sure at all times to keep it perfectly flat, till it touches the forehead just above the outside corner of the eye. Got it? Now pull your hand down fast. Up! Down! Fast! Up! Down! Fast! *Faster!*

"My *eye!*" Clifford Fowler cried out, and David exulted, without guilt.

During subsequent sessions, the chaplains were also instructed in:

Military Law: You don't lose any of your rights as a United States citizen when you enter the Service. It only *seems* that you do.

Management: Management involves the effective utilization of four things: men, matériel, time, space.

Administration: AFR, AFL, AFM, AFB, AFP, AFVA, AFR 5-2, AQE, ACB, AFJKT, DR, PERAM, OER, AFR 35-66, AFR 36-2, AFR 39-11, AFR 39-13, AFR 39-16, AFR 39-17, AFR 39-22—these are just a few of the terms and regs you must learn to start off with.

Classification and Assignment: In the Service, every man has not one number but *two.* The second one indicates his specialty, which is arrived at only after extensive testing, careful deliberation, and lots of luck.

History of the Chaplaincy: The name of "chaplain" goes back to a legend about Martin of Tours who gave half of his cape to a shivering beggar. The half that he kept, known as *capella,* became an object of veneration at court, and the French kings began to call their clergymen *chappelains,* the keepers of the cloak.

USAF Supply: If you want to get two of anything in the Air Force, you'd better ask for six.

Intelligence: A nation's capability to wage war is based upon its location, size and shape, topography, climate, natural resources, technological development . . .

Charity Drives: Since you are shepherds of flocks, bear in mind that sheep have to be sheared regularly as well as fed.

Chaplain Service Specialist: It's usually better to choose an atheist for an assistant rather than a lay preacher for the same reason that a wise man never marries a woman who thinks she knows more than he.

Problems on Officer Behavior: It is absolutely forbidden for an officer to accept any gifts from anyone connected with the Air Force. That's why last week General

Price's wife received as a present from the Landers Officers Club the finest pair of shotguns that you ever saw.

Funds and Facilities: Remember this name: the Central Post Welfare Fund. That's the fund that plays Santa Claus to a goodly part of the chaplain's program.

Chaplain's Supply: Always take a personal inventory of every piece of property that you sign for, especially when you're taking over the account of another chaplain.

Chaplain's Place in the Air Force: A chaplain has to strike a balance between his ecclesiastical authority and the military's authority, or else he's in for trouble.

Air Force Organization: The Air Force is composed of: CONAC, ADC, ATC, ARDC, AMC, ARTRC, Hq COMD, AU, APGC, USAF SS; also, SAC, TAC, and MATS for those who want Air Commands where frequent TDY's (Temporary Duty assignments) will take them away from nagging wives.

Leadership: The primary consideration in all military organization is *not* the men but the *Mission.*

Physical Training: Hup, two, three, four, *hup* . . .

Moral and Religious Education: Your religious education program must be nondenominational, and ideally your Dynamics of Moral Leadership Lectures should be nonsoporific.

Customs and Ceremonies: The salute is not a sign of servitude but a form of greeting exchanged between two people, or one person and a black Oldsmobile with a star on its license plate.

Worship and Pastoral Function: Here you proceed in the same manner as you did in the civilian ministry, except that you must conduct at least one major nondenominational service a week.

Drill: Surely you chaplains can do better than *that* for God's sake.

History of the United States Air Force: From the Wright brothers and Kitty Hawk to Buck Rogers and the moon may not be as far as you think.

As incidental information, the chaplains were also informed, soberly, that in the Air Force *everything* was considered a privilege. "Does that mean," Bentley Lane inquired, "that if the Air Force lops off your head, they're only withholding your privilege of living?"

Such was the efficacy of their indoctrination by the end of their first week of classes that none of the chaplains laughed. But a few were noted to rub their necks absent-mindedly.

"So in the Air Force everything is considered a privilege!" Bentley exclaimed to David after the session. "I'm beginning to think that maybe instead of enlisting I should have kept on looking for a church until I found one foolish enough to take me."

David was surprised. "But why wouldn't every church snap up someone like you—Yale, Phi Beta Kappa, two articles published in *The Christian Century*, and with two vertical dimples yet to titillate the sisterhood?"

Bentley ran his fingers through his crew-cut black hair. "Maybe because at all the church interviews I was subjected to, no one ever thought to ask me what I thought of God, Christ, religion, Christian education, or the function of the Church. Instead, one joker asked me whether I'd join him in denouncing the current trend of running Catholics for high offices, and I told him I'd rather denounce bigots instead. Then there was the dowager who, hearing my age, asked: 'But how could I ever bring my troubles to someone who wasn't even *born* when my troubles got *started?*' So I told her that it was time she got herself some *new* troubles. There was even the time I flunked out on an interview because of what I *heard*. What happened was that I went to meet this Westerner, on a buying trip in New York, and for no reason at all—except perhaps the six martinis that had preceded me into his suite—this pillar of the church starts telling me about this affair he's been carrying on with this size fourteen model for these past five buying trips. Later, he returned to his church and reported, I was informed, that they wouldn't possibly want to see me because I squinted, stuttered, fluttered, and picked my nose. But the prize one was the pulpit committee chairman who got up to tell me that his church wanted—and these were his exact words—a high-principled spiritual leader with a

56

dynamic personality who wouldn't be trying all the time to tell the congregation what to do, a man of conviction who was firm yet gentle, strong but mild. I couldn't help myself, I told him that he didn't want a minister—he wanted Ex-Lax. *Voilà,* the Air Force."

It was late the first Saturday night in the Chaplains' Barracks, and David had nothing better to do than sit at his desk and read a book on existentialism.

"Dave, are you getting stir-crazy here too? Or is it just that it's Saturday night and my old sailor blood is heating up?"

David looked up. Paul Smith was standing in the doorway.

"Want to go to San Antonio with me and paint the town red, white and blue?"

David laughed. "I'm game!" He put away his book. "Maybe some of the other fellows want to go too. Let's see."

But the first chaplain they asked said, "At *midnight?* Oh, you crazy Presbyterians and lunatic Jews." That effectively discouraged them from seeking more recruits.

The two of them set out for the city in Paul's car. Overhead, the stars of the night shone bigger and brighter than any David had ever seen. So brilliant and excessive were the heavenly hosts, so vast the desert they were driving through, so dark the night, so solitary the feeling, that David found himself automatically reciting aloud from the books of Psalms. " 'When I behold Thy heavens, the work of Thy fingers, the moon and the stars which Thou hast established— What is man, that Thou art mindful of him? And the son of man, that Thou thinkest of him?

" 'For Thou hast made him a little lower than the angels, and hast crowned him with glory and honor,' " continued Paul. " 'Thou madest him to have dominion over the works of Thy hands. Thou hast—' "

David interrupted. "What's *that?*"

Ahead of them on the dark road a light was flashing, moving sideways, then up and down, signaling.

Paul got his foot on the brake and the car slowed down. The light grew larger as they neared it. Now they could see that it was a flashlight, and waving it was a young man in a leather jacket and bluejeans.

"Help me?" the fellow was calling. He pointed to an old car with a battered license plate at the side of the road. "Flat."

David remembered something then, something he had read in the San Antonio newspapers. There had been several stories during the past week alone about muggings and hijacking of cars. Three drivers had been set upon by hitchhikers, and two cars that had stopped to help people supposedly in trouble had been overturned by gangs hiding in nearby bushes and their owners had been beaten up, robbed, and stripped.

"I need a jack," the fellow was calling as Paul's car drew closer. "Got a jack, Mac?"

Paul turned to David. "It's the Christian thing to do," he said, and he looked at David as if he expected an argument.

David thought of at least two rejoinders. One: Maybe. But *I'm* no Christian. Two: But wasn't it a gang of Christians—the percentages were in their favor—who knocked off those other cars and cracked their passengers' skulls?

Yet how could he, a rabbi, say such things to a Protestant minister? Paul might think him cowardly or uncharitable, possibly that he didn't want to help the stranger in trouble on the deserted road just because he didn't look Jewish. So instead he forced himself to say, "It's the Jewish thing, too, you know. Love your neighbor and all that."

"I suppose," said Paul, and he stopped the car several feet behind the other one.

But why, wondered David uneasily, did his neighbor out there have to look like a thug? And why did he have to get a flat in such a dark forsaken spot? And why didn't the nogoodnik carry his *own* damn jack?

Paul got out of the car and took a jack from the trunk. Then he came around to the front, stepping into the glare of his headlights. The stranger did not come forward to meet him but waited near his car while David wrestled with his mounting uneasiness. Deserted roads, dark midnights, and leather-jacketed strangers were decidedly not his glass of tea.

The fellow took the jack from the chaplain and, for some strange reason, raised it high above both their heads. He said something to Paul—David could not hear the remark, he was too far away—and the redheaded chaplain seemed to start. He hesitated for a moment, then slowly put his left hand in his back pocket and took out something. His wallet?

Things happened all at once then. The car ahead seemed suddenly to sprout heads—one head, two heads, three heads. David stopped counting at four as the silhouetted heads advanced toward his colleague.

"*Paul!* Watch out!" cried David.

As if the cry were the signal, Paul extended his hand, the one with the wallet in it, toward the leather-jacketed stranger. He grabbed for it. Suddenly Paul withdrew the wallet, did something with his other hand and his feet—too fast for David's eye to follow—and sent the stranger flying head over heels into the darkness, out of range of the headlights.

"*Dave!* Help me!"

David sat transfixed. *What to do?* The last time he had been in a fight he was ten years old, and then it had been with a nine-year-old girl. ("Jews don't fight," Tante Dvorah had repeatedly indoctrinated him, "not until they're married.")

A second stranger advanced on Paul and jumped him. Suddenly, Paul turned him into a cartwheel also and sent him spinning off into the blackness.

"I'm coming!" David cried, though what he really felt like doing was *going*. He started out of the car but, calling upon God and recalling Gideon, he paused for a moment to imitate his Biblical battle strategy. He pressed the horn several times, flicked on the radio, turning up the volume full force, and jumped out of the car, yelling all the while.

"All right, let's get 'em, men! Bentley! Roger! Albert! Jim!" He raced to Paul's side. "Clifford! Dan! Tante Dvorah! Unc—"

A sharp clout on the side of his head knocked his uncle's name completely out of his mind and sent him reeling off into the darkness beside the car. Before he could catch his breath, he was set upon by someone with three legs and at least two heads.

David, who knew less about the manly art of self-defense than about any other art known to man, thrashed about violently with every limb of his that he could move, like a child throwing a temper tantrum or an adult doing the Twist. How it happened he had no idea, but now he found himself on top of someone. His knee found a softly yielding human juncture, either an armpit or a groin, and he mashed it down as if he were putting out a cigarette. It was a groin, he concluded as one of his assailants yowled in pain and recoiled from him. David kicked out with all his might and pulled away, rolling into a ditch at the side of the road.

Above him the shadowy combatants fought on, grunting and cursing now. David looked up and saw Paul, his back to the license plate of the other car, still sending strangers spinning into cartwheels in all directions.

Then what was that bedlam? Who the devil was being mugged above him on the dark road? Whom were they beating up? It could only be, he reasoned, his assailants themselves. They were, thank God, mugging one another.

". . . surrounded now, trapped, defeated!" blared an official-sounding, self-confident, supercilious voice. "And this is how every bit of scum, every piece of dirt ends up—washed-up, destroyed, and down the drain!"

"Hey, you guys! Let's get the hell out of here!"

There was a scurrying of feet, a slamming of doors, a car starting up, and the muggers sped off, though not before they tried unsuccessfully to back over Paul who eluded them by jumping into the ditch.

"And who do we have to thank for this clean-up?" the radio called after the hoodlums.

"Mr. Clean! Mr. Clean! Mr. Clean! Mr. Clean!" a chorus gaily trilled.

David scrambled to his feet and ran to Paul. "You all right?"

He nodded. "Sure. You? Why, you're bleeding!"

David was surprised. "Am I?" He put his hand to his nose and felt the familiar sticky liquid. "It's nothing. I always bleed. I even bled the first time I kissed a girl. Come on, let's get out of here too!"

They returned to the car, turned off the radio, and headed back for the base.

"Boy, you sure were something," David said with admiration, his head tilted back and his fingers pinching his nostrils. "Where'd you ever learn to play with boys like that?"

Paul grinned. "I wasn't *always* a clergyman. I've told you—once I was a sailor. They taught us jujitsu."

"God bless the Navy," David said. "And Mr. Clean too."

Paul shook his head. "We sure are lucky the way things turned out. But I must say it was stupid of us to stop on a deserted road at midnight, especially after all those stories in the paper recently about muggings. David, why did you ever make me stop?"

David was astounded. *"I* made *you* stop?"

"Well, sure. You quoted me 'Love thy neighbor,'" Paul said. "You don't think I'd have stopped if I were *alone*, do you? Or with Bentley or Roger. I couldn't have a rabbi think badly of us Christians— *could* I?"

Paul phoned the police from the barracks as David took off his blood-spattered clothes. "There were about four, maybe five of them, I guess . . . I only saw one clearly though, the one who stopped me and demanded my wallet . . . About six foot, long black hair, broken nose . . . I don't know, early twenties, I should say . . . Black leather jacket, bluejeans . . . Car was a dark color, couldn't tell what exactly. I'm not sure about the make, it was an old car . . . Are you serious? Who had a chance

61

to look at the license plate? Everything happened so quickly, I—"

David interrupted. "Tell them six, five, three, dash, nine, six, six."

Paul paused, looked at him in astonishment.

David repeated the number.

Paul said into the telephone: "My friend says it's six, five, three, dash, nine, six, six . . . All right . . . You'll let us know? . . . Thank you." He hung up, then turned to David. "How did *you* know the license number of that car? You were just as busy as I was."

"Are you kidding?" said David. "Ever since we started that administration course, I automatically memorize any number with more than four digits in it. Don't you?"

Chapter : 5

THE police caught the four hoodlums the next day and Paul and David were able to identify the ringleader, as were several other victims of theirs from Landers and San Antonio. As a result, the thugs were put away where it would take them at least two years before they could return to ply their trade.

The verdict did not elate David. For by this time he was encountering his first problem in the Air Force, other than the Air Force itself: He was beginning to feel lonely—even in the midst of his twenty-nine fellow chaplains. For much as he liked the great majority of them and their warmth, geniality, intelligence, sense of humor and comradeship, not one of them was a nice Jewish girl for him to date. And when he took the bus to San Antonio's Jewish Center, he found to his dismay even fewer nice Jewish girls there than at Landers.

Approaching the problem tactically, David used his first paycheck to buy a used car which, according to Your

Friendly Used Car Salesman, belonged during its entire eight years of existence to an old maid who had been dead for a decade. Then he sped to San Antonio's largest synagogue where he reasoned that, if its congregants were *truly* Jewish, as soon as he'd walk in unaccompanied they would start matching him up.

David's logic proved to be perfectly sound, but only in theory. For in the synagogue he met a host of would-be matchmakers, all frustrated because there was not a single eligible girl for him in the entire city. (And they said *they* were frustrated!) It seemed that the San Antonio Jewish Community was not a large one, and the crop of girls born in the thirties had been a small one due to the Depression and the laws of chance. (Now if David were only a *girl*, he was told rather irrelevantly, could *he* make out!), and the few available girls had followed the Southern tradition of marrying at an early age. So, alas, ended David's quest.

For solace he turned first to solitary night walks, then to the impromptu religious discussions that had started up among the men in the barracks. Every evening found several of these discussions going on concurrently in various rooms, with the tacit understanding that it was no disgrace for the various faiths and denominations to go along together as far as they could; nor was it any disgrace for them to part company when a dividing path was reached, just so long as each continued to have respect for the other.

Soon these nightly religious bull sessions, which most of the chaplains considered the most valuable part of the Chaplain Training School, reduced the frequency of David's walks. Still, he could not bring himself to believe that, when God stated in the Bible that it was not good for man to live alone, He was advocating a communal celibate existence. "Be fruitful and multiply," the Lord had commanded, and David yearned to do his bit.

And so one Sunday morning when he was called by six different people and notified that Sandra Birnbaum was coming to town, he exclaimed, "Wonderful!" even before inquiring, "Who *is* Sandra Birnbaum?"

"She's single," each caller began by saying. Sandra had other virtues besides, it developed, but the twin facts that she was a girl and single were stressed most heavily of all, as if these were her own brilliant inventions.

David was also apprised that Sandra was a twenty-one-year-old college graduate with a fine Jewish background. Moreover, Sandra was attractive, intelligent, considerate, refined, charming, good-natured, and possessed so many other fine qualities that he was tempted to ask whether, in addition, Sandra's father was offering to take her future husband into his business as well. Sandra lived in Dallas but—how fortunate for him! everyone exclaimed in turn—she would be visiting relatives in San Antonio the following weekend.

David lost no time in telephoning the Birnbaum house. A voice that sounded suspiciously like at least two of the six people who had called him earlier answered the phone. She said she was Sandra's aunt and accepted the engagement for her niece as soon as she heard his name and before he asked for a date. "I suppose," Mrs. Birnbaum went on to say casually, "that everyone's told you already what a refined, attractive, intelligent, considerate girl my niece Sandra is?"

"Yes," he replied and, because he was refined and considerate himself, refrained from adding: "*You* have —twice before."

David told only Roger Allerton of his date, but came Saturday night and the rest of the chaplains guessed. On his way out of the barracks, David, attired in his most non-funereal-looking suit, passed through the dayroom. Immediately his friends surrounded him.

"Who is she, Dave?" Paul Smith asked.

"She?" said David, surprised.

"Your Sabbath was last night, and you didn't look half so good then," Jim Mackey commented.

Roger tried to rescue David. "A Jew is *supposed* to look twice as good after the Sabbath—that's a Jewish teaching—because the Holy Day of Rest refreshes his soul."

"The only trouble with that explanation," said Bentley Lane, "is that David doesn't look so much refreshed as *hungry*."

"Come on, David," Albert Cohen insisted. "Who is she? You told us there were no eligible Jewish girls in town. That's why I wrote my wife to alert all matchmakers she knew in neighboring states."

David laughed. "All right, fellows. She is an import all the way from Dallas. She is also my only hope here. So you'd better wish me luck."

"That all depends," said Dan Miller innocently. "What do you want us to wish you luck *for?*"

"Oh," David replied, "that she has a friend for you. What do you say, Dan? How about double-dating?"

Dan pondered the proposal for a moment, then said, "My Bishop just might not approve of my dating right now or even getting married. It would be bigamy. See?" He held up his breviary. "I have a wife already. And, bless her, she's the only wife I know who never talks back to her husband."

Bentley grabbed David by the shoulder and propelled him toward the door. "Well, come on, let's go."

"Where are *you* going?" David asked.

Bentley's deep-set black eyes widened in pretended surprise. "Why, with you, of course. To chaperone. You don't think I'd trust you alone with a lovely young Jewess, do you?"

"Don't worry," David laughed. "It's been so long since I've been with a girl, I don't even remember what to do."

Clifford Fowler spoke up. "I'll *bet!*" he sneered in a voice leering with innuendo, and all of a sudden the light banter among the chaplains was transformed into an off-color smoking-room story.

Silence fell upon the room. Even David did not reply to Clifford. He refused to allow himself to be drawn into a dispute minutes before his first date in two months. And so, excusing himself, he left the barracks.

Bentley accompanied him outside. "I'm sorry about Clifford," he said. "I would apologize to you for him, but that would involve me in apologizing for the whole damn human race. Because Clifford is fairly representative, alas, in his own unique way."

David stopped short. "How can you say a thing like that!"

"Easy," Bentley said. "Because it's true. Original Sin isn't just a Christian doctrine, you know; it's a factual description of human nature. Oh, I was like you, David, until I entered Divinity School. A regular people-lover I was until I took my first student pulpit, and people started telling me how superior our church was to all the other surrounding ones; asking whether I had ever been a Communist because I was inviting Negro families to attend our services during the fifty-one other weeks of the year when Brotherhood wasn't being officially observed; criticizing my sermons for making them feel that all was wrong with the world and that it was up to them to right things; apprising me of all the latest slander because they figured that it was only proper that I should know what dirty dogs their neighbors were since I wasn't able to learn it firsthand from a confessional booth. Good old New Haven! I'd be preaching to the congregation about God and His wondrous message and they'd be gossiping about the tight dress my wife was wearing—was Cathy being provocative or just pregnant? —and where had I gotten such an awful haircut? No wonder more ministers have nervous breakdowns than any other single group. All the henpecked husbands who couldn't even run a lawn mower, all the women whose husbands were ignoring them for good reason, all the old maids of both sexes—all of them were telling me how to run a church. It was a pain in the ass. Here as a minister I found myself forced to associate with a good many people, serve them no less, whom in other circumstances I'd have walked across the city to avoid. That's when I discovered something important about myself—I don't really want to serve, I don't yearn to help my fellow man. Because I hate him."

"Bentley!"

"I'm not ashamed to admit it. Other ministers, I know, have doubts about God. Not me. My faith in

66

God has never wavered. My doubts are all centered in my fellow man. Life is so short, and yet he concentrates on being so little! It always gets me, all those people who deny God. Me, I deny people. That's why I plan to go into Biblical scholarship: so I can be with my first, last, and only love who will never disappoint me—God."

David marveled aloud. "With an attitude like that, how did you ever fall in love and get married?"

"Oh, I just proposed to the first girl who said she hated me," Bentley said. "It meant that we were *simpático*."

David was not sure whether Bentley's words were meant to be taken seriously or not, but about Clifford he had no doubts at all, only questions. Driving to San Antonio he kept asking himself: Why was Clifford so perverse? Why did he have a prune for a heart and a pit for a soul? Why had he ever become a clergyman? Why had he taken such a wholehearted dislike to David? And why wouldn't the *momzer* leave him alone already?

As soon as he arrived at the Birnbaum house, however, David, in his eager anticipation over his date, put Clifford out of his mind, even when he found that Sandra was not yet ready. (Still another why: Why was it that women thought that being punctual was against their sex?)

Mr. and Mrs. Birnbaum were very cordial to him, also inquisitive. He was hardly seated before they started inquiring about his background, family, plans for the future, rabbis' salaries, how many children he planned to sire. (One more why: Why did girls' families always behave as if they were interviewing him for some unadvertised position?)

Finally Sandra appeared, just as it seemed that the Birnbaums were about to hire him. She was a tall, dark, shapely, extremely attractive girl, whose bosom mushroomed up pleasantly from her narrow waist, like an atomic explosion. "Hello there," she said.

David sighed. "Hello."

Behind him he could feel the Birnbaums already beginning to count their *nachus* from their niece. And, after two dateless months, this did not disturb him at all. Now he hardly minded giving away any amount of *nachus* just so long as it gave him the prospect of eventually cashing in on some for himself. "Oh, I'm so excited," he overheard Mrs. Birnbaum saying as he and his date were leaving. "I'm so excited! I've never been to a *military* wedding."

Alas, Sandra proved to be a good deal less excited than her aunt and, worse still, no more exciting. A high school music teacher, she behaved with David as if he were her principal come to observe her. On the way to the San Antonio Opera, she asked as many questions as had her relatives, but all her inquiries were strictly academic ones; not once did she so much as allude to how large a family he hoped to have. And after the opera, when he asked her to recommend a night spot, she guided him to an ice-cream parlor!

"You know," David commented wryly, "on occasion I do go to night clubs where I've noted that people listen to music and dance and actually enjoy themselves."

Sandra couldn't have been more astounded. "Really?"

"How about it? Would you like me to take you to a night club? There's a nice one on the south side of town, I've heard, with an excellent jazz combo. Would you like to go there?"

"No," Sandra said. "Let's order our sodas now."

They gave their orders to a waiter, and when their drinks were served there was nothing to do but drink them. Between sips of soda, they spoke of the opera, Chaplain School, and teaching music. But the talk always remained impersonal, as if the two of them were plucking scraps of information from one another, like two monkeys swapping fleas.

While David learned all about the Dallas high school system and music departments and that there just wasn't anyone who was *really* tone deaf, Sandra learned about the curriculum at Chaplain School and the courses at Rabbinical Seminary. Yet despite the tedious agenda, Sandra never seemed bored; she appeared content just so long as either of them was talking words or uttering sentences, so much so that David expected to hear her cry, "Bravo!" when he had completed a boring but lengthy paragraph on the organization of the Air Force. Silences evidently made the girl uneasy; during one such lull in the mutual interrogation, she took such a long sip of soda that her straw collapsed and she began to choke.

Happily David seized the opportunity to pound the girl on the back. And it felt, he realized as soon as his hand touched her softly rounded shoulder blade, wonderfully good—so good that he let his other hand join in the fun of pounding.

"*What*," sputtered Sandra, "are you *doing?*"

For a moment David was at a loss for an answer. Then, as he reluctantly withdrew his hands from the girl, who unfortunately was coughing no more, he remembered. "I was hitting you on the back. You were choking—"

"That's an old wives' remedy for choking—hitting someone on the back. Didn't you know that?"

"Yes, of course."

Sandra regarded him with surprise. "Then why did you do it?"

Go tell her! David hesitated, then replied, "Reflex action, I suppose. Man is a creature of reflexes and all sorts of fascinating drives—did you know *that?*"

But all that Sandra knew was that it was time for her to go home. This she informed him in such a business-like tone of voice that he almost said, "Okay, meeting's adjourned."

During the long drive back to the Birnbaum house, David tentatively raised his hand behind the girl and hoped.

"Oh, my windpipe's all unclogged now, thank you," Sandra exclaimed, and he swiftly dropped his arm to his side, feeling like an unmasked sex fiend.

Seeing Sandra to the door, he made no attempt to kiss her. (Who wants to kiss a girl with an unclogged windpipe?) Yet he asked to see her on the following night.

"Well . . . all right," she said, without indicating that the thought of seeing him again made her the least bit happy. Evidently, reasoned David ruefully, another one of Sandra's virtues was that she did not lie.

Some of the men were still awake when he returned glumly to the barracks. They were either chatting in each other's rooms or playing cards. "Lord, they're gambling—make them *lose*," one chaplain was praying aloud. "I need the money."

In no mood to engage in further dispassionate activities that night, David slipped unobtrusively into his room. What, he kept asking himself, had gone wrong?

There was a knock at the door. "Can I come in?" Bentley Lane asked.

"On one condition," David said. "That you don't ask me how it went tonight."

Bentley entered the room carrying a book by Reinhold Niebuhr in one hand and a slice of pizza in the other. "How did it go tonight, David?" he asked.

David shrugged. "Oh, I don't know. It was all right, I suppose."

"Wasn't the girl *simpático?*"

"Oh, she was very nice. Very attractive, refined, intelligent. Cultured, too."

"Then what was the matter?"

David threw up his hands. "That's just it! I don't know. She was so polite all evening long. Polite—and informative. Who's interested in the damn public school system of Dallas anyway!"

Bentley, shaking his head soberly, downed the last piece of pizza. "I think I know what was the matter. You're a rabbi."

"What?"

"Did you kiss her good night?"

"Bentley, what a question."

"Well, *did* you?"

David shrugged. "I thought I'd wait till tomorrow night."

Bentley sighed. "You'll find out then."

"Find out what?"

"That you're a rabbi. That's what was the matter, David."

"What are you talking about!"

"I've been through it myself, so I know," Bentley said. "David, you were double-dating tonight after all, only you didn't know it. There were the two of you, of course, but along with you were also the Rabbi and the Parishioness: your date's ideal conception of a Rabbi and the girl she thought the Rabbi would expect her to be. That's a tough parlay to beat." He paused to light a cigarette. "I remember that once I had entered Divinity School it wasn't easy for me, either, to find a girl who thought of me as—well, *me*. Clergymen are different from others in a few respects. The trouble is people think clergymen are different in *all* respects. People—girls, especially—think of a minister in terms of a stereotype. And it's to the stereotype they're usually reacting, not to you personally. And who can live up to someone else's ideal of you? Heaven knows it's tough enough trying to live up to your *own* ideal of yourself!"

"Come to think of it," David recalled, "Sandra never once called me by my first name tonight."

"That's what happens, David," Bentley insisted. "Girls just don't feel comfortable with a clergyman as a date. I remember they never used to act natural with me. For one thing, they used to feel so *safe* with me. Now that isn't natural. It's *aggravating!* Even a minister wants a girl to give him the impression every once in a while that she's going to have to fight him off, even if the only thing he attacks all evening is a bag of popcorn. Why is it girls suppose clergymen are *above* sex!"

Bentley put out his cigarette without realizing that he had been so engrossed in talking that he had not taken a single puff. "It's unfortunate but it's true, David. If there's one thing most people begrudge men of the cloth, it's a love life. Politics may excite us, wars may arouse us, and sin, of course, is supposed to keep us in a perpetual dither. But to the public mind we clergymen are supposedly as unattuned to the call of sex as we are

71

to dog whistles. Just because some people are *always* responding to it, they think we clergymen shouldn't *ever*. You should have seen how disconcerted my little New Haven church was when I told them Cathy was pregnant. If it weren't for a lingering atavistic belief in spontaneous generation, I think they'd have unfrocked me on the spot."

The next evening David took Sandra to dinner. Their conversation differed from that of the previous night only in that it tended to explore more shallow topics in greater depth.

"How about going dancing tonight?" David suggested after dessert. "I know you don't care for night clubs, but some of the chaplains told me about a dance that's run downtown every Sunday night. It's supposed to be very nice. They have a five-piece orchestra, and the chaplains who have been there say it's a very lovely place. Respectable too," he added as a final inducement. "How about it? Would you like to go there?"

"Well," Sandra replied with all the enthusiasm she might have summoned for a plane crash, "all right."

The San Antonio Ballroom was very crowded when they arrived there. Even so, when David took Sandra out on the dance floor, she managed to keep enough floor space between the two of them for another couple to dance on. A man cut in, and David surrendered the girl, then noted with chagrin that he could not see any space at all between Sandra and her new partner. Yet as soon as David claimed her for the following dance, the missing floor space magically reappeared.

Someone else cut in; this time it was, surprisingly, Jim Mackey.

David watched Sandra and Jim dance away, the gap between them diminishing with the speed of a jet. But suddenly Sandra pulled away from him—why?—and finished the rest of the dance at a discreet distance.

"I didn't know he was a classmate of yours at the Chaplain School!" Sandra exclaimed as soon as she returned to David. "He certainly doesn't dance like a clergyman."

David welcomed the opportunity to explore the topic. "And how are clergymen *supposed* to dance?"

"With their wives," Sandra said.

"But *I* am *single.*"

Sandra narrowed her big brown eyes. "Your friend isn't. He's married—with a wife and all. Did you know that?"

"Yes, but no wives are allowed up here at Chaplain School. So Jim had to leave his wife and baby behind in—"

"A baby yet!" Sandra exclaimed. "That makes it even *worse*—and him a man of God. Why does he ever come to these dances?"

"He likes to dance, I suppose. *I* like to dance—"

"It's not right for a man like him to do something like that."

"To dance?"

"To do *anything,* I mean—" She translated, "I mean, coming to a public dance, picking up strange women, dancing with them—"

"You mean it isn't right because he's married, or because he's a clergyman?"

"It amounts to the same thing, doesn't it? I mean—" Again she translated, "I mean, *after all.*"

"After all, *what?*"

"If a *clergyman* can't be trusted—"

"You know what the Talmud says? That *every* man is *always* suspect."

"Oh, I don't agree with that," Sandra declared. "Well, look—you're a rabbi; I certainly trust *you.*"

"You *do?*" David groaned. "It's getting late, Sandra. Maybe I ought to take you home now," he said, and gave up.

But not entirely. Seeing Sandra to her door, he tried to kiss her good night. Purely in the interests of research, he told himself, to test Bentley's theories.

Sandra made no attempt to push him away. She simply took two steps backward. "But you're a rabbi," she

73

exclaimed as he opened his eyes to find Sandra inexplicably even further away from him than when he had closed them. "You're a rabbi."

"Yes, I know I'm a rabbi," David said. "I'm a rabbi, not a priest."

"But rabbis don't do things like—like—they just don't. Rabbi Levy has been the rabbi of our synagogue for twenty-four years, and he's *never*—"

"I thought Rabbi Levy was a sixty-nine-year-old married man with five grandchildren."

"Well, even so . . ."

For a moment David considered paraphrasing Shylock's speech and explaining that even rabbis were capable of bleeding when pricked, but he quickly abandoned the idea. Who wanted to debate with a pretty girl on a beautiful moonlit night? "Well, thank you for going out with me, Sandra. Good night."

"Thank you for asking me out," she said politely. "It was nice."

David sighed. "Good-bye, Sandra." And ruefully he returned to Landers to resume his solitary nightly walks.

So solitary did David feel that when, during one midnight walk, he saw Clifford Fowler approaching, he did not avoid him. At least there was one thing the two had in common: no feminine companionship.

"Clifford," David said, "I don't imagine that the two of us will ever become friends—and maybe it's my fault because I impulsively lied that time about your peeking over my shoulder at that magazine—but do you think that at least we can stop being enemies?"

"Surely," Clifford replied without hesitation. "Just as soon as you turn from your prurience and lies and mockery and—"

David gritted his teeth, hoping that somehow Clifford could have been caught between his upper and lower molars. "Listen! I have an announcement to make," he exclaimed. "Clifford, I have just run out of cheeks."

The next night David happened upon pleasanter company, Dan Miller, and he wondered aloud why *he* was walking the dark streets.

Dan smiled crookedly. "You think rabbis are the only ones who ever get lonely?"

They walked along in silence for a few minutes. Then David, striving to sound completely academic, said, "Dan, I've always wondered: How do priests manage without wives?"

"Very well," Dan said.

David chuckled. (He did not want to appear too anxious.) "But still, Dan, don't you . . . Don't you ever uh . . ."

"That's why priests go to Confession too," Dan smiled, leaving David to wonder which of his unspoken questions Dan had answered.

"Dan, why *is* it that priests can't marry? What's the reason for the ban?"

Dan took off his horn-rimmed glasses and wiped them with a handkerchief. "So that the priest may concentrate completely on his work," he said soberly. "The priest takes the vow of perpetual celibacy to become truly 'all things to all men.' Also, there's the idea of sacrifice. The priesthood is such a sacred sacrament we feel we should sacrifice something precious for it, like a family of our own." He fell silent for a moment. "Sometimes a priest doesn't know *how* precious a sacrifice he's made until he leaves the Seminary and his friends behind him, and takes a parish full of nothing *but* families— other people's families—and learns that respect is not exactly the same thing as . . . affection." He cleared his throat. "Of course, precious as one's own family is, there are yet *more* precious things in life. And all of a priest's parishioners are his children . . . in a spiritual sense. Shall we head for the barracks now, David? It's almost midnight, and I have a six o'clock Mass in the morning."

They turned back. "And what happens when you . . . when a priest gets lonely, perhaps even feels the stirrings of . . . of . . . ?" David faltered.

"Why, we do what you're doing right now, David," Dan said easily.

David paused. "What am I doing?"

"Asking an older priest how he manages to—do without."

David persisted. "And what does the older priest usually say, Dan?"

"Well, you see *he* goes to ask an even *older* priest. And so it goes. By the time the answer gets back to you, you no longer care."

David laughed. Yet he still cared, very much. Alas, that was about all that he could do. He could not even return his car. Your Friendly Used Car Salesman had refused to refund his money.

Chapter : 6

You know, David, you're the first Jew I've ever really known," Roger Allerton remarked during the first week the two chaplains were rooming together, and David felt strange because he couldn't figure out *why* the remark made him feel strange.

"Well, I guess you're the first *Christian*," David pointed out in return, "that *I've* ever really known."

"I am?" Roger's blue eyes evinced surprise. "I guess I'll have to be on my best behavior then," he smiled. "I wouldn't want you to get the wrong impression about us Christians."

That was it, David suddenly realized. He felt uncomfortable being cast as The Jew; he much preferred being *a* Jew, like any other. The only thing worse than being just a cipher, he reflected, was becoming a symbol; neither was a flesh and blood human being. "Roger? Suppose we strike a bargain," David proposed. "I'll promise not to think *all* Christians snore just because you do—if you promise not to think *all* Jews are grumpy in the morning just because *I* am. Okay?"

"Okay," Roger laughed. "Here's *another* bargain: When we swap information about Judaism and Christianity, let's swap a *lot* of it. Otherwise it's liable to turn out like an interfaith experiment that was tried out back home in Idaho with a neighboring church. What a mess! We each learned just enough to prove to ourselves why the other's denomination was inferior to our own."

Right then David felt that the twenty-four-year-old blond, round-shouldered, introspective fellow bachelor from Idaho and he would be friends by February, when they would be graduated from Chaplain School.

Time was not proving his intuition wrong. And somehow mutual envy strengthened the friendship of the two. For Roger, despite his small-town upbringing, had a grasp of classical music that David, despite New York's Metropolitan Opera and Carnegie Hall, did not. He, on the other hand, had salami.

"Gee, I wish *I* received a salami from home twice a week," Roger exclaimed enviously several times before David pointed out: "But you've gotten sick every time I forced the stuff on you."

"I hope you won't think I'm anti-Jewish or something," Roger explained with a grin, "but I *hate* salami. I guess what I really mean is that I wish I had someone back home who was thinking of *me* twice a week." As David suddenly recalled that his roommate received little mail, Roger spoke ruefully of his childhood as an orphan being passed around from foster home to foster home. "As a kid, I was always not only the new boy on the block but always the new member of some miserable new family. You know," he reflected, "I find myself wondering at times whether I became a minister just to prove to everyone who mistreated me in the past that I'm better than they, to show them that I'll forever be with the right if not *in* it altogether, while they were all so wrong for having treated me, a minister of God Himself, so shabbily." He paused, exclaiming: "Wouldn't that be a terrible reason to become a clergyman!"

77

Most of the chats between the two men took place after they had turned out the lights at night and were lying in bed before drifting off to sleep. It was easier to give vent to personal feelings in the dark; there each could pretend that he was only thinking aloud.

"I often wonder whether I did the right thing in entering the ministry," Roger confessed one night. "I mean, whether I'm good enough for it, whether I've *really* been called. I think about God a lot—*worry* about Him is what I really mean—but I still don't know how close I am to Him. And a man can't lead others closer to God than he is himself. You can't lead people to a spot where you're not. And I keep wondering if I ever *will* get closer to God. I'd be a dreadful failure if I didn't! It's no credit for a minister to camp where his predecessor died. Because some man fought and died to get there, and you can't just hold on to what another man has won. That's not enough. That's not nearly enough."

As the two became close friends, formalities were dispensed with, sequiturs too, and frequently their nightly dialogues dissolved into pairs of monologues; thoughts alluded to by one, sometimes just a word, were picked up by the other and often developed independently, like improvisations on a theme or exercises in free association:

"Roger, who says there's no such thing as evolution? Did you notice it in our bull sessions? In the early discussions each of the fellows would say, oh so politely, something like, 'Now *my* denomination *believes* . . .' Later they would bust out with: 'Well, why *doesn't* your religion believe . . . ?' After a few weeks here they were agreeing, 'Why then, we *both* believe . . .' And now you can even hear a few of the chaplains conceding, 'I think I understand now. You believe . . .'"

"All except Clifford Fowler. He's still at the stage of: 'My denomination believes . . . and what was the name again of that group of infidels *you* belong to?'"

"One nice thing about Clifford—he hates *everyone*, *regardless* of their race, color or religion."

"That Dan Miller certainly surprised me, David. I

ever thought I'd hear a Catholic telling that joke. He said that this fellow had died and gone up to Heaven and was being shown around the place. 'In this room,' St. Peter pointed out, are all the Jewish souls, in this room all the Greek Orthodox souls, in this room all the Protestant souls. And now let's tiptoe quietly past this here room.' 'Why?' St. Peter was asked. 'Because,' he replied, 'in this room are all the Catholic souls, and they think they're the only ones here.' How *about* that? From a *priest!*"

"It's hard being a member of a minority group, hard for many of them to overcome the feeling that fifty million Frenchmen can't be wrong, and besides, why bother sticking to your beliefs—wrong *or* right—when the vast majority believes otherwise. It's like that old saw in elementary philosophy: Does a tree falling down in the middle of a distant forest make any noise when there's no one around to hear it? But God hears, He does."

"It's no easy thing to be a member of a majority either. It's so comfortable to float along with the tide without thinking for yourself. It's so much more difficult to strike out against the current, for who wants to risk ejection by his group and end up beached on a sand bar all by his lonesome?"

"Bentley Lane is the one who fooled me," said David. "I thought him so cynical at first. But an idealist always runs the danger of being taken for a cynic, I guess, specially by the majority who can't imagine that there are a few people who care deeply enough about things to get disillusioned. Did Bentley ever tell you that his first congregation wouldn't keep him because he referred to the church as the Duffy's Tavern of New Haven, 'the church where the elite used to meet to eat, and stay away from when it came time to pray'? Seems that the Ladies' Auxiliary, Men's Club and Young People's Society would always turn out in full force for luncheons and suppers and teas and weenie roasts and things like that, while the church was two-thirds empty on Sunday mornings and emptier still for Bible classes and lectures. So Bentley got up in the pulpit one Sunday and proposed that since the church's kitchen facilities were too small to accommodate its social gatherings and the sanctuary too large for religious meetings, the two should be switched, with the refrigerator, stove and freezer being installed on the pulpit, and the altar being placed next to the sink in the kitchen. And that was Bentley's last sermon in that church, by popular demand."

"My first church—what a thrill that was! Telling people how they ought to behave, thundering from the pulpit what the Lord required of them. Actually it was what *I* required of them, but I didn't tell them that because I figured that God's name carried more weight."

"The thing that bothers me is when somebody tells me they 'enjoyed' a sermon of mine. Who do they think I am—Sophie Tucker? I wonder how many people in Biblical times 'enjoyed' the prophets. I'd be a whole lot happier if after a sermon of mine someone would once try to stone me."

"My mother was always sickly. She had a heart condition. I always used to worry about letting her go to sleep at night because I was afraid she wouldn't be getting up in the morning. I remember as a child often waking up scared in the middle of the night and sneaking into her room to hold up a mirror to her mouth. And then one night there was no vapor on the mirror. I was the first to know, even before my father, and he was lying right alongside of her. My sobs woke him up. But not her, never her."

"My foster mother has a saying: 'When I die, I don't want anyone to say that Life was good to me. Better they should be able to say that *I* was good to *Life—halvai!*'"

"As if it weren't bad enough my being the newest boy everywhere, I also had to be the tallest one, looming like the Empire State Building over the rest of the boys my age. I tried to hide myself by going around with my head sunk in my chest, and it worked too. Soon they stopped calling me the Empire State Building and started calling me the Leaning Tower of Pisa."

"Me—I was fat. But in my neighborhood, *all* the kids

were fat. All those immigrant mothers shoveling all that food down us, making up for all those lean years in the Old Country, like they were afraid they were going to be deported in the morning and we were camels."

"Do you know what it's like being passed around from relative to relative, hearing them argue with one another, saying, 'Now I had him for six months, you got to take him for the next six'? It was like being in labor all my childhood with no one wanting to give birth to me. Maybe that's why I seized hold of God—at least *He* loved me."

"Nowadays, religion doesn't seem to demand anything more of people than does the AAA: affiliation," said David. "Modern religion breaks no current idols, it challenges no popular fallacies, it shakes no one up. It is simply there, welcoming one and all with the spiritual awareness and social consciousness of a headwaiter. The trouble is that religion has become too respectable, like corruption."

"I've never slept with a woman, have you? But that doesn't make me virtuous, only hard-up. I dream about it all the time, like Woman is the Promised Land and I'm the Children of Israel yearning for entry therein. I wonder how much this had to do with my proposing to Gloria when another fellow, more experienced than I, would simply have taken her to a drive-in."

"Temptations I can always resist. It's only my impulses that I'm always succumbing to!"

"You know what the cardinal sin is? No, it isn't selfishness—that's too positive a sin, and most people sin indifferently, without passion. The cardinal sin is thoughtlessness—not caring about another human being, not thinking of him, not sympathizing with him—and thoughtlessness is next to mindlessness. And mindlessness means you're an animal."

"Judaism teaches that the root of sin—or one of them —is taking people or things for granted. Indifference to the sublime wonder of life and the living, taking for granted the grandeur of the universe and the inherent good in each person, callousness toward the suffering of

81

others, neglecting our opportunities to help people—that's sin."

"Once when I was young, a teen-ager, I got the bright idea that the world would be well on its way to Utopia if everyone would keep quiet, no one talk at all. Then there'd be no nasty things said, no time wasted on trivialities, no gossip spread, no orphan's feelings hurt. I actually stopped talking myself for two days, but I had to resume when my Sunday School teacher called on me to get up and explain to the class why Catholics were no better than Jews."

"I'm afraid that I wasn't brought up with any great love for Christians. Uncle Asher came from a town where a family of nine Jews were slaughtered for supposedly draining the blood out of a Christian child to use in making matzos and Passover wine. And Tante Dvorah's mother was killed, along with thirty-four others, in a pogrom which took place on Easter Sunday."

"Is that why Jesus is anathema to so many Jews—a sort of guilt by association? I myself would think that every Jew would be proud to boast that Jesus, the Lord's only begotten Son, who has had greater impact upon the world than anyone else ever, was Jewish."

"Tante and Uncle weaned me on a saying of Theodore Herzl: 'If you will it, it is no legend.' You *can* make things, *good* things, happen—it's your *duty*. That's why when the State of Israel was re-established after a two thousand year interval—a miracle if there ever was one —Tante and Uncle weren't even surprised. 'You see?' was all they said to me. 'You see?' "

"I thought I was lonely before, growing up as the perennially new boy in the new household in the new school in the new neighborhood. But I'm even lonelier now as a minister. I find I have hardly anyone to talk to. I'm the shepherd, and a shepherd doesn't unburden himself to his sheep, for fear they might discover that he's all wool too, and a hundred self-doubts wide, besides."

"You know something? Sometimes I find that my most devout prayer during a service is that I don't make a fool of myself when I open my mouth to preach."

"A fool is what I made of myself over this girl. Can you imagine? Her father made twelve dollars more *per week* than I made all *year!* I asked her to marry me, and she accepted, *provided* I would give up the ministry—you can still preach somewhere on Sundays if you like, she said—and take an executive job in her father's plant. So I enlisted in the chaplaincy. I was afraid if I stayed around her any longer, I would gain Gloria and lose my soul."

One Sunday morning, Roger was asked to substitute for an ailing minister in San Antonio. Before leaving for the church, he invited David to join him there later at the service. "I'd count it as a personal favor if you'd criticize my sermon afterwards, also my delivery," he said. "God knows I need all the help I can get in preaching."

David readily accepted the invitation. He was eager to hear his friend preach as well as curious to see a Christian service for the first time. And if he had any feelings of uneasiness about attending a church, the reception accorded him there immediately dispelled them. For no sooner had he started up the walk to the small white frame building than a dozen people came up, smiling and with hands outstretched in greeting, to introduce themselves and welcome him, a stranger, into their midst.

Now why couldn't synagogues be as friendly to newcomers? fretted David, when inside the church even more parishioners greeted him warmly, obviously undismayed by his Jewish name. He took a seat in a back pew, and the people beside him said, "We hope this is only your *first* visit to us."

A few minutes later, Roger appeared in the pulpit and invoked the name of God, and the service began. As plain and simple and dignified as the unadorned church building itself, the service consisted of several prayers, congregational singing, a soprano rendition of two psalms, and readings from the New Testament. And then Roger started his sermon, preaching with earnestness and fervor, also with some of the awkwardness of a self-con-

83

scious speaker more intent on himself and his manuscript than on its message and his audience.

Yet Roger was interesting to hear even when he was rambling on about the consequences of sin, as he was doing now. For neither wordiness nor disorganized theme nor stiff delivery could dim his decency and dedication which shone through his sermon and compelled attention and respect.

Now, without any logical development, he was talking about the Jews. David listened carefully as his roommate began to tell the story of "the Wandering Jew," which David recalled as an unlovely medieval fictional justification of anti-Semitism.

Roger, his round shoulders seeming to hug the congregation as he leaned forward, reminded the people of the legend of Ahasuerus the Jew refusing to let Jesus, on the way to Calvary, rest for a moment against the wall of his house, consequently being condemned to wander eternally over the earth without rest or death, like another Cain.

What was Roger driving at? David wondered. And then he realized that his friend was doubtlessly repeating the legend of the Wandering Jew in order to demolish it. He smiled as he waited for Roger's conclusion, betting himself that it would parallel the sentiments expressed by both men during several of their nightly chats.

But now Roger was concluding, incredibly: "And the wandering Jews are *still* with us, still *cursed* to wander the earth forever, like Cain before them, still serving as the living witnesses of the consequences of sin . . ."

David gasped, tears starting to his eyes. He felt as if he had been dealt a physical blow. "And the wandering Jews are still cursed to wander the earth forever," his best friend at Chaplain School had said, "still serving as the living witnesses of the consequences of sin . . ." The words sounded and resounded in David's ears, blotting out the rest of Roger's sermon. ". . . still cursed . . . like Cain before them . . ."

David sat appalled and shaken, entombed in a frozen vacuum in which Roger's words continued to reverberate.

". . . the Jews . . . still serving as the living consequences of sin . . ." *How could Roger have said what he did!*

In the course of his rabbinical training, David had studied the religious, political, social, economic, and psychological causes of anti-Semitism until by now he knew everything about it, except how it felt. Raised in a ghettolike Jewish environment, his contacts with anti-Semitism had been meager—so meager that when, on two occasions while in high school, he had been refused summer employment on account of his religion, he had experienced neither hurt nor anger nor embarrassment so much as amazement. He had been dumfounded that for no logical reason at all one human being would deliberately and maliciously seek to harm another.

But those employers had been strangers to David—and ignorant, he had told himself. Roger was a friend of his, a fellow of intelligence and sensitivity. How could *he* be guilty of anti-Semitism? It simply was not possible!

But again Roger's words echoed in his mind: ". . . the wandering Jews . . . still with us . . . cursed forever . . . living witnesses of the consequences of sin . . ." And again he saw those gentle lips uttering the horrible words implying that God had murdered six million Jews to punish them for a legendary sin committed by a fictional personage who was supposed to have lived some two thousand years before. How could anyone level such a monstrous charge against the Lord God!

David felt cold and clammy and nauseous. Retrieving his service cap, he started to his feet. He had to get away from this plain simple church with its smiling, friendly people and the sincere, decent clergyman up there who worshipped a God who was a *devil*.

He moved sideways in his pew, but suddenly everyone in the row was standing, too, blocking his way. The people started to sing. They were singing, he noted, a hymn about love.

Impatiently he waited for them to finish and sit down again. "Amen," they sang at last, but they remained standing, now bowing their heads. He looked toward the front of the church. Roger, his earnest brow bent in meditation, was reciting the benediction, the ancient triple priestly one from the Torah, and there was loving devotion in his voice.

David could bear that sincere voice no longer. He pushed past the people on his right. But now everyone was moving with him. The benediction over, the service was evidently concluded.

Congregants all around were smiling at him.

"Lovely service, wasn't it?"

"There's a prayer meeting on Wednesday night. Hope you can come."

"Such an inspiring message, wasn't it!"

"You come back again real soon, you hear?"

David pushed forward through the crowd. Ahead of him was the door. He stepped through it, and the outside air chilled his damp face.

"David! I'm so glad you came."

Roger was standing upon the threshold of the church shaking people's hands as they filed by him. Now it was David's turn to shake the hand that had written that his people were cursed living witnesses of the consequences of sin. "What did you think of the sermon?" Roger asked, and he held out his hand.

David saw the long, tapered fingers extended toward him, and somehow it surprised him that they appeared so clean. He looked up into the earnest face with its honest blue eyes and high intelligent forehead and reflective expression, and he felt sick to his stomach.

"David . . . ?"

Tell him what you thought of the sermon, David urged himself. Tell him what you think of him too.

He turned away from Roger.

"David!"

Tell him! *Now*. Tell him how it feels to be cursed not by God but by one of His self-appointed prosecutors. Tell him it was sermons like his that instigated pogroms in the towns of Tante Dvorah and Uncle Asher. Tell him of Anne Frank and all the others. *Tell him!*

He broke into a run.

"David!"

He ran to his car and jumped in, jamming the key in the ignition lock and twisting it. The car leaped from the curb as he jabbed his foot on the gas pedal, and he raced the car through the city streets as if fleeing a strafing.

In a matter of minutes he was outside San Antonio and hurtling through the bleak desert that surrounded it. He passed few cars there, hardly any vegetation and no people, and he liked it that way. The land was flat and desolate and uninhabitable, but that was all right with him; the desert had never pretended to be otherwise.

For hours David sped on, purposely driving so fast that he was forced to concentrate all his attention on the road. He wanted to forget, he *had* to forget Roger and his sermon and his church and his congregants and their friendliness and his God and his friendship and Chaplain School and Brotherhood Week and the National Conference of Christians and Jews, *everything*.

Tens of miles hurtled into a hundred miles, a hundred miles became two hundred, and still he sped on, away, his most pressing concern to make the next curve without turning the car over.

The road signs looked different, he noted. It took him a while, and another twenty miles, to realize that all the signs now bore the imprint of the state of Louisiana.

It was time to turn back.

He drove, more slowly now, to San Antonio, arriving there a few hours after dark. Still, it was too early for Roger to have gone to bed, and David could not bear the thought of seeing his roommate that night. Parking his car in the city, he went to a movie and took a seat in an empty corner of the darkened theater, paying scant attention to the images on the screen, periodically talking to himself:

—All right, David, all *right!* Isn't it time you calmed down already?

—I can't believe it! I still can't believe it!

—Is it so inconceivable?

—*Yes.* That's why it hurts so terribly.

—You're so naïve. You're a child—

—But Roger is my *friend*. I *thought* he was my friend. Of all the people in the world, I'd never have suspected Roger to be a—a—a—

—Why do you hesitate to use the word? Say it: anti-Semite.

—But he *couldn't* be, not *Roger*. He's an intelligent fellow, kind, sensitive, decent, cultured, educated. He invited me to his church. I told him about Judaism. He taught me about music. We confided in each other. He said I was the first person he had ever really talked to in his entire life. How could *he* be an *anti-Semite!*

—You've studied enough about anti-Semitism to know that education and culture are irrelevant to it. Look at Germany—one of the world's most educated, civilized, cultured countries. Look what *they* did.

—Germany's a nation; Roger is one individual, and a *friend*. If someone like him can turn out to be an anti-Semite, who can be trusted?

—You're not the first Jew to be fooled.

—But *such* a fool! I fooled myself into believing there could be friendly relations between the different faiths. Those other friendly chaplains—what do I know of their *real* feelings toward Jews?

—Can't you guess now?

—It's all so—so—so irrational. I wish Roger were dead!

—*David!*

—It's true! I could kill him myself!

David sat in the dark theater until the last show ended and the lights were turned on and the ushers came down the aisle to sweep up. Then he left and drove back to Landers, certain of one thing only. He would have to get his room changed in the morning. He could not bear rooming with Roger any longer; it would be difficult as it was for him to stay on in the same barracks with all the others.

It was after one o'clock when he reached his darkened room. Entering, he discerned Roger's sleep-curved form in bed. He undressed and got into bed. But he could not sleep; the acid hatred within him gnawed at his stomach, cramping it.

"David . . ." It was Roger's voice, earnest and hesitant—and despicable. "David . . . ?"

He turned his back on his roommate and faced the wall, not trusting himself to reply. All that hate within him would spill out.

"David, it was an old sermon," Roger said, and there was a pleading note to his voice. "It was one I've given a few times before—that doesn't excuse it, of course—but I've given that sermon so many times already I didn't think about it any more. I guess I never really thought about it even when I wrote it . . . David, the way you *looked* at me!"

David turned around and burst out bitterly into the darkness: "Did you really expect me to shake your hand after what you said? Did you!"

"I did—I mean, until that moment I didn't realize what I had said. It wasn't until you ran from me . . . Then I remembered my sermon—and the reference to your people. I remembered it then, as everyone kept shaking my hand and telling me how much they had enjoyed my message. David, afterwards, when everyone had gone, I went back inside the church, alone—when I realized why you had run from me—and I delivered that same sermon again, to the empty pews. Only this time, this time, every place where I had written the word 'Jews,' I substituted your name. It was horrible! I found myself accusing my friend David Cohen of not letting Christ rest on the way to Calvary. I was saying that God had cursed my friend David Cohen with eternal punishment. I was condemning my friend David Cohen for committing sins he is no guiltier of than I. I was justifying— It was horrible! David, you know how highly I think of you . . ."

"You mean I'm a freakish Jew? An exception to my people? A rarity in my religion?" David exclaimed. "No, thanks, Roger. I can get along very well without being highly thought of."

"I didn't mean *that!* David, please try to understand. Where I come from—Idaho—there are no Jews. Oh, there were a few Jews in town, I suppose, but our paths never crossed except in a Jewish clothing store, maybe, or once or twice in a jewelry shop. David, you're the first Jew I've ever actually known. And so up till now when I read about the Jews in the New Testament or preached about them, it was never really the Jewish people I was thinking of, but Them, the villains, the incarnation of all wickedness, the evil people who are always with us trying to destroy the good, the devils. And I labeled these symbols—that's what they really were to me: symbols— I called these symbols 'Jews.' I've never thought of Jews as being real people, like my family and friends are real to me. Jews were mythological creatures to me. What else could they be when I had never known them except as the name for some characters in the Bible or in some derogatory joke? That's why, strange as it may seem, I never identified you with my Jews. Until I saw your face outside the church today—it was the face of my father when he awoke to find Mother dead—"

David put a pillow over his head. He did not want to listen any longer. If he heard any more explanations he might find himself accepting them, and that he would never forgive himself for doing.

But Roger's voice penetrated through the pillow as he continued, impassioned: "The implications of that sermon terrify me! All day long now while I've been waiting here for you to return, all that time I've been wondering whether my Christ is any more real to me than my Jews. Or whether Christ was only a mythological symbol to me, too, a symbol of the Good Guy fighting the Bad Guys and getting even with them in the end by becoming Divine, much like I had become a minister. It's a terrifying thought! If my God has no more reality to me than that, I'm no more Christian than you are, David, and I don't belong in His ministry! Surely there must have been a reason why Jesus was born a Jew and spoke only to the Jews, and it couldn't have been just to give them enough rope to flagellate them until eternity. My God of Love isn't like that. His ministers *can't* be like that."

David pushed the pillow away from his head and spoke out with vehemence. "Before you speak to me about love, Roger, let me tell you something about hate. Roger, had I been able to press some sort of button today that would have struck you dead, I would have done so—quickly and with satisfaction."

"David," Roger said, "if I had found that button first, I would have beaten you to it."

"I *mean* it, Roger. I felt like killing you. And there's another thing that's worse still. Even now, I can't feel the slightest shame or remorse for conceiving such a monstrous thought against you. Yet I know I'd never try to pass off these murderous feelings of mine as religious ones, voicing them in a pulpit in the name of God."

Roger cried out: "I know! I know! I'm no better than all those people I've condemned in the past; I'm guilty of my own cardinal sin—thoughtlessness. If only I had worried less about my soul and more about my tongue! I've always been so sensitive for myself; it's time I took into account other people's feelings as well. David, I know I'll never be able to unpreach that sermon—all those minds I infected!—but I do offer you now my apology for it, inadequate but sincere. Will you accept it?"

David answered him with silence. He wasn't going to make it as easy as all that for Roger. For he remembered more than his roommate's sermon. He remembered all the abuse and indignities and persecutions and tortures and murders inflicted upon his fellow Jews by people as devout in their religion and as sincere as Roger. No apology would restore even one of the victims to life. It would be a sin to forgive what was unforgivable.

But Roger would not accept his silence for an answer. "David," Roger said, "maybe my religion has given me some sort of excuse to hate your people. But it has also provided me with the means to overcome such unjustifiable hatred. And from what I've learned about your own religion in the past months, Judaism is no different in that respect. Can't we use those means then to bridge hates and prejudices and my thoughtlessness? Can't we, David?"

A scornful laugh welled up in David's throat. But it was checked by a sudden alarming thought. He caught his breath as the realization smote him that he did not want to relinquish his hatred for Roger because of a feeling that he wasn't being offered anything of comparable worth in return.

But *why?* Roger's contrition was evidently sincere, his explanation reasonable enough. Why was David so reluctant to accept them? Was he afraid of being deceived? Or could it be that he was finding some strange unanticipated satisfaction in hating Roger?

David bit his lower lip. Was he happy at last to be able to find in the person of Roger a focus for all his hatred, his foster parents' too, of the persecutors of his people through the ages and in his own time? Was he transforming Roger into anti-Semitism incarnate, a bloodless symbol, his own private scapegoat?

No, of course not!

Then why, immediately he asked of himself, why didn't he accept Roger's apology? Thoughtlessness was not the same thing as anti-Semitism, and surely Roger, now that he realized the evil that he had done, would never repeat it. Or—David was appalled by the thought—was he *enjoying* his hatred for Roger?

Shaken, David said, "We can try, Roger."

That answered Roger's question, but not his own. It gnawed at him, like a sin one refused either to acknowledge or to renounce. *Was he himself capable of succumbing to an irrational and unreasoning hatred?*

With compelling urgency, David added, "Roger, we *have* to try!"

92

Chapter : 7

CLASSES at Chaplain School continued unabated, but the interest of the chaplains did not. By the middle of January, with almost a month more still remaining till the end of the course, the men were growing restless. Most of them, veterans of a minimum of seven years of higher education, were weary by now of any additional schooling; their *sitzfleisch* had clearly been worn to the bone. All of the men were now anxious to enter the active chaplaincy, instead of merely continuing to talk about it.

Chaplain Radcliff, sensing the men's growing impatience, sought to stimulate them with a surprise. "Fellas, I have good news for you," he announced one morning. "Base Operations has agreed to take you all up on a flight this afternoon. They're going to fly us around the area for an hour or two in a Gooneybird. Now what do you think of that?"

The class, with a single exception, responded with enthusiasm. And for the rest of the morning that single exception fought off a spiraling feeling of nausea.

During lunch hour David, slowly losing out to the nausea, went on Sick Call. There a comic in a white coat informed him that he had neither fever nor morning sickness and sent him back to duty and the flight, armed with two aspirin tablets.

Fortunately, by the time he reported for the afternoon formation, his nose was bleeding, possibly because he had blown it just a little too hard all the way back from the hospital. Clutching to his nose a handkerchief carefully folded to display the maximum amount of fresh, bright bloodstains, he took his place in formation.

Chaplain Radcliff picked up his cue. "Maybe it would

be a good idea for you to go lie down in your room, Chaplain Cohen. I know how much you must have looked forward to flying today, but—"

"That *is* a good idea," David said and raced to the barracks. By the time he reached his room, his nausea had disappeared; only now it was replaced by a gnawing sense of shame. Here he was an Air Force chaplain, and he was afraid to fly—it was simply too *absurd*.

Alone in his room he brooded until the group returned two hours later and described the flight. Then, somehow, he was greatly comforted hearing about which chaplains had vomited during what had turned out to be a rough flight, how often, and upon whom.

His colleagues had additional news for him. Chaplain Radcliff had come up with another lively idea. Would the chaplains like to put on their own talent show? he had asked during the flight. The response of the majority of men had been rousingly affirmative.

Clifford had been among the dissenters. "My only talent," he had said pointedly, "lies in preaching the word of God."

And yet Clifford showed up at the talent show, as did all the other chaplains, on the following Saturday night. The first one on the bill was Chaplain Radcliff himself.

Stepping onto the improvised stage set up in a corner of the dayroom, spotlighted by thirty flashlights lying on the floor in a semicircle, the Director held out a coiled rope in front of him, saying with a grin, "I never met a Christian or a Jew that I didn't like."

His hands worked swiftly with the rope, and in a few seconds he had made it into a lariat. This he skillfully twirled over his head and lowered slowly until it was spinning around him, grazing his barrel belly. Then he raised the lariat over his head and cried, "Now watch this!" The rope whirled through the air and, in the batting of an eye, Paul Smith, sitting in the back of the room, had been lassoed and was being pulled to the Director's side. "Now where's my branding iron?"

The men laughed and applauded as Chaplain Radcliff freed Paul.

"When I was nineteen I graduated from punching cows up near the Panhandle," the Director said. "I started punching people instead." And he proceeded to give a demonstration of professional rope-jumping. White hair flying and red face growing crimson, he jumped rope forwards, backwards, running, skipping, on alternate feet, arms crossed in front, legs crossed in back—all the while huffing and puffing like a Santa Claus whose reindeer had left him to pull the sleigh all by himself.

The chaplains cheered him on until he jumped himself out of breath. Gasping, he continued, "When I took to boxing there was only one thing I hadn't figured on—my Ma had warned me and she was so right—all those fellas I'd be punching, they were punching me right back! It wasn't like cows at all, nohow." He looked out beyond the audience and mused aloud: "It's funny how some people come to God. There I was one day, a nineteen-year-old whose only aim in life was to become the world's heavyweight champion, as close to God as hardtack is to caviar, and all of a sudden I'm all alone in a hospital room with nothing between me and eternity but a plastic oxygen tent—it was divine retribution, just as my Ma had predicted—wheedling Him not to take me to Him, not yet, horrified that I could have knocked someone else into the afterlife just for a shot at money and fame. That's how I was reborn—in a hospital bed, appropriately enough. Funny how sometimes only death can give a fella the right perspective on life. The way I figured it then and there, still do, is that dying for nothing worthwhile is downright criminal compared to living for something like God. Because when you come right down to it, touching a man's soul, as mine was touched by Him in that hospital, is a darn sight better goal in life than clobbering a man's kidneys."

He paused then, suddenly apologetic. "But I didn't mean to offer up any testimony here, fellas, forgive me! I only wanted to do a few rope tricks—show you how, starting out as Paul, a persecutor of the Gentiles, I ended up like Peter—" Again his hands worked swiftly, weaving the rope this time into a makeshift net which he cast out over the heads of the audience. "—a fisher of souls," he concluded as the net dropped over Clifford's head.

"Looks like Radcliff missed," Bentley commented as Clifford snorted in annoyance and disentangled himself from the rope.

The next man on the bill was Jim Mackey who confided to the group in a monologue how he planned to subvert the Catholic Church and its priesthood by going around hugging and kissing his wife in drive-ins while wearing his clerical Roman-looking collar. But Dan Miller proved he was of a forgiving nature by dedicating to Jim two Irish ballads which he sang while Roger Allerton accompanied him on the guitar. Afterwards, David and Albert Cohen taught the men how to do the Hora, and all of them joined in the dance.

And then it was Bentley's turn. Borrowing Roger's guitar, he strummed a few jangling discords and chanted:

> *Oh, when you're lonely and blue,*
> *'n' envy animals in the zoo,*
> *For heaven's sakes, why don't you*
> *Cuddle up in the lap of the Lawd?*
>
> *When you're down in the mout'*
> *Cussing yourself out,*
> *Don't sit and pout like a lout—*
> *Cuddle up in the lap of the Lawd!*
>
> *A mighty pillow is the lap*
> *Of the Big Guy in the Sky;*
> *When you crave a comfy nap,*
> *Remember: His lap is always standing by.*
>
> *Even when one sins or strays,*
> *It really nearly pays,*
> *'cause afterwards you can always* .
> *Cuddle up in the lap of the Lawd!*
> *I mean, that happy lappy of the Lawd!*

The men applauded good-naturedly when Bentley was done, but not so loudly that it drowned out Clifford's considered judgment which he delivered at the top of his voice. *"Blasphemy!"*

David came to Bentley's defense. "That's unfair! All these current pseudoreligious pop songs are so nonsensically nauseating that parodying them is a *mitzvah*, a good—"

But Clifford cut him short. "Blasphemers of a feather," he said, "stick together."

David flushed and started toward Clifford, but a chuckle from Bentley stopped him short. "Clifford, your trouble," Bentley remarked, "is that, spiritually speaking, you've been much too strictly toilet-trained."

"Oh!" exclaimed Clifford. *"Oh!"*

Chaplain Radcliff intervened. "You fellas are beginning to sound like husband and wife. Cut it out now, will you! Or would you prefer to settle this matter in the ring with boxing gloves?"

There were no takers.

The talent show continued, its spirits dampened if not killed, and at its close the Director announced still another plan of his—whether it was spawned by the unanticipated failure of the talent show, it was hard to tell—to further enliven the dry academic proceedings at Chaplain School. He suggested that, for the sake of practice, the class conduct a mock military funeral during the following week. Accordingly, he assigned each chaplain a part in the undertaking as either pallbearer, honorary pallbearer, chaplain, funeral director, usher, relative, friend, lodge brother, or even widow.

The chaplains, taking their assignments seriously, began studying military funeral procedure the following day, reminded of the fact that the activity had not yet been imagined for which the Air Force did not have a manual. Meanwhile, Chaplain Radcliff went around busily extending invitations for the mock ceremony to the Landers Band, an Honor Guard, the cadets, the officer-candidates, the Public Information Officer; then, to make the funeral even more realistic, he replaced

Bentley, originally cast as the "widow," with a Waf. A day before the event, the first of its kind at Landers, General Price himself announced that he would attend, possibly because nearly everyone else on base was going to be there and he did not want to feel left out of things.

"Fellas," the Director warned on Wednesday, "tomorrow at noon I'll come over with the General, scared to death but bragging. If you goof on this, start running. Don't even look back."

Bentley had his own view of the proceedings. "You think paganism is dead?" he remarked to his colleagues as they rehearsed that evening in the dayroom. "Just wait till you see this military funeral tomorrow, with its fussing detail over the flesh to the complete neglect of the departed Christian spirit. With its Mardi Gras parade, blaring band, high-stepping color guard, floats of gawking spectators, the firing squad's fireworks—the only thing missing will be a live human offering!"

Clifford inquired: "You want to volunteer for the job, Bentley?"

Everyone laughed, and Clifford flushed with pleasure; he was being approved of.

"Now *there's* an idea!" Bentley exclaimed. "I've been working on an article on the apocalyptic literature, and this would fit right in: I Was a Corpse for the Chaplain Corps."

At precisely 1200 hours on the following day, the Landers Band marched up, brass whining and drums banging, to the base chapel. Behind them followed Jim Mackey's station wagon containing the "deceased" in an old fruit crate which was covered by an American flag. As the car pulled up before the chapel, whose entrance was flanked by six honorary pallbearers and a growing crowd of curious spectators, the band segued into a bilious dirge.

The six pallbearers, David among them, opened the back door of the "hearse" and pulled out the "coffin." It proved to be surprisingly heavy.

"I think they forgot to take the oranges out of this

thing," David muttered to Roger, another pallbearer.

Roger smiled. "Maybe they put a cadaver in here for effect."

The pallbearers carried the flag-shrouded crate past the Honor Guard, between the honorary pallbearers, and through the spectators whose whispers were audible to everyone save, possibly, the "corpse."

"But isn't that a *fruit crate* they're carrying under that flag?"

"I'm as liberal in my religion as anyone, but substituting a *station wagon* for a *hearse*—"

Once inside the chapel, filled with chaplains representing family, friends, lodge members of the "deceased," all the invited guests, and several curious interlopers, the pallbearers deposited the crate in front of the railing, then took their assigned seats.

Clifford, the "chaplain," rose from his seat and inched his way into the pulpit. From that elevated position he looked down upon his fellow chaplains, which for months he had been able to do only figuratively. Then he sonorously declaimed: "The church service is hereby concluded."

"Am I mistaken," David commented to Roger as they stood up with the other pallbearers, "or does Clifford look sorry that this isn't for real?"

The pallbearers returned to the railing, took hold of the "coffin," and carried it back up the aisle.

Outside the chapel, the band wailed anew, sounding as if they were blowing live cats through their brass. On every side now there gathered increasing numbers of onlookers, all expressing their curiosity about the "deceased," who merited the presence of thirty chaplains, a color guard, platoons of cadets and officer-candidates, and the starred automobile.

"It's General Price, poor guy. I remember someone telling me he dropped dead yesterday."

"Do you think we'll still have to go on saluting that damn Oldsmobile of his?"

"Did you ever see such a widow in your life? She's chewing gum!"

99

After the "coffin" was returned to the "hearse," the entire entourage proceeded to the "cemetery," a nearby parking field, where the "coffin" was unloaded and carried to a previously assigned location.

"Where's the hole? They just can't *leave* him there."

"I hear they mean to cremate him, then sprinkle his ashes all over Landers."

"But isn't that *unsanitary?*"

Clifford stepped forward, frowning at the whisperers as if he feared that their chattering might restore the "corpse" to life. He waited until everyone was silent and then he declaimed: "The graveside service is hereby concluded."

The Firing Squad stepped forward, and Clifford, following the funeral manual's suggestion, cautioned the "widow" not to be frightened by the rifle volleys. The Firing Squad came to attention, raised their rifles to their shoulders and opened fire.

And they really *did* open fire!

David, who knew that blanks were used on such occasions, had always been under the impression that blanks were not only empty cartridges but silent ones as well. Consequently, when the Firing Squad began blasting away behind him—*at* him, it seemed—he was so startled that he leaped into the "grave" before him, barking his shins on the "coffin."

Blushing with embarrassment, he exclaimed softly to no one in particular: "I'm sorry! I'm sorry!" And so completely rattled was he that he imagined hearing the "coffin" respond, "Oh, that's all right, David."

Taps began to sound, the mournful notes imparting a painful semblance of reality to the mock proceedings, as David scrambled back into position, stealing embarrassed glances to either side. But the other pallbearers, considerate men all, were staring straight ahead, as if they had missed seeing him bound into the "grave" like Hamlet in Act Five.

And then, above the elegiac bugle, David heard labored breathing coming from the direction of the "coffin." He turned his head sideways and saw with a start

100

that Clifford was glowering at him so hatefully that the swollen vein in his forehead seemed to be pumping pure venom into his stabbing black eyes.

Taps ended, its echoes hanging on the air like black wreaths, and the two chief pallbearers folded the flag into a bulky triangle and handed it to Clifford. Only then did he unfasten his murderous gaze from David. Accepting the flag, he brought it to the "widow" who, to show her grasp of the seriousness of the occasion, stopped chewing her gum.

Instead of handing the flag to the Waf, however, Clifford clutched it tightly in his hands and burst out: "I know it would be a breach of my duty as a man of God were I not to express my thoughts regarding the deceased on this most solemn of occasions." He twisted the flag until his knuckles whitened and squeezed a rush of words from between his pinched cheeks. "At a time like this it is customary, of course, to say complimentary things about the deceased, especially one who may have died nobly in the service of his country. But what of one who has lived ignobly in the sight of God in whose service all of us are enlisted from birth? Isn't it a minister's duty to point out—and publicly too— wherein the deceased has strayed from God's path so that others, still living, might yet take heed of their sins and trespasses and turn from the evil of their ways while there is yet time?"

"What's he doing?" Roger whispered. "That's not in the manual."

A chilling premonition struck David. But it was too absurd to voice, even to himself.

The acting chaplain continued with a passion that he clearly was not faking: "The deceased here has sinned— it pains me to say this, but say it I must out of love for him because his sins are as a burning fire shut up within my bones—he has *sinned*. And I shall now enumerate the ways, painful though they be to me personally and to him too, if he is listening."

"If he's listening?" Roger repeated, bewildered. "A *corpse?*"

But David was not bewildered, only very much apprehensive.

"This man was lascivious, collecting prurient pictures," Clifford intoned, now clicking off the words like an adding machine. "He was a liar, implicating innocent parties in his sins. He was a mocker, scorning all authority, military and civilian, ecclesiastical and secular. He was a blasphemer, poking fun at the Lord Himself. Not even a funeral was sacred to this man. For he used it as still another occasion to deride that most awesome moment in a man's life, his death, the time when he appears before the throne of judgment."

"Is he saying what I *think* he's saying!" Roger exclaimed softly to David.

"He *couldn't* be," David said, even as he noted that the eyes of everyone there were now shuttling between him and Clifford like observers at a tennis match.

Vein throbbing, Clifford turned abruptly from the "widow" and sent his next words flying straight at David. "Jumping like a jack-in-the-box into an open grave, dancing upon a coffin—"

There was no doubt about it now; the incredible was true! Clifford was preaching a eulogy over David's still warm, erect body. And such a eulogy! Could Genghis Khan have lived up to it?

"The Lord is long-suffering and plenteous in mercy, but never for scoffers, never for deriders, never for lechers!" Clifford cried. "And yet the Lord is forgiving too. If only a person repent of his sins, confess his iniquity, implore the Lord for forgiveness, mend the evil of his ways—"

David, exploding with fury, exclaimed, "I'll repent *you!*" And oblivious to everyone around him—his fellow chaplains, Chaplain Radcliff, General Price, the crowd —he started with a rush toward Clifford, intent on garroting him with his own vein.

"*Don't!*" Roger clawed at David's jacket, but he pulled free.

"I'll repent you all right!" He headed for Clifford

and the malicious tongue he would still just as soon as he could get his hands on it.

But then another hand grabbed hold of him, and suddenly everyone was screaming at once, like a hallelujah chorus gone berserk. David paused, startled by the frenetic reaction of the crowd which was now recoiling from him as if he were death and taxes combined. He turned to shake off the clenched hand, and then he too yelled in fright.

For the hand that was clutching him was reaching up out of the "coffin," like Judgment Day come to earth!

The "widow" reacted exactly as the real widow might have done under the circumstances. She shrieked—as the top of the "coffin" fell open to reveal a man inside: crew-cut, dimpled, and wearing a Yale sweat shirt— and fainted on top of Clifford, knocking him to the ground.

No one picked up the "widow" of the "corpse" who, on closer scrutiny, turned out to be Bentley Lane, alive; everyone was in flux—backwards, sideways, down, or up. Five women onlookers fainted, men shrieked, some cursed, the bugler put his foot through the drum, one guard put a blank through the "hearse," while everywhere people were scampering in all directions like poisoned mice.

Bentley looked on, surprised. "David," he scolded, "*now* look what you've done!"

Even before the crowd had stopped running, Bentley, Clifford and David had been marched into the Administration Building and were standing at attention before Chaplain Radcliff who, crimson-faced and furious, looked like he regretted ever having hung up his boxing gloves. "I've been all over Hell and half of Texas, and I've *never* seen the likes of what happened today. *Explain!*" He pointed at Bentley. "You first, you *ghoul*."

For the first time in his life, Bentley seemed at a loss for words. He swallowed hard. "I was only trying to make the funeral more realistic," he said, "that's all."

"By clambering out of your grave before you were

decently buried?" Chaplain Radcliff roared. "Play that somewhere else, don't sing it to me!"

"It was a reflex," Bentley explained. "I didn't plan to get up out of the coffin till after the whole pagan thing was over. But I heard Clifford and I saw David go for him and, without thinking, I reached out to stop him, completely forgetting I was dead. I didn't want David to get into any trouble."

David, touched, looked from the chaplain who professed love for people and showed it by publicly condemning them at every opportunity to the chaplain who demonstrated his professed hatred for the human race by jeopardizing himself in an effort to aid another person.

"So," the Director said, *"you* didn't want *David* to get into trouble."

"I didn't want to get myself into trouble either, believe me!" Bentley said in earnest. "I'm very much interested in Biblical scholarship—that's one reason I enlisted in the chaplaincy: so I'd have more time for studying and writing—and I know no one would take me seriously if I went around popping out of caskets at funerals, like chorus girls out of punch bowls at stag parties. You do believe I didn't *plan* to disrupt your ceremony, don't you?"

Chaplain Radcliff gave Bentley a growl for an answer and passed sentence upon him, confining him to Landers until he would be ordered elsewhere at graduation, and dismissed him. Then he turned his wrath upon the other two.

"Now who do you two think you are anyway?" He singled out Clifford. "If you'd only learn to stop judging everyone, hastily and aloud, you wouldn't be here now being judged by me. The world wasn't created, nor the people in it, just for you to vent your disapproval of them. The normal reaction to seeing Cohen jumping into the grave like he'd been goosed by a cannon would have been amusement; the *Christian* reaction should have been compassion for his embarrassment. But you see everything as a personal offense, some kind of sinful plot against you."

Clifford bristled as David sighed in relief. "That's exactly the way it was," he said. "I never—"

Chaplain Radcliff turned on David, interrupting him. "And as for you, you have to learn that the Air Force isn't Brooklyn, and you don't start a rumble here no matter *what* the provocation."

David flushed.

"Now aside from confining you two to Landers for the remainder of your stay here, this is your punishment: Both of you are to remain in this office, closeted together, until you apologize to each other—even if it takes all year. How can you expect Russia and the United States ever to make peace if two men of God can't!" He started to go.

Both men began to speak at once in protest.

"You'll find food outside the door every Monday and Thursday morning," the Director said and left the room.

Then began two contests: Who detested the other more, and which one could stay silent longer while in the same room with someone he despised?

The contests ended almost as soon as they had begun. Clifford swiftly lost the second one because he was the easy winner of the first. Facing David, he burst out:

"I don't care what anyone says! I'll *never* apologize for doing what I know was right, and necessary too. I can only pray that you profited from the experience."

"Not nearly as much as you," David retorted. "I've never seen you more cheerful than when you were shoveling all that dirt over me."

Clifford's hollow cheeks puffed out with indignation. "Do you think I spoke out like that for my *own* benefit —do you?—when I knew only too well how I might be condemned for it! The trouble is that no one today takes their religion seriously. That's why every Sunday morning is a talent show in church, with more jokes coming out of the pulpit than from a television set. I thank God that my father isn't alive today to see how religion and its servants have so debased themselves.

105

Do you know what my father would have done had he seen someone drooling over a pornographic magazine, leering about women, mocking God, blaspheming Him in song, cavorting at a funeral, deliberate or not—"

"You forget—I've heard this speech before." David strode to the door.

Clifford followed behind and caught him by the arm. "And you need to hear it again and again until you cry out: 'Yes, that's me you're talking about—*me*—and I repent! I repent!'"

David shook off the restraining hand and grabbed the door knob, twisted it and pulled. But the door would not open. It was locked, from the outside. True to his word, Chaplain Radcliff had locked the two of them in together. "Damn!" He turned back to Clifford. "There's something else you can add to your list. Occasionally I use four-letter words. Sometimes, when I get real mad, even *five*-letter ones."

Clifford did not bristle at the taunt. Indeed, his whole manner suddenly changed, softened. "David, I know how you feel now, I do," he said not unkindly, as if he suddenly wished to convince David more than to berate him. "Shame and guilt warring in your soul against pride and self—that's how it is with you." The words were the same, it occurred to David, but the melody was different, almost gentle now. "I know you, David. Because I was you once. That's why I've taken such an interest in you—once I was you. Only there was even more reason to condemn me than there is you because my father was a preacher, the saintliest man in my home town. He was a man of fiery, vengeful wrath, my father, like the God of the Old Testament."

David began to protest, then thought better of it. What was the use? Clifford was no Roger; reason was alien to him, so how could he convince him that his image of God was a specious stereotype?

"Like you, David, I used to buy pornographic literature and sneak it into my room. Like you, I was a scoffer and mocker outside of Father's earshot. Since he was so strict at home, whenever I stepped outside I was the biggest wise guy you ever heard, making fun of the church choir for singing off-key, scoffing at the bans on drinking and dancing, deriding everything. Once I even went so far as to imitate Father's thundering manner in the pulpit!" He winced as if in pain. "And then one night—it was a wintry Saturday night after junior choir rehearsals, two weeks before my sixteenth birthday, I'll never forget it— Father found me out for what I was. David, I tell you this, my shame, to prove to you how sincere I am in my wish to help save you." He lowered his eyes. "It was in the church basement. Father discovered us there, a member of the junior choir and I—like animals!—my hand touching her bare breast. I tell you, David, I was *just* as bad as you!"

The insult glanced off David. "What happened?" he asked, fascinated. "What did your father do?"

Clifford said in a voice whose calmness was belied by the vein throbbing in his forehead: "He denounced me from the pulpit the following morning. He told the entire congregation about the terrible sinful thing I had done."

David gasped.

"It was the best thing Father could have done!" Clifford exclaimed, too loudly. "That's when I was reborn, I'll never forget it. I had run away and stayed out all night in the fields, afraid to go home. But I returned to town the following morning and went to church, praying for a miracle to make everything all right. And Father passed that miracle with his sermon. He began it with a graphic description of the fires of Hell and the sins of the flesh that were sure to consign one there. Then he held up some pornographic pictures—those he had found in my room—and he told of what sinful boys did with them and the worst things they did with girls in God's own house right before His eyes. And all this time I didn't dare walk out of church for fear everyone would guess Father was referring to me. Yet I couldn't remain either, because Father was liable to identify me as the subject of his sermon. I was so *torn!*" Sweat glistened on his brow. "And then, thank God—I'll never forget it—Father finally pointed at me and thundered: 'And it's my own son, my own sinning son, I've been talking about all this time, God forgive him!' At that moment I was re-born, baptized in a sudden burst of tears and sweat—I'll never forget it—and I was up in the aisle, down before the pulpit, on my knees before Father, crying, 'I repent! I repent! I repent! Forgive me!' "

David stared at Clifford, horrified. For his imagination had conjured up the scene of Clifford in church, sitting there, sweating, listening in mortification to his small, childish sins grow great and black and unbearable, afraid that leaving the scene would expose him and afraid to stay lest his father publicly condemn him, afraid even to cry, so terrorized that he finally welcomed his own public denunciation and found relief in confessing his shame aloud before everyone. It was like *Darkness at Noon!* David shuddered. How fortunate he was to have been raised by an Uncle Asher who, had he found David fondling a bare breast in a cellar during the win-ter, would first have bawled him out for being so incon-siderate as to expose the girl to a chest cold.

"And he did forgive me, I'll never forget it. In front of the entire church Father forgave me for my sins! Be-cause I had repented. I'll always remember that day, I'll never forget it." There was a moment of silence then, as if in memoriam for that awful day of a decade ago. Then Clifford turned to David, imploring him, "David, can you understand now that what I did today, what I have al-ways tried to do for you, is out of love, the love a father has for a son, the love a fellow should have for his brother? I wanted you to experience the same catharsis that I did, the same cleansing of the spirit, the same re-birth. Do you understand that? Do you?"

David felt his eyes grow hot and salty. "I under-stand," he said, wishing that he did not, for it would have been less painful to continue detesting Clifford, hoping that he could help Clifford, knowing that he could not. "I understand."

Clifford's face lit up as if in acquittal. "Thank God!" He sank down wearily in a chair and fell silent, wiping his brow with a handkerchief.

David kept quiet too. What was there for him to say?

The door opened and Chaplain Radcliff, who had evidently been waiting outside for the first sound of silence within, stepped inside the room. "Well?" he said. "Have you two apologized to each other?"

The light fled from Clifford's face. "Apologize!" he repeated, indignant again.

"Apologize?" David looked at Clifford whose color was rising once more in his hollow cheeks. What Chaplain Radcliff did not realize was that he might as well have asked Clifford to apologize for his father, or for being Clifford, or for having so successfully fused the two into one.

"Well?" the Director asked.

"Yes, we apologized," David said with a rush. "May I be excused now?"

Chaplain Radcliff nodded and David hurried out of the room. It was only poetic justice, perhaps some form of atonement, he reflected, that his relationship with Clifford, which had begun with a lie to save himself, David, should end now with a lie to save Clifford.

But Clifford refused to be saved. "*I* never apologized to Cohen!" he exclaimed loudly enough for David to hear him down the hall. "That's still *another* one of his sinful lies."

Clifford Fowler, mused David sadly, he's my albatross here. But sympathetically he realized something else, too, that Clifford labored under a worse handicap: He was his own perpetual cross.

Chapter : 8

'GENTLEMEN," twanged Chaplain Radcliff after Dan Miller's invocation and General Price's message of congratulations to the class—and to David this was the equivalent of receiving his diploma, for until that moment the Director had never called the men anything but fellas—"you are now full-fledged chaplains. But instead of congratulating you, let me warn you—because you have a dual allegiance now, a twofold loyalty. For your mission remains exactly the same despite the change in your clothing and the shift in your titles from Father, Reverend, or Rabbi to Chaplain, First Lieutenant.

"You men are still servants of God Almighty before you're servants of anyone or anything else, and your conduct must always conform not only with your silver bars but also with your cross or your tablets.

"Don't ever forget that you're clergymen. You're going to have to say that to yourselves many times. The road is devious and dangerous. There will be times when you'll want to take off your cross or tablets because you'll have a strange feeling of not-at-homeness in some military environment. And I don't mean out of a feeling of ostentatious, sanctimonious piety, than which nothing stinks more.

"I've been in the Service for eighteen years now, and I still can't understand how any clergyman can feel wholly adjusted to military life. Whenever I hear a commanding officer say a chaplain is perfectly adjusted to the military, I smell trouble. God help the chaplain who ever feels completely at home in the Air Force! Even the military has nothing but contempt for such men.

"For the chaplain is not only a chaplain. He is something more. Just because he wears the same uniform as other officers and is subservient to military command and is paid by the government, these things do not mean that he is to be an apologist for the military.

"The chaplain is, first of all, a spokesman for God.

"That is why in the military the chaplain is always a displaced person. And he must forever remain a D.P. if he's to be any good as a chaplain. This is not a call for insubordination, mind you, but a reminder that you should never set your sails to catch the winds of command. For a chaplain's value is determined by his ability to walk the tightrope between military authority and ecclesiastical authority. This is no easy task. It is, however, a rewarding one."

The Director paused for a moment and a faraway look came into his eyes. "I remember reading somewhere—in Gibbon, perhaps—that the friars used to walk up and down the streets of Europe during the Middle Ages, asserting that anyone who met one of them would have a spiritual adventure. I hope that those who meet you in the Air Force shall have that experience. Then, gentlemen, I am sure that a spiritual adventure will be yours too."

How strange! thought David. Here was an ex-cow-puncher and ex-people-puncher, to use the Director's own words, a Texan who had grown up on a ranch and in a ring, the product of a rural Baptist seminary, a twenty-year military man, and yet he had the ability to inspire David.

The new graduates rose to their feet as Chaplain Radcliff led them in reciting the Chaplain's Pledge responsively.

"Chosen, trusted, commissioned . . ." the Director began.

"I will be true," the chaplains responded.

"The opportunity I have was given to me . . ."

"I accept it humbly and gratefully."

"Mine is an important assignment with grave responsibilities . . ."

"I will do my best."

"As a commissoned officer of the defense forces and a chosen representative of my church . . ."

"I will serve both with all my ability."

"Since service to others is my goal . . ."

"I will seek no personal credit."

"Recognizing that chaplains of other faiths have motives similar to my own . . ."

"I will co-operate with them."

"As the chaplain of men and women of many faiths . . ."

"I will serve all with equal sincerity."

"Believing that what I am is more convincing than what I say . . ."

"I will live worthily."

"Since I have been appointed to preach . . ."

"I will strive to become a worthy spokesman of God."

"As a chaplain I represent mothers and fathers and all Americans of good will . . ."

"This I will always remember."

"Because I am chosen, trusted, commissioned for tasks beyond human limitations . . ."

"I will seek the guidance of God and will trust utterly in Him."

Such a beautiful pledge, so meaningful! reflected David, conceding to himself the possibility that he might have erred in harboring so negative an attitude toward the chaplaincy. Hadn't he profited already from his three months at Landers, perhaps not so much from the courses as from getting to know people he would never have met in Brooklyn or in a synagogue. Maybe the chaplaincy would turn out to be a spiritual adventure for him after all—*halvai!*

Roger Allerton stepped forward to deliver the benediction. "Our Father in Heaven," he prayed, "we thank Thee for using this Chaplain School, where representatives of all religions have met and lived together in peace and amity, as an instrument to teach us that in Thy house there are indeed many mansions, all seeking Thee, Thy wisdom, Thy understanding, and Thy blessing. May we all prove ourselves deserving of them and of Thy love. Amen."

"Amen," echoed David.

As the men were seated, Chaplain Radcliff called Jim Mackey to come forward for his orders. The chaplains stirred restlessly, anxious to discover whether their preferences in bases, which they had been requested to indicate on one Air Force form, had been honored. David had asked for England, France or Italy. To which one of these exciting places would he be assigned?

As Jim Mackey went down the aisle, Chaplain Rad-

112

cliff announced: "You've all been assigned to wonderful bases!"

It's France, David felt sure, France! Uncle Asher had been so right in urging him to enlist.

With a chuckle the Director added, "Every single one of them is in the Air Force."

David settled then for Italy, or even England.

As everyone moved forward to the edge of his seat, Jim Mackey received his orders for France, Paul Smith for Florida, Clifford Fowler for Japan, Bentley Lane for Iceland, Dan Miller for California, Roger Allerton for Labrador, Albert Cohen for his birthplace, Germany.

Finally David's name was called, and he hurried forward. To England? France? Italy?

"And you, Chaplain Cohen, are assigned to Fairfield Air Force Base," the Director said, holding out a sheaf of mimeographed orders. "That's a SAC base."

David still remembered SAC and the movie with Jimmy Stewart but . . . "Fairfield?" he repeated, wondering where in Europe it was located.

"That's right outside Fair City."

England! Fair City sounded so English. *Didn't* it? "Fair City?" He reached for his orders.

"That's in Mississippi." Chaplain Radcliff handed him the sheaf of orders.

Join the Air Force and see—*"Mississippi?"* But he had requested England, France or Italy. Surely there must be some mistake. He looked to Chaplain Radcliff for a word of hope, some explanation, at least an apology.

The Director sighed. "That's the way the Air Force cookie crumbles, Chaplain Cohen."

David returned to his seat, despairing and inconsolable. Who had ever had a spiritual adventure in Mississippi!

Chapter : 9

THE first thing that David learned upon reporting to Fairfield Air Force Base, Mississippi, was that this was—it sounded so redundant—Mississippi. This was imparted to him when he was welcomed to the base by its commander, Colonel Stratford, who unaccountably reminded David of General Price's Oldsmobile, though the one was big, black, sleek and smooth, and the other short, wiry, pasty-faced and pock-marked.

In informing David of his geographical location, Colonel Stratford had leaned forward confidentially, narrowed his green gimlet eyes, lowered his gruff voice, and generally so behaved that David had excitedly anticipated some startling revelation like, "We attack in the morning," or at the very least, "Khrushchev is restless tonight." But all that the Commander said, so authoritatively, was: "This is Mississippi."

David was more disappointed than bewildered. "It *is?*"

Soberly Colonel Stratford replied, "Yes."

"Oh," said David.

"Chaplain, you're from up North, aren't you?" the Commander inquired, and all at once the picture swam into focus.

David nodded. "From New York. Brooklyn, really."

"That's exactly what I mean," Colonel Stratford said. "That's why it's so important for you to remember that this—" Was he going to repeat it? "—*this* is Mississippi."

"Mississippi," David echoed, for want of something to say.

"I won't beat around the bush, Chaplain. I'm referring to the race problem down here," Colonel Stratford said dispassionately. "Of course, you know that discrimination is outlawed in the service. Off base, however,

114

things go on that may disturb a Northerner like yourself. Last year there was a chaplain here who was troubled by the race problem in Mississippi. In fact, he was so troubled that he was moved. To Thule. Because he forgot that there's nothing the Air Force can do about off-base discrimination. Nothing. The military has no right to interfere in state affairs. Chaplain Cohen, you come from New York but this—always bear in mind—is Mississippi."

That was the *first* thing that David learned when he reported to Fairfield. The *second* thing was that there was a Negro Jewish airman on base.

Between announcements, David was conducted on a tour of Fairfield by a Sergeant Andrews of the Adjutant's Office who told him that the base had originally been a cotton plantation which had been purchased by the citizens of Fair City some twenty years before and donated to the Federal Government as a site for an airfield. This patriotic gesture had, not unexpectedly, paid off. A military community of five thousand employed men plus their ten thousand consumer dependents had not proven at all detrimental to Fair City's business life.

The base itself was beautiful. It had wide boulevards lined with redbud trees, now in bloom and tinting Fairfield with the rosy hue of dawn all day long. The Fairfield homes—whether large, stately French colonial houses or smaller, modern duplexes—were framed by thick, springy St. Augustine grass and evergreens and flower beds, as verdant and well kept as any country estate that David had ever seen in the movies.

Sergeant Andrews informed David that Fairfield was a one-Wing base supported by a housekeeping unit called the Air Base Group. The Wing consisted of three squadrons containing forty-five B-47's (medium six-engine jet bombers capable of flying 550 m.p.h.) and one Air Refueling Squadron of KC-97's (tankers which served as flying gas stations for the B-47's). In addition, the Wing contained other squadrons which maintained, equipped, and periodically checked all the planes.

The mission of the Wing was threefold, Sergeant Andrews went on to explain in a precise manner which suggested memorization. First, the Wing had to be capable of conducting long-range operations on any part of the globe at any time. Second, it had to be able to provide combat units capable of sustained and intense combat operations in all parts of the world. Its third mission was to train strategic bombardment crews and units.

The mission of the Air Base Group was to support the Wing by housing Fairfield's personnel, feeding them, paying them, supplying them, doctoring them, transporting them, entertaining them, even incarcerating them, providing law enforcement and traffic control, guarding aircraft, and maintaining facilities for the entire base. All in all, Fairfield was as self-contained and self-sufficient a community as any city in the United States, except for a scarcity of susceptible girls for the single airmen.

On the way to the bachelor officers' quarters, Sergeant Andrews pointed out a large compound surrounded by several high barbed-wire fences and a wide trench. "That's Littlefield Base, Chaplain. It's Top Secret. All I can tell you about it is that if you question anyone on base about it or so much as mention its name in Fair City, you're in trouble. Serious trouble."

"*Another* base *inside* of Fairfield!" said David. "Why? What's Littlefield for? It isn't for nuclear weapons by any chance, is it?"

Sergeant Andrews looked grim. "You've already forgotten, Chaplain. No questions at all about that place."

At the B.O.Q. David was assigned a private two-room apartment which the Base Chaplain had thoughtfully reserved for him. The telephone rang as he started to unpack. He picked up the receiver.

"Is this Rabbi Cohen?" a man's voice inquired.

"Yes," David said, wondering who the caller was. He had not been addressed as "Rabbi" since he had entered the chaplaincy.

"*Shalom aleichem!*" the man said. "This is Rabbi Arthur Garfield of the Fair City Synagogue. The Jewish Welfare Board wrote me you were due today, and I thought I'd call to say hello. After all, how often do I have the opportunity to greet a fellow rabbi? Once a year at the Convention, that's all. I'm very happy that you're here, David, probably happier than you are to be here."

David laughed. "Look, I'd like to come out to see you, but with Passover coming up next Monday night and with our Community Seder and all, I won't have the chance to shmooze with you for a while yet."

"I'll come over to see you then," David said.

"That's why I'm calling," Rabbi Garfield said. "I know you don't have time now to set up your own Seder for the Jewish boys on base, so I'd like to invite you and your whole congregation to join us at our Community Seder. And at the Seder I'd like you to lead us in the *Kiddush*."

"Thanks very much," David said gratefully, "but you've never heard me sing."

Rabbi Garfield laughed. "You've never heard *me* sing! Besides, this will give my congregation a chance to get a good look at you. And then, if you'll preach to us on the following *Shabbas*, there won't be a Jew in Fair City who won't know you. Well, how about it?"

"I accept, of course. I'm very grateful to you. You've made me feel very much at home here already."

"Good. That's the way it should be. David, if there's anything I or my congregation can do for you or the other Jewish people at Fairfield, just let us know. Except for one thing. The Jewish Welfare Board wrote me that you're single. I'm very sorry, but there's no one here to change that status for you. We only have sixty Jewish families here. The most eligible girl in town is my daughter Betty, and she's eight years old."

David tried to mask his disappointment. "So if she's as nice as her father, I'll wait for her."

Rabbi Garfield laughed. "I'll see you and your people at the Seder then. On Monday night. Seven o'clock. Happy Passover."

Somewhat cooler was the reception accorded David by the base chaplain, a Methodist major by the name of Mitchell Wrightson. A pale, thin man in his early forties with a heavily lined face and a distant air about him, Chaplain Wrightson said all the appropriate things but with little warmth and less conviction.

Ill-at-ease, David mentioned he still had not completed his clearing-in and asked to be excused.

"Forgive me, Chaplain," Chaplain Wrightson said, and he rubbed his red-rimmed eyes. "I haven't been very cordial to you, I know. Not that I'm not very happy to see you, only . . ." He grimaced, and even more lines furrowed his face. "One of our B-47's crashed early this morning and I've been out with the searching party. I only just returned from picking up the pieces." He pointed to a chair. "Please have a seat. I think I could use a chaplain myself to talk to right now . . ."

David sat down, annoyed with himself for having misjudged the base chaplain.

"We found only one of the men alive—none of them could get out in time—" David shuddered and Chaplain Wrightson noticed it. "Chaplain, if you haven't been used to death, get set. And don't be too upset if your theology takes a turn, changes. It's going to. I've buried a great number of men whose entire body I could have carried in the palm of my hand. There are times when you have to go out and search an area a mile square and pick up as many pieces as you can find. Yet the man isn't dead until the flight surgeon says he's dead. Then you have to go see the wife, as I'll be doing as soon as Colonel Stratford comes by, and you have to tell the woman her husband is not coming home any more . . ." He fell silent.

David could think of nothing to say. Suddenly he found himself thinking of the automobile crash that had killed his parents.

A voice on the intercom broke the silence. "Chaplain, Colonel Stratford is waiting for you outside."

"Tell him I'll be right out, Sergeant," Chaplain Wrightson said, then turned to David. "Chaplain Cohen, you should make a good chaplain. You listen as if you really cared. That's half a chaplain's job. When you're faking an interest instead of really taking it, the men spot that right away. And then you're useless. Remember that."

The following afternoon, Chaplain Wrightson—"Suppose you call me Mitchell," he said, "and I don't want to see you ever salute me again; even if I do outrank you, we're still colleagues"—told David how happy the Jewish personnel would be to see him, since they had been without a Jewish chaplain for more than a year.

"How large a congregation do I have here?" David asked, expecting the number to be around a hundred. "How many Jews are there at Fairfield?"

"Well, from our records—and they're far from accurate, what with transfers and discharges—I'd say about thirty or so." David's mouth fell open. *Thirty!* "Of course, on your Passover Holy Days and New Year that number quadruples . . ." David laughed with relief; evidently Mitchell had been referring to the weekly attendance at Sabbath Services which could be increased. ". . . because on those days I see to it that all Jewish personnel are exempt from duty, so all of a sudden everyone on base is a Jew."

David exclaimed, "You actually mean there are only thirty Jews here *in all?*" Was he supposed to devote two years of his life to serving *thirty* people, all of whom could be easily accommodated in Rabbi Garfield's synagogue?

"I can imagine your disappointment," Mitchell said sympathetically, "but perhaps our records are all wrong. Maybe there are other Jews on base who are not registered at the chapel, like that Negro Jew we stumbled on accidentally when Clark Herford heard him singing at the Service Club and tried to enlist him in our choir. I never knew before, David, that there were Negro Jews. How does that happen?"

David, who had never met a Negro Jew, told Mitchell that Negro Jews were believed to be descendants of Jews who settled in Egypt some twenty-five hundred years before, after the First Exile, and then moved to Abyssinia. There they had intermarried with the inhabitants,

119

yet had remained more or less faithful to their religion. Some of these people had emigrated to the United States, settling in Harlem.

"Fascinating!" Mitchell said, and he handed David a list of names. "Here's a list of the Jewish personnel. Airman First Class Harris is the Negro."

David spent the remainder of the day telephoning all the people on the list. As it turned out, he did more phoning than talking, because the majority of the people were no longer at Fairfield. Of the thirty men on the list, no more than thirteen—*thirteen!*—were still stationed at the base. Of these, only ten, including Harris who seemed somewhat reluctant, promised to attend Sabbath Eve Services on the following Friday night. To describe David as feeling disheartened would be like saying that the Jews in 586 B.C. had been annoyed when the Babylonians razed Judea and carried off most of her inhabitants. In both instances, Jews, through no fault of their own, found themselves in exile.

On Friday evening nine Jewish men, including David, came to chapel—together with three wives, one abnormally fat daughter in her early twenties, and two small girls—which was one shy of the required quorum necessary for a Jewish religious service. As the group (composed of the installations commander and his huge daughter, a doctor and his wife who were soon leaving the service, two R.O.T.C. lieutenants, a sergeant and his wife and two children, an airman and his wife, and two single airmen) waited for the tenth man to appear, someone remarked that what the congregation lacked in quantity it made up for in paucity, and David felt too disheartened to muster a smile.

The tenth man to arrive was Airman First Class Ben Harris, whose color left no doubt as to his race. He was a tall, pleasant-looking fellow, about twenty-two, with a shy smile and a New York accent.

"Look!" exclaimed the older of the children, and she pointed in Harris' direction. "He's wearing a *yarmulke!*"

"Lots of people wear skullcaps," said the child's

mother, equally surprised. "Don't you remember seeing the Pope on television wearing one?"

"But the Pope's Jewish," said the younger child, a seven-year-old, "else he wouldn't be wearing a *yarmulke.*" She stared in fascination at the colored airman. "Why is *he* wearing it?"

"Ssh!" said the mother, mystified. "I'll explain later."

The Negro stirred uneasily. "Was there—is there supposed to be a service tonight?"

David came forward quickly. "Thanks to *you*, there is. We've been waiting for you, Airman Harris, to complete our *minyan.*" He shook the fellow's hand. "We're very glad you came. Now we can begin."

The service was like no other that David had ever conducted, and not because a Negro happened to be in the congregation. The difference was that in the three-hundred-seat chapel the sixteen Jews seemed more like a club than a congregation. They were hardly able to raise an echo, let alone their voices, in the large chapel. And when David delivered his sermon, he felt that he was preaching to 285 empty seats rather than to fifteen people. He had experienced more response in the past when talking to himself.

After the service was concluded, David shook everyone's hand in turn, wishing each one a Sabbath of peace, and extending Rabbi Garfield's invitation to attend the synagogue's Community Passover Seder on the following Monday night. When David reached the installations commander, a Major Gordon, standing beside his enormously fat daughter Dena, the major took David aside.

"Maybe it would be better," he suggested, "to speak about Rabbi Garfield's invitation at another time, when the Negro boy isn't around. He'll feel bad when you invite everyone else here but him."

"But I mean to invite Harris too," David said. "The synagogue's invitation was extended to *all* Jews on base."

"You're not serious!" Major Gordon exclaimed. "You know as well as I the synagogue had no idea . . . They didn't mean it for . . . Look, Chaplain, I'm not the least bit prejudiced, believe me. I just want to remind you that this is Mississippi. Here there are laws to—"

"Major," David said evenly, "in Judaism, too, there are laws—*higher* laws."

"Can breaking one of the Jewish laws get you shipped to the Arctic?"

"Now no one's getting shipped anywhere," David replied with an assurance he was trying to achieve. "Because I'm not going to make a great big issue out of this thing."

"How are you going to avoid it!"

"Major, the trouble with people is that everyone thinks he has to have an opinion about *everything,* especially about things he knows nothing about. Now I don't intend to let a soul in the synagogue know that I'm bringing Harris, because then everybody there would think he'd have to take some kind of stand, which in this case would mean acting the way he thinks others *expect* him to act. And after the Seder, if there's any adverse comment in Fair City, the congregation can blame it all on me, that radical from New York."

"Chaplain, they'll transfer you to Thule, the Siberia of the Air Force," Major Gordon warned. "That's where they sent a former chaplain from here who was considered a troublemaker. And what's the point of it all? Bringing a Negro to a white Southern Seder—what do you hope to accomplish by doing that?"

"Nothing very great, I realize that," David conceded. "Nevertheless, it will be an achievement, tiny though it may be. A Negro will have eaten with a white congregation in Mississippi without having 'contaminated' them in any respect. That's a good memory for people to have in the backs of their minds with integration coming to the schools and—Major, if the synagogues and churches don't take the lead in solving the race problem, *who will?"*

Major Gordon shook his head. "I don't understand you at all,. Chaplain. Why run the risk of starting a ruckus and getting yourself shipped to Thule? For what? You yourself admit that the results, even if successful, will be meager. Is it worth the gamble?"

"Let me quote from the Talmud," David said. "'It is not incumbent upon you to finish the work, but neither are you free to desist from it altogether.'"

Major Gordon shrugged. "I'm afraid that has more meaning for you than it does for me."

"Perhaps this will make it clearer. Major, I'll be very frank with you. I was never wildly enthusiastic about entering the chaplaincy. But if I *have* to be a Jewish chaplain, I'm going to *be* a Jewish chaplain. For *all* Jews." He added, "And I hope you don't think I'm trying to be some kind of hero. Because that isn't the case at all. It's simply that I learned a long time ago that it's easier for me to explain to others why I'm doing something I know is right than to explain to myself afterwards why I did something wrong."

Major Gordon shrugged. "Have it your way, Chaplain. It's your fu—" He checked himself.

David felt himself shiver. "My funeral? No, Major. This will be nobody's funeral, but a truly Jewish Seder for all." At least, that was what he *wanted* to say, but somehow the words never left his mouth. For all at once he found himself thinking of Chaplain Radcliff's parting words to his graduating class, something to the effect that a chaplain in the military was a displaced person and that his value depended upon his agility at balancing himself on the tightrope between military authority and the religious imperative. Was he, in the active chaplaincy less than a week, *already* losing his equilibrium?

"You two can stop arguing now." It was hulking Dena Gordon, interrupting. "When the Negro airman heard my father explain how really unprejudiced he was, he left," she said. "Could be the fellow prefers being hated to being tolerated. I know *I* do."

David, ashamed that Harris had been made to feel uncomfortable, immediately excused himself from the group and went to seek him at his squadron barracks. There he was told that the Negro Jew was married and lived off base, at 210½ Pinto Drive in Fair City. Nor could the C.Q. have Harris report to the chapel on Monday morning because Harris would not be returning to his squadron any more, for he was clearing the base prior to being discharged. Since Harris had no telephone, there was only one way to contact him, and that was to go to his home.

With a map of Fair City at his side, it did not take David long on Sunday to find Pinto Drive, the heart of the Negro ghetto, which consisted of rows of broken-down cigar-box houses, attached like railroad cars, with smaller cigarillo outhouses behind them and muddy roads in front of them. Each rickety wooden structure had a porch and a swing which looked as if anyone sitting on either would bring the ramshackle house down on his head. David, walking to the door of 210 Pinto Drive, felt sick to see human beings living in places where no self-respecting farmer would keep livestock. He knocked on the door.

A Negro man of indeterminate age came to the door and opened it. He made a motion as if to shut it as soon as he saw David. "What do you want?" he asked suspiciously.

"I'm looking for an Airman Harris," David replied. "He's an airman first class from Fairfield and I'm—"

The man interrupted. "Never heard of no Harris."

"But his address is 210½ Pinto Drive. I'm a chaplain from—"

"This is *210*, Mister."

"Well, where is 210½?"

"Don't know. Never heard of it."

"Where do you suggest I look?"

"There is no 210½. You musta made a mistake."

David started away, then paused. "Is there a policeman around here who could perhaps help me find—"

"Wait a minute!" the man exclaimed. "I remember now. A soldier used to live here with his wife. But they moved. To 21 Pinto Drive. Try there, Mister."

The tenant at 21 Pinto Drive did not even open the door. As soon as she saw David through the screen door, she retreated.

"I'm looking for an Airman Harris from Fairfield—"

"He don't live here."

"I was told he did."

"Ain't so."

Maybe the grocery store on the next block would know where Harris lived, David reasoned, and started toward it. A screen door squeaked behind him. He turned around in time to see a woman's head pull inside 21 Pinto Drive and the door slam shut.

As he entered the grocery store, all life inside came to an abrupt, silent halt. There were nearly a dozen people in the store and yet not one person was talking. No one looked directly at David, but everyone had his eyes fixed on something in his vicinity.

"I'm looking for an airman named Harris," David began.

"Never heard of him," the storekeeper said, then turned to address his customers. "Anybody here ever hear of a Harris?"

The quiet people shook their heads.

And then, at last, David understood. These people were *afraid* of him! The thought sickened him. "Look, Mister," he began, and the storekeeper looked at him strangely. David recalled then that no white man in the South addressed a Negro as mister. "I'm a chaplain in the Air Force, a rabbi—that's a minister, a clergyman. I'm not out to harm this fellow Harris. I just want to talk to him." He could see that no one believed him and somehow, confronted by the obvious disbelief on all those silent faces, he found himself doubting his own story.

The storekeeper shook his head. David gave up.

He left the store and walked toward his car, conscious now of dozens of eyes following him, eyes peering out of windows, faces looking out of doors, people on the street turning around to watch him as he passed by, all silent, all observing, all suspicious . . . There was something so very familiar about it all.

Suddenly he remembered. He recalled witnessing men hanging back against walls before, women shushing their children, people peering out of ramshackle wooden buildings, a town falling silent, eyes watching fearfully . . . And then the villain would appear, striding down the noiseless streets, and a child would begin to whimper, as one was doing now. *That* was why this scene seemed so familiar: He had seen it before in scores of Western movies. And here now, on Pinto Drive, *he* was the villain. The color of his skin had convicted him.

"Man, are *you* lost!" Even before David turned around, he recognized the New York accent. It was Harris, smiling. David almost whooped with joy to see a set of teeth on Pinto Drive. "What are you doing here, Chaplain?"

"I came looking for you," David said, "but no one would tell me where you live."

"I know," Harris said. "They told me. But when a white man comes looking for a black man here, it means only one thing: trouble. They thought you were a cop."

"But I explained to them—well, that doesn't matter now. I came to talk to you about the synagogue Seder tomorrow night. You left Friday before I had a chance to invite you."

Disbelief, not unlike the expressions of it he had seen on the other Negro faces, appeared in Harris' eyes. "Are you kidding?" he exclaimed.

Yet even when David convinced the airman of his sincerity, he demurred. "What's the point, Chaplain? It's not as if I'd be around after next week to make anyone feel uncomfortable. I'm being discharged in six days. Why are you so anxious that I go to that Seder anyway?"

"I'm a rabbi," David said.

"You're also a chaplain, first lieutenant," Harris responded.

"I know it—you don't have to remind me!" David exclaimed loudly, possibly to drown out his own thoughts to the same effect. "That's *my* problem."

"It's my problem also. Chaplain, this is Mississippi."

The familiar phrase goaded David to anger. "I certainly don't intend *forcing* you to go to the Seder. If you want to attend, if Passover means something to you —then I want to take you. If being a Jew means nothing o you, say so. But please *don't* tell me that this is Mississippi!"

Harris was taken aback. "What are you getting so teamed up for?"

David knew the answer—he was a D.P. many times over: a chaplain in the Air Force, a civilian masquerading in military dress, a Brooklynite in Mississippi, a Jew among gentiles, a white man in a Negro ghetto, a bachelor without any girls—but he said instead, "Look, I've got to get back to the base to practice the *Kiddush* for the Seder, and I don't have the time to—"

Harris interrupted. "You know, I used to sing the *Kiddush* myself at home when—" He checked himself, then said abruptly, "Let me talk it over with my wife. I'll call you at the chapel in the morning. Okay?"

"Fine," David said, somehow relieved that the discussion was at an end. "Just one thing now before I leave. Just for curiosity's sake—where the devil *do* you live?"

Harris grinned sheepishly. "You had the right address, all right—210½ Pinto Drive. It's at the back end of 210. The landlord partitioned the house in two, then knocked a door into the back wall. And that's 210½."

"It sure would make a good hide-out from the cops!"

"Maybe it'll come in handy then tomorrow night after the Seder," Harris commented.

David forced a wan smile.

The next morning Harris called to say that he had decided in favor of attending the Seder. He added that his wife would not be accompanying him. It seemed she felt very strongly that while Northern Negroes could think of sitting down and eating with white people, as far as *she* was concerned, this was *still* Mississippi.

David was leaving his apartment on Monday evening when the phone rang. It was Dena, Major Gordon's huge daughter. "I just wanted to tell you I'll be saving you and Airman Harris two seats at our table," she said. "We'll be sitting in the back—near the fire exit. There's an ax there, just in case."

Dena Gordon's words did not cheer David at all; for

a moment he even felt like taking her ax to her for depressing him when he needed all the courage he could manufacture. Nor was he exhilarated by Harris' opening remark when they met across the street from the Fair City Synagogue.

"Chaplain, are we *really* going to go through with this?"

David threw up his hands in anger. "I don't know. *Are* we? You tell me." But when his hands fell back to his sides it was in something bordering suspiciously on relief, and this knowledge spurred him to add in a tone of voice that was perhaps two shades too loud for what he had to say, "I'll tell you why *I* want to go through with it, Harris. Because some two thousand years ago one of the rabbis proclaimed: 'Act like a man one day before your death.' And when he was asked by his disciples how anyone could possibly know on which day he would die, Rabbi Eliezer's reply was: 'Exactly. For that reason, we ought to live *every* day as though it were our last.'"

Loud as were David's words, Harris did not seem to hear them. He was otherwise occupied, staring intently ahead of him at his car in an apparent effort to hypnotize it. But suddenly his lips began to twist and turn as if unseen fingers were pulling at them, and he burst out: "Chaplain, my wife's sick and she's going to have a baby and she's worried I'll get into trouble here tonight with only four more days remaining and—" He checked himself and abruptly strode to his car, opened the door and jumped inside.

David gritted his teeth in anger, and this time it was directed against himself for having been more concerned about the principle of the situation than for the person caught up in it. He followed Harris into the car, saying, "I didn't mean to put you on the spot—especially at a time like this. It wasn't fair of me."

Harris turned on David. "You'd better get out of my car," he said gruffly.

Wincing, David accepted the rebuke implicit in Har-

128

ris' tone of voice. "I'm sorry! I hope you'll forgive me," he said shamefacedly, stepping out of the car.

Harris reached out and caught him by the arm. "What are you apologizing to me for?"

For preaching to you before instead of listening to you, thought David. For thinking of you as a problem rather than as a person. For not knowing your wife was pregnant. For not perceiving you're more anxious than I about tonight. For not realizing that, this being Mississippi, you're running the greater risk. For not noticing that there was something more distinctive about you than a shy smile, white teeth, and brown skin. "I can't blame you for not wanting me in your car," he said aloud.

Harris' liquid brown eyes opened wide, and his thick black brows arched over them in surprise. "Who said I didn't want you in my car?" he exclaimed. "It's against the law in Mississippi for a Negro and a white man to be in the same car. Didn't you know that? Just like it must be against the law for us to eat at the same Seder. That's why I lied to you—" His voice broke. Lowering his eyes, he forced himself to continue. "My wife isn't sick, Chaplain, and she's not having a baby—she isn't even pregnant. I lied to you. And yesterday when I told you I wanted to consult her about coming here tonight— that was a lie too. My wife went to New York last month to get herself a job. Everything I ever said to you was a lie, and I'm so ashamed! Because I'm *scared*, Chaplain. I'm scared to go into a house of God like anyone else— and that shames me."

Harris' confession did not relieve David's sense of guilt any; to him there was only one thing worse than confessing one's shame, and that was witnessing another's. "Harris, suppose we go to my quarters now," he said hurriedly, getting back into the car. "I have some Passover provisions there. We can make our own Seder, just the two of us. How's that?"

Harris shook his head. "Chaplain, I told you it's against the law here for us even to sit in the same car, much less drive together."

"Oh, the *hell* with Mississippi law!" David exclaimed. "Come on, we're going back to the base now and—"

"*No!*" He raised his dark brown eyes to David's and burst out with sudden determination: "We're going to the synagogue. If you can drive back to the base with me, Chaplain—well, I can go to the Seder with you." He waved aside David's attempted protest. "Like you said before, we ought to live every day like it was our last day on earth."

"*I* didn't say that—"

Harris interrupted, his round, smooth face set but his eyes smiling. "And like Rabbi Eliezer said: The *hell* with Mississippi law!"

David hesitated. "I don't want to get you into any trouble even if your wife isn't pregnant—"

Harris bounded out of the car. "I *want* to go to the Seder, Chaplain. Come on!"

David smiled, happy about Harris' decision but happier still that Harris' decision had *made* him happy. He stepped out of the car, saying, "Let's wait till they're all seated at their tables inside. We don't want to make our entrance while people are standing. Then it would be just as easy for them to walk out as to sit down. Once they're seated, though, it will take an action on their part to remove themselves from the premises. You see, I'm counting not only on our religion for help, but also on inertia."

"Thanks," Harris said quietly, then explained, "You said 'our.'"

The two men waited for the shadows of evening to lengthen and darken, and as they waited they talked. David asked about the synagogue in Harlem and learned that it was thirty-five years old and its membership, most of whom claimed descent from the legendary union between King Solomon and the Queen of Sheba, numbered some twelve hundred people which, David ruefully noted, was a hundred times as many people as in his own Fairfield congregation. Harris revealed that he had sung in the Harlem synagogue choir for several years and that this experience had given him the idea to become a pop singer in civilian life, especially since he felt that show business was about the only field where a Negro was judged on the basis of merit alone. "Look how far Sammy Davis, Jr., has gotten," he said, proudly adding, "He's Jewish too, you know, just like us."

"Thanks," David said, "for the 'us.' "

Harris' teeth flashed in a smile.

A church chime nearby sounded the hour, seven o'clock. "It's time now," David said.

The two men crossed the street and entered the synagogue. Inside, on the door to the sanctuary, was an arrow marked SEDER, and they followed it down the vestibule to a closed door which muffled the sounds of people milling about beyond it.

David opened the door and looked inside. He saw a long festively decorated hall with some two hundred people in it seating themselves around a score of tables, all decked in white linen tablecloths and floral centerpieces and wine glasses and holiday candles whose softly flickering yellow light made all the people in the hall look young while at the same time it somehow imparted a look of age to the Seder platters containing the ancient Passover symbols: the bitter herbs, the parsley, the roasted egg, the shankbone, the *charoses.*

Observing the traditional setting, David felt impressed, as he never failed to be on Passover, more by the antiquity of the holiday than by the beauty of its symbols and ritual. For much as he valued beauty, he felt it was something that existed only horizontally in time and temporarily in space while the religious ideals of Judaism, as manifested in its holy days, existed vertically for four thousand years of past history at the same time that they were being projected forward into the future by his people, whose greatest hope it was to help bring about God's Kingdom on earth.

And thinking in terms of millenniums and absolutes and the world, David suddenly felt his anxiety slipping away. For wasn't it foolish of him or even of Harris to worry about this single moment in a tiny corner of the world when one man would sit down with other men at a Seder for a fraction of time? So what if this was Mississippi? This—the overriding eternal factor—was the Passover, thank God.

Rabbi Garfield, at the far end of the hall, rose to his feet and motioned for silence. At the same time David spotted Major Gordon sitting at the table nearest the door and waving to him. "Harris, remember," David said, "we're not sneaking in. We're walking in. Because we belong here. *Now!*"

With Harris close behind him, David stepped inside the hall, steeling himself for any possible outcry.

Suddenly a girl cried out and plates crashed to the floor. David sucked in his breath and stopped short.

"Oh, how stupid of me!" Dena Gordon, at the other end of the hall, was exclaiming over and over again as she continued to drop plates to the floor like an expert juggler who had mistaken Down for Up. "How clumsy!"

"Come on!" David said, and he pulled Harris to Major Gordon's table where they were greeted warmly but quietly by all the Fairfield personnel there. They sat down swiftly while everyone was looking, many laughing, at the fat girl now stooping to retrieve her plates but somehow managing to drop more than she picked up.

Rabbi Garfield waited for Dena Gordon to quiet down, as she did when she saw that David and Harris were seated; then he said, "Let us turn to page five of our *Haggadahs.*"

The chair next to David groaned as if in protest as Dena Gordon sat down beside him. "I read somewhere that magicians always use beautiful assistants to distract the audience's attention," she whispered. "Now, I may look more like the Beast than like Beauty, but I sure know how to break plates!"

The rabbi raised a silver goblet of wine. "The new chaplain at Fairfield, Rabbi Cohen, was supposed to lead us in the *Kiddush,* but evidently he has been detained. And so—"

David called out: "I'm here, Rabbi."

The congregation turned to look at David, and Harris

moved back from the table into the shadows cast by the holiday candlelight and bowed his head.

"I'm so happy to see you, Chaplain," Rabbi Garfield responded. "Would you kindly lead us in the *Kiddush* now?"

"It will be a great honor." David started to rise from his seat, but a hand upon his arm restrained him. It was a dark brown hand.

"Just like I really belong here," Harris said, then stood up with the rest of the congregation, and began chanting the *Kiddush*.

There were several startled exclamations, but they were drowned out by David and Major Gordon and the other Fairfield personnel who were quick to join in the chanting. Rabbi Garfield added his tenor voice to the singing and soon other members of the congregation were chanting in unison with Harris whose reedy though powerful baritone did not, unfortunately, augur well for a career in show business.

"Lord our God," Harris was chanting, "out of love Thou didst give us festivals for happiness, holy days and seasons of joy. This Passover season, our festival of freedom, is a holy assembly called together to remember the exodus from Egypt." And by the time he completed the *Kiddush,* most of the people in the hall were chanting along with him.

Everyone fell silent as Harris emptied his wine glass and sat down. Suddenly there was an ominous scraping of a chair, and a dark, portly man at a nearby table took his woman companion by the arm. "Come!"

All at once people were turning to their neighbors and whispering. More chairs scraped, and when the couple started for the door, an argument broke out between two men at the far end of the hall.

Rabbi Garfield spoke up above the noise: "Now we take the parsley and we dip it in the salt water which reminds us of the bitter tears our forefathers shed in Egypt because they were slaves there, and we say the blessing."

The whispering died away as the congregation joined

133

the rabbi in the Hebrew benediction. Undeterred by the holy words, the couple left the hall, followed by a second couple. But all the others took their seats.

David turned to Harris. "Don't let those people bother you one bit. *They're* the ones who don't belong here."

There was no reply.

Rabbi Garfield held up a plate of matzos as he continued the thirty-three-hundred-year-old ritual, intoning the ancient words from the *Haggadah:* "See the bread of suffering which our forefathers ate in Egypt. All you who are hungry, come, eat with us. All you who are in need, come, celebrate the Passover with us. This year we are here; may next year find us celebrating the Passover in Israel. This year men are enslaved; may next year see them free . . . ."

Chapter : 10

AT the appointed time of 1500 hours on the following afternoon David rapped once on the door of the Base Commander's office, opened it, marched to Colonel Stratford's desk, halted, clicked his heels together at attention, and saluted. Then, recalling what he had heard about the Colonel since arriving at Fairfield (to someone who had once ventured to remark, "Nice day, Colonel, isn't it?" the Commander was reported to have replied, "Goddammit, when I want your opinion, I'll *ask* for it!"), he faltered, "Chaplain Cohen reporting as ordered —Colonel."

Grudgingly the Commander returned the salute. "At ease," he said, and David assumed the position though he did not at all feel it.

Colonel Stratford spoke unhurriedly in a flat tone of voice. "Chaplain, it's most unfortunate that you chose to disregard my previous excellent advice to you on how to conduct yourself off base here in Mississippi. I've been informed by one of the leading citizens of Fair City, who happens to be a Jew himself, that you brought a Negro airman along with you to a communal supper at the local synagogue last night. Fortunately, after the two of you left the premises, all the people present swore not to breathe a word of what you had done, so it looks like the incident will be hushed up. Now I have summoned you here to tell you that if you ever plan to flout local laws again, or my advice, you had better pack all of your belongings *beforehand*. That is all, Chaplain."

David flushed. "May I say something?" he said, having spent the night memorizing Chaplain Radcliff's words about the necessity for a chaplain to maintain his dual status. "Colonel, what I did last—"

The Colonel interrupted, his green eyes raking David. *"No."*

"Pardon?"

"You asked me if you might say something, and I said *no*," the Colonel explained, the narrowing green eyes in his pasty, pock-marked face glinting like mold on a piece of Swiss cheese. "Good afternoon."

Fuming at the curt dismissal, yet relieved that in the first clash between his silver bars and his Tablets of the Law he had escaped with only a warning, David returned to his quarters. He arrived there in time to answer a phone call from Rabbi Garfield regretfully withdrawing his preaching invitation.

"David, I'm afraid you're too controversial now," he said apologetically. "If you were to speak from our pulpit now, people would think the synagogue officially endorses your racial views. Now personally I share your sympathies, as do most of the Jews of Fair City; had I been in your position, most likely I'd have done what you did. Still, this *is*—"

David filled in: "Mississippi."

"Now please understand *our* position. We live here in Mississippi. You live there in the Air Force. It makes a big difference. You can afford to be liberal; we can't.

Every single Jewish family here—mine is the only exception—is in some sort of business that's easy to boycott and *would* be boycotted if we got involved in the race problem. There's nothing that we as Jews can do to help the Negroes, unfortunately. We're a minority here ourselves, only one per cent of the population of Fair City. And it's no virtue to invite prejudice and reprisals against ourselves when we can't even hope to achieve anything by it."

Thereafter, David's contacts with the members of the synagogue were at all times polite, and little else. Whenever he went to the synagogue now, he was treated like an old and familiar member of the family—the crazy uncle on temporary leave from the attic.

On base too there were hardly enough Jews to reassure him that he was indeed a rabbi. When Harris was discharged, David lost a full ten per cent of his congregation. Even on those Sabbaths when a *minyan* came, the dozen people in the three-hundred-seat chapel looked more like an underground band of saboteurs than a religious congregation; and preaching to such a tiny group gave him the uncomfortable sensation that he was being overheard while talking to himself.

As a result, one Friday evening when the required ten men did not show up and Major Gordon commented that coming to chapel did not seem to him—with no aspersions on David, he should understand—like attending a real service in a real synagogue, could David disagree? He could only discuss the matter with his tiny congregation and finally concur—Dena Gordon was the only dissenter—that it would be better for them to resume their religious activities at the synagogue in Fair City.

On the following Monday morning, David went to Mitchell and explained the situation to him, that he couldn't feel any more useless had he been assigned to be chaplain to the Knights of Columbus. The base chaplain, sympathetic, immediately sent a TWIX to Headquarters USAF requesting that David be reassigned to another base with a larger Jewish population.

136

Four days later a reply came from Washington. The answer was clear and very much to the point; it was no.

David now found himself in the peculiar position of being a religious functionary of, for all practical purposes, nothing. Sadly he reasoned that he might as well have been a witch doctor as a rabbi at Fairfield, since there were only a dozen fewer cannibals on base than there were Jews.

—David, there's no getting away from it. As a rabbi, you just *ain't*.

—Careful now, you're talking to yourself. And you know what they say about people who talk to themselves.

—Who *else* can I talk to? Who else would understand?

—That's true, too true. Alas!

—Here I prepare myself for four years to become a rabbi because there are great things I wanted to learn and to teach, things worth saying and worth hearing . . .

—And where do they send you once you become a rabbi? To a place that has as many Jews as Notre Dame or Darien, Connecticut.

—It's like being assigned to be the house doctor of a mausoleum.

—You just don't feel needed.

—Exactly.

—Don't agree! Whatever you do, don't agree. I feel bad enough as it is. *Argue.*

—All right, all right. There's the Chaplain's Six-Point Program they taught us about in Chaplain School. Remember?

—I remember.

—Well, the first point of the Chaplain's Six-Point Program, Worship and Pastoral Functions, is ruled out. We know that. But what about the second point?

—Half of it, Religious Education, doesn't apply either. The two Jewish kids are better off attending the synagogue's religious school.

137

—The other half of the second point: Moral Education—

—You mean Moral Leadership Lectures? Telling the boys to keep chaste, sober and thrifty?

—Now you're getting sarcastic—that doesn't help any. What about the third point, Personal Counseling?

—I can't even solve my *own* problem! Besides, who's there to come to me for counseling? Don't people always go to chaplains of their own faith?

—There's the fourth point, Humanitarian Services—charity drives . . .

—Am I to be a collection agency for two years?

—The fifth point, Public Relations.

—After the synagogue Seder? Next point.

—Cultural Leadership.

—You mean, put on plays and movies and such? Is that why I studied for four years to be a rabbi—to become a small-time Josh Logan?

—We've run out of points! Except, of course, for your making yourself available generally for aid and assistance.

—What? Living with gentiles for two years—all right. But *serving* gentiles for two years? I'm a *rabbi*.

—Surely there must be *something* you can do at Fairfield for two years.

—There is. I can get in an awful lot of praying.

Mitchell tried to help out with some occupational therapy; he assigned David to deliver his first Dynamics of Moral Leadership Lecture whose topic for the month, he conceded, sounded like something suggested by Ma Perkins: The Need for Wholesome Thinking. "Still," the Base Chaplain added, "these talks are a great improvement over the old World War II Sex Lectures when we chaplains would get up and tell the boys *not* to, only to be followed instantly by the medics—with pictures, slides, plaster casts, everything but live models—showing the boys exactly *how* to."

But the lectures did not cheer David any, for he found them to be nothing more than contests between him and the Sandman for the eyelids of men. These kept closing during the lectures (attendance at which was compulsory for officers and airmen alike, and consequently resented by officers and airmen alike) and so remained for the duration of the talks. Some men came as much as twenty minutes early, he noted with chagrin, just to avoid the risk of his husky voice keeping them from falling asleep.

Yet it was not the sleepers that annoyed him so much as their snores. Beginning as a buzzing overtone to his lecture, they would gather so much tempo, volume and nasality that toward the lecture's end, David himself was stifling yawns, while ruefully conceding that the benefit the men seemed to derive from his talks was of the kind they could get simply by refraining from banging their heads against curbstones.

Take, for example, the effects of his second lecture, Clean Speech, upon the men's speech habits. Most of the comments on the lecture itself that David heard afterwards, on the way to the base theater's exit, were vulgar, except for those that were obscene. If this was the men's initial reaction to a lecture on Clean Speech, he wondered at the time, what would they do immediately after hearing the one on Chastity?

By his third lecture, David was sufficiently frustrated by his audience's snoring to try anything to rouse them. And the means he finally chose were three raw eggs. These, as he began his talk by repeating the familiar tale about the milkmaid who had achieved immortality by counting her chickens before they had been hatched, suddenly slipped from his hands and broke with a dull squash at his feet behind the podium.

David grimaced, and the audience howled so loudly it startled the sleepers awake. Automatically they struggled drowsily to their feet, believing the lecture to be over, and started for the exits. They were pulled down by their chortling buddies, who gleefully informed them of the broken eggs.

David hesitated, as if torn between continuing the

lecture and leaving to change his trousers, then began anew.

This time not a snore was heard; everyone was too eager to catch a glimpse of his egg-splattered uniform.

David gave his talk and, upon concluding it, remained on stage behind the podium. "You're dismissed," he said to his watchful audience.

But nobody moved. For once the men did not dash away as if he had been trying to sell them diseases.

David smiled at the brightly eager faces turned toward him, all so intent upon enjoying his embarrassment to the full, then bent over. When he straightened up and stepped aside in a clean uniform, he held in his hand a large pan which he had placed behind the podium before the men had assembled and before he had deliberately dropped the eggs into it. "Men, as you may recall," he said, "the topic for this month's lecture is Plan Ahead."

The audience roared approvingly.

During subsequent days, to his great delight, dozens of men stopped David on the street. Some of their comments were: "That stunt with the eggs—that was something!" and "You sure fooled us with those eggs!" and "I thought I'd die laughing at that last lecture of yours!" and "Chaplain, you're a *gasser!*" '

His delight died with the comments. What are you anyway, he asked himself, an egg-dropper or a speaker? a clown or a chaplain? a con man or a lecturer? Maybe next time you'll be dropping your pants?

Yet he did not regret having stooped to scrambling eggs. At least he had proven to himself that the men could be interested in the lectures, certainly when they were *im*properly presented.

One immediate result of the lectures was that a goodly number of personnel coming to the chapel surprised David, also pleased him, by requesting to be counseled specifically by "the tall, dark, curly-haired chaplain," or "the Jewish chaplain," or—would he never live it down! —"y'know, the one who drops eggs." For Air Force people seeking counsel were usually unconcerned with a chaplain's religious affiliation, perhaps because the great majority of their problems were not of a religious nature.

Certainly once David started counseling in earnest, he discovered that not all men were as interested in acquiring Religious Truth or Moral Law as they were in avoiding Unpleasant Assignments. Indeed, some men tended to equate Moral Law with Fat Deals Like My Buddy Got, and when David tried to distinguish between the two, several men threatened to take their problems elsewhere.

There was one thing that all the problems had in common, and that was gamut:

Adjustment:
—Suppose we work out a nightly schedule for you that will keep you too busy to get homesick.

—You should have come to see a chaplain *before* you decided to go AWOL for the third time while stealing Colonel Stratford's car from the motor pool.

—If you study hard and pass those proficiency tests, we'll get you that job that you want.

—No, I really don't think that the base psychiatrist has a dirty mind.

Administrative:
—I'm afraid you can't just resign from the Air Force, even if the recruiting sergeant *did* lie to you.

—I'll see what can be done about getting you an administrative discharge instead of a homosexual one.

—You may be right. Maybe the people in Washington *don't* know how to run an Air Force. But going AWOL for 254 days is *not* an effective means of protest.

Alcohol:
—But why do you *have* to end up in a bar every night?

—No, alcohol does *not* make everything look better. Do you see, for example, what it's making *you* look like?

141

—A.A.'s address is 176 Hill Street.

—Isn't it foolish for you to start drinking, Ma'am, just to try to forget that your husband's a lush?

Discipline:

—That's not the way the Air Force works. They don't just dock you a few days' pay when you go AWOL to take your girl in Chicago to a prom.

—The Air Force is a dictatorship, and the sooner you realize that, the better for you.

—I sympathize with your distaste for hillbilly music, but that was no reason to swipe your buddy's radio and hock it and buy two cases of beer with the money.

—I'll check with your C.O. to see if your first sergeant knows the difference between discipline and sadism.

—No, we don't hit our commanding officers in the nose even if they *do* rub us the wrong way.

Family and Marriage:

—*Why* do you want to get married?

—*Why* do you suppose you prefer beating up your wife to sleeping with her?

—*Why* did you have children when you're obviously not interested in their welfare?

—*Why* do you want a divorce?

Finance:

—Suppose we work out a budget now and see if you can afford to buy a brand-new air-conditioned Chrysler when you make $92 a month.

—The Air Force Aid Society or the Red Cross may be able to help you. No, I can't loan you $110 . . . I am *not* cheap.

Moral:

—Why do you insist on saying that you're married in the eyes of God when the more correct term for the relationship is simply "shacking up"?

142

—Personally, I feel there are much better reasons for getting married than pregnancy.

—Chastity has been defined as "emotional sincerity in human relationships." Are you trying to tell me now that with all sixteen of these girls you've been emotionally sincere?

—No matter what your buddies in the barracks say, it is not abnormal for a fellow of seventeen to be a virgin.

Morale:

—I'm telling you: It is *not* abnormal for a fellow of seventeen to be a virgin.

—I wasn't aware that Negroes couldn't get their hair cut by white barbers at the base barber shop. I'll certainly look into it.

—To tell you the truth, I wouldn't enjoy emptying garbage cans all day long myself. We'll see what can be done about it.

Religious:

—I'm sorry but, offhand, I don't know the recipe for kosher sour pickles, Mrs. Reilly. I'll write my aunt though and ask her.

All of the counseling cases did not come to David's office voluntarily. Some, like the wife-beaters, were sent to him by the Staff Judge Advocate's Office; others, like the airmen whose only illness was found to be homesickness, were recommended by the Flight Surgeon's Office; others, like sufferers from mild depressions, were referred by the base psychiatrist; and some, like the lower-grade airmen who wanted to get married, were sent by their squadron commanders.

A dismaying number of these young airmen appeared to be intent on marrying the identical girl, Her. Either that, or the youngsters had studied the identical script:

—*Why do you want to get married?*

—I love Her.

—*Why do you love her?*

—I have to have some kind of reason?

—*It helps.*

—I just love Her, that's all.

—*But why?*

—Because she's—Her, that's why.

—*What do you mean by the word "Love"?*

—I don't know. That's a tough one to answer.

—*Try.*

—I guess it means I want to marry Her.

—*Why?*

—I already told you—I love Her, that's why.

—*You know what you're saying? You're saying you want to marry her because you love her, and you love her because you want to marry her!*

—That's it *exactly.*

—*How old are you?*

—Nineteen, in a few months.

—*And your girl?*

—Sixteen, in a few months.

—*How long have you known her?*

—Oh, quite a while.

—*How long is that?*

—Almost three and a half weeks.

—*Are you two churchgoers?*

—We like to spend our time in other ways.

—*How?*

—Well, for one thing, we like to sleep late on Sundays.

—*How else do you spend your time?*

—Drive-ins . . .

—*What do you two do together?*

—At the drive-ins?

—*On other nights.*

—Sometimes we go to one of those places that have a jukebox, and we dance. Or fool around with some friends. Or watch TV. Or, when we get tired of TV, we go to another drive-in. We go to a lot of drive-ins.

—*Do you own your car outright?*

—Are you kidding? I pay forty-five dollars a month on it.

—*And how much do you make as an airman-third?*

144

—Almost a hundred dollars a month. But then there'll be a fifty-dollar allotment. And she's quitting school to get a job.

—*What happens when she gets pregnant?*

—Pregnant?

—*Maybe you'll have a baby.*

—Nah.

—*And if by chance you do?*

—We'll get an allotment for the baby, I guess.

—*It's very little, you know. Can all three of you live on forty dollars a week?*

—We'll manage.

—*With prices as high as they are—with rent, food, clothing, car payments, insurance, a baby?*

—We'll manage.

—*What makes you so sure?*

—We're in love, and that's what counts.

—*What do you mean by . . . Never mind. Did you graduate from high school?*

—School bored me. I quit.

—*What makes you think, if you couldn't finish high school, you'll be able to stick out marriage, which is a longer course?*

—Because marriage couldn't bore me as much as school or these rotten barracks here.

—*Your girl—what kind of family does she have?*

—A rotten one. A snotty kid brother and a father who's always coming home drunk and beating her up.

—*I wonder, could it be that the two of you are bound closer together by hate than by love?*

—Huh?

—*I'm suggesting that perhaps your dislike of barracks life and her unhappy home life are the prime reasons why the two of you want to get married.*

—Nah.

—*Do you realize that six times as many divorces occur among teen-age couples, and that short engagements and no money make the chances for a successful marriage even slimmer?*

—Our marriage'll be different.

—What makes you so sure?

—Because we're—*us.*

—Do you two have a lot in common?

—Sure. We like the same movies, same TV programs, same jukebox music, same cars . . .

—Is that all?

—What else *is* there? I mean, that's what we do together—go to drive-ins, drive around, dance, watch television. Do married people do more? And we got something in common that lots of married people, including my folks and hers, don't have.

—And what's that?

—Like I told you, we're in love. And we want to get it regular, y'know what I mean?

In the belief that there should be a more stringent requirement for marriage than the ability to survive a wedding ceremony, David tried at first to reason against these ill-fated teen-age unions and, as such reasoning inevitably failed, finally to stop them. He soon learned, however, that Air Force regulations stipulated only that a lower-grade airman had to be counseled by a chaplain before his marriage; nowhere did it state that the chaplain had to be willing to give the groom away.

And so these youngsters were wed even as their married counterparts, or their wives, were coming to David with marital woes or divorce plans, suggesting that Love conquered all but married life. The most common reason given for the marital distress was:

—I just don't love Her.

—You loved her when you got married.

—That was a long time ago.

—How long ago?

—Last year.

—And now?

—She bores me. We fight. We argue about everything —money; what movies to see. We can't afford to go anywhere any more or do anything. And I think she's stepping out on me.

—How come?

—Because she's just **no** good, that's how come. And I hate the lousy bitch.

—*What would you like to do?*

—Figure out what to do with the baby, and then . . . I don't know . . . but *something*. You just can't live with somebody you don't love. Especially when she don't give it to you regular no more.

Not all of David's counseling was conducted in his office. Some people, ashamed to come to the chapel and openly confess that they had problems, would waylay him, as if by chance, in the street, library, cafeteria, duty stations, to say:

—I've been so anxious for my tour to end, but now that I'm getting out next month—I don't know what to do with myself in civilian life.

—My first sergeant hates me.

—Can you loan me two hundred dollars?

—Can someone inherit a nervous breakdown?

—This girl friend of my buddy's—she just happened to get pregnant the other day . . .

—How can I get along better with people?

—My C.O. discriminates against me just because I have a much higher intelligence quotation than him.

—How can I get into a new career field?

—I'm going to kill my first sergeant.

—I want to attain faith, but how?

—There's these checks I accidentally forged . . .

—How can I get out of the South?

—My wife keeps nagging me to leave her.

—I'd like to go to school under the G.I. Bill, only I don't know what to study for.

—How come it was a religion, Judaism, that invented judo?

—I love her very much, but we're of different faiths.

—Did Methuselah *really* live 969 years?

—How can you tell when you're really in love?

—The recruiting sergeant told me such lies!

—Okay, can you loan me *five* dollars then?

—Could you sum up the essence of your religion in a few words?

—Where did we all come from if Adam and Eve only had two children and both of them were boys?

—My wife threatens to leave me if I go on another TDY [Temporary Duty assignment away from home].

—I don't know what to do with myself on weekends.

—They want to throw me out of service just because I got a little high and beat up my C.O. thinking he was my wife.

—Are there any facilities in Fair City for a—a—retarded child?

—How can one think only clean thoughts all the time and forget about women?

—How can you prove there's a God?

—Remember my buddy's pregnant girl I told you about the other night? Well, she isn't my buddy's . . .

—Would you know of any adoption agency that doesn't discriminate against service couples?

—Why did my mother have to die?

—What makes men—impotent?

—I don't know whether to stay in service or get out.

—Is it better for an unhappy couple to stay together for the children's sake, or should they get a divorce?

—Can a baby be baptized if his parents just didn't have a chance to get married before he was born?

—I drink too much.

—Colonel Stratford is a dirty rat, *isn't* he?

In addition to counseling people in his office, on the street, in the cafeteria, in the library, and at duty stations, David even tried to counsel a person at home— just once. He went there in answer to a telephone call from an obviously distraught woman. "Chaplain Cohen, please come over immediately! It's an emergency! My husband's just come back from TDY and I need some counseling desperately!" The woman, her words tumbling thickly over one another, sounded as if she were on the verge of something which David could not quite define.

"Of course, I'll be right over," he said. "Tell me, what's your name and address?"

"Oh, didn't you recognize my voice?" The note of urgency in her voice gave way to disappointment. "This is Mrs. Ainsley—Joanna Ainsley. We met at the last Air Base Group Dance. Don't you remember?" David did not. "That's why I thought of you now. Chaplain, you must come over right away. The address is 435 Fairfield Boulevard. I *need* you, Chaplain!"

David drove quickly to Mrs. Ainsley's home. He rang the doorbell. "Come in, come in, come in," a woman's voice called. "It's open. Come in, come in."

He opened the door and stepped inside. He was in the living room. "Chaplain, that's you, isn't it?" the voice called. "I'm here. Come right in."

David followed the woman's voice to a bedroom. Mrs. Ainsley was lying in bed under a quilt, and she was not alone. Beside her lay an empty bottle that looked too large ever to have contained perfume.

"Mrs. Ainsley . . ." he began nervously, with a swift change of venue in mind.

Mrs. Ainsley, a striking platinum blonde with black eyebrows, smiled languorously. "It was very good of you to come, Chaplain, but everything is under control now. He's locked up in the closet."

David started. "He *is? Who* is?"

"It's my husband." Mrs. Ainsley picked up the empty whiskey bottle beside her, then let it casually drop to the floor where it knocked over another liquor bottle, this one half full. As whiskey gurgled through her open-toed bedroom slippers, the blonde went on to explain: "Frank's always like a wild man when he comes back from TDY at Goose Bay. He's been drinking ever since— Say, what day is this anyway?"

"Tuesday."

Mrs. Ainsley ran a wet pink tongue over her wet pink lips. "I always *liked* Tuesdays."

"I'll remember that," said David, edging out of the room. "And now, if you'll excuse me—"

"Oh, but you *can't* go! You got to protect me from

Frank. He's crazy, that husband of mine. He was trying to eat me up before. Yes, he was! He came after me with a knife and fork. That's when I locked him up in the closet and called you."

"And don't think I don't appreciate it. But if your husband is locked up in the closet there," David paused to explain carefully, "he can't very well eat you up, can he? You're safe now until both of you sober up." *That* was a mistake, he realized as soon as the words left his mouth.

"*Both* sober up?" Mrs. Ainsley exclaimed, so indignant that she sat bolt upright in bed, letting the quilt slip from her shoulders and revealing a backless lace nightgown whose color was hard to determine because she was wearing it backwards. "How *dare* you suggest that I'm drunk!" she cried, her bare breasts bobbing like apples one went ducking for in the parlor game.

"I didn't mean to suggest that at all," David said, trying to direct his gaze upward. "My English, I realize, is sometimes rather ambiguous—"

"*Oh!*" Mrs. Ainsley jumped out of bed, sloshed through the whiskey on the floor, and darted to the closet door which she swiftly unlocked and flung open. "Frank, did you hear what he called me? *Ambiguous!*"

"Well, good-bye now," David called over his shoulder as he hurried toward the front door. He was stopped there, however, by a series of high-pitched screams. I'm a fool if I go back to that bedroom, he told himself as he turned around and went back to the bedroom.

There he saw Mrs. Ainsley, her bare bosom bouncing in time to her staccato screams, standing in the closet over the inert body of a stark-naked, bald-headed man in whose right hand was a knife and whose left hand held a fork.

"He—he isn't *dead*, is he?"

Mrs. Ainsley stopped screaming long enough to say, "Of course he isn't dead. He's only passed out, that's all." She took a deep breath and resumed screaming.

"*Then what on earth are you screaming about?*"

Mrs. Ainsley's wet mouth fell open. "What's happened to Frank? What's happened to my husband?"

"You just *told* me: He's passed out." For corroboration David bent over and prodded the bald man in the ribs. He responded with a hiccupped obscenity.

"But *that* isn't *Frank*," Mrs. Ainsley wailed. "That's *Major Albright*, Frank's aircraft commander. What's he doing in my closet with a knife and fork? Where's *Frank?*"

David uttered an oath, although he retained enough presence of mind to use a Yiddish one. "Lady," he called over his shoulder as he raced for the front door, "I got my *own* troubles."

Chapter : 11

As the days passed by without any dates to keep the nights from skittering thoughts of ducking for apples, David wrote Tante Dvorah accusing her of not having nagged him enough for *nachus*, then called Dena Gordon to ask her out to dinner.

The girl responded with disbelief: "You mean, you're asking *me* for a *date?*"

"Well . . . yes, what else?" said David, though it was not exactly a date that he thought of in connection with Dena. For the grossly fat girl fulfilled only half of his three requirements for feminine companionship. Dena was Jewish, but she was no more desirable as a girl than *he* was; and she clearly was not eligible. That her monolithic obesity proclaimed quite clearly, and she said as much herself. "Can you imagine me married to Farouk?" she remarked once. "We'd be able to kiss only when the servants would hold us at right angles."

Still, Dena was of the right sex for him, David told

151

himself, despite the fact that her appearance almost belied it. A few years younger than David, she outweighed him by several pounds, also two chins. Years of monumental overeating (certified to by Major Gordon's words and her own gluttonous deeds) had made the girl a figure of rectangular proportions whose only curve was to be seen when she bent over to tie a shoelace. Her ruddy face was not ugly but so well larded that it looked like the face of any other fat woman—or fat man. And her closely cropped reddish-brown hair did little to clarify her sexual status.

"You know, April Fool was *last* month, Chaplain."

David asked lightly, "Playing hard to get?"

"No one who's hard to take," Dena replied, "plays hard to get."

David winced. "I'll pick you up at seven tomorrow night. Okay?"

"Brave man," Dena remarked. "Sure hope you don't break anything."

It was then that David decided that the girl, huge and strong as she was, needed protection. And indeed she did, for on their date there was not a familiar "fat joke" that Dena did not tell upon herself, as if trying to use her cutting humor to pare herself down to normal size. Or was she only trying to beat everyone to those jokes so that no one else could use them against her? David could not tell, but by the end of the evening he had concluded that it was foolish for him to think he could succeed in protecting the girl against herself; she was far too quick for him either to defend or to parry.

"Why did you take me out tonight?" she asked abruptly during dinner.

"You're good company, Dena."

She smiled crookedly. "And you're a bad liar."

"I am not!"

Dena regarded him innocently. "You mean you're a *good* liar?"

David resolved not to see the girl again. Yet a few

weeks later he found himself calling her for another date, uncertain whether he felt sorrier for Dena and her self-deprecating tongue or for himself and his lonely evenings.

He took the girl bowling, and it was not at all a happy choice. For as soon as they reached the bowling center, she began comparing herself disparagingly with all the slim girls there with trim figures. "I'll bet no one here ever saw a bowling ball bowling before," she remarked, slapping a cylindrical thigh.

"Dena, you're a very self-centered girl," David said, acting annoyed. "You're so busy saying nasty things about yourself you never have time to say nice things about me."

Dena turned color, and for the rest of the evening no more self-deprecatory remarks were heard. Yet when he took her home, she repeated her question of the first date. "Why did you take me out tonight?"

David flinched. "You're good company, Dena. I've told you that before."

Dena snorted. "You must have read *Mein Kampf*. Hitler also believed that if you repeat a lie long enough, people are bound to believe it."

Why not? David thought afterwards. If Hitler, using repetition, could get people to believe lies, why mightn't he be able to make Dena believe a few truths? After all, she *was* good company, intelligent, vivacious, and kind to everyone but herself.

Thereafter, he called Dena for dates several times a month. He found that when she was not busy deprecating herself, she was a quick-witted conversationalist who did not speak very much about herself and never at all about her mother who had died many years before.

Dena, on the other hand, learned a good deal about David's personal life, especially about the girl he had left behind, to whom he was going back, who of course and alas did not exist. Dubbed Barbara, she had sprung into being full-grown from David's mouth, in response to Dena's remark that the only reason he dated her was to make people think chaplains never sullied their minds with thoughts of sex. Impulsively his tongue had given birth to Barbara in an effort to prevent Dena from thinking that she was unappealing to him as a woman. (Who could get romantic about a girl who was continually saying that she looked like a female Tony Galento and, what was worse, *did?*)

At the end of each date, David usually took Dena to an ice-cream parlor in Fair City in the hope that one night there she would publicly renounce banana splits forever and go on the wagon. But, like the girl who says she shouldn't even while she does, Dena objected to chocolate fudge sundaes only between mouthfuls.

One night, however, she abruptly said, "You know, David, there are a lot of things about you I can't understand. One of them is that you're the only person I know who hasn't advised me to go on a diet. Instead you seem to be doing your best to make me *fatter!*"

"Dena, if you want advice," David said casually, "you'll have to come see me at my office during duty hours. I'm not working now."

"But don't you think I *should* go on a diet?"

"That's entirely up to you, Dena."

"Well, do you think it would make me more attractive—if such an impossibility can even be contemplated?"

"Most people look better when they're thinner."

"Would *you* find me more— I mean, do you think I should go on some sort of diet and waste myself away to only a ton?"

"Dena, you know I think you're nice the way you are."

"But what about the *shape* I'm in?"

"What about it?"

Dena threw up her tubular hands. "Oh, you're no help at all!"

David acted surprised. "In what way do you want me to help?"

"Say that you care—" Dena faltered. "I mean, say that you'd care to see me svelte like a salamander."

"Then what?"

"Well—maybe I'd go on a diet . . ."

"You mean, for me?" David shook his head. "No, Dena. A thing like that you don't do for anyone else. You have to want to do it for yourself alone. Taking off a lot of weight, I've heard, is torture."

"Thanks for the tip," Dena said dryly. "If ever I contemplate suicide, I'll make sure to avoid discussing it with you. You'd probably *encourage* it." He chuckled. "David, why are you always saying things like that and stuffing me with the gooiest sundaes when you know how I hate myself for being so fat?"

"Dena, did you ever think," David remarked, "that maybe you don't hate yourself *for* being fat, but that you hate yourself *by* being fat?"

Dena was not deceived by his casual demeanor. "Everyone's a psychiatrist nowadays," she said sharply. "A person who wants to enjoy a good old-fashioned neurosis doesn't stand a chance any more."

He laughed. "Oh, I have no psychiatric pretensions. The base hospital and the chaplains have an understanding. The hospital doesn't give lectures or serve Communion, and we don't psychoanalyze anyone. They have a pretty good psychiatrist there who handles that department."

"Don't you dare—*counsel* me!" Dena exclaimed. "David, I'm no candidate for a couch and I won't be propositioned for one!"

"Dena, please!" David exclaimed lightly. "The way you talk—people around us might get the wrong idea." He cleared his throat. "However, since you were the one who brought up the subject, what's so terrible about seeing a psychiatrist?" Dena reddened, and he hastened to add another lie to his saga of the nonexistent girl he had left behind him. "Deborah was in analysis when I first met her. Coincidentally enough, she was somewhat overweight too—"

Dena interrupted. "Let's talk about that some other time. Here come our sundaes." The waitress approached with their heaping dishes of three scoops of ice cream, topped by whipped cream, chocolate syrup, nuts and cherries. "Business before pleasure, you know."

On the way back to the base Dena was very quiet, and David made no attempts at conversation. Let her think about what he had said, and perhaps . . .

"David, I've been thinking about what you said in the ice-cream parlor," Dena suddenly remarked.

"You mean about the psychiatrist?"

"About that overweight girl. David, who is Deborah?"

David was surprised. "Deborah is my girl. I've told you about her before. She's the girl I'm going back to in Brooklyn."

"But I thought," Dena said, perplexed, "that your girl's name was *Barbara*."

"Oh . . . !" David exclaimed. "Well, you see, Deborah is Barbara's *Hebrew* name. All Jews, you know, have a Hebrew name as well as an English one. Unless they're Frenchmen. Then they wouldn't have an English name, of course . . ." He ran out of words.

"Oh . . ." Dena was silent for a few minutes, then said, "David, tell me about her."

"About who?"

"About your girl."

"Oh. You mean Barbara." Or had she meant Deborah? What *was* that girl's name!

"What's she like?"

"Oh, she's really very nice."

"I'm sure she must be to have you for a fiancé. What does she look like, David?"

"Tall, dark, and—and pretty."

"Is she slim?"

"Uh-huh."

"I don't suppose you'd marry her if she wasn't slim, would you?"

"I don't think I'd put it that way . . ."

"Do you love her very much?"

"Oh, yes."

"How long have you two been going together?"

"Oh, for years."

"And when do you plan to get married?"

"Oh, when I get out of the Air Force."

"Why wait so long? I mean, if you've known Barbara for years and love her so much, why wait any longer?"

David, at a loss for lies, changed the subject by deliberately speeding through a red light and then debating with Dena whether or not to turn himself over to the police. By the time they reached her house, he allowed himself to be convinced that he should try to get away with it.

Seeing the girl to the door, he prepared himself for the inevitable query, phrased in any one of a dozen ways. But this night she had a different question in mind.

"David, we've been going out together for so long now, and we're such good friends and all, I feel—I wonder, could we—when we say good night from now on, could we—could we shake hands?"

"I don't think Barbara would object," David replied, then reddened as Dena giggled and he realized that he had been tricked.

She called him the next day. "I want to atone for last night, David. Tell me, what do you want most of all? Never mind, I'll tell you what I got you. I've had my father get you an invitation to pinch-hit for Rabbi Garfield at the synagogue."

"What happened to Rabbi Garfield?"

"Nothing. Well, something. His father died, and Rabbi Garfield has to go home to St. Louis for the funeral. You do want to help out, don't you?"

David was delighted with the opportunity to preach again. To show his appreciation, he invited Dena to the movies that night.

"If you think I purposely mentioned your name to my father just to get you to reciprocate," Dena said when he came to pick her up that evening, "you're right."

The base theater was crowded when they arrived, but they managed to find two seats up front and sat down. Suddenly Dena disappeared from view; there was a splintering sound and her seat, which must have been previously damaged, collapsed with a crash beneath her.

157

"Tim-*ber!*" someone shouted, and the audience laughed.

David tried to aid the girl, but he succeeded only in wedging her further between the arm rests. An usher came over to help and between the two of them they managed to get her to her feet and to an adjoining seat.

"Did you see that?" someone nearby exclaimed. "Imagine what she'd do to a *man!*"

The audience howled, and Dena's face turned the color of Passover wine.

David tried to make light of the incident. "We'll sue, of course," he said to her as the theater darkened. But she did not reply. He longed to say something, to do something that would alleviate the hulking girl's embarrassment, but what? Her hand was lying on the arm rest beside him, and impulsively he seized it in his.

She clasped his hand tightly for a moment, then pulled away. "That's not where I hurt, Chaplain," she said dryly, and that was the last word she said to him until the movie ended, despite repeated comments from him.

When the lights went on again, he noticed several welts on her arm. "You're all bruised!"

"Oh, I have built-in shock absorbers, or haven't you noticed?" And she stepped out ahead of him into the aisle full of people surging toward the exits.

An airman up ahead asked loudly enough for half the theater to hear, "Why do you suppose the chaplain would date an elephant like that?"

"Maybe it's another stunt, like with the eggs," was the reply, equally loud. "Or do you think he's doing it for penance?"

David, his face burning with embarrassment for Dena, could do nothing but pretend he had not heard the remarks.

Finally Dena and David reached the exit and stepped outside. Gesturing toward the crowd behind them, he groped for words. "You know, if I had my choice, I'd choose to be heavy rather than hardhearted every time. One's only a condition, but the other is a sin."

She turned away from him. "Take me home, David, would you, please?"

"Sure. After our usual sundaes and—"

"No, *now!* I want to go home right away!"

They drove in silence to Major Gordon's house while David tried to think of some way to alleviate Dena's distress, but without success. He saw her to the door and there he held out his hand.

"Shake? We're friends, Dena—remember? And friends don't ever get embarrassed in each other's presence."

"Elephants don't, at any rate." She turned away, her green eyes shiny with tears. "We pachyderms have such thick hides."

David grabbed the girl by her chunky shoulders. "Dena, *don't!* I won't let you tear yourself down any more—"

She shook off his hands. "I don't have to. There will always be others to do it for me."

"That's not true! So you're overweight—what of it? You're also intelligent, quick-witted, excellent company—"

"—and as desirable as Old Dog Tray."

"Dena!" At a loss for something comforting to say, David acted impulsively. He seized her in his arms and planted a kiss on her mouth, trying to make the kiss say what his tongue could not: If you were any more desirable, rabbi or no rabbi, I'd ravish you right here on your front doorstep amid the two milk bottles.

Somehow his unspoken message must have become somewhat garbled in transit, for Dena's response was to throw her meaty arms around his neck and fasten them there.

"David, sleep with me . . . ?" There was a gulp then, like the sound of a tongue being swallowed.

"Of course, Dena, anything you say," David said, hurriedly acceding to the imploring tone of the request before he had quite appreciated its contents. *"Pardon?"*

She disengaged herself from him with the speed of a

159

blush. Slipping away, she flung open the front door and dashed into the dark house.

"Dena!" David, hating himself for his initial reaction (*Pardon?* he had exclaimed, as if she had asked him to jump off the Brooklyn Bridge, backwards), followed the girl inside the house and into the pitch-dark living room. "Dena, where are you?"

There was a muffled sob at the opposite end of the dark room. "I'm so *ashamed!*"

Guided by the sound of the sob, David started across the room. "Dena, there's nothing to be ashamed of—"

"I'll never be able to face you again—"

"Dena, I know exactly how you feel, believe me—" He stopped short, nursing a bruised knee, as he walked into a coffee table in the dark.

"You're lying again! You *couldn't* know how I feel—"

"But I *do*. What kind of a man would I be if I didn't?"

"I don't believe you!"

"But it's true, Dena, I swear it. You only voiced what I have felt—many times."

There was a sharp intake of breath. "You've felt the same way?"

"Of course. I'm a man, aren't I? And it's perfectly natural—" He carefully side-stepped the coffee table and stumbled into the couch. "Now will you put on the light before I break my neck in the dark!"

"You mean you actually *want* to make love to *me?*"

David took a quick step back behind the coffee table. "Oh!" No, that wasn't what he had meant, not at *all*, at least not in regard to Dena. Yet how to phrase his feelings without hurting hers? A fine girl like Dena offers herself to him, and he can't very well say, No, thanks all the same, but you don't carry my brand.

"Dena, what I *meant* to say was that it's perfectly natural—and understandable—for—for—" He faltered, his tongue flailing at words that were not there. "—for anyone to want to—to sleep with—with anyone," he finished lamely, cursing himself for his ineptitude.

"I see! You're telling me that even a fat cat may look at a chaplain."

"That's not what I said at all!"

"Or did you mean that making love to an elephant would be sodomy?"

"Dena!"

A gulping sob rent the black stillness of the room. "I wish I were dead!" The bedroom door opened and Dena, her right hand dabbing at her eyes, was silhouetted in the doorway as she turned to close the door behind her.

David started forward again, again stopping short as he hit his same knee against the same coffee table, and impulsively he cried out at the top of his voice, hoping the loudness would drown out the lie: "There's nothing in the world I'd like more than making love to you right now, only—"

"I don't believe you!"

But the bedroom door did not slam. Dena held it ajar as she paused to ask in a tremulous voice, *"Should I*—believe you?"

David cleared his throat and dislodged another lie. "Well—yes."

Dena was silent for a moment, but her fluttered breathing was audible. "All these weeks you *have* been telling me what a lovely girl I am, how much you like me—*haven't* you?"

"That's true."

"And you didn't *have* to say what you did just now if—if you didn't mean it, *did* you?"

"That's true, too," he conceded. "I really didn't *have* to—"

"Then you really *meant* it?"

David stirred uncomfortably. "Well, of course—"

She lowered her voice to an insinuation. "You mean—tonight? Right now?"

"Tonight? Right now?"

Dena heard only his words, evidently, and not his punctuation. *"Oh, David!"* She emitted a small cry. "I'll be ready in a minute!"

161

Swiftly she shut the bedroom door behind her, plunging the living room again into darkness and David into something akin to shock. She had *believed* him, she had *actually* believed him—it wasn't fair!

David ground his offending tongue between his teeth. All those times he had told Dena the truth—about how nice she was, how vivacious, what good company—she had thought he was lying. Now, the one time he had patently lied to her, she had believed him. Worse still, right this minute she was getting ready to call his bluff!

And what could he do about it now?

"Run!" a voice within him advised. *"Fast!"*

—But I couldn't do a thing like that to Dena!

—Well, could you do anything else?

—With *Dena?*

—Why not with Dena?

—Because.

—Ethics?

—Well ...

—Well?

—Aesthetics too.

—Aesthetics?

—Who wants to make love to a whole squadron of a woman!

—So what's the problem? Leave. Quick.

—I *can't.* How would Dena feel if I ran out on her now?

—How will *you* feel if you *stay?*

—Rotten. But either way I'll feel rotten.

—Serves you right for getting involved! Don't you remember what they taught you in pastoral psychiatry? That a rabbi must be clinical and impersonal and detached in his counseling of people ...

—But it helps when you get involved, it does. Look at Dena—a few months ago she'd never have offered herself to anyone like this. She didn't have enough confidence in herself then. I ask you: Doesn't this show she's improving?

—Oh, I see. When a girl turns bad, to you that's good.

—I'm serious. A few months ago Dena never thought herself good enough for anything at all.

—And now all of a sudden she's developed a specialty, and that makes you happy?

—It's true. Dena has an inferiority complex that's bigger than she is. She's just shot through with feelings of self-hatred. That's why she's so fat—she doesn't care enough for herself to keep slim and normal looking. But now, tonight—

—And when did *you* get a license to practice psychiatry?

—I don't have to be a psychiatrist to see that her ego needs a tremendous lot of bolstering and propping up.

—David, a phallus was never intended to be used as a *jack*.

—Still—

—Do you think that going to bed with Dena is a *mitzvah*, a good deed?

—Isn't it a good deed to show a girl who hates herself that she really isn't hateful?

—David, they have a name for a man who makes it his life's work making unhappy girls happy, and the name is not "rabbi."

—But I wouldn't be *taking* anything from Dena, nothing but *nachus*. I want to *give* her something. And didn't Emerson say, "The only gift is a portion of oneself"?

—Good heavens, man! Even Emerson wouldn't have wanted you to take him so *literally*.

—Maybe you're right! Oh, I don't know . . . I'm damned if I do, and Dena's damned if I don't. I'm so *confused*.

—*You're* telling *me*? You're so confused you don't realize that, aside from everything else, you'd be thrown out of the Air Force Chaplaincy should anyone find out about this personalized counseling service of yours.

—I would? I guess I would at that! Oh, why couldn't Dena be like that Sandra Birnbaum who wouldn't even let me so much as pound her on the back? What is it about a clergyman that either repels women or provokes them?

—Look, we have no time to get psychoanalytical. This is serious business here. This is no joke.

—That's it! That's it!

—What? What?

—Maybe all of this *is* just a joke.

—A joke?

—Maybe Dena's only playing another practical joke on me. Like the time she wanted to shake hands but made me believe she was going to ask for a kiss. You know what a peculiar sense of humor Dena has!

—Do *you* think this is all only a practical joke?

—Are you kidding? Would I be talking to myself like this if I did!

—Then we're right back where we started from, aren't we?

—No, we're not. The minute Dena said she'd be ready in—it's just about up.

—And what have you decided to do?

—*God!* I only wish I knew!

The bedroom door opened, flinging across the living room a shaft of light which struck David in the eyes, momentarily blinding him. When his vision cleared, he saw Dena outlined against softly beckoning lamplight, and not joking at all.

There she stood in the bedroom's doorway, looking, in her billowing dressing gown, like a bologna with a loose casing. She raised her sausage-shaped arms toward him.

"David . . . ?"

Suddenly—how could he have forgotten!—he remembered his out. "My fiancée," he said, exulting.

"Oh, I know all about her." Was Dena *chuckling?* "What was her name again?"

David's exultation died a swift death, and he expelled nothing but dead air when he opened his mouth to reply. For—it wasn't possible!—were his life depending upon it at that moment, he could not recall his fictitious fiancée's name. Was it Sandra? Laura? Cora? Deborah? Cassandra?

"David . . . ?"

"Your father—"

"He's asleep."

"Your mother—?"

Dena let out a gasp.

It was only then that David remembered Dena's mother had been dead for some twelve years. "Darling!" he exclaimed to atone for his blunder. He took a deep breath, so deep a breath that he choked on his next words: "I'm coming—" Stretching out his arms he stepped energetically forward as far as his legs would reach.

Before him loomed Dena's broad face, her arms reached out for him, there was a sudden stabbing pain in his lower extremities, a sense of the floor giving way beneath him, a crash as of cymbals, a jarring jolt to his head, and David found himself sprawled over the coffee table, his nose in a dish of hard candy and his stomach impaled on a chromium cigarette lighter.

"*David!*"

He groaned.

She ran to him, her dressing gown ballooning behind her. "Are you all right? Are you?"

He rolled over on his back and put both hands to his face, now wet with a familiar liquid. "Yes," he said, rejoicing as his hands came away sticky and his tongue tasted salt, "I'm bleeding."

"You're *bleeding!*"

"My nose—"

"Oh!"

"Don't worry, it'll stop soon. I've had these things before. In a half hour or so—"

Dena regarded him incredulously, and suddenly she was shaking all over, her flesh shimmying like Jello in a squall. From her quivering lips escaped a whoop of laughter, high pitched and thin.

"What's the matter? What happened?" The light was

flicked on, and Major Gordon appeared in the room donning a bathrobe.

David restrained a shouted hallelujah though it would not have been heard anyway, for Dena's wild, raucous laughter would have drowned it out.

The major rushed to David. "You didn't hurt yourself, did you?"

Dena's laughter gained momentum, swooping down and up like a roller-coaster. Convulsed, she dropped into a chair, gasping for breath yet still whooping.

Major Gordon helped David to his feet, then turned on his daughter. "What are you laughing at!"

She roared, "He's bleeding!"

"My God!" the major exclaimed. "My own daughter —and she's crazy!"

David bent his head backward. "I'm all right. Don't worry about me." He pinched his nostrils together between his right forefinger and thumb.

Major Gordon recoiled at the sight of David's red face and jacket and the blood oozing out between his fingers. "Come on, Chaplain. We're going to the base hospital." He grabbed a coat from the hall closet and took David by the elbow.

"There's no need—" David began, then thought better of it. "If you insist—" He let himself be steered to the door. There he turned around toward the whooping girl. "Dena—"

All at once her laughter skidded to a halt and her face froze. "It was just one of those things, David," she said with an elaborate shrug. "You know—a trip to the moon on elephant wings."

"Dena! How can you be so heartless!" her father exclaimed. He pulled David by the arm. "Come on, while there's still some blood in you."

He pushed him through the door, guided him to the car, and helped him inside. Behind them they could hear Dena again, only now it didn't sound as if she were laughing. David winced.

By the time they arrived at the hospital, the bleeding

166

had stopped. David asked to be taken to his quarters, instead, and the major complied.

"There's one thing I can't figure out," he said as David removed his bloodstained clothes in the BOQ. "How did you ever manage to trip over the coffee table? I never heard of anyone doing *that* before."

"Neither have I," replied David, his head now throbbing with a painful regularity, as if someone were applying a tourniquet to his throat. "And now if you'll excuse me while I rest for a while—"

Major Gordon departed, and David was left with a dozen questions. Had he been right in his impulsive decision to make love to Dena? And why was he forever acting upon impulse? Wasn't he lucky that this time his impulse had been aborted? Or *was* it luck? Had his subconscious, which must have known damn well that the coffee table was in front of him since he had bumped into it some three times before his fall, deliberately sought to render him unconscious? Was he sorry now or glad about the way things had turned out? And what was Dena's reaction to the hapless events of the evening?

With the aid of three aspirins and two cups of Passover wine, he was finding success in postponing the answers when the telephone rang. And it rang and it rang and it rang, alternating with his head-throbs, until he picked up the phone just to silence it.

The caller did not wait for his hello. She started speaking immediately. "You know, you didn't have to try to commit suicide just to escape me, a fate worse than death. All that you had to do, David, was say that it was all a mistake, and I'd have understood. Really I would have. I may be fat, but I'm not *thick*. You didn't have to go into that swan dive, almost break your neck—"

"Dena, I—"

But she cut him short. "I suppose you expect me to thank you now for saving my virtue, and say that it's all turned out for the best. Well, I won't. Because I don't think a girl's virtue is worth very much if she can't even *give* it away! And as for you, I never want to see you again—"

"*Dena . . . !*"

"Oh, I didn't mean *that!* What I meant was that I don't want to see you again until you can see *me*, David—I mean, *really* see me. Maybe it'll take five months, maybe it'll take longer. But don't call me—as the saying goes—I'll call you. When I'm no longer a slum you regard as some sort of personal reclamation project, when I'm as worthy of a man's love as that girl you called Barbara, I'll phone you and then, *you'll* see, I'll tantalize you into propositioning *me*—*that'll* be a switch!—but I'll turn you down, of course, because, of course, I'll have plenty of other offers by then from plenty of other—" She was sobbing now, uncontrollably.

David cut in, pleading. "Dena, will you listen to me? That was no dive I took, honest! You must believe me when I tell you—"

But she had hung up.

He called her back the next day, the next week, the next month. But she was never at home, not to him. So, sorrowfully, for only then did he discover that he was fonder of Dena than he had realized, he stopped calling and waited, hopefully.

Chapter : 12

DAVID was one Jew to whom *Exodus* automatically meant the second book of the Bible and not the novel. And it pained him that for a good many Jews it took a best seller and Otto Preminger to teach them about the significance of Israel, to make them aware of the agonizing struggle for the ancient Jewish homeland, to instill in them a sense of pride in the state's establishment.

"Did this *really* happen?" Jew after Jew would ask

him, referring to one recent historical incident or another recounted in the novel and, upon receiving David's assurance of the historicity of the event, would exclaim, "I never *realized!* How come I never knew this *before?*"

David successfully withstood replying to the first score of rhetorical questions, but one person he finally answered. This man had said, "You mean that hundreds of thousands of lives could have been saved in the thirties, had there been a Jewish state in existence? That no other country would take them in? I never *realized* it all the time I opposed the creation of the state of Israel! *Why* didn't I know all this *then?*" And David had replied, "Because you're an obtuse, self-centered, ignorant Jewish jerk. Does *that* answer your question?"

David could not recall a time when Israel was not part of his being. He remembered studying about Israel in sacred Jewish writings ever since he learned to read; always facing East when praying, for in the East lay the holy city of Jerusalem; building a booth on the holiday of Succos in commemoration of the time the Israelites wandered in the desert on their way to the Promised Land; every spring observing Passover and the Festival of Weeks, which correspond to planting time and the harvest in Israel; as a child, collecting pennies and nickels and dimes which he solicited door-to-door and in the streets and on the subways, monies which would go toward the purchase of land for Jewish settlers in Palestine; making speeches on street corners, as a youngster, urging people to wire President Truman to support the establishment of Israel; sobbing with joy on May 14th, 1948, Israeli Independence Day.

Above all, he remembered Psalm 137, the poignant psalm relating the Israelites' vow of eternal fealty to Zion, a vow made more than twenty-five hundred years earlier, as the people of Israel were being exiled from Judea to Babylonia:

By the rivers of Babylon,
There we sat down, yea, we wept,

When we remembered Zion.
Upon the willows in their midst
We hanged up our harps.
For there they that led us captive asked of us words
    of song,
And our tormentors asked of us mirth:
"Sing us one of the songs of Zion."
How can we sing the Lord's song
In a foreign land?
If I forget thee, O Jerusalem,
Let my right hand waste away.
Let my tongue cleave to the roof of my mouth,
If I remember thee not;
If I set not Jerusalem
Above my chiefest joy.

And so when the synagogue's bulletin editor called the week before May 14th, asking David for the topic of his sermon for the following Sabbath, he immediately told her: "My Heart Is in the East," a line from a poem by Yehuda Halevi.

The next morning Hugh Marshall, Jr. telephoned. He paused after announcing his name, as if he expected David to recognize it. David responded as if he expected Mr. Marshall to remind him who he was.

"I'm calling as Vice-President of the Fair City Chamber of Commerce. I could also be calling as President of our Interfaith Society; I wear so many hats in this city I hardly have time to look up to see which one I have on. I'm calling to invite you to be my guest for lunch today at the Club so that the three of us—you, I, and Fair City—can get acquainted. Would you like to join me?"

David thanked the man for the kind invitation and readily accepted it.

"That's the Fair City Social Club, of course," he said before hanging up. "Anyone can tell you where it is."

A dignified man in his late forties, with erect carriage, dark hair graying at the temples and an aristocratic manner, Mr. Marshall looked even too distinguished to pose for the Men of Distinction advertisements. He came forward quickly to greet David as he entered the Fair City Social Club, a huge ante-bellum Southern mansion with tall white columns, framed by century-old oak trees and a lawn as large as a baseball field.

"How do you like our little Club?" he asked with obvious pride as he led David through a high arched doorway into the paneled dining room and to a table near a real fireplace.

David surveyed the elegant furnishings: the oriental rug, the silk brocade on the paneled walls, the crystal chandelier, the rich tapestries. "Beautiful, just beautiful!" he exclaimed. "I keep expecting to see Clark Gable come sweeping down both sides of that divided staircase there any minute now, dragging Scarlett O'Hara behind him."

Mr. Marshall smiled politely. "I'm so glad you like our little Club. I hope you like the lunch as well. I took the liberty of ordering it before you came." He nodded to the waiter who filled the crystal wine glasses on the table. Mr. Marshall sipped his drink decorously and David followed suit. "How do you like it?"

David thought the wine as tasteless as it was colorless. "Fine, fine."

"It's Château Yquem '57," Mr. Marshall said meaningfully.

"Really?" said David, who knew enough about wines just to be able to distinguish them from whiskies.

"Yes. I do hope you like your pompano amandine as well. They make it very well here, and it's about as kosher a food as you can get in Fair City."

David smiled appreciatively. "That was very considerate of you—to bear my religious eating habits in mind."

"Not at all," Mr. Marshall said graciously. "You're not the first rabbi I've eaten with. There have been quite a few rabbis here in recent years and, of course, there were Jews in Fair City even before I was born."

171

"How old is the present Jewish community here?" David asked. "Oh, but I don't suppose you'd know that."

Mr. Marshall surprised David. "Indeed I do. For the most part, the Jews here are the children and grandchildren of German and East European immigrants who came to Fair City around the turn of the century, when the Massachusetts textile mills moved South. Later, other Jews came to open retail stores here."

David wondered aloud, "How do you know so much about the early Jews of Fair City?"

"Well, my father was a manufacturer here himself," Mr. Marshall replied, "and after all, owning Marshall's Department Store—"

"*You* own Marshall's?" David interrupted. "I should have made the connection, I guess, but it never occurred to me."

"I'm surprised." Mr. Marshall seemed offended. "I thought you knew. Everyone does."

David apologized. "I'm sorry, Mr. Marshall, but I haven't had that much to do with the city since—" since the Seder, he almost said, "—since I've come to Mississippi. Fairfield is a kind of community unto itself, you know."

"Perfectly understandable," Mr. Marshall said, adding casually, "Oh, in regard to Fairfield, I was wondering. Do you have many dealings with our Christian brethren on base?"

David smiled. "If I didn't, I'd be talking to myself all day long. There are only a dozen Jewish personnel at Fairfield."

"I hope those Jews are making a vital contribution to the base, nevertheless," Mr. Marshall said soberly. "I mean, there are only sixty Jewish families in Fair City, but they're all very active in the Community Chest, Red Cross, hospital drives, and all other local projects, including even raising money for church-building funds."

"Really?"

"Oh, yes," Mr. Marshall said. "That's one reason why our daily newspaper is so liberal in writing up the Jewish holidays and events, and the synagogue socials, and even, occasionally, wise sayings of the rabbis. What's more, the Jews mingle with the best people of the city, too, perhaps not socially as yet, but in our Civic Club, our Interfaith Society, many charitable organizations, and the like."

So what? David was tempted to ask. "How nice," he said instead.

"And just last year this Club invited me to become a member," Mr. Marshall said proudly.

David could not follow the *non sequitur*. "What's so unusual about that?"

Mr. Marshall looked triumphant. "I am the very first Jew they've ever invited to join the Club."

David was taken aback. "You—Jewish!"

"Didn't you know?" Mr. Marshall laughed. "You mean you really didn't think I was Jewish?"

"No," David said, and wondered why he had not realized it before. Was it because of Mr. Marshall's facial characteristics? No, David had stopped categorizing people according to their appearance ever since his first night in Chaplain School with Albert Cohen. Was it because of Mr. Marshall's soft Southern speech? No, that was not it either. Then what was it? The name—so completely Anglo-Saxon—that was part of it. Then the answer came to David: Never once during his discourse on the Jews of Fair City had Mr. Marshall said, *"We* Jews." It was always *"the* Jews." But it was *"our* Club" and *"our* Christian Brethren" and *"our* Interfaith Society." Finally, there was the unmistakable look of pleasure on Mr. Marshall's face when David expressed surprise that he was Jewish. When Mr. Marshall had discovered that David was unaware of his ownership of Marshall's Department Store, the man had been offended. Yet when David expressed astonishment that Mr. Marshall was a Jew . . .

"You mean you never realized I was Jewish?" Mr. Marshall repeated, and there was no mistaking the childish delight in his voice. "Really?"

"Really," David said.

"As a matter of fact," Mr. Marshall chuckled, "my

two sons don't look Jewish either. That's what everyone tells them, and here I am a member of the Board of Trustees of the synagogue!"

"Is that what everyone tells them?" David said.

"Oh, I'm not ashamed that everyone in Fair City knows we're of the Jewish faith, you realize. Why, it even makes me feel more comfortable, if you understand what I mean. I don't have to give that any thought any more. You know, I even close Marshall's on the High Holidays. How many of the big Jewish department stores in New York do that?"

"Not any that I can think of," David replied.

"See? And other Jewish stores here do likewise, just as our Christian friends expect," Mr. Marshall continued. "What's more, Fair City Jews give more, and more of them give, to Jewish charities, percentagewise, than you New York Jews. And that's in addition to contributions to the Community Chest, Red Cross, churches, and the like. There's probably something else you don't know. There are more synagogues in the South and more members in them, percentagewise, than up North. Percentagewise, Jews have just as many churches in the South as do our Christian brethren. I tell you all this—about what a fine Jewish community there is here in Fair City—so that you'll understand better that—that—" He faltered.

"Yes?"

"Well, our Interfaith Society, for one thing." David noted the reappearance of the possessive pronoun for the Interfaith Society where none had existed for the Jewish community. "Our Interfaith Society is a splendid organization—even more social than religious, really—where all three faiths meet as equals, full of understanding for one another. And it's this spirit I hope you'll be emphasizing in your sermon at the synagogue, this lovely spirit of brotherly love. Because, as it happens, on this Sabbath my nephew will be becoming *bar mitzvah*, and so many of my brother's friends and mine who will be attending the service are not of the Jewish faith, of course."

174

"To tell the truth," said David, "I haven't been thinking along those lines at all. I mean, for my sermon."

Mr. Marshall motioned to the waiter, and he refilled the wine glasses. "Well," Mr. Marshall said, after taking another thoughtful sip of wine, "what *were* you planning to say, Chaplain?"

David quickly sipped his wine again. "I'm not exactly sure as yet. I haven't had the time to work on—"

Mr. Marshall interrupted. "The title has something in it about the East, I've been told. What does that signify? Are you going to be talking about Russia perhaps?"

"Russia?" said David in surprise. "Oh, I see—the East. That reminds me of the time I announced I'd be preaching on Jewish Sects, and there was a record turnout at the temple, Christians among them too. Everyone thought, it came to light later, that I'd be talking on Jewish Sex." He chuckled.

Mr. Marshall did not even smile politely. "Russia and godless communism would make a splendid topic. Reverend Fielding has been giving a series of sermons on that very topic for the past month. But that makes no difference, of course, because it's such a big topic. There's so much to say, so much to condemn."

David said, "The East I'll be talking about is the *Middle* East. It's the anniversary of the founding of the state of Israel this week."

"Oh?" Mr. Marshall hesitated for a moment, and the general quiet pervading the room emphasized his silence, so that when he resumed speaking, it seemed as if he were raising his soft Southern voice. "Is *that* what you're thinking of talking about, Chaplain? I should think that would be one topic to avoid at this time. You know, of course, that Israel was just censured by the United Nations as well as the United States for her recent attack on Syria."

"That's right." David shook his head sadly. "I'll have to mention that too in my sermon—how terrible it was for the U.N. and the United States to censure Israel

175

for retaliating against Syria's machine-gunning of Israeli fishermen."

"Chaplain Cohen!"

David looked in surprise at Mr. Marshall, heretofore a study in gray with his Oxford-gray suit, charcoal-gray tie, dapple-gray eyes, dun-colored hair, silvery temples, trim black mustache, pearly complexion, and noticed that his cheeks were almost pink now. "What's the matter?"

"You're not going to come right out in public and say something like that before a group of Christians!"

"Wha—?"

"Of course, I suppose I must expect you, as a rabbi, to be inclined toward Israel even despite what she has done," Mr. Marshall said, clipping his words short. "But you must bear in mind that this Sabbath you will be speaking to people who can't be expected to view the Middle East through Jew-colored glasses."

David reddened. "Mr. Marshall, being a rabbi does not distort my vision. It *clarifies* it," he said evenly. "It clarifies it to the extent that I realize the State of Israel is not my religion. *Judaism* is. And just because I'm Jewish—"

"—you have a Jewish bias," Mr. Marshall concluded. "It's only natural, I suppose, for a Jew to have a Jewish bias."

"Is it really?" David remarked. "You seem untainted."

Mr. Marshall flushed. "I've overcome my Jewish bias." Before David could inquire whether it had been much of a struggle, he continued hurriedly. "Chaplain Cohen, you must understand my position here. And it's not only *my* position but that of the entire Jewish community as well. On the Sabbath you will be representing Fair City's Jews before a congregation that will contain more Christians than Jews, just as I in this Club represent the Jewish community here, which fact I always bear in mind—so much so that I am careful to overtip and even deliberately lose at cards on occasion. Chaplain, you simply can't affront the audience with your private Jewish attitude toward Israel. Perhaps a few

176

Jewish extremists might be in agreement with you, but all the others there will not be."

"Need I ask on which side you will be?"

"The only side I am ever on," said Mr. Marshall firmly, "is the side of our United States Government. Now I don't care to argue the matter with you. The point is that you simply *can't* talk about the Middle East."

"Can't?"

"If need be, I'll just have to see to it that your invitation to preach is withdrawn."

David slapped the table, and Mr. Marshall's empty wine glass tipped over. "Why, you're—you're *threatening* me!"

"Chaplain, *please!*" Carefully Mr. Marshall looked around the room to see if the handful of other people there, dining quietly, had taken note of David's outburst. If they had, they were politely overlooking it.

"Mr. Marshall, you cancel my sermon just because we happen to disagree," exclaimed David, "and I'll raise my voice in other places besides this Club of yours."

"Chaplain Cohen, can't you see that I'm looking out for your own good as well?" Mr. Marshall asked with patent hostility. "Have you forgotten that you are an officer in the United States Air Force?"

"That doesn't make me an apologist for the military," David retorted, "any more than my religion makes me an apologist for Israel. As a chaplain—damn it, as a *human being*—my first allegiance is to God, not to any government."

"You can be *court-martialed* for voicing criticism of your superiors, don't you know that? You remember what happened to General Walker's aide, who did just what you're thinking of doing!"

David faltered. "Court-martialed?" He rallied as he recalled something he had learned at Chaplain School. "The Air Force does not censor sermons. I may have to clear *talks* through the Office of Public Information, but not *sermons*."

"You New Yorkers!" Mr. Marshall exclaimed, then

177

swiftly lowered his voice to a hiss. "You *enjoy* making trouble—just like when you brought that Negro to the synagogue Seder. I warned Colonel Stratford *then* that you were a troublemaker. If the congregation hadn't hushed it up . . . But now, *this*. Why couldn't Israel have waited for Syria to openly attack her in force?"

David countered, "And why couldn't Rabbi Garfield's father have died at a time more convenient for you?"

"Chaplain, I won't let you jeopardize my position in the community by—" Mr. Marshall checked his outburst as the waiter approached with their luncheons.

Neither man spoke—Mr. Marshall tried to look amiable and David tried not to feel disgusted—until the waiter withdrew. Then David said, "I think I'd better leave. We'd probably both end up with indigestion if we ate now. Where do I get my check?"

Mr. Marshall sneered at him. "Haven't you ever been to a private club before? Private clubs do not give checks. You are my guest."

David rose to his feet, flushing. "Thank you, Mr. Marshall. I'm sure your fellow members here must tolerate you with as much graciousness as you have tolerated me. If you'll excuse me now, I have a sermon to write."

Mr. Marshall smiled coldly. *"Talk."*

David retorted, "You bet I will!" He had, alas, mistaken the noun for the verb.

The phone rang as David was completing the last paragraph of his sermon two days later. It was Captain McGurney, the Public Information Officer, calling. "Chaplain, will you clue me in on what to do in a Jewish synagogue? I've never been to one before. I promise to remember not to cross myself every time I stand up, if you tell me when I'm supposed to genuflect or whatever."

David laughed. "Okay. But tell me first, what's the occasion for your going to a synagogue—a wedding?"

"Don't you know?" the captain asked in surprise. "Didn't you get the announcement from the synagogue in today's mail?"

"What?" Quickly David turned to the pile of mail on his desk and shuffled through it until he came to a letter from the synagogue. He opened it, then swore at the enclosed invitation:

You are cordially invited to attend
DECORATION DAY SERVICES
at the Fair City Synagogue
on Saturday morning
at 9:30 A.M.

Address: "Decoration Day Today"
Colonel Thomas Stratford, Commander of Fairfield AFB

Talk: "What America Means to Me"
1st Lieutenant David Cohen, Jewish Chaplain

The word "Talk" was circled in red and underlined twice.

"Mr. Marshall set up the program with me just yesterday," Captain McGurney was saying. "He's the owner of Marshall's, you know, also some kind of deacon at the synagogue. A very fine gentleman, isn't he? Oh, the real reason I called you: Can I see a copy of that talk of yours before the end of the week? You know I have to pass on all talks."

David faltered, "I haven't finished it yet."

"Well, I don't suppose it matters too much. Just so long as you don't get political. But anyway, all these Decoration Day orations are about the same," the captain said. "Only usually these ceremonies are held closer to Decoration Day. Why do you suppose the synagogue is jumping the gun by two weeks?"

David waited until 9:29 A.M. before entering Rabbi Garfield's study, then hastily donned his skullcap, prayer shawl and robe as he exchanged hasty greetings with Colonel Stratford, Captain McGurney, Mr. Marshall, his brother and nephew.

"I am looking forward to your talk, Chaplain," the Base Commander said.

David grimaced politely.

"I thought you would," said Mr. Marshall, smiling darkly.

A minute later they marched out into the sanctuary, Mr. Marshall and Colonel Stratford on either side of David, and Captain McGurney behind them, as if they were escorting him down the last mile. He ascended the pulpit, announced the page, chanted the opening psalm, and the service began.

It was fortunate that David knew all the prayers by heart, for he found it impossible to concentrate on the service. He led it automatically—twice he lost his place in the prayerbook and continued by rote until he found it again—while his thoughts kept circling around Colonel Stratford and his possible reaction to the sermon. Correction, *talk*. (And circle that in red and underline it twice.)

Every once in a while a verse would rise up from the prayerbook and strike him with new pertinence, inspiring him with courage: "May it be Thy will, O Lord our God, to lead us in Thy ways, that Thy name may be honored and Israel be blessed by our actions . . . May we walk according to the precepts of Thy law and may we never fall into temptation or shame . . . May our better nature always prompt us to discharge our duties faithfully and to do good with a willing heart . . . Grant, O Father, that by our conduct we may win favor in Thine eyes and in the eyes of our fellow men . . ."

But there was also one Biblical verse in the prayerbook that sent chills skittering up and down his spine: "The sacrifices of God are a broken spirit; a broken and contrite heart, O God, Thou wilt not despise."

David took the Torah from the ark, the congregation rose, and the choir sang: "Thine, O Lord, is the greatness and the power, the glory and the victory and the majesty. For all that is in the heaven and in the earth is Thine. Thine is the kingdom, O Lord, and Thou art exalted above all."

The silver ornaments and the blue velvet cover were removed from the Torah, and it was placed upon the reading table. The congregation sat down, various men recited the blessings thanking God for giving the Bible to the people of Israel, and David read the portion of the week from the parchment scroll.

A youngster of about thirteen appeared beside him, and David wondered what he was doing there. Suddenly he remembered: This was the *bar mitzvah*, the lad who was being admitted into manhood on that Sabbath and accepting the responsibilities and obligations of Judaism, as Israel had welcomed them some thirty-three hundred years before at Sinai. Distractedly David said, *"Mazel tov.* You did very well."

The youngster, a clean-cut blond boy who smelled of too much of his father's cologne, looked perplexed. "What are you congratulating me *for*, Rabbi? I haven't done anything yet."

David reddened and mumbled something which he hoped the boy would be able to make sense of, for he himself could not. His mind was too occupied with other things.

The youngster chanted the blessings in a voice that started off as a soprano, developed into an alto and ground to a halt as a bass; he seemed to age arithmetically before the congregation while David felt himself aging geometrically beneath Colonel Stratford's watchful gaze. Then, in Southern-accented Hebrew, the boy read from the Torah, chanted a chapter from the Prophets, and concluded with a short speech on the significance of Judaism to a youngster becoming *bar mitzvah* in the modern world.

Somehow the Torah found its way back into the ark and a few minutes later Colonel Stratford was standing before the lectern and speaking about Decoration Day.

David listened intently and heard nothing. His mind was busy alternating between berating himself for considering changes in his sermon and wondering whether to deliver it exactly as written.

Suddenly he heard his name mentioned, and he realized with a start that the time had arrived for his irrevocable decision. He rose slowly to his feet as Mr. Marshall completed his introduction.

Mr. Marshall, on his way back to his seat, whispered to him, "I hope you remember that now you also have something to lose, Chaplain."

"Only my self-respect," David retorted, and he strode forward angrily, his mind finally made up. How could he start compromising his ideals at the untimely age of twenty-four? What would then be left for him to do in his thirties, forties and fifties? There would always be a Colonel Stratford to be angered by his outspokenness. Possibly next time it would be the president of his first congregation or the wife of a trustee or a committee chairman. If he were to start running his ministry on the platform of No Offense to Anyone Ever, he might as well have studied for four years to be a writer of deodorant ads.

David began speaking even before coming to a halt at the lectern. With a vehemence unwarranted by his words and directed not at the eyes out front but at Mr. Marshall behind him, he shouted the introduction of his sermon as if it were one lengthy word:

"General Stratford has spoken so eloquently on the meaning of Decoration Day and loyalty to our country," he said, his anxiety promoting the Base Commander by several ranks, "that it would be anticlimactic for me to talk on the same topic. I should therefore like to preach on a second love that American Jews have besides their great love for our own country. I refer, of course, to their historic religious love for the land of Israel."

He paused to gulp down air, then licked his parched lips while drops of perspiration raced each other down his tightening spinal column. *God!* He had never realized that his back had so many muscles in it.

He forced himself to read slowly from his manuscript.

'A Jew's *ultimate* loyalty is to God alone. For only He is divine; governments are not notoriously infallible."

All at once, he realized, in an effusion of cold sweat, that he had inadvertently skipped three paragraphs of his sermon. What must the congregation be thinking!

"Christianity too could believe no other way," he continued. "For while we all pledge allegiance to our country and love it, we realize that it is entirely possible for our country to err. And when it does err morally, we are obliged to call attention to the lapse." He took a deep breath and blurted out: "And err morally, I believe, our government did recently when it supported the U.N. censure of Israel for retaliating against Syrian troops that had murdered fishermen in the Israeli Sea of Galilee, because this immoral vote can only serve to encourage Arab aggression and terrorism and—"

There! It was said. The rest would come easier now. He looked up at the congregation—they were only individuals assembled together, he realized now, and not some collective monster—and pushed away his manuscript. He did not need it any longer; what he wanted to say he knew in his heart.

"It took more than fifteen full years of errors and equivocations in the Middle East to produce the present tragic situation there. Our contributions to the current state of cold war between Israel and the Arab nations have been our vacillation and preoccupation with sops rather than solutions.

"The United Nations' establishment of Israel in 1947 created vast moral and practical problems that the world organization promptly proceeded to ignore. For example, the U.N. failed to insure Israel's survival against repeated Arab incursions. It also neglected to develop practical plans for aiding the Arab refugees on a permanent basis and to move ahead with a regional economic development program, like the Jordan Valley project.

"Because we all shirked our responsibilities at the outset, a state of warfare has existed in the Middle East since 1948. Recent events served only to pull the scabs off the sores festering beneath, with the ceaseless invasions of Israel, murder of her citizens, blockade of her ships, the Arabs' arms dealings with Russia and their well-advertised ambition to complete in Israel what Hitler began in Europe.

"Could we expect Israel to submit to annihilation without representation when we ourselves fought a war to protest mere *taxation* without representation?

"Listen to these words, which set Israel's attack against Syria in perspective:

Peace is generally good in itself, but it is never the highest good unless it comes as the handmaid of righteousness; and it becomes a very evil thing if it serves merely as a mask for cowardice and sloth, or as an instrument to further the ends of despotism or anarchy. We must bear in mind that the great end in view is righteousness, justice as between man and man and between nation and nation.

"Were these words spoken last week by Prime Minister Ben-Gurion to justify Israel's action? Not at all. Those were the words of President Theodore Roosevelt upon the occasion of his acceptance of the Nobel Peace Prize in 1906.

"Yet only a moral delinquent would deny that warfare, even when self-defensive and justified, is at best only tenth-rate justice. *First*-rate justice requires discussions of problems, negotiation of common concerns, a willingness to sit down at conference tables to iron out differences with words instead of trying to stamp them out in blood."

He paused for a moment, and behind him he heard Captain McGurney exclaim quietly, "He never cleared *that* talk with *me*, Colonel!"

David continued speaking, unperturbed. What more could he lose now?

Hardly had David's lips met to begin the second syllable of the Amen in the parting benediction than he

184

started for the nearest exit. I am *not* running away, he told himself; after all, Colonel Stratford knows damn well where he can find me.

"That was a real terrific sermon, Rabbi!" someone exclaimed, and David paused. The *bar mitzvah* young man had grabbed his sleeve, and out of relief David could have kissed him. "It was just as good as *Exodus* with Sal Mineo and President Kennedy's brother-in-law, honest! And shorter too."

"Thank you, thank you very much," said David gratefully. "And *mazel tov* to you—for real now. You did do very well." He started away but all of a sudden Mr. Marshall was there, blocking his path.

His gray eyes glittering coldly, Mr. Marshall called over his shoulder, "Colonel, what did you think of Chaplain Cohen's *talk?*"

David stood his ground—trapped. That damned tightrope between the military and the religious! Below him he could see Colonel Stratford's angry green eyes coming up on him fast, his mouth opening wide.

"I think Chaplain Cohen is pushing his luck, that's what I think." The Colonel turned on David and addressed him icily, as if he and not the Russians were the enemy. "This makes Strike *Two*, Chaplain, doesn't it?" He walked away from the smugly grinning Mr. Marshall.

And David was left alone with but one hand now on the slippery tightrope.

Chapter : 13

SOON David was marking his first anniversary of service in the Air Force with a two-foot-long strudel from Tante Dvorah and lingering feelings of insecurity. So uneasy did the Base Commander make David feel, that during a subsequent encounter he had to restrain himself from blurting out, "Come now, Colonel—not even *one* ball?"

Less harrowing, because it was safely predictable, was David's work. For he awoke every morning at 0630 to face problems that were here today, here tomorrow. He could always feel reasonably certain that though yesterday's counselee may have gone, the problem itself lingered on for someone else to usher into his office on a succeeding day. Indeed, sometimes it seemed that instead of people coming to him with problems, it was the reverse—the same problem would frequently return to him with different people.

Usually awaiting David in his chapel office each morning was at least one airman, summoned the day before in response to a letter or phone call from his mother saying that her son (1) hadn't written home in ten months, and she was worried; or (2) hadn't written home in three days, and she was worried; or (3) was going to get married, and she was worried; or (4) was returning with his wife to live with her, and she was worried; or (5) was getting court-martialed for the fourth time, and she was worried; or (6) seemed to be getting along so surprisingly well in the Air Force —*that* worried her.

By the time David was finished speaking to the airmen and writing their mothers, the mail would arrive. He would then answer the inevitable letter from a cast-off sweetheart who, after naming her boy friend (sometimes, places too) and telling how much he meant to her (a whole lot, a good deal, the most, or too much), would ask David to find out whether the reason her boy friend no longer wrote her was (1) he had lost her address, or (2) he had done something so awful that he was afraid she couldn't love him any more, but yes she could, or (3) he was working a full twenty-four hours a day, or (4) he was dying and didn't want her to know, or (5) his secret undercover work prohibited letter-writing, as he had once mentioned, or (6) he had found out that she was pregnant: (a) by him, or (b)

186

by someone else whom she never really loved anyway.

Never once did an ex-sweetheart suggest the possibility that the negligent boy friend might be (1) married, or (2) unconcerned, or (3) might have enlisted in the Air Force just to get away from her. It was not at all unusual for one of these letters to start out by saying how much the writer loved the airman in question, to continue with the comment that he was the worst kind of miserable scum for ignoring her now, yet to conclude by asking the chaplain to talk the dirty rotten scoundrel into writing the girl or, at the very least, marrying her.

By now David had become so adept at replying to these lovelorn girls that five of them had written back to comment on his understanding, and three girls had written to inquire whether he was single. One had enclosed a picture of herself attired in a tight choir robe.

The next few hours, except for time taken out for lectures and lunch, were devoted to counseling. Following that, David went around visiting the various squadrons, chatting with the men about their work, their families, their plans, their problems. In this manner he got to know a good many of the men, and they came to feel that in the vast impersonal machine that is the Air Force there was at least one man who took a personal interest in them. The lower-grade airmen, in particular, took a liking to him for taking the trouble to remember their names and concerns even while he managed to forget everyone's rank.

Near the end of the duty day at 1630, he would visit patients at the hospital where he made a point of avoiding the psychiatrist who, on first being introduced to David, had remarked, "I'm so glad to meet you, Chaplain. You see, you're the first clergyman I've ever met whom I wasn't treating." (If David had been harboring any desire, even subconsciously, to discuss his flying phobia with the psychiatrist, he quickly repressed it then, consciously.) A surprising number of flyers, he found, were hospitalized for back trouble (due to cramped seating arrangements in the B-47) or ulcers (caused by the tension of their jobs).

After leaving the hospital, David would usually drop by the library to read *The New York Times* and a few magazines, then check out another one of the four hundred Great Books which he was sorely afraid that, by the end of his tour at Fairfield, he would have read at least once.

When he was not spending the evening at the home of a married friend, he dined at the Club with a single one. Afterwards he would retire to seek the excitement he wasn't finding at Fairfield in a Bible commentary or one of the Great Books, or try to ascertain once and for all why the hi-fi set he had built with Roger Allerton's instructions refused to produce any sound whatsoever. Failing that, as he always did, he would turn off the lights at about midnight and sleep.

Unless he was duty chaplain that evening. Then he could reasonably expect to be roused some time during the night by a telephone call (1) from the hospital advising him of a serious illness or death, in which case he notified the chaplain of the same faith; and/or (2) from the Air Police notifying him of an automobile accident, in which case he went to the hospital to visit the victim; and/or (3) from an airman who had been brooding all day long and only now, in the middle of the night, finally decided to talk to a chaplain, in which case he would either see him then or the first thing in the morning; and/or (4) from a wife whose husband was beating her up, in which case David wanted to know what she expected him to do about it; and/or (5) from the husband taking time out from beating his wife to grab the phone to tell David to mind his own business, in which case he did.

And by then it was 0630 again, the start of another similar day with no surprises greater than that still another twenty-four hours had passed without his having incurred Colonel Stratford's further displeasure.

One morning Mitchell had not only a surprise for David but also a proposition. "Now, this is Top Secret, David. There's a three-month TDY to Goose Bay leaving on January 15th. Usually we send one of the Protestant chaplains along because most of the TDY men are, naturally, Protestant, and I'm here to carry on the Protestant activities at Fairfield. But I've been thinking. Now, I've never heard of a Jewish chaplain going along as a SAC TDY chaplain before, but it just might be possible for me to arrange it if you'd care to go—"

"To Goose Bay? Labrador?" Wouldn't David have to *fly* all the way up there, and fly all the way back too?

"You know, the more I think of it," said Mitchell, warming to the idea which chilled David's blood, "the more I like it. Because there are several Catholic and Protestant chaplains at Goose Bay anyway to conduct religious services there and take care of any religious problems that may arise among our men. And you can do there what you've been doing so well here at Fairfield—counseling, lecturing, morale work, serving as an advisor, maybe even flying with the men every once in a while to boost their spirits. Just because a Jewish chaplain has never before been utilized as a SAC rotational unit chaplain, that doesn't mean he shouldn't be."

But David had not heard past ". . . flying with the men . . ." "Now I certainly appreciate the offer, Mitchell, I really do," he said hurriedly. "But I certainly wouldn't want an Air Force precedent to be made just for *me*."

So ashamed did David feel for not having been able to muster the courage to say, "Go TDY to Goose Bay which is only a mere ten hours flying time from Fairfield *one way?* What a question! When do I leave?" that he passed up the next Great Book at the library to go to the Officers Club that evening, thinking all the way there that if only he were a drinking man, *boy!* would *he* get drunk that night.

And by the time he reached the Club his thoughts had gradually progressed from would he to could be, and thence, with hardly any effort at all, to what the hell. So just as soon as he had dropped his hat on the rack, he made straight for the cocktail lounge where he stepped up to the bar to declare: "I'd like a drink."

The bartender stared at him. "What *kind* of drink?"

"Oh," David said. "Manischewitz?"

The bartender looked puzzled. "What was that?"

"It doesn't really make *that* much difference to me. Anything will do."

The bartender shrugged. "Anything it is." And he plunked two ice cubes into a glass and sloshed some colorless liquid over it as David contemplated what joy it would be to possess the sweet solace of Lethelike forgetfulness about things with wings.

He lifted the glass and gulped down its contents. Then, as the tasteless liquor spilled down his throat and set fire to the lining of his gastrointestinal tract, scorching it from top to bottom like a long internal hot foot, he recalled why he had never cultivated a taste for alcohol: It upset his stomach terribly.

Inside him fluids were now flooding his stomach—he could hear their gurgling—to douse his inner conflagration, while he wondered: This is enjoyment? This is solace? This is Lethelike forgetfulness?

"The hell with *this!*" he exclaimed and left the bar. Clearly it was less disturbing for him to remain sober. Drinking would only do to his system what the thought of flying did, so what would it profit him to get drunk?

Glumly he returned to the vestibule for his hat. What kind of man was he anyhow? He couldn't fly and he couldn't drink, he didn't even smoke—what on earth was there left for him?

Above the hat rack was a big sign that proclaimed: BINGO TONIGHT, and impulsively he made a detour to the game room. Maybe Bingo would succeed where alcohol had failed; at the very least, like the vows made by buffered aspirin, it wouldn't upset his stomach.

But his bad luck held good even at Bingo; he lost every game that he played and himself not once. So, after four rounds of one person yelling "Bingo" while hundreds of others cried "Dammit" and even shorter words, he retired to the lounge where he leafed through a copy of *The New Yorker*. This time, however, the cartoons failed to amuse him, and one by Charles Addams depressed him.

From the lounge he wandered into the card room which, on Tuesday evenings as well as Thursday mornings and Sunday afternoons, was occupied by Fairfield's bridge fans, who behaved like members of some austere religious sect. Attired in their Sunday best, the players met religiously three times a week in their own private chapel, the card room; greetings were exchanged briefly at the door, announcements were made, a collection plate was passed around for dues; then everyone sat down soberly at his table, sometimes graced by the presence of a Bridge Elder, called a Life Master. At the conclusion of the evening a few words of wisdom, contaminated by no more arrogance than is found in some clergymen's sermons, were graciously imparted by the evening's winner. Then the devotees would depart feeling uplifted, especially if they had won part of the pot, and vowing to meet again before the week was out.

David was acquainted with the rituals of the game —he knew everything about bridge except how to bid —but it never appealed to him. The game was so grim. All the participants were so deathly serious about it that less conversation was exchanged during an evening of bridge than during an hour's church service.

Stationing himself behind an acquaintance—she barely turned aside from her devotions to acknowledge his existence—David watched her play. Naturally, there was no talking.

Suddenly a voice broke the silence to exclaim, "Tell me, dear, do you eat your peas with a knife too?" All eyes, including David's, focused on an adjacent table. "Well? Do you?" The speaker was an immaculately groomed red-haired woman with a fair complexion and a florid tongue which seemed to lick her caustic words with relish before spitting them out of her thin mouth.

Her partner, a small, pregnant brunette in her early forties, mumbled, "I'm sorry, I'm terribly sorry. That was an awfully stupid play."

191

"Yes," the redhead said, "it was."

The games at the other tables continued without a pause, even when the same voice commented acidly during the following game, "You seem to give as much thought to your cards as you do to planning children, dear."

This time the brunette did not reply. Blushing, she sucked in her lips.

David, tempted to intervene, wondered why nobody in the room took exception to the redhead's rudeness. Yet he controlled his impulse. If the brunette did not care to speak up for herself, there was no reason for him to defend her. Perhaps nasty remarks were some of the rites of bridge with which he was unfamiliar.

Several rubbers later, David, now observing the redhead's table from afar, saw a crisis brewing. The lady at the brunette's right had led her a card, and the brunette was deliberating what to play. Evidently it was an important move, for the three others were watching her closely, and the redhead was heaving her looks which clearly said: You'd-better-play-it-right-this-time or-else.

Reluctantly and with an anxious glance at the redhead, the brunette finally threw out a card. Their opponent gleefully trumped it, and the brunette, catching her breath sharply, put out her hand to grab it back.

"Idiot!" the redhead cried, and she tossed her cards in her partner's face.

The brunette burst into tears, jumped to her feet and ran out of the room.

This time everyone stopped playing. Still, no one said a word.

Not so David. Impulsively he stepped up to the red-headed woman, now fumbling to light a cigarette. "Ma'am," he exclaimed in reflex action, his words dropping like glistening diamonds on the black velvet of silence, "you are a *bitch*."

The cigarette lighter slipped through the redhead's fingers and dropped to the floor.

The resultant clatter, punctuated by a chorus of gasps

from the players in the room, brought David sharply to his senses. Appalled by his own rash words, he hastened to add, "What I *meant* was—"

"Did you hear what he called Mrs. Stratford!" someone exulted, and David was struck dumb.

Mrs. *STRATFORD?*

"Here's where the crap *really* hits the fan!" someone else exclaimed as Mrs. Stratford opened her narrow mouth to emit a jagged scream of outrage.

David let out a groan.

Strike Three!

Chapter : 14

THIS trip to Goose Bay, courtesy of Colonel Stratford, *was* necessary, several officers kept insisting at the Air Refueling Squadron's preflight briefing, to maintain combat efficiency and readiness to fly on an hour's notice to any base in the world from which they could refuel SAC's jet bombers in the air, thus saving them precious time and fuel which would enable them to get to their targets that much sooner.

David heard these protestations several times, plus the example to which all pointed with pride, namely, the squadron's participation in the famous air-refueling of the three B-52's that flew all the way around the world without ever landing once, which feat had all kinds of awesome implications—as a warning to Russia, for American defense, and as a booster to SAC's power, which was the key deterrent striking force of the United States and the free world. But what impressed him most of all was that he hadn't even seen his plane yet, much less flown in it, so how could he *already* be airsick?

The briefing ended, mercifully, but his gastric torment did not. As he descended with the others from the briefing room to the hangar below, it seemed to him that all the juices of his body were draining out of his weakening extremities and flooding his stomach which bubbled like some huge cauldron of stew about to boil over from all apertures. And his twenty pounds of arctic clothing (quilted pants and parka, wolverine-hair trimmed hood, and woolen helmet and muffler all on top of his regular woolen uniform and flannel under wear, plus three pairs of double-layer duffel socks, felt insoles, and knee-high canvas muk-luk boots) only added more fuel to the stew.

A whistle sounded and the men, waving good-bye to their wives and lugging their belongings behind them in foot lockers and duffel bags, began to line up. To David's apocalyptic eye (as far as he was concerned the moment he'd set foot in an airplane—*that* was the end of his days), the hangar in its state of human flux resembled a supernal way station where people were being consigned to either Heaven or Hell. And the way he was feeling there was no doubt at all in his mind where he was being sent; he felt, as a matter of fact, as if he were there already.

The whistle blew again, and his line moved forward into the shadows of evening that lay in wait for them outside the hangar. David followed behind, hearing, as he stepped along, his intestinal juices slosh around inside him and slowly rise as though his body's defenses had all sprung leaks and it would now be only a matter of time before he would be drowned inside. Following his group into a bus, he surrendered himself to the conveyance which took him along with the others inevitably, as in a Greek tragedy, to his nemesis, a twenty-ton four-engine KC-97 tanker.

Everywhere around them, as they left the bus, the air was quivering with the roars of twenty-five aircraft warming up, their propellers slashing viciously at the night in ever-quickening sweeps, as if straining to break free from their engines and get at the people nearby. There were so many planes warming up, so many engines roaring, so much air vibrating that it seemed possible he entire airfield, hangars and all, might yet take to the air.

Someone announced that his plane was now loading, and David ran to the head of the line, scaled the ladder leading up into the cavernous side of the aircraft, and dashed into the latrine. The only thing that cheered him when he finally emerged from his haven was that he was able to secure the seat closest to it.

But then, feeling ashamed, he began to reproach himself:

—Come on, cut it out. This whole thing—it's all in your *mind*.

—Maybe it is, but now it's in my stomach too. I can feel it. (He swallowed two Dramamine pills.)

—I know it, I know it. But there must be *something* we can do to help . . .

—Like for instance? (He swallowed two Bonamine pills.)

—Maybe if we can figure out *why* flying terrifies you so. Maybe if we probe to the root of your phobia, dissect it, examine it . . .

—All this in the ten minutes we got before the plane takes off?

—You have something better planned for these ten minutes? Like maybe a return trip to the latrine?

—All right, all right. Probe, dissect, examine. Go ahead.

—This phobia, there's one thing I've always suspected about it—you had it even *before* that plane crash of yours, didn't you?

—I *was* upset when I got on the plane that first time, that's true. I remember that.

—But why? Why? You had never flown before.

—Well, *that's* why. It was my first flight. Everyone is scared on his first flight, isn't he? I mean, it's natural.

—But everyone doesn't take out $62,500 in flight insurance policies as you did. *That* isn't natural.

—So I was a little nervous.

—A "little" nervous? *Five* insurance policies?

—Well, it isn't everyone's father and mother who go and get killed in a plane crash, you know.

195

—But Mother and Dad were killed in an auto wreck.

—Say, that's right! Why did I think it was a plane crash?

—You tell me. This is significant.

—Well, they were driving to the airport when it happened. Maybe that's why.

—Could be.

—They were going to fly to California. It would have been their first flight too.

—How did you come to think they had died in a plane crash?

—Well, I remember them telling me they were flying to Los Angeles, and they never came back to me after they left for the airport.

—Did Tante Dvorah and Uncle Asher tell you what happened?

—Not till a few months later. They just told me that Mother and Dad had gone away to Heaven, instead of to Los Angeles. And I remember I kept asking when Mother and Dad were returning from Heaven, when the plane would bring them back.

—That's it! That *must* be it!

—What?

—As a kid you got the idea that whenever anyone goes away in an airplane, he's never coming back, that something happens to prevent him from returning, just as your parents were prevented from coming back from Heaven. Don't you see?

—Sounds reasonable, it seems reasonable.

—Of course, it sounds reasonable. It's the *answer!*

—You know, I really believe that may be it!

—You see! It *helped* to probe, to examine, to understand—

—You're right. That's true. There's only one thing that bothers me now though . . .

—And what's that?

—My stomach. Why do I feel sicker now than before?

—You mean, after all our probing, examining, understanding your phobia, you don't feel better?

—I feel worse. Oh, I feel *awful!*

—In that case, you'd better take those sleeping pills right now. This is going to be a long flight.

As David swallowed two sleeping pills—the first ones he had ever taken in his life—someone handed him a tangled web of straps, belts and buckles, saying, "Your parachute harness," then helped him put it on.

Though David knew nothing about parachutes, he knew enough to ask for his parachute pack. He recalled the horror story—true or not, it was still a horror—a pilot had told him of the navigator who bailed out of a stricken plane without remembering beforehand to attach a parachute pack to the harness. He had pulled at his rip cord only to find that he had none. "Oh, nuts!" he had exclaimed, the pilot reported to David. All the way down, oh, nuts ...

David sat down on the canvas seat and buckled himself in it, but he was quickly unbuckled, then re-buckled by an officer who came around inspecting all harnesses. "If you ever tried to bail out, you'd have to take the whole plane with you," he said. "You buckled your seat belt to your harness."

"I'm sorry," said David.

All of a sudden the plane slid forward, and automatically he popped a third sleeping pill into his mouth. Then, in an effort to take his mind off his mind, he tried to concentrate on the conversation of the men in the canvas seats behind him. One of them was saying:

"I've had it! My separation date is four months from now, and I'm grabbing it with both hands. I'm too old for games. I want to get out of the Air Force before my kid is old enough to ask me questions about what I do for a living. What can I tell him? That I play games? This is what I do for a living, son: I play TDY, Camping Out, Sortie, Ringelevio, Alert, Let's Pretend, Refueling, Hide-and-Seek. And how can I make the kid understand that I have to leave him so often just to go to some hell-hole to risk my life practicing at air-refueling bombers which don't go anywhere anyhow. What sense of accomplishment does it give a grown man when the most he can hope for in his job is that everything he does is for *nothing*, and that he *continues* doing it for nothing? I've had it, I'm telling you. Thank God this is my last TDY at ..."

Someone was rattling David, but he shook him off. What was that? "... land in a few minutes ... Goose Bay ..."

Land? Goose Bay? David stirred himself, and the insides of his head thudded dully against one another.

Stretching his eyes open one at a time, he gasped to see a huge yellow eye, like that of a Cyclops, glowering balefully upon him. The eye was pressed to a hole that had worn itself through the gray murk outside the window. The eye grew larger, yellower, and more menacing, as David stared at it, hypnotized.

"There's the sun!" someone cried. "It's morning—our first day at Goose Bay. Only eighty-nine more to go now!"

"Fasten your safety belts," someone else was calling. "We're landing."

It was the truth too. Several minutes later, even before David had time to terrorize himself with the knowledge that he had been flying for nine hours, the plane landed. He uttered a prayer of thanksgiving; now, at last, he could start worrying about the flight back to Fairfield.

Still groggy from the sleeping pills, David stepped out of the plane and immediately he was jolted awake. *Man, it was cold!* He felt as if he had stepped into a swimming pool filled with nothing but shaved ice.

The biting cold wrung tears from his eyes as he climbed down from the plane, and the tears froze on his cheeks. There he stood in the sandy snow weeping icicles and feeling his nostrils contract as the moist cilia inside froze, hair by hair, into icy stalactites. In front of him he could see his breath freeze and then, as it was blown back, he could hear the ice crystals tinkle like bells as they broke against his ears.

Stamping his tingling feet, he surveyed the vast desert

of snow around him and the milky sky above it. With all the snow and ice and whiteness, Goose Bay looked like nothing so much as Hell frozen over.

Impatiently he looked back at the KC-97 to see if all the men had disembarked so that they might proceed to an indoor shelter. He saw something extraordinary happen then. One of the last men to step out of the plane, shocked by the icy wind, turned his head aside. In doing so, his face came close to the plane's passageway and his nose brushed against the metal skin of the aircraft. And there it froze! His nose stuck to the plane and, try as he did, the man was unable to pull it away.

The man began, understandably, to yell. David did too. So did everyone else. One man nearby, dashing to the rescue, tried to pull the airman away from the plane and, in the attempt, nearly succeeded in pulling the airman away from his nose. The airman continued to scream, nasally now. He also waved his arms.

The pilot appeared in the passageway and hollered, "Cigarettes! Cigarettes! Cigarettes!"

The airman screamed something which sounded like, "I don't smoke!"

Still, the pilot continued to yell, inexplicably, for cigarettes. Someone threw him one and he yelled for more, lighting them as quickly as he got them. Then he carefully applied the burning cigarettes to the plane's skin around the airman's nose. In a few moments they heated the metal and the man was able to pull all of his nose away from the aircraft.

"You *idiot!*" the pilot hollered. "Don't you know enough never to touch any metal up here with your bare skin? We *warned* you that skin freezes to metal in this minus-fifty-degree temperature!"

So this is Goose Bay, David said to himself. Lord preserve us! When does that sweet plane fly us back to Fairfield?

The insignia of the Strategic Air Command was an impressive one: a mailed fist, outlined against a bright blue sky, clutching thunderbolts together with olive branches. On the door to the Goose Bay Visiting Officers Quarters, an old off-white wooden barracks, one of whose two stories was as yet unburied in snow, David spied a cartoon paraphrase of the SAC insignia: Rising up through a Goose Bay snowdrift was the same mailed fist; only here it was squeezing a turnip from which dripped a dozen bright red drops of blood.

"Amen," David breathed as, defrosting, he made his way upstairs.

Behind him someone was expressing his feelings in somewhat less religious terminology: "If the world ever needs an enema, this is the place they'll probably shove the tube!"

Entering his assigned room, David swiftly noted that, in addition to a desk, a chair, two closets and two beds, the drab room also contained a body, with empty whiskey bottles standing at its head and feet, like candles at a bier. Sprawled on its back in one of the beds, the body was clothed in a shoe, two socks, a wrist watch, dog tags, the imprint of a beer can, and was presumably warm.

If he had any doubts as to the body's sobriety, they were swiftly dispelled when its owner hiccuped back to life, smiled up at him and his lower lip, and belched: "I'm drunk."

"But we only just got here! How could you possibly have gotten drunk so fast?"

The man (with his curly blond hair, cherubic face, cloudy blue eyes, small, pudgy body and wiggling toes, he looked more like a boy) smiled with his other lip. "Oh, I've been drunk for— Say, what day is this anyway?"

"Thursday."

The lieutenant closed his right eye, then his left one, then his mouth, then his right eye again. "I've been drunk for four days," he concluded.

"Too bad!" David shook his head sadly. "You must be left over from that last TDY here. The squadron was taking off, returning to the States, when we landed."

"You don't *mean* that!" The fellow sat bolt upright in bed. "They couldn't've gone and left me here—they couldn't've! That's why I'm drunk—to make this damn

200

TDY pass quicker. But I couldn't've been drunk for ninety-four days; I just couldn't've!" He made a grab for David and nearly fell out of bed when he missed. "Tell me fast, what base are you from?"

"Fairfield. What's *your* home base?"

The pudgy body fell back, belching in relief. "What were you trying to do scaring me like that—sober me up? I'm from Fairfield too. I was sent up to this hole in the Advance Party to pave the way for you bastards, assign rooms and things like that. A few sonofabitches thought my job included lining them up some pieces of ass, but I told them to go—"

Swiftly David introduced himself. "So glad to meet you, Lieutenant. I'm Chaplain Cohen."

The curly blond head nodded. "Welcome to Goose Bay, Captain. What say we burn this hole to the ground when I sober up? My name is Winkler, Alex Winkler. I'm only a lieutenant, a co-pilot. That's *another* reason to get drunk. A co-pilot is sort of the Air Force's middle son. He's not the pilot, and he's not the navigator —no status, you know what I mean? Gives a guy all kinds of complexes, especially when he's nursing one to begin with. Oh, I've taken some psych courses—went to college. I'm R.O.T.C., but don't tell on me. Say, how can you be a captain when you're wearing silver bars, same as me?"

"I didn't say captain. I said—"

Lieutenant Winkler waved a few fingers in David's direction. "*Now* I know who you are. What a blooper!" The cloudy blue eyes opened wide. "You're the *chaplain.*"

"That's right," David said. "And I've made a blooper too. I must be in the wrong room. I'm supposed to have a private room." He turned to go.

Lieutenant Winkler shook his head once. "No, Chaplain. Colonel Kingsbury gave me special instructions to assign you as my roommate."

David paused. "What was that?" he demanded.

"Colonel Kingsbury—you know, he's the A.R.S. Commander—he wants me to room with you, or you to room with me. I don't know which it is. But at any rate he wants us to room together. Why doesn't Colonel Kingsbury like you, Chaplain?"

"I never met the man," David said grimly. "What reason did the Colonel give for putting us two in the same room?"

The lieutenant snickered. "You must be even newer than me to the Air Force, Chaplain. If there's anything you never ask a C.O., it's questions. And as for *reasons*—well . . ."

"According to regulation," David explained, "chaplains are supposed to have private quarters, for counseling purposes."

Lieutenant Winkler looked up plaintively at David. "What's the matter, Chaplain? Don't you like me either? Colonel Kingsbury doesn't like me, but he at least *knows* me. Why don't *you* like me? Just because I drink? Well, I have a good reason, a damn—I mean, a darn good reason. How would you feel if you had to spend your honeymoon with five hundred guys, instead of with your bride? Or are you a priest?"

"I'm a rabbi," David said.

"A rabbi?" Lieutenant Winkler said. "Can rabbis get married?"

"Yes."

"And do you have a wife?"

David sighed. "No."

"Then you wouldn't understand; no one would," Winkler said mournfully. "Here my girl Marge and I send out our wedding invitations, and a week later I find out the squadron is going on a ninety-day TDY to Goose Bay on the 27th of July, and we're getting married on the 26th of July! In the evening yet! And we can't change the date, not just because all the arrangements have been made, but because it would be violating security even to drop a hint when the A.R.S. is going on TDY! So we go ahead with the wedding plans, and then at the last minute Marge refuses to honeymoon before the wedding—I mean, well, we get married, but the whole squadron's there thinking it all one big joke, because at the end of the evening I leave with them instead of going off with Marge. What a honeymoon *that* was!" He grimaced horribly. "Then, no sooner do I get back to Fairfield and Marge than bam! that damn Alert, and I'm sharing the shower again with a hundred other guys for another month. And now, only six weeks later, we're back again for *another* ninety days. By the time I get back to Marge, I'll have been married for almost a year, but a husband for less than three months. Now I ask you, isn't that reason enough for any man to drink?"

"You mean," David asked, "you never used to get drunk like this before you got married?"

The boyish lieutenant shrugged. "So if I did get drunk a few times . . . a week?"

"And what was the excuse then?" David asked.

"Who needed excuses? I wasn't rooming with any chaplain then."

"Maybe Colonel Kingsbury will remedy that," David said. "I'll go ask him about it now." He started out of the room.

Lieutenant Winkler called after David. "Say, would you bring me some beer on your way back? All this talking—it's made my throat awful dry."

Colonel Kingsbury was a tall, dark and dour man in his late thirties, with graying sideburns, broad, powerful shoulders, narrow hips and sharp features. He mustered a convincing display of indifference when David entered the room and introduced himself.

"Oh, yes, I remember now. Someone did tell me a chaplain was coming along with us." The man was so unreceptive—he did not even stop unpacking to talk—that David faltered. "What is it, Chaplain? Has one of my men already come to you complaining about me? The way it usually works is I find some foul-up in the organization, so I chew out my adjutant, who goes and chews out the first sergeant, who goes and chews out an airman, who goes moaning to the chaplain, who then comes complaining to me. Isn't that what's called 'a vicious circle,' Chaplain?"

"You don't seem to be particularly fond of chaplains," David noted aloud.

"How could I be?" the Colonel remarked dryly. "It was a chaplain who married me. But I can't hold that against you, I suppose," he added, unconvincingly. "What do you want to talk to me about?"

"Well," David began, "it's about my quarters here—"

"You mean, Winkler?" The Colonel's thin lips twisted into a crooked smile. "If I were you, I'd hide my shaving lotion. That boy drinks *everything*."

David began again. "Colonel, it was my understanding that the Base Chaplain had sent you a DF explaining how important it is for a chaplain to have his own room up here so that he can counsel men in privacy. That's set forth in Air Force Regulation 165-3, I believe."

Scowling, Colonel Kingsbury stopped unpacking and faced David. "Chaplain, you're a religious man, yet you quoted a military reg to me. I'm a military man, but I'm going to quote a religious reg to you. 'Love thy neighbor as thyself.' Now tell me, does *your* neighbor have to be *sober* before you can love him?"

Here was a switch, thought David wryly. Colonel Kingsbury had assigned him the role of villain before he could cast the Colonel in that part.

"Chaplain, Winkler is as important a counseling case as will ever come to you up here, with this one exception: Winkler would never come to you for counseling. That's why I put him in with you, so he doesn't *have* to come to you because he's already *there*. As you've already seen, I take it, Winkler drinks too much. Especially since he got married, or maybe it started when his plane cracked up here. I'm not sure which it is—I suspect it's his marriage though—but I do know that his drinking impairs his efficiency, and it's going to get him in serious trouble if it continues. That's what I want you to prevent, and that's why I gave Winkler to you."

"Colonel," David said evenly, "I am not A.A."

"I didn't think that you were," Colonel Kingsbury replied, his black eyes frowning. "But then, Winkler is not an alcoholic, else he'd have been thrown out of the

Air Force long ago. He's only a kid who drinks too much. And I'm giving him to you to rehabilitate, Chaplain." He attempted a smile but his dour face refused to play host to the stranger. "Why, you ought to feel grateful for the opportunity."

What could David say? The Colonel had pitched him an oddball—and not entirely for the beneficent reason given, of this he felt certain—and he could do nothing but take him. Excusing himself, he left the Colonel, grimly envisioning a lost weekend ninety days long with himself serving as a male nurse, hiding shaving lotion in light fixtures. The only therapy he could recall from the movie was Jane Wyman's taking the bottle away from Ray Milland and offering him her lips instead. And what did David have to compare with that?

Passing a room where several men were standing around drinking beer, he paused on the threshold. "Have any extra cans?" he asked.

"Sure thing," said one of the men, pointing to an open case of beer near the door. "Help yourself."

David dug his wallet out of his pants pocket. "How much is it a can?"

"No charge," was the hospitable reply. "It's on the house."

"Well, thank you," David said and picked up six cans. He turned to see startled looks all around him. "These are for a friend," he explained. "You're sure now you don't want me to pay for them?"

Dumbly the men shook their heads, and David left with his arms full of beer. Behind him he heard several surprised exclamations.

"But wasn't that the *Chaplain?*"

"Sure," someone snorted, "but this is Goose Bay!"

"Didn't you hear? The last man to go AWOL from here was the Deputy Base Chaplain."

"*Still*—to go ape so *soon*. Pretending they were for a friend—"

Winkler was still in bed, playing with his dog tags, when David returned to the room and dumped the beer cans on the desk. The boyish lieutenant nodded his curly blond head in their direction. "Say, what's all that, Chaplain?"

"Beer. You asked me to bring you back some—remember?"

"Did *I* ask *you* to do *that?*" Winkler asked in shocked tones. "Why, I must have been stoned!"

David looked around the room. "Where's the can opener? You couldn't have drunk that too."

"You mean you also like beer?" Winkler asked in pleased surprise.

"No, beer always reminds me of diabetes tests," David said. "These cans are all for you."

Gallantly Winkler declined them. "There'll probably be a briefing later on today. There always is. If I drink any more, I'll never be able to make it."

David found an opener on the co-pilot's bed, took it, and opened one of the cans. "Oh, you'll enjoy the beer better than the briefing anyway," he said, and held out the can.

Winkler's blue eyes opened wide. "Say, what kind of chaplain are you anyway? Are you trying to get me *drunk?*"

"Isn't that what you want?"

"Yes—I mean, no—I mean, a chaplain getting me drunk—that's like my sister pimping for me—I mean, are you *sure* you're a chaplain? Where's your damn cross?"

David pointed to his tablets. "I told you. I'm Jewish."

"Jewish?" Winkler regarded David suspiciously. "Is that what Jewish chaplains do—go around getting Protestants drunk?"

"That's what Jewish chaplains do, all right," he said soberly, "to those damfool Protestants who let us."

"What do you mean?" Winkler exclaimed.

"Look, Lieutenant," David said, serious now. "I'm here to help you. I'd *like* to help you. And I'm *going* to help you—in any way you want me to. We're going to be rooming together for ninety days, and if you want me to keep you drunk for ninety days, I'll oblige. Now, with my help and Colonel Kingsbury's distaste for your drinking, you may not last a full ninety days up here, but I'll help you with your immediate wish; I'll keep you drunk till they toss you out of the Air Force. On the other hand, if you want to stay sober, I'll be happy to help you there too. I'm always available to you, any time of the day or night, to talk over anything that might be troubling you and see if we can find a solution for it that's not one hundred proof. We can even draw up some regimen to keep you too busy to drink by utilizing the gym, chapel, library, flight line, USAFI courses, movies. Whichever way you want it—drunk or sober—I'll help to the best of my ability. Now, which is it to be, Lieutenant?" David held out the opened can of beer. "Which do you want?"

With mouth agape, Winkler looked from David to the can of beer, then back to David. "I want to get out of here, *that's* what I want!" he cried. "You must be a souse yourself or something!" He jumped out of bed, groaning as his feet hit the floor. "Oh, my head . . ." He staggered to the door with his one shoe, two socks, dog tags, and wrist watch. "I'm going to see Colonel Kingsbury!"

"If that's what you want," David said amiably, "I'll help you to his room. But first let me help you put on your other shoe."

Winkler looked down, then grabbed a pair of shorts. "Chaplain," he cried, "what are you trying to *do* to me!"

"God help me," David muttered, as Winkler tripped while trying to put on his shorts and fell on his face, "I'm trying to love you."

Chapter : 15

THE only nice thing that David could discover about Labrador was his old roommate, Roger Allerton. He was the Deputy Base Chaplain at Goose Bay. "There's no truth to the rumor," he told David with a smile after he greeted him at the chapel, "that I deliberately instigated the previous Deputy Base Chaplain to desert just so I'd inherit his position."

"Then he actually *did* go AWOL," said David. "What ever for?"

"Because he's human, I suppose. Some chaplains are, you know," Roger replied. "He'd been in Goose Bay for three months, which is about ninety days more than most sane men can stand. It's like living in a deep freeze up here. You get to feel after a while in all this snowy cold that you died a couple of years back but, through the miracle of modern science, you're being kept from disintegrating into dust and ashes."

What do old classmates do at a reunion? They gossip, naturally, about those who are not there. David was reminded of their nightly chats at chaplain school as they swapped news. Roger began:

"Did you hear what happened to Clifford Fowler? He's been bounced clear out of the Air Force. He was stationed in Japan, you recall, and there he took it upon himself to tell the Japanese that Buddhists and Shintoists, with their shrines and incense and statues, were all pagans, the whole lot of them. And with his usual delicacy, he added that that was why God had dropped those A-bombs on Japan, to punish them for their paganism. And then, when he was reprimanded by the Chief of Chaplains—this was after he was saved from being lynched by the local townspeople—what was Clifford's reply? He told the Chief that he couldn't afford to talk since he and his ilk used even more statues and incense and bells at their services than did those pagan Japanese."

"Dan Miller is Stockade Chaplain at Edwards in California. He's become so interested in the subject that he's now taking a degree in penology at the university nearby. He's just hoping that his Bishop won't recall him after his initial hitch ends."

"Jim Mackey got into something of a bind in France.

eems that his French cleaning lady came upon his
lerical collars and spread the word around town. And
ow, despite his repeated tries at explanations in frac-
ured French, half the town sneers at him whenever he
ppears anywhere with his wife and daughter, and the
ther half leers."

"Albert Cohen is in Germany, the one place he swore
ever to see again in his whole life. He never sets foot
ff base because he can't help thinking of every single
German that he meets: 'Here is one more accessory,
till another murderer. Six million people could never
ave been destroyed by even ten thousand Hitlers. He
ad, alas, hundreds of thousands of eager helpers.' "

"Bentley Lane is doing fine since he stopped playing
ide-and-seek in coffins. He's making a name for him-
elf in the scholarly journals. And he just signed a con-
ract with a publisher to expand one of his articles into
a book. The title is 'Sex Is a Summer Festival'—what-
ver *that* means."

"Paul Smith is the most popular man at Orlando. The
oung airmen at his base found out that, thanks to his
Navy training, he can outjudo, outdrink, and outswear
ny man there. So they listen to him with all the devo-
ion and respect that the squirrels showed St. Francis
f Assisi."

Inevitably the conversation wound its way back to its
wo participants. "And what's new with old Roger Aller-
on?" asked David.

"Nothing much," Roger replied with pretended casual-
ess, "except that he's getting married."

"*Married? Wonderful! But to whom?*"

"Gloria. I know, I told you I enlisted in the chaplaincy
ust to escape her. But that's exactly the reason she's
narrying me! She told me last time I was home on leave
hat if I had accepted her proposition to go into her fa-
her's business after marrying her, she'd never have gone
hrough with the wedding. Because she couldn't have
gone on respecting me. But when I turned her down flat
nd enlisted—that's when she decided she simply *had*
o marry me, and on my terms. Can you figure out wom-

en! Now I have to start boning up on all those sex book
I've been recommending to all the about-to-be-marrie
airmen." He paused. "Oh, there's something I've bee
meaning to ask you, David, ever since I came back fror
leave. We've set the wedding date for when my tou
here ends. That's also when your hitch ends in the Ai
Force, and I was thinking that on your way home t
Brooklyn—David, would you mind being best man a
my wedding?"

"Best man?" David was taken aback. But your denom
ination specifically forbids a member of another faith t
take part in any way in a religious service of yours, h
was about to say. He checked himself, however; surel
his friend knew what he was doing. "I'd be *honorea*
Roger." He added wistfully, "And jealous too of you
good fortune. But I'm sure the *nachus* I'll be gettin
from you will counteract my jealousy." And then he ha
to explain what *nachus* was, its implications, ramifica
tions and Tante Dvorah.

Exactly five days after the Fairfield Air Refuelin
Squadron had landed at Goose Bay, disaster struck. Dis
aster, to be exact, did not *strike;* it was *delivered.* O
Monday the first batch of mail arrived from the States
and its effect upon some of the men was completel
demoralizing.

A letter from one wife amounted to exactly two words
"Love," and her name scrawled on a packet of bills sh
was forwarding to her husband. Another wife wrot
that she now found home so unbearably lonely tha
she spent all her free time away from it, night as well a
day, which news impelled her distraught husband t
implore David to get him shipped back to Fairfiel
because his wife was going to have a baby, and h
wanted to get home in time to be its father.

At subsequent mail calls, there were at least a scor
of wives whose letters amounted to little more tha
carefully detailed dossiers of their latest aches an
pains with their locations (one sent along her newes
X-rays) and the children's maladies and broken bones. A

ew wives even made a point of including a death notice r two (". . . and the day before he dropped dead, he ooked healthier than you," wrote one wife), sometimes ot even of a family acquaintance, but of someone vhose obituary in the Fair City *News* had sounded in- eresting.

But the worst offender, by far, was the wife who vrote her husband five letters warning him not to be- ieve a word everyone else was writing him about her, or he would leave him forever. When the distraught hus- and showed the threatening letters to David, he asked he obvious question:

"Well, what *has* everyone been writing you about our wife?"

"That's just it!" the man moaned. "That's just it! No one's written me a *word* about my wife. The only etters I keep getting are hers telling me not to believe vhat other people are writing—*and they're not writing ne at all.* I tell you I'm going out of my mind!" he cried, and David believed him.

When he was not busy reading mail pressed upon him by distressed men, or writing Mitchell asking him to mplore the Fairfield wives to do anything to their hus- bands but write them, he tried to do his bit in aiding he maximum efforts of the squadron, when all its planes took to the air for large-scale refueling operations.

On these occasions David always came along to see the men off, usually around midnight. Then, while wait- ng for the planes to return from three to six hours later, he would fill up a truck with jugs of hot coffee and trays of sandwiches coaxed out of an obliging mess sergeant. This food he brought to the maintenance crews, and with them he waited up in the minus-ten-degree hang- ars for the planes to return; then, as each plane landed, David would drive out to meet it and give its men cups of hot coffee and one-ounce bottles of whiskey cajoled from the Flight Surgeon's Office.

The crews, for their part, tried to express their appre- ciation of David's efforts by inviting him to fly along with them on subsequent sorties. It goes without saying that he declined all such gracious invitations with a great deal of thanks and no less trepidation.

All this time the letters continued to pour into Goose Bay, and few of them were as morale-boosting as the ones from Tante Dvorah ("Try and arrange to go back to Mississippi by *train*, you hear me? . . . Stay out of drafts. . . . How's your nose? . . . Don't talk to strangers . . . Do you remember to wear your rubbers and hat outdoors? . . . Only nine more months and you'll be home, believe it or not! . . . I've picked out a nice assortment of girls already for you to select from. . . . Those *meshuganah* astronuts—some fine mothers they have! Any *real* mother would have stretched herself out in front of those capsules just to stop them from getting inside. . . . I can hardly wait to see you, David. . . .") and from Uncle Asher ("How did you enjoy your first airplane ride? Wasn't it tremendously *exciting!* I've always wanted to see Labrador, but isn't there any more to the country than the snow and ice and cold you keep writing about? We miss you, especially on your birthday we missed you. To celebrate it, Tante planted ten trees in your honor in Israel, and I ran a big special on McIntoshes and Bartletts. You should see the girls your Tante has lined up for you here! Better you should marry some Eskimo up there. . . .").

Each successive mail call brought the hard-working, lonely, miserable, bored, freezing, depressed, restless men up at Goose Bay further news from Fairfield about colds, and measles, and how the household was falling apart without its head, and bills, and stomach-aches, and obscene anonymous phone calls, and broken vacuum cleaners, and how the children were always killing each other, and broken television sets, and the latest accident with the car, and wasn't it awful the way so many planes were crashing lately? and guess who was pregnant at Fairfield and her husband had been in Japan for eleven months now? and broken washing machines, and how nice it was for husband's friend to try to keep her from getting too lonely, and diarrhea, and how other wives were stepping out on their men, and pregnancies, and things were so boring, and rain, and how wonderfully well the family was now getting on without any man around, and damp drive-ins, and Mother had warned her never to marry a serviceman, and more bills, and a separation like this gave a person a chance to see if they really missed the other, and why didn't she feel that she did? and the baby almost died last night but she was perfectly all right now, and how she hated being cooped up in the house all the time, and Bingo's latest winners, and was the rumor true that the TDY was being extended for still *another* ninety days?

Meanwhile, David was having his own troubles parrying the ever-increasing flying invitations. He appreciated the thought very much, certainly much more than the invitations themselves which he did not appreciate at all. Yet he could hardly say, "Thanks all the same, fellas, but I have this flying phobia, you see." And so each invitation was declined with a different excuse but with the same devout hope that, after his first twenty refusals, someone would realize there were, roughly, two million things he would rather do than fly. However, so accustomed were the men to regarding flying as a function as natural as walking or getting drunk, that the invitations continued unabated.

Even without a phobia, David would have hesitated to fly for no good reason, especially since a recent rash of aircraft accidents in the States made *not* flying seem so much more attractive. Equally disturbing was the fact that a man bailing out of a stricken plane over Goose Bay was likely to freeze to death in the air before he even reached the ground to freeze to death.

The Fairfield A.R.S. itself was not exempt from accidents. A propeller reversal malfunction had caused one of the KC's to skid into a snowbank, fortunately with no injury to anyone. Three days later a fire broke out in the lower cargo compartment of another KC; it was spotted, again fortunately, before take-off and the flight was aborted safely. Several other such narrow aborts—

usually the extreme cold was a factor in each—gave impetus to talk of a "black cloud" hovering over the squadron, and all the while flying invitations to David mounted ominously.

Casually he kept reminding the men of what had happened to a ship when a fellow named Jonah once boarded it. None of the men, however, seemed to be Biblically minded; some even expressed the superstitious thought that a chaplain could somehow dissipate the "black cloud." Possibly they reasoned that he could cause no harm to an aircraft that could not be corrected, as with Jonah, by tossing him overboard.

As invitations to fly soared, David became the fastest man on base with an excuse to stay on the ground. No woman ever defended her virtue more zealously, or with greater success, than he guarded his phobia.

Then one day the squadron was assigned to a special exercise consisting of three consecutive turn-around missions with no rest in between. For twenty hours David busied himself on the line seeing the planes off, scrounging food for the maintenance men in the hangars and the crews as they returned, pooh-poohing "black cloud" talk which was multiplying as aborts were increasing, and parrying flying invitations.

While waiting for the exhausted men to make final preparations for the third consecutive mission, David, exhausted, dozed off on the floor of the office in the Big Hangar. Before he could savor much of his sleep, however, he was shaken awake by a large, powerful hand.

Groggily looking up, he saw Colonel Kingsbury towering above him looking, with his white sideburns, like a young Alp. All the Colonel's swarthiness now seemed to be concentrated in blue-black half-moons beneath his dark eyes; the rest of his face was chalky and drawn, sharpening his already sharp features into caricatures of themselves. "Come on, Chaplain."

"Wha—?"

"You're flying with us on this last turn-around mission."

David gagged.

"The bus is leaving for the aircraft in ten minutes." The Colonel leaned over and pulled him, struggling, to his feet. "Come on, you can sleep on the plane, Chaplain. You'll have nothing else to do aboard anyway."

"I can't!" David exclaimed. "I mean, I—I don't understand ..."

"It's simple enough," the Colonel explained impatiently. "We want you along for luck."

"For luck?" David said, with manufactured indignation. "For *luck!* Colonel, what am I—*a rabbit's foot?*"

"Yes," Colonel Kingsbury replied. "If some of the men are foolish enough—perhaps 'exhausted' is the correct word—to believe in this black cloud business, they're just as likely to believe that you're a rabbit's foot."

"But—but—but that's nonsense!"

To David's consternation, the Colonel conceded the point without relinquishing his argument. "Of course, it's nonsense. But what with three grueling missions in a row and this spate of aborts and near accidents lately, the men's morale is scraping bottom. And that's serious."

"What can *I* do about it, other than what I have been—?"

"Same thing I'm doing, even though I have no aircraft of my own," the Colonel replied. "Come along on this last mission tonight. It's not very much really, but if it gives the men a little lift, it's worth it. Isn't it?"

David faltered. "Colonel, I—I—I—"

"We don't have time to talk. We have to board our planes now." He grabbed him by the arm.

David pulled away. "I'm not going . . ." he said, and both men were startled.

Colonel Kingsbury looked at David incredulously. "What do you *mean*, you're not going?"

"I—I—I mean, I don't see the necessity, Colonel. I'm a chaplain, not a witch doctor. And then I know nothing about planes. I'd only be in the way in case of trouble and—"

Colonel Kingsbury interrupted, scowling darkly. "Who said there'll be trouble? Don't tell me you believe in that black cloud too!"

"Of course not," David said, "but . . ." His words faded away as he realized that his phobia was just as ridiculous as any superstition. Surely he could manage this one flight, much as he dreaded it. With God's help . . . "Of course not," he repeated.

"All right then. Let's go." The Colonel propelled David toward the door. "You know, Chaplain, it may not be a bad idea for you to fly regularly with the men after this. Much as I dislike chaplains, you seem to have been of some help here because, strangely enough, the men like you and—"

"Fly *regularly!*" David stopped short, horrified. "I *can't.*"

The Colonel paused. *"What* did you say?"

He doesn't have any authority to make *me* fly just because he happens to be a colonel and I'm only a lieutenant, David told himself. He's just another man, that's all, and I'm just another—coward? Yet coward or no, even Strike Two or no—"Colonel, I just can't."

The Colonel glowered hatefully at David, but before he could speak, Alex Winkler burst into the room.

"The bus is leaving in five minutes. Come on, Chap."

Colonel Kingsbury cast a contemptuous glance at David. "The Chaplain isn't coming with us."

Alex's pudgy face fell. "He *isn't?*" he said strangely disturbed. "Why not?"

"Ask him," the Colonel sneered and stomped out of the office.

Alex looked beseechingly at David. "Chaplain? Aren't you coming with us?" David hesitated, then shook his head without saying a word. *"Why* aren't you coming with us?"

David lowered his eyes. "Why such a fuss about having me along anyway?"

"You're a chaplain and—" Alex checked himself.

"Yes . . . ?"

Alex bit his lip. "Forget it." He turned to leave.

You're a chaplain—the words echoed in David's ears and made him flinch as he noted for the first time that Alex's cherubic face was lined with exhaustion and his childishly full lips were constricted with tension. And suddenly he found himself thinking that it was one thing to pretend to be denying military authority, but it was something altogether different—and reprehensible—to refuse a request put to him as a *chaplain*. What reason could he offer himself for that, other than that he was taking himself not only off the tightrope but out of the entire ball game as well? He was a chaplain, and he had to act like one now.

"Okay, Alex, maybe you'll explain it to me on the plane."

"You mean, you're coming?" Alex exclaimed.

David forced a smile. "Would I joke about something like this?"

The men on board the bus greeted David warmly.

"Say, Chap, where's our whiskey?"

"Why do you always make us wait for it till we return?"

"You'll be sure to put in a good word for all of us when you get up there now, won't you, Chaplain?"

"Where do you think I'm going tonight?" David asked. "I only volunteered for a flight, not the Pearly Gates."

Everyone laughed but David. He felt too tense, so tense that he began to wonder whether it was possible for *rigor mortis* to set in *before* death.

Colonel Kingsbury was the last man to board the bus. He addressed the group, "Men, I know I told you the Chaplain would be coming along on this last mission, but —but I couldn't locate him in time to invite him to—"

David quickly interrupted. "Here I am, Colonel. I got your message." He offered no explanation, because he had none—even for himself.

Colonel Kingsbury's face mirrored surprise, but no trace of a pardon. "I'm glad you were able to make it, Chaplain," he said tersely. "Let's go, driver."

The bus started off, gliding forward like a sled on the snow-packed terrain.

"Say, Chaplain, who are you flying with?" someone called.

Alex spoke up quickly. "The Chaplain is coming with us. Aren't you, Chaplain?"

"That's right. I'm going with Major Givney," David said, wondering about Alex's insistence.

The bus stopped in front of a plane, and the driver called out its number. As its crew rose to their feet, the flight surgeon stood up to make an announcement. "I'm giving you all some pills to take now," Dr. Shannon said, distributing one white capsule to each man. "You men have been without sleep for twenty-five hours now, and you won't be able to get to bed for at least another eight. These pills will help eliminate fatigue and keep you from falling asleep."

The men all around David swallowed their pills, and automatically so did he. And then, just as the pill was clearing his esophagus, the doctor's words registered upon his consciousness. "O my God!" he exclaimed softly.

"Chaplain," Alex said, regarding him curiously, "why are you sticking your finger down your throat?"

"Oh," said David, as he removed his finger from his mouth. "Am I?"

"Well, bottoms up." Alex swallowed his capsule and said, "They're really very effective, these goofballs. I know I can't get to sleep for almost thirteen hours after taking one—"

David let out a groan.

"—without those sleeping pills Doc gives us when we land."

"Sleeping pills!" *Sleeping pills*. That was it, he suddenly remembered, he had a whole bottle of them back in his room, the same life-savers he had taken on his flight to Goose Bay.

Inevitably the bus reached Major Givney's plane, and the Major, Chuck Conte the navigator, Sergeant Banks the flight engineer, Sergeant Cribbs the boom operator, Airman Second Class Slevin the radio operator, and Alex Winkler headed for the door. But David stayed behind, explaining, "There's something in my room that I have to go back for."

Colonel Kingsbury came up to him. "Take-off time is in one hour," he said suspiciously. "You're liable to miss it if you return now to the V.O.Q. What is it that you have to get there?"

David faltered because he could think of nothing to say except the truth, and what would the others think about his taking pills to make him sleep when all the others had to resort to goofballs to keep them awake?

"He needs his arctic survival equipment. Ours is already on board from our previous flights," Alex noted as he disembarked.

Colonel Kingsbury nodded, and the bus moved on, continuing to discharge its other passengers. Finally, even the Colonel got off the bus, and David was left alone with the driver, a dubious look the Colonel had thrown him upon departing, and his phobia.

The bus, turning around, headed for the V.O.Q. as David debated with him whether to pray for a blowout, a whiteout, or a small wreck. But before he could make up his mind, the bus reached the V.O.Q.

Alighting from the bus, David dashed toward his room —why hurry? he asked himself suddenly, and slowed to a shuffle—got his bottle of sleeping pills and bundle of arctic survival equipment, then ran all the way back to the bus. He couldn't miss the plane on *purpose*, he had sullenly decided in the room—that would be *cheating*, dammit.

The bus returned to his aircraft, passing on the way (he noted not without aggravation) two other buses which had broken down in the snow. For David, Fate had turned out to be a sturdy bus.

He boarded the plane and found the latrine with no difficulty at all. There he disgorged everything, it seemed, save a few vital organs. Then he swallowed two of his pills, one to counteract the goofball and the other to put him to sleep.

Emerging finally from the latrine, he said to the crew nearby, as casually as he could force it, "I hope you fellows don't take it personal if I fall asleep on you during the flight. I'm really tired."

Major Givney ran up the engines. "Just wait till we take off, Chaplain. It's a whole lot safer to stay awake during take-offs and landings."

David restrained himself from asking why. Better, he figured, that he shouldn't know. He had enough to worry about as it was.

He walked back to the cavernous upper deck, donned a parachute harness and chest pack, and strapped himself into a canvas seat. Then he wiped his wet palms, neck, forehead, the backs of his knees, the insides of his elbows, and the small of his back. And when he had finished wiping the sweat from his back, it was time to start drying his damp palms again.

Suddenly the plane lurched forward across the snowy field with the gathering momentum of a snowball sliding down a mountainside. A quick spurt of speed and the plane took to the air while David exulted: We made it, we made it! But his exultation evaporated as soon as he realized exactly what it was that had been made. The plane was now airborne and would remain so for the next six hours unless, of course, it crashed. He shuddered, wiped his forehead and bit off half of another sleeping pill, then prayed for sleep to engulf him.

Almost an hour later David was still awake, still perspiring, still nauseous, and wondering now whether sleeping pills worked only through the power of suggestion. He thought of taking still another sleeping pill, even considered for a moment swallowing the entire bottle, then compromised by nibbling on the second half of his third pill.

At last the barbiturate began taking effect, but in easy stages. Or was it his cramped sitting position, with all his arctic clothing and the parachute, that was putting first his left leg asleep, then his left arm, then his right arm? He could hardly wait any longer for his churning stomach to doze off too.

Sergeant Cribbs chose that moment to become friendly. "How's it going, Chaplain?" the boom operator asked and slapped David on the left thigh, setting off an agonizing reaction of tingling nerves throughout his sleeping extremities, which gave him the excrutiating feeling that small boys were racing through his flesh running boards against the picket fences of his body fibers.

David yelled out in pain, and the sergeant laughed. "You bet, Chaplain. Geronimo! Come on now. You want to see the refueling, don't you? We'll be hooking up pretty soon."

"Refueling?" Why not, thought David. It would certainly help him take his mind off his phobia. "All right." He unbuckled his seat belt which, he was annoyed to note, he had buckled to his parachute ring.

Sergeant Cribbs led him forward to the navigator's station and down a ladder there to the lower deck, then walked back with him to the tail section. There on the plane's underside, a few feet forward of the tail, was a glass-enclosed pod which contained a panel of instruments and a leather pallet on which the sergeant stretched out prone. Below him, through the glass bubble, David saw what must have been the sky but looked like gray sour cream.

The sergeant strapped himself into a shoulder harness, then pushed a stick, and a long steel tube with two small black wings at its end dropped away from the aft end of the pod. "That's the boom," he said, pointing to the tube. "It's through this that we give them the gas, about five hundred gallons a minute. It's operated with this control stick. With it I can fly those two little wings like a miniature plane." He pushed the stick in four different directions, and the boom responded accordingly. "See?" He pressed something else, and suddenly the boom doubled in size. "See that? I can extend this baby too. Only I have to be very careful, because it's done with such power that I can wreck the receiver. Hey, look—we're breaking through the soup now. What do you know? It's daytime already . . ."

David looked through the glass pod at the earth below, swathed now in soft pastel colors, and thought that he could almost estimate its age. For Labrador was a vast birthday cake iced in white frosting, with evergreen trees dotting its crust like birthday candles.

A light flashed on in the pod, and the sergeant pointed to it. "They've found us. That light means we're about to make contact."

"Go ahead," David sighed.

Major Givney's voice was heard: "The receiver is coming into position."

"Ready for contact," Sergeant Cribbs said.

"Receiver ready," said an unfamiliar voice which must have belonged to the pilot of the B-47 that would soon be refueled.

Suddenly a gigantic silver form dropped out of the sky above them, so gigantic it looked as if a piece of sky had broken off. A monstrously large plane which dwarfed the KC-97, itself huge, the receiver was a couple of hundred feet wide and the tail was taller than the apartment house David lived in back in Brooklyn.

"What's *that!*" he exclaimed. "That's no B-47."

"That's its big brother, the B-52," the boom operator said. "Big, ain't she?"

Stealthily the B-52, some one hundred feet below now, crept up on the KC-97, growing larger all the while, until it seemed to David that the bomber would do to the tanker what the whale had done to Jonah. But Sergeant Cribbs remained unperturbed. "Forward eighty feet, up forty feet," he said, and the B-52 advanced so much that David had to restrain himself from yelling, "Look out!" Yet in the midst of his inner turbulence he felt, like the eye in the center of a hurricane, remarkably calm. For in this situation he at least knew what he was afraid of.

"Right height . . . closing rapidly . . ." Sergeant Cribbs continued. "Forward forty . . . to your left, four . . . forward twenty . . . down two . . ."

Now, with the sergeant manipulating the boom toward an alley on top of the B-52's fuselage, it almost looked as if the two metal birds were courting, and with such grimness that their lives might have depended upon the success of their mating which, David realized with a start, they did if the coupling was not managed with the utmost precision.

Despite its gigantic size, the B-52 was proving to be the shy one of the pair, ducking as the tanker kept rising above the bomber, as if both were as reluctant as David for their union to be consummated. "You see," the sergeant explained, "the upwash from the 52 pushes our tail up, and the downwash from our tail pushes the 52 down. So both pilots have to be crackerjacks at this job." Then, into his radio: "Forward ten . . ."

In a sudden, *too* sudden burst of speed, the bomber moved in almost close enough to ram the tanker and, as the boom elongated, David felt himself shrivel inside his skin. Tearing his eyes from the relentlessly oncoming B-52, he fastened both his hands to the metal ring of his parachute.

"To your right, three . . . fifteen feet from contact . . . ten, eight, six, four, two . . . hold it there."

The boom inched forward into the bomber's alley as David uneasily noted that the two aircraft were so close together now that he could see where the receiving pilot had cut himself while shaving that morning. Abruptly Sergeant Cribbs pushed hard on his control stick, and the boom buried itself in the bomber's receptacle with a crash like that of a train wreck.

"Contact!" the sergeant cried, and another light flashed on in the pod. He turned toward David. "That's all there is to it."

"That's *all?*" said David, his eyes riveted on the thirsty B-52. "That's *enough.*"

Sergeant Cribbs chuckled. "Now we just give them the gas, making sure they keep their distance of thirty feet all the time. Major Givney now has to keep increasing the speed past 340 miles per, but gradually, because the more gas I give them the heavier they get and the faster they have to fly to keep from stalling and—"

David, his eyes still fastened to the B-52, interrupted. "I know it's only my imagination, of course, but right now it looks to me like—" He pointed to the bomber which, to his untutored eye, seemed to be inexorably overtaking the tanker.

Sergeant Cribbs faced forward and his face blanched. Now David could see the reason why: The boom, at an obtuse angle to the B-52 and the earth below, was rapidly moving into perpendicular position, a graphic indication that in seconds the B-52 would be ramming the KC-97.

"Breakaway!" Sergeant Cribbs cried.

"Breakaway!" the receiver pilot shouted.

"BREAKAWAY!" David yelled too, and he yanked his parachute ring.

Swiftly the boom leaped out from the bomber's receptacle, so swiftly that the boom almost tore off from the tanker and flew away on its own. At the same instant, the B-52 dropped into a dive and the KC-97 veered into a climb, sliding the floor away from beneath David's feet and knocking him into the pod.

In a moment he was sliding over the boom operator —feet, knees, waist, shoulders—and falling toward the plane's tail. Blindly he grabbed the sergeant's head, anchoring his hands around his throat. Cribbs reached out and caught hold of him, also by the neck, and the two of them clung together, head upon head.

"Hold on!" he shouted to David—as if he would ever let go!

Gradually the pressure on David's throat eased, and the boom operator's throat relaxed; the tanker was leveling off. They released each other's necks, and David got unsteadily to his feet.

"Now we go home?" he inquired hopefully.

Cribbs massaged his throat without erasing the finger-marks from his flesh. "In a while. When we finish our job." He turned his attention to maneuvering another hook-up. "Forward . . . left . . . up . . ."

Contact was made again, under David's watchful eyes. The tanker's gas poured into the bomber while he automatically began to recite from Psalms.

Sergeant Cribbs called out in the middle of the

Twenty-Third Psalm: "Tanker ready to disconnect."

"Receiver ready to disconnect."

The boom telescoped itself with a crash as the sergeant pushed a switch. "Bye-bye, mother." He unstrapped himself from his harness and stood up, stretching. "*Now* we go home." Suddenly his body stiffened. "Hey! *Don't* do that—" And his arm shot out and grabbed David's hand.

"Wha—?"

"Why, you almost opened your chute there. Playing with your ring like that— What is it? All of a sudden you don't look so good."

David let out a gasp.

"Chaplain?"

David swallowed the rapidly rising lump in his throat without diminishing it. "I just remembered. Before, when everyone started yelling 'Breakaway'—well, I yanked the ring."

"You're joking!"

David shook his head dumbly and pulled the parachute ring with all his might. There was no discernible result this time either, except for the ring's coming off in his hand.

Cribbs whistled. "Say, there *is* something wrong with your chute."

"Oh," said David.

The sergeant unfastened the defective parachute, then picked up another pack from a pile of them near the pod and handed it to him.

"Thank you, but suppose we *test* this new pack first—"

The boom operator shook his head.

David stopped buckling on the pack. "No?"

"We can't, Chaplain. I mean—well, we can test the chute all right to see if it opens when you pull on the ring, but if it *does* open—I mean, *when* it opens—I don't know how to repack it for you to be able to use."

David shrugged. "Hardly seems worth all the trouble to put it on."

"You *have* to put it on," said Cribbs. "That's the regulation: Everyone *must* wear a chute."

"Even if it doesn't open?"

"It doesn't say anything in the reg about the chute opening," the sergeant replied, and he fastened the pack to David's harness, "but, of course, it's *supposed* to."

"I see." He thanked Sergeant Cribbs for the refueling demonstration, then left him and hurried back, nauseous as before, to his seat. There he gulped down his fourth sleeping pill—or was it his fifth?—and tried to talk himself down into slumber.

Relax, damn you, *relax*. Go to sleep now, and stop toying with your chute ring again, and stop wondering whether this pack also is a dud. You'll never know if it is anyhow. So reeeelax. Just try to go limp now, all over, and go to sleep. Everything is all right. You hear? Everything is all right. Stop worrying already. Go to sleep . . . everything is all right . . . one, two, three, four, five, six, seven, eight, nine . . . lullaby and good night . . . all right . . . everything is . . . sleep . . .

Someone was fighting him, pulling at his belt, grabbing at his shoulders, shaking him by his harness, hitting, shouting, yelling—such a pogrom of a dream! Go away, leave me be, let me sleep, one, two, three, four, five, relax, stop worrying, everything is all right, sleep, just sleep, lullaby and good—What? You *still* here? Aw, leave me alone, let me sleep, come on . . .

". . . white smoke!"

"Relax . . ."

". . . magnesium fire!"

"Stop worrying already . . ."

". . . alarm bell!"

"Everything is all right . . ."

". . . sixty seconds to jump!"

"Relax . . ."

". . . jump!"

"Jump . . ."

". . . *Chaplain!*"

"Alex . . ."

". . . CHAPLAIN!"

"Ssh, everything all right . . ."

Finally! No more grabbing, shaking, pulling, shouting,

elling—no more dream. Now, just to relax again . . . to
top worrying . . . to sleep . . . everything all right . . .
ne, two, three, four . . . lullaby and . . . sleeeeeeeeeee . . .

Hands pulling at him, unbuckling him, helping him
ut, talking, chattering, jabbering away like. Sentences
url ed at him, whole paragraphs, curving away, out of
each. His head so heavy, neck so weak, tongue so thick,
why didn't they leave him alone?

A sudden blast of freezing air startled David half
awake. Gasping, he stepped back to get out of the draft.
But they kept pushing him from behind through the
open doorway in front of him. All that empty space out
there, he mused, soon to be filled by him and his faulty
parachute.

And then dimly, as in a nightmare, he recalled: *faulty
parachute!* And he cried out: *"Oh!"*

But they—who were They anyway?—paid him no
heed. All They did was to continue pushing him forward—toward all that void.

Frantically he yelled, "My parachute—it doesn't
work!"

"What a kidder," someone laughed. "Always joking."
And someone else gave him a shove which sent him
tripping even closer to the great freezing empty beyond.

"Look!" In desperation David yanked at his
parachute ring, remembering too late that he shouldn't
have done that because if the parachute did open, by accident, no one would be able to repack it for him.

But—should he feel grateful or what?—this time too
the chute failed to open, for he had—now he could feel
it—yanked his parka pocket instead of his parachute
ring because—God!—the ring was nowhere to be found.

And how could he bail out of the plane without knowing where his ring was! Frantic, he felt his chest,
his stomach, his legs, his back, but there was no ring
there or anywhere. He could not even find his parachute
pack. All he had was his parka and its wolverine-hair-
trimmed hood and himself—nothing more. They were
making him bail out without his parachute! The care-

less, thoughtless, inconsiderate, dirty . . . What a way to go—damn!—all the way down . . . oh, nuts . . . and then, chopped liver, like canapés all over the landscape.

"Wait!" he cried. "Please?"

But They didn't. A final shove and he was outside the plane plunging through the subfreezing air, falling fast. Good-bye, Tante Dvorah, good-bye, Uncle Asher, good-bye . . . But he wasn't dead yet, and where there was life —maybe there would be a snowdrift for him to land on, a *big* one. Ground below! This was it . . . coming up fast now . . . people all around, awaiting him, watching for the splash . . . coming . . . coming . . . slowly now . . . slowerly . . . landing . . . land—*Land!* He made it— *alive* yet!

Stairs? Careful now, slippery . . . one, two, three, four, lullaby and—

People in front, people behind—why were They all hitting him? Surprised just because he had made it without a parachute. Flaring the nostrils—that's what did it. Broke the fall.

". . . white smoke . . . black smoke . . ."

What were They all babbling about?

". . . alarm . . . jump . . . sleeping . . . refused . . . coolness . . ."

And who cared?

"Aren't we *ever* going to get to bed today?" someone yelled.

Laughter, more slapping. "You bet, Chaplain!"

Finally!—the bus, thank God.

On.

Moving.

Pills.

"Take."

Took, swallowed.

Slowing down.

Someone: "What for?"

Answered: "Counteract those goofballs."

What?

Stopping.

"Sedative . . . make you sleep now."

228

SEDATIVE? *"Oh, no!"* David cried, not even sure that his cry had been voiced. No! He was off the bus now, running between snowdrifts toward the V.O.Q., running, slipping, sliding, gliding, he dared not stop . . .

No . . . no . . . no . . . not *another* sleeping pill! He so wanted to be able to wake up *sometime*.

Chapter : 16

DAVID, opening his eyes to behold naught but inky blackness, was not so much disturbed by his first thought— Where am I?—as he was by his second one—*Who* am I?

Summoning all his strength, he raised his right hand. Automatically his rubbery fingers found a light switch on the wall. He pushed hard with all his might and flicked the switch. (Such a little switch, but what a *racket* it made!)

Everything remained dark.

Perhaps if he were now to pry his eyes open . . . That did it—light, at last. Too bright! Close eyes. Now to open them slowly, an eyelash at a time. Thataboy . . .

Staring at him from across the room was a long, olive-drab fellow, dressed in an overgrown snowsuit, with hooded eyes, curly black hair, a belligerent nose, and a soggy hand on a light switch. He recoiled at the sudden confrontation, and when the other fellow recoiled too, all at once David realized he was looking into a mirror. So *that's* who he was.

He had the feeling that he was dissolving. Sweating freely in the overheated room, he methodically stripped off his blouse, quilted flying pants, woolen shirt, woolen trousers, muk-luks, sweater, felt liner, woolen socks, another pair of woolen socks, a third pair of woolen socks, a pair of cotton socks, underwear, earmuffs.

Struggling to his feet, he took off his scarf, then grabbed a robe and a towel, and headed—upstream, it seemed—to the shower room. He found two other officers there who greeted him with enthusiasm. "Geronimo," he responded politely.

He turned on the shower and stepped under it—warm at first, then increasingly cooler until it was ice cold and he felt sober. Relinquishing the shower, he began to dry himself haphazardly, trying to make sense of the others' allusions to the previous day's max effort. But about all he could understand was that it was now one o'clock in the morning and that—there was no doubt about it now—he had survived his flight.

Parrying further invitations (*"Of course* I'll fly with your crew," he said, "the very next time I feel like flying again!"), he returned to his room. There he found that Alex had returned and was drunk again. Else why would he be looking under the beds and calling, "Come out, come out, wherever you are . . . Chaplain?"

Alex, hearing the door close, looked up at David, and suddenly he was no longer playful. "Well, if it isn't the hero himself!" he exclaimed sardonically.

David flushed, taken aback as much by his roommate's tone of voice as by his appearance which, with the chubby face now haggard, the full lips drawn tight in a sneer and the blue eyes almost purple from the reflection of their bloodshot settings, presented the startling appearance of a degenerate cherub.

"Well, Chaplain," Alex was saying mockingly, and it was hard to tell at which of them his derision was aimed, "now at least you know *why* I get drunk, don't you?"

David shook his head in perplexity, and his head seemed painfully to shake itself back at him.

A sound like a moan fell from Alex's lips. "But I wasn't always like that—the way you saw me yesterday—and that's the *truth!* I *loved* flying. I was the one R.O.T.C. boy who was going to make the Air Force a career. Because all my life I've always wanted to be part of something *big*. Lots of guys are always railing against people becoming little cogs in big machines. But not me. I never minded being a cog—wanted to, as a matter of fact—provided the machine was only big and important enough. Like SAC is. SAC's bigness, its importance rubs off on a fellow, gives him size, dimension, if you know what I mean." He paused. "*Do* you know what I mean, Chaplain? About how important it is for a fellow to become part of something important, maybe even try to help it along in his own small way—"

David nodded. "Yes, I know what you mean, Alex," he said. "That's one reason why I became a rabbi."

Alex heaved a sigh which materialized as a very fine spray whose high alcoholic content stung David's eyes. "Gee, I envy that. I mean, being able to make religion your life. Religion gives a fellow magnitude, if you know what I mean—purpose too. At least that's what they say. I never could feel it myself that way—religion, I mean. Or about the family farm either. And you can't force those feelings, can you? You either feel them or you don't. Oh, farming is okay, I suppose. It gives people food and milk and stuff. It's necessary, all right. But it's not *exciting*. It's not *important*. It's not *big*. It's not *SAC*."

David could not resist a smile. "I never thought I'd live to hear anyone wax romantic over SAC—and in Goose Bay yet!"

Alex's lips twisted into a smile, too, but there was no pleasure in it. "Everyone gets romantic over something he's lost. You can't help it."

"Lost? What are you talking about?"

But Alex did not hear the question. He was staring straight ahead and saying, "If it wasn't for that crash . . . that damned rotten crash!" His smooth face crumbled like a cookie in a child's hands, and he turned away.

"Crash?" David repeated, at a loss. Then he remembered. Colonel Kingsbury had alluded to it during their first conversation together; subsequently other men had mentioned it, but Alex himself had never spoken of it

231

before. "Oh, yes. Some of the other fellows—they told me about it."

Alex turned on David. "Did they also tell you how it feels to be hanging by your heels from a plane that's exploding? Did they?"

"Do you want to tell me about it?" David asked quietly, as he sat down on his bed.

Alex shrugged. "What's there to tell? Our number one prop never reversed, and we swerved into a ditch. The landing gear sheared off. And the plane caught fire." Suddenly, Alex was pacing the floor, his crooked path betraying his double burden of memory and alcohol. "On my left, Major Givney and Chuck Conte were diving out their front window, and Banks jumped through the window in front of me. And I just sat there—frozen with fear!" His pace quickened, yet his path became less erratic. "Then I heard them below calling my name, Alex! Alex! Alex! and I dove head first through my window. Only my chute caught on something inside, and I got hung up. And the right wing is ablaze, the flames licking at the fuel tank. The plane's going to blow any minute, and I'm hanging, hanging, hanging upside down from it!" Beads of perspiration glistened on his forehead. "Major Givney is on the ground below me, but he's too far away to help. Then I remember the knife in my shoulder scabbard. I—I manage to get it out. I hack at the damn harness, hack at myself, keep hacking away, and the flames getting closer to the fuel tank all the time. And then I'm loose! I fall. I'm running, yelling, 'Look out, she's going to blow! Look out, she's going to blow!'" Abruptly he stopped pacing and wiped his forehead with his hands. When he resumed talking, it was in a voice drained of all emotion. "I was still running, still yelling when they caught me. Only by that time the plane had already exploded. And if I had still been hanging there . . ." He shuddered and dropped down on his bed.

"Praise the Lord," David said softly, before inquiring, "Did they ever find out what caused the accident?"

Alex fell back on the bed and closed his red-rimmed eyes. "Oh, yes. They had an accident-investigating board and all that. They found ice crystals in one of the decreased solenoid valves—this damn cold! They made it impossible for the prop to reverse. Oh, they found out what happened to the plane all right, but not what happened to *me!*"

"Were you hurt badly, Alex?"

Alex sat up, his bloodshot eyes stabbing at David. "You saw! You saw for yourself yesterday on the plane . . ."

David flinched. "Alex, you're going to have to—to remind me. Those sleeping pills—I mean, the one Dr. Shannon gave us—well, I can't remember a thing about yesterday's flight."

Alex regarded him with wonder. "Can it be that some people are heroes by reflex, while others, like me, are—are—" He broke off.

"Alex, what did happen yesterday?" David insisted. "You've got to tell me."

"You mean you actually don't know?" David shook his head, and Alex shrugged. "Why not? Everyone else knows." He averted his gaze and looked out the window at the snow blowing outside. "It happened about an hour after the refueling. I spotted white smoke coming out of the number four engine. That's the first and last sign you get of a magnesium fire, an induction fire in its advanced stages. A fire like that burns an engine off a plane, just like that. White smoke means you have one minute—exactly sixty seconds, no more—to abandon ship before it blows." He jumped to his feet and began pacing anew. "I notified Major Givney. He feathered the engine, activated the CO_2, also sounded the alarm bell. I ran back to the escape hatch to prepare for bailing out. Then I saw you there in your seat—"

David grimaced. "Fast asleep . . . !"

"Yes," Alex nodded. "I ran over to wake you. I shook you hard, telling you about the fire, and you looked up and said—so calmly I'll never forget it!—'Don't worry, everything's all right.' But I was too panicky to listen. I yelled at you and unbuckled your seat belt, and all the time you're telling me everything's all right!" Savage-

233

ly David bit his lower lip. "And then—all of a sudden—everything *was* all right! No more white smoke! The scanner called out that it had changed to black. And just in time. Because in a few seconds more we'd all have bailed out. I know *I* would have. And it took a chaplain with zero flying hours to show me up for what I am—a—a *coward* . . . !" Alex's hands shot up to cover his face.

David jumped to his feet. "Alex, that doesn't make sense! You didn't do anything wrong . . ."

Alex's hands fell to his sides, and he cried, "You don't understand, Chaplain. You don't *know*. No one does, not even Marge. Yesterday wasn't the first time I've seen a magnesium fire. I've been seeing all kinds of things wrong with that plane ever since—the accident."

"And did you report those too?"

"No," Alex conceded. "I had more self-control before. All those other times weren't third turn-around missions. Besides, after the minute was up I knew they really hadn't been magnesium fires after all." He laughed humorlessly. "But this time—this time I was so exhausted I—"

David interrupted. "This time there really *was* a magnesium fire, or what looked like it at first. The others saw it too, didn't they?"

Alex shook his head. "You still don't get it, Chaplain. What I've been trying to tell you is that—that—" He slumped down on his bed, and lowered his eyes. "Chaplain, I'm *scared* of flying." David caught his breath. "Flying—it terrifies me now. Every time I have to go up, it ties me in knots inside . . . the thought of another accident . . . another plane exploding under me. I'm too scared to even drink before a flight, so I do it afterwards —as you've seen already—to unwind. I go to chapel every Sunday, but you know all I pray for? That we abort on the next couple of take-offs, even that our KC is put out of commission for lack of parts. I'm a pilot, but I'm scared to fly! And you're only a chaplain, but you're a hero . . ."

"For crying out loud, cut out that hero business. It's getting on my nerves!"

234

Alex sighed. "You're even *modest* like a hero . . ."

David gritted his teeth. "Look, Alex, about this problem of yours—why don't you go talk it over with someone? I'm sure that would help—"

"I *am* talking it over with someone."

"You are?" David felt relieved. "Good. Who—?"

Alex stared dumbly at him. "You."

"*Me?*" David faltered. "But—but there are *better* people to consult: one of the other chaplains, *any* of the other chaplains, perhaps the psychiatrist back at Fairfield, or even Colonel Kingsbury."

"No!" Alex turned on David. "No one else must know. I'm only telling you because we're friendly, and after I saw how brave you behaved—"

"*Again* with the brave?" David groaned. "Alex, *stop* it!"

"It's the truth—"

"The truth? Alex, the truth is—" David checked himself, in time. "The truth is I think you should discuss this matter with Colonel Kingsbury. I really think you should. He has eight thousand flying hours, and he's been in two crashes—"

Suspiciously Alex retorted, "You keep trying to palm me off on the Colonel. What's the matter? You want him to ground me? Or is it that you just can't understand how anyone could be terrified to take a plane up?"

"I wish I *didn't* understand!" David exclaimed. "I mean—Alex, not only do I understand, but I have the greatest *sympathy* for anyone in such a predicament, *believe* me."

"I bet!" Disconsolate, Alex dropped on his bed. "Even with all that excitement on the plane, you were fast asleep before we landed. And you've been sleeping fifteen hours straight without twitching a muscle or going to the john even once. All day long I was watching you from this bed, until the bar opened. All day long and you didn't move once. I thought you were dead! And I kept wishing *I* was."

David, feeling Alex's shame (it was his own), burst out: "Alex, four sleeping pills could make you, too, sleep like a dead man. That's my secret weapon. Alex, you think flying bothers *you? I'm* so scared of planes—it's *ridiculous!* You see, I have some sort of stupid phobia about flying. So whenever I go up I gorge myself on sleeping pills. Yesterday I took three or four. *That's* why I was so heroic: I was half-dead. One more sleeping pill, and I'd have been a *suicide!"*

Alex fixed David with an incredulous look. "You expect me to *believe* that?"

David hesitated. After all, he had tried, hadn't he? Did he *really* want to convince Alex that a childish phobia held sway over him—a mature, rational person, a rabbi and a chaplain?

Alex slumped back on his bed. "You're just trying to make me feel better. But it won't work, Chaplain. Because I *know* you're lying. I *saw* you yesterday—a hero—"

"Oh, shut up already!" David forced himself to go to his closet and open it. From his parka pocket he took out the half-empty bottle of sleeping pills. "Alex, if you ever tell anyone about this—" he warned his roommate and tossed the bottle on his bed. "Read the goddam label."

He turned then and grabbed the doorknob, twisting it hard, pulled open the door, and bolted out of the room.

Chapter : 17

DAVID was a veteran of so many service movies and war novels that he was not unprepared for most eventualities and inevitabilities at Goose Bay. One thing he had expected, and which surprised him by its initial absence, was horseplay in the barracks. Yet during the first half of the TDY, the men behaved as if they were completely unaware of what was anticipated of them.

The tameness of the officers coincided, unsurprisingly, with the great number of sorties the crews were flying. For the first six weeks, the hectic flying schedule left them too tired to do much else besides rest up for the next sortie.

With the end of the final maximum effort, however, the schedule was drastically reduced, and now the crews flew no more than twice a week. This afforded the men the opportunity to write more letters, read more books, see more movies, attend chapel more frequently, work out more in the gym, take additional USAFI courses, and gripe with greater regularity. Only the men were not particularly interested in writing more letters, attending chapel more frequently, reading more books, working out more in the gym, taking additional USAFI courses, or going to see another *Francis, the Talking Mule* film, which was the invariable feature at the base movie.

Of course, when the ensuing hi-jinx finally did begin, not all the officers participated. Most of the senior officers acted their age, but, alas, a few of the junior officers acted their age too. (One, a drunken Pgymalion of sorts, fashioned himself a snow-maiden in front of the V.O.Q. one moonlit night and then, overwhelmed by his creation, tried to mate with her. Fortunately, the resulting case of frostbite cleared up completely.)

Later the same week, the commencement of capers was officially inaugurated early one morning with, appropriately enough, the clash of what sounded like warped cymbals. David and Alex were startled awake to hear someone shout, "La Conga!"

David turned on the desk lamp and looked inquiringly at his roommate. "La Conga?" He looked at his wrist watch. "At three in the morning?"

Alex shrugged. "The two cheapest things up here, Chaplain, are liquor and dancing. So if you're not getting drunk on a conga line, you're simply losing money."

A chorus in the hall chanted, "One, two, three . . ."

"La Conga!" someone shouted, and cymbals clonged.

"One, two, three . . ."

"La Conga!"

Clong!

David got out of bed and went to the door. He opened it and looked out. At the other end of the hall was a conga line of four, equipped with garbage-can covers, bobbing and weaving its way toward him. Periodically they would stop at a door—though standing, they'd still be bobbing and weaving—open it, and inquire politely within, "La Conga?"

The responses ranged all the way from an epithet to a shoe. Yet the conga line proceeded forward, undiscouraged.

Alex smiled. "The second from the end—that was my spot on the last TDY. See what a ghastly fate you've saved me from, Chap?"

(That remark was as close as Alex had come to referring to his confession of the week before. He never mentioned the subject while he was sober, and neither did David, for since that night Alex had never gotten drunk.)

"How shall we greet them?" David asked. "What do we have here that's nice and soggy?" He picked up a pitcher of ice water on the desk. "Now this may not be the most Christian thing in the world to do . . ."

The One, Two, Three, La Conga! *Clong*, paused outside the door. "La Conga?" a malign voice inquired benignly, and the knob turned.

Before the door opened and David could respond aquatically, another voice in the hall called out: "No, that's the *Chaplain's* room." And, much to David's surprise, the conga line moved on as someone else hiccuped, "You wouldn't want the Chap to put a *hex* on us, would you!"

Another occasional early morning highlight was Urine Call, at which time a group of highly spirited bad Samaritans would go around awakening sleeping colleagues to remind them to respond with alacrity to the call of nature. If the roused colleague, unappreciative of the consideration being afforded him, chose to ignore the suggestion or offered an original one of his own in turn,

238

the ungrateful fellow would be hauled away bodily to the latrine. And no one was so foolish as to lock his door against the midnight intruders after one lieutenant ended up in a shower tied to his door, which had been deftly unscrewed from its frame.

After a while David grew so used to the pranks that he slept through them undisturbed. Of course, the cotton in each ear and the pillows over his head helped too.

Then one night one young drunk remembered that the Chinese had, centuries before, invented gunpowder, and David was awakened by what could only have been gunfire.

He sprang to open the door. Upon hearing further explosive reports, however, he locked it. This time Alex was flying and therefore unavailable to reassure David that no one would molest a chaplain, even to shoot him.

Several more shots sounded, all accompanied by gleeful laughs and shouts. Or were they moans? David *had* to see what was happening. He unlocked the door and opened it. Someone should get those guns before a man got killed, he told himself, even as he decided that that someone would not be he.

Down the hall several sodden souls were cheerfully lighting firecrackers—then they weren't guns, thank heaven!—and rolling them under closed doors. Sharp reports followed, then muffled oaths, and the pranksters gleefully moved on to their next victim.

They pushed more lighted firecrackers under another door and playfully poked their fingers into their ears as they awaited the explosions. This time, however, all remained quiet. No explosion, save a hiccup. Even David was mystified.

The pranksters lit six more firecrackers and rolled them under the same door. Still no sound, even after five minutes. Quietly one of the pranksters opened the door and stepped inside the dark room to investigate.

This time the result was both immediate and loud. The prankster was catapulted out of the dark room as if by some giant slingshot, ricocheted against his cohorts, knocking them down, rebounded off the wall, then fell in a heap on the floor.

The squadron adjutant, Captain Leonetti, appeared in the doorway and genially inquired, "Next?"

Just then the four pranksters seemed to lose all interest in firecrackers. They swiftly vanished from sight, leaving behind two cigarette lighters, a little blood on the woodwork, and their glee.

After that incident, things quieted down a good deal in the V.O.Q. No firecrackers exploded under anybody's bed, bladders filled up undisturbed, and the conga line staggered on only sporadically.

All antics had not ceased, however. David found out soon enough that all friskiness need not necessarily be performed with one's colleagues, or be accompanied by loud noises, or be enacted in public hallways.

He made this discovery one morning on the way to the shower room when he met a woman in the hallway. He greeted her cordially—up till then the Goose Bay V.O.Q., unlike Fairfield's B.O.Q., had been without maid service—and she responded amiably in return.

"Am I glad to see *you* here!" David said. "We certainly could use a woman's touch around here."

"You're a charmer," laughed the woman, a rather unattractive brunette in her twenties, thirties or forties.

Immediately, David returned to his room to tell the good news to Alex who was sweeping the floor unenthusiastically. "You can turn in your broom now!"

"You swept yesterday, don't you remember? It's my turn today."

"From now on, it's neither of our turns. We have maid service, starting today. How *about* that, Alex?"

"We do? You sure?" David nodded, and deliberately mussed up his made-up bed for emphasis. "Happy days!" Alex exclaimed, and ran out of the room. He soon reappeared without the broom and sprawled on his bed. "You know, I don't mind sweeping so much as making my bed. I guess it goes back to the time I was in flight school. They used to be so strict about the way you made up your bed—they would gig you for the slightest deviation—I used to sleep on the floor most of the time. Who told you about the maids, Chaplain?"

"I just ran into one in the hall now." David smiled. "She called me a charmer. She must be Canadian, I guess, like most of the other women employees here. You know, it's beyond me why any woman in her right mind would come to live at Goose Bay to work here for—"

Alex interrupted. "Chaplain, did you meet this woman near Major Albright's room?" David nodded, and Alex sighed. Then he got up and left the room without a word. He returned shortly with the broom and sadly resumed sweeping the floor.

"What's the *matter* with you, Alex? Didn't you hear me tell you that we had maid service now?"

"Chaplain," Alex said, "the service performed by the woman you met is not that of a maid."

"Oh . . . !"

"You mean you actually didn't know? You take showers here, don't you? How do you suppose Major Albright and the others got those fresh scratches on their backs—from shaving?"

"And how long has this been going on?"

"As long as TDY's have been going on, I guess. There are always a few married guys who fool around. They used to bring the women into the barracks here, until chaplains started coming along with us and inhibited them. Then they moved their base of operations elsewhere—to that deserted barracks near headquarters. But the heating system there went on the blink last week, and Major Albright keeps coming down with colds."

"I see." Suddenly David recalled where he had last seen Major Albright and his bald head and fork, and under what circumstances.

"The worst part of it is that it's usually a senior married officer like him who plays around like that—just the one who should be setting examples for us younger guys. But, to listen to them talk, all they care about is setting *records*. What are you going to do about it, Chaplain, now that you know?"

David hesitated. "I'm not sure."

"Can I make a suggestion?" Alex asked eagerly. "You have another Moral Leadership Lecture coming up, don't you? How about springing it on them there? I remember in that movie *David and Bathsheba*, that scene where the prophet—I think it was Raymond Massey—points his finger at Gregory Peck and shouts, 'Thou art the man! *Thou art the man!*' It was really quite effective. Of course, Raymond Massey had a long white beard, and it was in Technicolor and all—well, what do you say, Chaplain?"

"I'll think about it," David promised.

—Well, what *do* you think? he asked himself as soon as he could without being overheard.

—It's not so much a question of what *I* think, but—

—You mean, what Colonel Kingsbury thinks?

—Uh-huh. He's had a worse cold this week than Major Albright.

—But you don't know for *sure*—

—You want me to go ask him how he caught cold?

—Guess not. There's something unkosher about his married life, from the comments I've heard, which makes me very much afraid—

—That this may turn into another Strike Three?

—Could happen. It already *has* happened to you, twice now, because you clashed with the powers that be. Maybe, for a change, you ought to just keep your mouth shut.

—David! I'm a *rabbi;* I *can't* keep my mouth shut.

—Well, just look what's happened every time you've opened it—your foot's slipped right in there. You never would have been forced into the Air Force in the first place, you know, if you hadn't spoken up to that doctor at the Army physical. And you'd never have been exiled to Goose Bay in the second place if you hadn't assaulted the entire Stratford family. And now, in the third place—

—But I *have* to speak out for what I know to be right.

—You mean, you think you're another Raymond Massey?

—No, I don't even think I'm a house detective. But Alex wasn't completely off. It *is* my duty at Moral Leadership to tell the men what's right and what's wrong.

—You don't think Major Albright and the others know that already?

—Then I can lecture them on what's done and what just *isn't* done.

—And how much effect will that have, I wonder, on men who are doing it and *liking* it?

—If I can only figure out some way to really get through to them!

—There still remains that other thing to figure out— Colonel Kingsbury.

—What can he do to me? I can't get court-martialed for talking on adultery, and he can't ship me back to Fairfield because Colonel Stratford won't accept me. So even if Colonel Kingsbury *is* involved in this adultery mess, and even if he *does* take offense, what can he possibly do to me?

—That's what makes me so nervous—*I don't know.*

That same day David had still another problem to figure out. A few officers were again good-naturedly badgering him to fly along with them when Colonel Kingsbury, standing nearby, interrupted to say, "Why don't you men lay off the Chaplain?" Surprisingly there was hardly any sarcasm in his voice. "A chaplain can't play house mother to *every* sortie of ours."

Afterwards, David puzzled over the Colonel's remark. Could it be that he had gotten wind of his planned attack at the lecture and was trying for some kind of reciprocal deal? Yet that was impossible. How could Colonel Kingsbury have heard what David planned to do when he himself still did not have the faintest idea?

"Chaplain Cohen, your Moral Leadership Lecture, please."

Grasping his notes tightly, David strode down the

center aisle of the base theater toward the stage, desperately trying to outdistance his growing feeling of uneasiness.

Suddenly he paused near the third row and bent over. When he straightened up, there was a letter in his hand. He held the letter up and asked, "Anyone here lose this?"

The men shook their heads, murmuring negatives.

David climbed the steps to the stage and walked over to the podium. He held the letter up again. "Does this letter belong to anyone here? There's no name or anything on the envelope."

No one in the audience spoke up, and David took a sheet of paper out of the envelope. "It's to someone named Frank. Sound familiar?" There was still no response from the assembly. "I think I'll read a little bit of it to you. It may be something important. As soon as you recognize it, just speak up and I'll hand it over. It starts:

Dear Frank,

Well, the worst is over now. We flew our last max effort day before yesterday, and what a job that was! It was our third turn-around mission in a row, which meant we were flying without sleep for thirty-six hours. But now the tension's over, and I can relax a little. And you know what relaxation means to me. Yes, you guessed it. I found myself a nice little piece.

The men gasped.

David looked up. "Someone recognize the letter?" The audience laughed gleefully. Some suggested names.

David hesitated for a moment, then shrugged and continued:

Well, to tell you the truth, she's not so nice and she's huge, but still she's a piece. And who am I to look a gift horse in the mouth? Besides, in the dark they all look alike anyway.

Again there was laughter. This time, however, it was drowned out by whispering and restless stirring.

Just one thing though—I wish she'd stop asking me if I love her every time. Why do women always ask that before? It should be enough that I—sex her. Besides, she knows I'm married. I didn't *tell* her I was married, of course—as a matter of fact, I told her I was single. But she's no fool. She *must* know I'm married.

David paused, and looked up inquiringly.
In the audience, several men were slumped down in their seats, counting their knees. Others, smiling, were poking one another and pointing at someone.
David resumed:

This time my conscience is clear though. I never made her any promises. I'm sure she enjoys it as much as me, so where's the harm? I just don't look forward to my last night at Goose Bay. It always ends up in tears. As if she'll remember my name next month! I know it's all I can do to remember hers now. But just as long as I remember to be careful, I'll be satisfied. My roommate has been sweating it out with his girl the past few days.

The audience was perfectly still now. Everyone was attentive, listening for clues as to the identity of the letter writer.

I miss Mary a lot, and the kids too. The boy starts school in the fall, and Mary can hardly wait. He can really tear up a house. The girl is almost ten now, and as pretty as her mother. She's going to be a temptation to the boys; I can see that right now.

Mary writes me pretty often because she knows how lonely it is up here. She's really very understanding. I'm sure she'd even understand if she found out about the girl. But that doesn't mean I'm fool enough to tell her! But then, I don't suppose Mary tells me everything either. I don't mean anything like playing around, or something like that. Mary knows how I'd feel about such a thing— how *any* man would feel. I'd take a gun to her and—

Got to finish this quick now. The Chaplain is going to give us another one of those Moral Leadership Lectures, and while he's talking I want to catch up on some of my lost sleep.

David looked up. "That's all there is," he said to the most attentive audience he had ever had.

"The signature!" someone bawled from out front. "You forgot to read us the signature, Chaplain!" A dozen men guffawed, and two men started taking bets.

David was taken aback. Hadn't they understood? He opened his mouth to speak but Colonel Kingsbury, sitting in the first row, spoke up first, scowling. "After you give your Moral Leadership Lecture, I want to speak to you privately about the morality of reading a personal letter in public like that."

"But, Colonel, this was *it*." David held up the sheet of paper he had been pretending to read and turned it over. It was blank on both sides. "That *was* my lecture."

Colonel Kingsbury broke into a spasm of coughing and exclaimed, *"Sonofabitch!"* But David chose not to take the remark personally.

A collective "Oh!"—part delight but mostly disappointment—echoed through the theater. It was followed immediately by at least a dozen "I told you so's," several "I don't believe its," an assortment of "Well, I'll be a . . .'s," and one loud "I don't care *what* the Chaplain says—I *know* who wrote that letter!"

Afterwards, on the bus returning to the barracks, David was congratulated for his lecture by all the faithful husbands aboard, two fiancés, and one captain who knew that David knew his wife. These men, however, clearly did not add up to the total number of men on the bus, leaving him to wonder about his letter's effect upon the others, especially after Major Albright commented, "Say, Chaplain, what are you trying to do—make adultery unfashionable?" Then, when he spied Colonel Kingsbury gazing thoughtfully at him, his lips framing the same four-syllabled word over and over again, David began wondering about his letter's effect upon himself.

The following evening there was some indirect direct response to his lecture. Returning to his room from the line, he found on his bed two unsigned notes addressed to him. The first note was so gratifying that it almost dispelled his sense of uneasiness. It read simply: "Thanks, Chaplain, for the lecture."

The second note, however, said: "Hearing you read that letter yesterday has taught me a very important lesson. From now on, Chaplain, I'm going to lay off writing."

Anxiously, David searched his room for a third note, a signed message from Colonel Kingsbury—but there was none. Not yet, anyway.

Chapter : 18

"CHAPLAIN!"

Alex Winkler, waving a snapshot, burst into the room one day as David was trying to defrost a salami which had frozen stiff en route from Brooklyn. "Chap, have I got a surprise for you! Guess what? I've got you a *wife!* Well, she's only a girl now, but—"

David stopped attiring the frozen salami in his heavy woolen socks. "What are you talking about?"

"Look at this!" Alex handed David the snapshot. "I took it myself just before with my Polaroid, to give you a preview. What do you think? Not bad, huh?"

David examined the photograph. It showed a slender girl with curly black hair and dark eyes much too large for her thin face. "Who is she?"

Alex laughed with delight. "She's yours, Chap, all yours. I know you'd like to get married and—well, anyway her name's Ilona Lazarus and she's twenty-something. I found that out from the other girls at the BX. Maybe you've seen her there. She works at the record counter and, Chap, she's *Jewish*—one hundred proof!"

David smiled. "Oh, Alex. Goose Bay is a long way from Brooklyn."

"It's true," Alex insisted earnestly. "Let me tell you how I know. For the last month or so a lot of the guys have been trying to date her, even some of the bachelors too. But she's been turning them down right and left, with all kinds of different excuses. Then yesterday she confesses to Chuck Conte that the real reason she doesn't go out with anyone here is because she's Jewish and dates only Jewish fellas. I thought it was some kind of gag myself, so this afternoon I went over and asked her for a date myself—for *your* sake, understand—and sure enough, she shows me a Star of David, like the one on your chaplain's insignia, and then she says she dates Jews only. It's a fact. And that makes her all yours, because you have a corner on the Jewish market up here, so to speak. Chap, you have it *made!*"

David regarded Alex with disbelief. "It doesn't make sense. What would a lone Jewish girl be doing at this forsaken base?"

"I don't know. All I found out from the other salesgirls is that she's from Hungary originally, but lately from England. She was flying to the States—they refuel here, you know—and she came down with pneumonia or something. So when the plane stopped here, they hospitalized her. Now I guess she's waiting for another flight. Which means you got to work fast, Chap.

I've always wanted to see what a Jewish wedding was like."

David laughed, but wistfully. *"Halvai* already!" he said under his breath, then felt prompted by something other than idle curiosity to ask, "What makes you so sure she's the girl for me?"

"Because she's not the least bit apologetic about being Jewish," Alex replied, then caught himself. "Oh, that didn't sound right! What I meant was, when she said she's Jewish, she didn't even bother to look at me, or pretend to look away from me, if you know what I mean. Now I don't know very many Jews, Chap, but a good many of those I've met, when they've mentioned their religion, especially the first time, they were hesitant, almost cautious. It's like they were watching for my reaction, to see what kind of difference it would make to me, because they always seem so sure it *will* make a difference. And *that* makes a difference to me—their watchfulness, I mean. It makes me feel kind of embarrassed for them, sometimes even sorry." He stopped short and a look of concern creased his smooth round cheeks. "What I just said—that wasn't anti-Semitic or something, was it?"

David laughed. "About as anti-Semitic as your try at matchmaking." He hastened to add: "Not that you stand any chance at succeeding, Alex. There's only about a month left to our TDY here."

The girl in Alex's photograph stood behind the record counter absorbed in looking ahead of her into blank space. Of medium height and slight build, she had short, wavy blue-black hair and very pale, almost translucent skin, stretched so taut over high cheek bones that she looked incapable of smiling. Her eyes, especially in comparison with the drawn face, were unusually large and the color of wet violets. Yet so expressionless was their setting that the girl looked neither pretty, nor even plain, but frozen—not unlike the salami in David's room.

"Miss . . ." David said, then cleared his throat. "Miss . . ."

Rousing herself from her reverie, the girl turned to him. "Can I help you?" she asked mechanically.

"Oh, I don't want to buy anything," David replied. "You see, I've been told that you're Jewish and I—"

The girl interrupted him. "That is correct," she said curtly, and took out a Star of David—across it was engraved the name Eva—that had been hidden behind her neckerchief. "And I only go out with Jewish men."

David smiled. "Well, I'm Jewish myself."

The girl seemed surprised, but not the least bit interested. "Are you?"

She did not believe him, David figured. "Would you want me to chant the *Kiddush* for you?"

"All right," the girl said. "So you are Jewish."

David was taken aback. "As a matter of fact," he began, "not only am I Jewish but I'm—"

She interrupted him, her face impassive. "So you are also a bachelor."

"My being a bachelor is beside the point," David said. "What I wanted to say was—"

Again she interrupted him, and now for the first time her voice evinced an emotion—extreme impatience. "Evidently someone has told you that I do not go out with non-Jews. That is true. But there is something else which they have *not* told you. I do not go out with Jews either."

"What?"

"The only reason I tell people I go out only with Jews is because they told me there were no Jews at Goose Bay. The truth of the matter is that I go out with no one, regardless of his religion."

"What makes you think I wanted to take you out?" David asked, annoyed now.

"You do not? Good." And there was no doubting the sincerity in her voice. "If you do not want to buy records, you will have to excuse me now."

"Listen, Miss," David said coolly, "all I wanted to tell you was that I am a chaplain—a rabbi. I was under the impression that, as a fellow Jew, you might be interested."

The girl hesitated for an instant, but the pale, taut

250

face did not change expression. "I must go now, Rabbi. A customer is waiting." And she left.

The Jewish girl's chilly reception (his frozen salami couldn't have been any colder) irritated David so much that, on his way out of the BX, he bought three cartons of Herbert Tareyton cigarettes which were selling for fifty cents per carton. It was only when he returned to his quarters and Alex expressed surprise at the purchase that David remembered he did not smoke.

Then Alex asked, "Well, Chap? How did you make out?"

David shrugged. "Well, she seemed to be a nice girl. Pleasant looking, refined. Self-possessed. But, of course, I didn't go to see her for any reason other than that I'm a rabbi and she's a Jew. However, I do appreciate your thinking of me."

"I'll be damned!" Alex exclaimed. "You mean, she wouldn't date you *either?*"

David saw the girl several times that week in the BX. Still, no more than a dozen words passed between the two of them and these only when he bought records for his silent hi-fi set. It was not that the girl was rude; she was completely indifferent to him—and, worse still, uncalculatingly so—even when he once offered her the address of Uncle Asher and Tante Dvorah, explaining that she could have his old room when she entered the United States.

The girl spurned his offer. "Thank you very much, Rabbi, but I do not need the address of anyone in America." And she left him to wait on another customer.

The next time David saw her was at the movies. It was on one of those rare nights when a plane had gotten through from the States with a film about people, instead of talking mules. When the movie ended, he saw the girl leaving the theater ahead of him. Impulsively he followed her into the nearby cafeteria.

He got a cup of coffee and went to the girl's table, where she was sipping a malted. "Looks like all the other tables are filled," David said. "May I join you?"

Pointedly the girl looked at a table nearby which was empty. He reddened, and the girl apologized, but without regret. "I am sorry, Rabbi. I did not mean to be rude. Please sit."

He sat down, and the girl said, "It is unforgivable of me. I want so much to be left alone that I find myself being rude all the time. But you Americans are so friendly, and so hard to discourage. There! I am afraid I have offended you again, when what I wanted to do was to tell you of my appreciation for offering me your uncle's address. I should have given you the reason but, again, I am afraid that I was rude when you were only trying to be a good rabbi."

A rather strange girl, David thought, as he said, "You don't owe me any reason." The cafeteria cat came up to him and rubbed its soft body against his leg. "Please don't feel obliged to explain." He pushed the cat away from him.

"It is nothing personal," the girl said, "so there is no reason why I cannot tell you. I do not wish any address in America because I have decided to stay at Goose Bay indefinitely."

"Really!" Stranger and stranger!

"Yes." This time she offered no explanation. The cat rubbed against her leg and the girl's face changed expression. She grimaced as she pushed the cat away from her, exclaiming, "Cats taste so horrible!"

David smiled. "You mean, cats *smell* horrible. Oh, please forgive me for correcting you, but I was sure you wouldn't mind because you speak English so well. I've been meaning to ask you—where did you learn it?"

"In Budapest. My father was planning for us to go to America, but my mother—" She faltered for a moment, then continued, "She could not leave the country. My father and I studied English at home, in secret. Then I've lived in England for a while."

David hesitated, then asked, "Are your parents still in Budapest?" Was that why a pretty Jewish girl would

252

choose to remain at a miserable place like Goose Bay, to await her parents?

"My mother is dead, and the Hungarian Secret Police sent my father away to a Russian concentration camp," the girl answered with no trace of emotion in either voice or face. "And please do not say that you are sorry. I am sure that you are. There! I am again rude. It seems I cannot help myself. I am not good company for people. Please excuse me." She rose to her feet.

David rose too. "Suppose I walk you back to your quarters. They're near mine."

"Please do not bother," the girl said, as she paused to draw on her mittens. David noted with a shudder that a serial number was tattooed on her left forearm.

"May I see you on another night?" he asked. "There's a good movie playing Thursday."

"Rabbi," the girl said quietly, "you seem to think we have something in common simply because we are both Jews, and alive. That is not so. All my ties are to *dead* Jews—my twin sister who was killed by the Nazis, my father who was killed by the Russians, if he was fortunate, and my mother who was killed by the Hungarians. And if perhaps I sound contemptuous of people who belong to a family that at least three separate countries did not cooperate in exterminating, I do not mean to. Although there was a time, I confess, when I did feel contempt for people without numbers tattooed on their arms." She shrugged her thin shoulders. "No more, though. I have no feeling at all any more toward—outsiders. And Judaism is no bridge for us, Rabbi. Despite our common religion, we are two different species. I do not make myself clear, I know. Perhaps this will help. When *you* see a cat, you think of how they smell, but I still remember how they *taste*. No, I did not make a mistake before. Good night, Rabbi." She left him then, shuddering still.

He would have to see the Jewish girl again, David decided as he walked back to the V.O.Q. Ilona Lazarus intrigued him. What inner strength and resources she had! To be content to settle in a desolate spot like Goose Bay, to be so self-sufficient, so secure, so self-contained. Somehow, despite her tragedy, he envied her. Would he, with a faith that was so strong partly because it was relatively untested, have been able to weather adversity as well as she?

Five nights later David saw the girl again in the cafeteria, after spending five successive nights there waiting for her to appear. He waited till she sat down at a table, then joined her. "So we meet again," he said casually.

The girl received him politely this time, and they chatted. David asked her how long she intended to remain at Goose Bay, and she said until she had read all the books in the base library. He laughed, but no smile appeared on the girl's face. It was then that David recalled that, except for that momentary flash of impatience, he had never seen the girl express any emotion at all. Her pale, drawn face was an impassive mask through which her violet eyes peered out at the world and its inhabitants without allowing anyone to look in.

"Why would you want to stay at Goose Bay indefinitely?" he asked finally. "You couldn't actually like this miserable place."

"No," the girl agreed. "And that's why I like it so much."

"Pardon?"

"The library has good books. The BX has good records. By now I have been rude to enough people, so no one bothers with me. The weather too is helpful—it discourages sociability. I have a private room to myself. But, best of all, one can never become attached to a place like Goose Bay or even like it, so if it blows up one day or I am forced to leave, it will not matter."

As David puzzled over the girl's strange reasoning, he felt a familiarly soft, warm body rubbing itself against his leg. Quickly he pushed the cat away, recalling the girl's words with a feeling of revulsion. The cat sidled over to her leg. She, again with a grimace of distaste, pushed the cat from her. The cat moved away.

254

Suddenly a piercing cry silenced the noisy cafeteria. Everyone turned toward the next table. There some major had chosen to chase the pesky cat away from him by grinding its tail into the floor with his heel. The cat emitted another nerve-rasping, almost human cry and streaked through the cafeteria yowling pitifully. The major and a few airmen laughed, and the cafeteria was noisy again.

Impulsively, David jumped to his feet and started toward the major. All of a sudden the girl was on her feet too, her face distorted by tears. She darted out of the cafeteria.

"Ilona!"

He ran outside and caught up with her.

"*That Eichmann!* The cat—the door was open—the cat—" she was crying incoherently, "it will freeze to death outside . . ."

Again he felt a soft body rubbing against his leg. He looked down and saw the cat. Smiling with relief, he picked it up and showed it to Ilona, and she wiped the freezing tears from her thin face and almost smiled.

He returned the cat to the cafeteria. Yet when he turned around, Ilona was not at his side. She had left without a word.

Emboldened by Ilona's expression of emotion, David went to the BX the next day to ask her to have dinner with him that evening at the Officers Club.

Ilona, as composed as he had ever seen her, declined politely. "What purpose would it serve?" she said.

He left the BX to ponder the question. Why indeed was he so anxious to see Ilona again? Was it possible that his interest in this very attractive girl with the beautiful violet eyes was not entirely rabbinic? After all, in what way was he seeking to aid her? Ilona wasn't even overweight. Of the two of them, he was the discontented one. And why? Perhaps because the girl seemed completely capable of leading a satisfactory life without him. Was it only vanity that prompted him to wish that he might come to mean something to her? Yet what other reason could there be? For in three weeks he would be leaving Goose Bay, and Ilona, forever.

David was still pondering these questions in the cafeteria that night as he waited hopefully. Ilona appeared finally and did not seem displeased to see him there. However, honesty compelled him to admit to himself that she did not look overjoyed, either, when he joined her. Yet she stayed in the cafeteria till closing time, chatting with him about a variety of things, none of which touched upon the tattoo on her arm, the deaths of her parents and twin sister, or her hysterical reaction of the night before.

"I don't think I've ever talked this much in my entire life!" David exclaimed at one point. "Believe me, I'm not usually such a blabbermouth."

Her face softened.

"But what about *you?* You haven't said a word about yourself all this time. I don't mean to pry, but I *am* interested—"

She stood up. "It is getting late."

Two nights later Ilona returned. They talked about books and politics and movies and David and the rabbinate. Thereafter, never with any appointment, the two of them met regularly in the cafeteria.

Afterwards David would continue their conversation, completely one-sided now, as he lay in bed. And when he finally fell asleep, he would dream one of two dreams of Ilona: either he was burning her with kisses, or she was dreaming of him concurrently.

One morning he awoke calling her name.

"You got it all wrong, Chap." His roommate was standing over him, chuckling. *"My* name is Alex."

Soon David's nightly date became the focus of his day at Goose Bay. And he learned to tolerate sunrises only because they were sure to be followed by sunsets ten hours later—and Ilona.

"You look especially lovely tonight," David remarked on a subsequent evening. (It was remarkable, he thought, how much prettier this unusual girl grew with each meeting.)

Ilona shrugged. "I look like I always look."

David smiled. No vanity in this girl at all. She did not waste her thoughts on trivialities. Suddenly he realized that *everything* about the girl pleased him. Even what he would have considered faults in another girl were somehow transformed in Ilona into virtues.

"What are you smiling about?" she asked.

"I can't help smiling—when I'm with you." He sighed. "But it doesn't seem to work both ways. Do you *ever* smile?"

"Smile?" she repeated, as if that were one English word she had never learned.

"And when are you going to start telling me about Ilona Lazarus, woman of mystery?"

She gave him a blank look. "No mystery. I do not talk about myself because there is nothing to tell. Not any more."

"Ilona—"

"But I do listen now—a little—since you have come to Goose Bay." She paused, then added wistfully, "It has been such a long time since I *could* listen." She seemed surprised by her own words. Quickly she added, "But you must not ask for more than I am capable of. Please do not ask too much of me."

David exulted to himself: I've had some effect on her, after all! She knows I'm alive, she responds to me, she *listens!* Hesitantly, for she had always turned him down before, he asked for the seventh time, "Can I see you home tonight?"

"All right," she said, and David felt he had scored a monumental triumph.

A gale outside made conversation impossible, but David did not care. He did not need to talk to Ilona any more or listen to her. Just being with her satisfied him. Her presence—the bestowal of her company upon him— made him feel complete as a man, and proud.

"See you tomorrow night, David," she said matter-of-factly at the door of her barracks.

"Yes! Tomorrow night!" (Never before had Ilona referred to a future date of theirs, nor had she ever called him by his first name.) She went inside, and he confided with a shout to the gale: "And the next night, and the night after that, and the night after, too!"

That night he had a different dream. This time Ilona was swathed in snowflakes, standing beneath a bower of flowers and fruits and vegetables. Tante Dvorah and Uncle Asher were there too—one, crying; the other, dancing. And David was stamping upon a wine glass. It shattered, its contents staining Ilona's gown red. She cried out, and he swept her up into his arms and tenderly carried her off into the snow which melted before them, steaming with each of his steps. And Ilona was *smiling!*

When he awoke, Alex was waiting with a comment. "I don't know, Chap. The way you carry on lately in your sleep—I'm beginning to wonder whether I'm safe here alone with you."

David blushed and swatted his roommate with a pillow.

The meetings did not escape the squadron's attention, and soon the men were teasing David about them while Alex proclaimed hourly that he had been the matchmaker. Even Colonel Kingsbury had a comment. "Chaplain, I've never seen a more devoted clergyman," he remarked dryly, "or, for that matter, a better stacked congregation." And David discovered one evening that Chuck Conte, the squadron entrepreneur, was taking bets among all the officers on whether or not David would marry Ilona and, if so, when. "Chaplain, marry the girl this week," Chuck counseled, "and I'll split my winnings with you fifty-fifty, and you'll be able to furnish your whole living room right away."

What disturbed David in particular was that so many men in the squadron had bet on his plans even before he had been conscious of them. For he had made up his mind to propose to Ilona only that night. Yet on the way to the cafeteria a familiar voice (his own) asked him a familiar question, also his own:

—*Why* do you want to marry the girl?

—Because I love her, of course.

—Of course. And what do you mean by the word "love"?

—I mean—well, I *love* her. It's hard to explain really . . .

—I'll be patient.

—Well, before I met Ilona—well, you know how restless I've been even though I enjoy my work and feel I'm a real part of the Air Force now . . .

—I also know that here at Goose Bay you've been cooped up, isolated and lonely for three months. And do you know that at Goose Bay not only did you have the market cornered on Ilona but she had the market cornered on you?

—My love for Ilona has nothing to do with geography or economics.

—Then what *does* it have to do with? Have you forgotten that in the beginning you actually *disliked* the girl?

—Never!

—You *did*.

—Well, perhaps I did. But only because I felt so *inferior* compared to her. And shut out. But now I love her and I want to marry her.

—Are you sure you're not just do-gooding again?

—I'm sure. What I'm trying to do now is good for *myself*. I know enough to realize I could never marry someone I pitied.

—But how long have you known the girl?

—We've been TDY here for eleven weeks now.

—But how long have you known the girl?

—About five weeks.

—And how long have you been seeing her steadily?

—Almost four weeks.

—And what do you know about her now that Alex didn't tell you five weeks ago?

—Well . . .

—Well?

—We avoid talking about Ilona's past. It's too painful for her.

—How do you know? Did she get emotional that time she mentioned her family being killed?

—Well, no. But that's why I think Ilona needs me.

—Have you ever seen her display any kind of emotion?

—That time with the cat. That showed me she had a heart full of compassion—

—For cats. Has she ever shown as much compassion for you, any sign that she feels toward you the way you feel, or *think* you feel, toward her?

—She keeps coming back to the cafeteria every night . . .

—Where else can she get a cup of coffee at that hour? Has she ever let you so much as hold her hand?

—I've never *tried* to hold her hand.

—Why not?

—In the cafeteria? With half the squadron there looking over my shoulder and betting on me?

—Does *your* gamble make any more sense? Why risk everything on a girl you've known for less than a month, in a miserably lonely place like Goose Bay—a girl who has told you less about herself than any man in the A.R.S.?

—Because I *love* Ilona.

—Oh, come now. Surely you should have a better answer than that no-answer answer; that's the one you don't accept from all those lovesick kids you're always trying to discourage from marrying.

—Maybe there *isn't* any rationally acceptable answer —for *any* marriage. Maybe it's all a matter of faith alone. And maybe I didn't realize that before.

—Maybe. Or maybe the only hunchback you ever see is the other fellow's.

—But the TDY ends this week, and I can't leave Ilona forever.

—That's a reason to make a lifetime purchase instead of taking out an option? Why can't you arrange to meet Ilona in New York in seven months, when you get out of the Air Force and she tires of Goose Bay? There you can get to know the girl under normal circumstances without having to meet any deadlines. Isn't that what you advised those two airmen who wanted to marry two Newfoundlanders they met up here? You believe it's sound advice for them, so why not follow it yourself?

—Because Ilona and I—we're different.

—Not if you give me a stock answer like that, you're not.

—Perhaps—perhaps—oh, I don't know!—perhaps you're right . . .

—You *know* I'm right.

Thus, reason prevailing over emotions, the only proposal David extended to Ilona that night was an invitation to have dinner with him at the Officers Club on Saturday night, the night before the A.R.S. Dining-In Dinner and two nights before the squadron's return to Fairfield.

This time she accepted the invitation, and without hesitation.

When David came to call for her on Saturday night, he found that she was refreshingly un-American: She was ready on time and waiting for him. And, in a new hair-do of blue-black clusters of curls that surrounded the drawn face and softened it, and in a dress the color of her velvety violet eyes, she was beautiful!

So beautiful did she look that he insisted on taking pictures of her right there, and he returned to his quarters to borrow Alex's Polaroid camera, while avoiding his questions: "You're going to pop the question tonight, aren't you? We leave here in two days, you know. Well, Chap?" David hurried back to Ilona and took half a dozen pictures of her, but none of them came out nearly as well as she looked.

"No, I don't want these pictures of you, Ilona," David said impulsively. "I want *you*. Will you marry me?"

"Oh, David . . . !"

The impenetrable mask slipped from Ilona's face and revealed tears in her eyes, like dew on a pair of violets. She turned away from him quickly, and rushed out of the barracks. He hurried after her and, taking her gloved hand in his, they walked in silence to the Officers Club

261

as David's reason congratulated him on his good fortune every step of the way.

At the Club they checked their coats and started toward the dining room. But Ilona took him aside and led him to a dim corner of the lounge. She sat down on a couch there with David and suddenly, her eyes looking everywhere but at him, she was telling him about her past life.

Ilona spoke briefly of her childhood in Budapest, of her twin sister Eva, of her mother who had been a concert pianist, of her father, a college professor and the president of his synagogue. She alluded to the harrowing life under the Horthy dictatorship, of how her father had sought fruitlessly to take his family out of Hungary, of the many times he had tried to get visas for Palestine only to be refused each time by Great Britain, who would allow no more than fifty Hungarian Jews a year into Palestine.

In 1941 Hungary joined forces with Hitler, and Professor Lazarus had to take to performing odd jobs while Mrs. Lazarus gave piano lessons. In 1944 Horthy petitioned for an armistice, and the Nazis seized him and occupied Budapest. The Lazarus family went into hiding in the cellar of a fellow professor, but they were betrayed a few weeks later by the professor's wife in exchange for medicine for her critically ill son. The Lazaruses, together with thousands of other Jews, all stripped naked, were herded into cattle cars which were then sealed. After a two-day trip in the sealed cattle car, so crowded that no one was able to sit down when tired or even fall down upon death, the train reached a concentration camp whose name Ilona had never been able to recall.

All this was recounted in a voice as mechanical as the weather officer's at premission briefings and with no trace of emotion on her drawn face. It was David, not Ilona, whose body was shuddering.

She continued her emotionless recital by listing the methods of execution favored by the Nazis in the concentration camp. These included crushing people in cement mixers, throwing victims to famished dogs, thrusting hot pokers down the throats of others, burying people alive, drowning, shooting, gassing, electrocution, and binding the legs and hips of pregnant women with ropes and belts as soon as they started to go into labor.

A feeling of nausea swept over David, and his eyes burned with unshed tears. He had to restrain an impulse to rush away from Ilona and the horrifying pictures she was conjuring up in his mind.

Of all the Nazi methods of torture, Ilona dwelt on only one, the one which had been employed upon her mother. Mrs. Lazarus had been forced to tell the authorities which of her twin daughters she wanted buried alive. She had refused to make the choice, until she had been informed that in that case *both* her daughters would be buried alive, and she had randomly chosen to save Ilona. Mrs. Lazarus had then been forced to watch her other daughter, Eva, being buried alive in a huge pit with some forty other children.

David was benumbed. Despite his stinging eyes, the horrors that issued forth so matter-of-factly from Ilona's lips no longer penetrated to his emotions. In some ghastly manner the ways of men had equaled the ways of God: Both now surpassed his understanding.

Tonelessly, Ilona related how her mother afterwards kept saying that she had chosen Ilona to live only out of a sense of guilt because she had always loved Eva more. Later she told Ilona that she had mistaken one twin for the other and had really meant to save Eva. Finally the demented woman began to insist that Ilona was the one who had been buried alive, and that Eva was the surviving twin. After that Mrs. Lazarus never called Ilona by any other name save Eva. The war ended and the family, three in number now, returned to Budapest, but Mrs. Lazarus had never recovered from the effects of the concentration camp. One night, yelling "Murderer!" she had attempted to stab Ilona to death in her sleep.

Ilona untied the neckerchief she always wore around

her throat, and David gasped to see a jagged pinkish scar on the left side of the girl's neck.

"Trust a chaplain to stake out the darkest corner of the lounge for himself!"

Startled, David looked up to see Colonel Kingsbury standing in front of him with some woman.

"Miss James, I'd like you to meet the A.R.S. chaplain, Chaplain Cohen, and a friend of his who, from what everyone's been telling me, could only be Miss Lazarus. Miss Lazarus, Chaplain—this is Miss James."

Ilona and the woman exchanged greetings but David, forgetting in his distress even to rise, only grunted in the woman's direction.

The Colonel chuckled. "Chaplain, you don't have to look so grim. Whatever sins I commit, you can rest assured that adultery isn't one of them. I can't—I'm not married. Or are you scowling at me because we interrupted something here?"

"Not at all," Ilona said so calmly that for a moment the thought hopefully occurred to David that maybe she had been fabricating the entire story as some kind of gruesome practical joke.

"I only wanted to ask you to deliver the invocation at the Dining-In tomorrow night. Would you do that for us, Chaplain?"

"Surely," David replied, and the Colonel and Miss James withdrew, mercifully. It was only then that David realized why there had been no repercussions after his fake adultery letter at Moral Leadership: The Colonel was a single man. But now David no longer feared what *might* happen so much as he dreaded what Ilona would reveal *had* happened, irrevocably and forever.

For the first time since they had entered the Club, Ilona turned to look at him. "David . . . ? Should I continue . . . ?"

He took a deep breath and nodded slowly.

Quietly the girl went on to say that, on the advice of doctors, her mother had been placed in a Jewish old-age home, outside of Budapest, which took care of mental patients as well. While Mr. Lazarus hoped for his wife's recovery, he taught himself and Ilona English in preparation for his dream of migrating to America one day. ("Who could bear to go to Israel after the war," she said, "and live with six million ghosts?") But that day never came. On the sixth of July, 1956, the AVO (the Hungarian Secret Police) came and arrested Mr. Lazarus as a spy because someone had reported that he could speak English. Mr. Lazarus was deported to a Russian slave labor camp, and Ilona prayed that he had died.

When the Hungarian uprising started spontaneously on the twenty-third of October, Ilona found herself caught up in the battle. As Russian tanks joined in the fray, someone shoved a homemade gasoline bomb in her hand, and suddenly she was fighting the despicable Hungarian Secret Police and the hated Russians, Nazidom's twin heirs. She even managed to destroy a Russian tank before being disabled herself by a bullet in the shoulder.

Six days after the start of the unexpected uprising, the Russians withdrew from Budapest in alarm, leaving the city in the hands of the freedom fighters. Joyously Ilona went to the Jewish old-age home, outside of Budapest, to tell her mother the wonderful news.

She arrived there in time to attend Mrs. Lazarus' funeral. Hungarian mobs had taken advantage of the temporary withdrawal of the central Russian authority to run riot through the town. The first place they had attacked had been the Jewish section of town. The mob had beaten up several inmates of the old-age home, turned them into the streets, and then had set fire to the home. Ilona's mother and another woman had been caught in the blaze.

David bit his dry lips as Ilona concluded by telling of her escape to Austria later on through swamps and drainage pits—she was vague about the date and all that had happened since her mother's murder—and her subsequent wanderings through Europe. Then, abruptly, she asked, "David, can we return to my quarters now?"

They got their coats and started out of the Club, running into Chuck Conte and Alex Winkler and others from the squadron in the foyer. "Remember, Chaplain, your whole living room," Chuck said. And Alex exclaimed so proudly, "And guess who was the matchmaker!"

Outside it was snowing now, but the sportive wind, hardly allowing the snow to touch the ground, created the illusion of snow falling upwards. Gloved hand in gloved hand, the two of them walked through the whirling snow back to the women's barracks, again in silence.

David had no idea of what Ilona was thinking, and he knew his own thoughts even less. Her incredible account of successive horrors had not moved him so much as benumbed him. He could hardly think of words to describe their ghastliness, much less imagine them. And what if she were to ask him, as a rabbi, for the meaning and purpose of these tragedies?

In front of her barracks Ilona squeezed his gloved hand tightly for a moment, then said quietly, "Too bad *you* did not create the world, David. Good-bye." She started away.

"Ilona!" He caught her arm. "I've been so—stunned by—by—I've almost forgotten. We haven't made any plans yet. I leave day after tomorrow, and tomorrow night is that Dining-In, so I may not be able to see you then. We only have tonight and tomorrow to talk things over. Do you think we can set a date before I leave? I can get a furlough as soon as I return to Fairfield, so we can get married in two weeks—if that's all right with you. I don't want to rush you, but I'd like to make it as soon as possible because—now, I don't have to give any reason for wanting to marry you fast, do I!" He smiled, and for a moment it surprised him that he was still able to smile.

No companion smile appeared on Ilona's face—only an expression of anguish that he had never seen before, not even earlier that evening at the Club. "Oh, David!" she exclaimed softly. "Did I not make myself at all clear? I am not marrying you . . ."

Somehow the whining wind and the blowing snow and the parka hood had combined to distort Ilona's words, he told himself as he yanked the hood away from his head.

"David, I *cannot* marry you."

"*What are you saying!* I proposed to you before, and you said—I heard you say—"

Ilona interrupted. "David, that first night we talked—I *told* you then that we were two different species, despite our Jewishness. Why did you not listen? David, we have nothing in common. Nothing. Not even Goose Bay. You, I know, see in Goose Bay only waste and isolation, but to me Goose Bay is Heaven—because I have already learned what Hell is. It is people. You, David, look at the world and see order and purpose and the handiwork of God. I look at the world and see chaos and madness and an officer crushing a cat's tail for sport—still *another* Eichmann. I recognize a hopelessly fat neurotic, and you envision her transformed by a little kindness into a slim, healthy beauty. I spend the entire evening explaining why I cannot be your wife, and you hear me telling you why I shall marry you. As a rabbi you talk about love and peace and the Messianic hope and God, but I know only of hatred and war and despair and—*devils*. You speak of—*there* is the difference between us —you speak and you feel and you believe and you hope and you pray. But I *know*, David. I wish that I did not, but I know!" She ground her eyes shut, and tears spurted from them. "You pray, and you ask God to forgive you for your sins. But I *never* pray, David, because I can never forgive God for *His* sins."

David seized the anguished face, glistening with tears and snow, between his hands. "I know too! I know I love you, Ilona. I know no one else can ever love you more. I know I want to make you happy. I know no man will ever try harder. I know you must trust me now, believe in me, and—"

"Oh, David, you do not understand what you are asking of me," she sobbed. "You have no idea! I no longer believe in *God*. I no longer believe in *civilization*. I no longer believe in *law*—it was all *lawful* what they did to us, every disgusting, horrible thing. *How* then

267

can you expect me to believe in *you?*" She broke away from him and darted through the swirling snow toward the barracks.

"Ilona!" David ran after her and caught her by the arm, forcing her to face him. "Ilona, I'll *make* you believe in God. And I'll *convince* you to marry me . . ."

She shook her head, her face again a taut mask. "David, do you not understand? If you have to *convince* me," she said, her voice again a monotone, "then *already* it is no use."

David's hand slipped away from Ilona's and fell to his side. God, where were the words? The hundreds of thousands of words learned, spoken, read, studied; English words, Hebrew words, Yiddish words, French words, Latin words—where were they all now? Among them surely sentences to explain, phrases to convince, words to communicate—surely, *something.*

But no word came—what word other than *God* had ever existed that could transmute suffering and anguish into something meaningful, and that word she denied; worse, condemned—and David stood mute beside Ilona, so close yet never to touch, so in love yet never to love, condemned to life without Ilona yet unable to speak in his own defense. *The words, O God, where were the words!*

Slowly she walked away from him and disappeared into the barracks, leaving behind nothing more tangible than a set of footprints. And these the snow filled in one quick swirl. Soon even her traces had vanished, and it was impossible to tell that any living person had entered the barracks just a few moments before, or had ever set foot outside it.

And still he stood there in the clawing wind—he did not know why—as the tips of his ears slowly turned white with frostbite.

Chapter : 19

AT precisely 1855 hours the following evening, all officers of the Fairfield Air Refueling Squadron, having carefully memorized the Air Force Manual on Dining-In Procedure, were standing at ease behind their chairs in the private dining room of the Goose Bay Officers Club. At the head of ten of the eleven tables in the room stood the senior table officers who faced the empty head table. Opposite each senior table officer stood the keeper of the wine.

At exactly 1900 hours Captain Leonetti, the adjutant, called the officers to attention and then followed Colonel Kingsbury, General Symons (the base commander), David, and the six senior squadron officers into the room and to the head table. They too stood at attention until David stepped forward. All bowed their heads as he delivered the invocation, looking, with his frostbitten ears, like an angel whose wings had been clipped.

The prayer ended, the men at the head table sat down. The senior table officers took their seats, and the other officers followed their example. All of this was done in complete silence.

Colonel Kingsbury picked up a spoon to eat his fruit cup; the senior table officers followed suit; and everyone started eating and conversing. Except for David. All his thoughts were focused on what he had found at Goose Bay, and lost.

Before the second course of the dinner was served, Captain Leonetti rose to his feet and said, "Gentlemen, I propose a toast!" Immediately all the officers were on their feet with their wine glasses extended at precisely half an arm's length. "To the Commander-in-Chief of the Armed Forces of the United States!" the Adjutant said.

"To the President!" all officers responded in unison, then drank their toast. The officers at the head table took their seats again; the other officers sat down too; and the dinner continued while the keepers of the wine refilled the glasses.

During the course of the dinner, additional toasts were proposed and drunk to: the Chief of Staff of the United States Air Force, the Commander-in-Chief of Strategic Air Command, the Commander of the 22nd Air Force, and the Commander of the 222nd Bomb Wing.

During dessert Colonel Kingsbury proposed a toast to the Commander of Goose Bay, and he responded with a toast to the Commander of Fairfield's Air Refueling Squadron. Then the Colonel stepped forward again, before the men could resume their seats. "Gentlemen," he said, "if I may depart from tradition and propose one final toast—to Goose Bay Air Force Base . . ."

The response to the toast was vastly unenthusiastic. Indeed, there was a decided note of incredulity in the voices that echoed, "To Goose Bay . . . ?"

". . . which, according to official word I received only yesterday, we shall never see again," Colonel Kingsbury concluded innocently, and drank his wine.

The men responded with wild cheers, mutual pummeling, and accidental though reciprocal staining of uniforms with wine. One man, carried away even further than the others, dashed his glass against the nearest wall. The sound of shattering glass quieted the men, and they looked inquiringly at Colonel Kingsbury. He, in turn, looked questioningly to the General.

General Symons threw up his hands. "It's all right with me if you all don't want to come back to Goose Bay," he said. "I don't own this damn base, you know." And he smashed his own glass against the wall behind him.

The assembly cheered and immediately the air resounded with so much breaking glass, the contents running riotously red over the four beige walls, that it did not seem at all unlikely that the room would soon be launched and slide smoothly over all the wine into the waters of Goose Bay.

"Gentlemen!" Colonel Kingsbury held up his hand for silence, and the gathering quieted swiftly. "Before you're billed by the Club for breakage and cleanage," he said, and the men laughed, "in appreciation for your excellent performance on this TDY, this last one at Goose Bay, the drinks in the bar are on me—provided you reach it before Chaplain Cohen burns down that wicked place."

A roar, compounded of cheers and laughter, issued from the men, and they hurried out of the room toward the bar as Major Albright spurred them on with the cry, "Last one to get drunk is a rotten egg!" And in a few minutes the room was empty save for David, Alex, and General Symons who was speaking to Colonel Kingsbury.

Alex came over to David. "Chap, now's a good time to announce your engagement," he grinned. "While the drinks are still on the Colonel."

"There's nothing for me to announce," David said tersely. "I think you'd better go to Chuck Conte now. He's going to need a lot of consolation." And he turned to leave.

Alex caught him by the arm. "But, Chap, didn't you pop the question last night? I could have sworn—" Brusquely David pulled free. "Gee, I'm sorry, Chap! I'm such a stupid—I'm so sorry!"

"Forget it." David started for the door. "I'm going back to the V.O.Q. now to pack my things."

"Wait!" David kept walking, and Alex came running after him. "I think I'll go pack now too," he said.

David paused. "But you're *already* packed."

"So are you, Chap," Alex said quietly.

David grimaced and fell silent.

"Of course, if you want to be alone—" Alex hastened to add.

"No!" David cried out, louder than he intended. "Not

tonight I wouldn't. Alex, I'd be very grateful for your company tonight."

"No sweat, Chap."

The two of them walked in silence to the door, David not wanting to talk and Alex not knowing what to say.

"Oh, Chaplain!"

The two men paused and turned around. It was Colonel Kingsbury, now alone, who had called to David. "Chaplain, there's something I want to ask you," he said, his husky voice strangely rising and falling as if in tune to the wail of an imaginary siren.

Alex said, "I'll wait for you near the cloakroom, Chap." And he left the room.

David went over to Colonel Kingsbury. "Yes, Colonel?"

"Chaplain, aren't you going to apologize to me now?"

David was taken aback. "Apologize?"

The Colonel grinned broadly, as if he had just discovered a new use for his teeth. "For all the names you'd have called me ninety days ago if you weren't a chaplain, when you found I had boarded you with a drunk. But it seems to have worked out pretty good. *Too* good, I think. I never asked you to make Winkler a *teetotaler!* He's the only one here, other than yourself, who didn't take me up on my free drinks."

"I'm afraid I didn't have too much to do with Lieutenant Winkler's going on the wagon," David said. "And as for tonight—"

Colonel Kingsbury interrupted. "You found out what his problem was, didn't you, when I was so sure it was his marriage. And you got him to talk to me about it . . ."

"You mean, Alex *did* go to see you?" David asked, surprised. "He never told me."

"That's right, he wouldn't!" Before David could ask the reason, Colonel Kingsbury continued, "And now that I've accepted your apology, Chaplain, let me make one of my own. I'm afraid my motives for boarding a chaplain with a drunk were not entirely without malice. You see, I hate chaplains."

272

The last remark was uttered so genially that the Colonel could only have been jesting. "Do you? *Why,* may I ask, do you hate chaplains?"

"I've told you before," Colonel Kingsbury said pleasantly. "Because a chaplain once married me. That sounds like a joke, doesn't it?" He chuckled. "But it's only a tragedy. Isn't it funny that it was a chaplain who ruined my life?"

The sound did not at all match the picture, and David was disconcerted by the discordance. But then, looking into the Colonel's dilated and watery cavernous black eyes, noting the odd tilt of his head, and recalling the drinking at the bar that had preceded the dinner and the multitude of toasts, David realized that Colonel Kingsbury was drunk. He also noted that alcohol decidedly brightened the Colonel's normally sullen disposition, and he wondered whether it would be amiss for him as a chaplain to suggest that the Colonel get drunk more often.

Colonel Kingsbury fixed his black eyes, whose pupils seemed to have completely devoured their irises, on David. His tone of voice sounded even more amiable as what he was saying grew uglier. "It happened on another TDY, Chaplain. Of course, on a TDY—where else! We were sent to England then, supposedly for two months, as soon as the Korean War broke out. Very inconsiderate of the Commies to attack just then, because I was getting married three weeks later. In England the two-month TDY became a three-month TDY, and the three-month TDY became a four-month TDY, and the four-month TDY became a five-month TDY, and the five-month TDY became a six-month TDY, and —I got involved with some English girl—like the one in that letter of yours, just a piece of— Well, anyway, she got pregnant, as some girls do, and she went to my C.O. when I refused to marry her. He referred us to the chaplain who talked and talked and talked to me about responsibility and the baby and God and duty and my career—oh, he didn't miss a weak spot—and I married the girl. I got her to the States before she gave birth, and we named the baby Roy, Jr., although perhaps TDY would have been more appropriate. Oh, Gwen was a faithful wife—as faithful as she had been virginal. I knew, of course, that I hadn't been the first man in Gwen's life, but after the first few TDY's I found out I was always the next-to-the-last man. *Damn these TDY's!* Chaplain, do you know how many marriages in the squadron busted up on that seven-month TDY to England? Almost twenty-five per cent! *Damn* these TDY's!"

Colonel Kingsbury shook his head. "No, that's not the reason either, I suppose. TDY's don't usually bust the good marriages. They just bust up those that were falling apart at the seams anyway. Like me and Gwen. I managed to stick with her, for the boy's sake, till I came back from one TDY to hear little Roy—my own son!—talking about Uncle Eddie who had been staying over at the house while I was here at Goose Bay. Two years ago I finally got a divorce, and Gwen married Uncle Charlie, some hot-shot major. Then just before we came up to Goose Bay this time, she came to ask me to take her back. True love?" He laughed sarcastically. "I'd been promoted to L.C. in the meantime, and poor Uncle Charlie had just lost his spot promotion and was only a captain again. What a girl, that Gwen! I threw her out of course, and you know—I never even asked a chaplain's permission first."

The familiar scowl reappeared on the Colonel's face, and suddenly he grew sober. "But meanwhile my son is an orphan with a mother who's unfit to care for him, and a father who's unable. I love my son, but that doesn't mean I don't know he'd have been a hundred times better off being put up for adoption when he was born. Which is what would have happened if not for your colleague's help. Well, what do you think, Chaplain? Do I have enough motivation to become a drunkard myself? Maybe I should have you room with *me* on our next TDY."

Suspecting that it was the liquor rather than the Colonel that was confiding in him, David hastened to

.hange the subject. "Where is the next TDY going to?"

Colonel Kingsbury heaved a sigh. "There's still an-other sad tale. Now this is Top Secret, Chaplain, and it's o be kept especially from the Squadron for the next ew months. Because from now on our TDY base will be a base that'll make the men think Goose Bay was the Garden of Eden."

"Thule!"

"Thule," the Colonel nodded. "But at least the men will have five glorious months to celebrate the last of Goose Bay before they learn the bad news about Thule —that's something. I don't have even that. Let me tell you, a fool's paradise looks damn good to a man who knows damn well he's never going to get into any *other* kind. Well, Chaplain? Will you be coming along with us?"

David stalled. "To Thule?"

Colonel Kingsbury grunted. "We still have to satisfy that reg requiring us to take along a chaplain, and it might as well be you. There's only one chaplain I'd *really* like to take with me to Thule anyway, and that's the chaplain who made me marry Gwen. But I can't take him. Know why? Because he got kicked out of service two years ago. Know what for? For screwing around with one of his Sunday School teachers! But did *he* have to marry *his* bedmate? Not on your life. Because he was shrewd—you see, he was *already* married. And that's the God's honest truth!"

David grimaced. "I know, Colonel. I heard the story in Chaplain School."

"Then it *is* true?" Colonel Kingsbury's face fell. "I was hoping it wasn't! Somehow it makes everything seem so much worse. My poor son . . ." He cleared his throat. "Well, Chaplain? Want to come to Thule with us? You won't have any cause to fake any letters there. The only females around are seals and they never grow that desirable, not even on a TDY."

David's heart throbbed like a mashed finger. Here was his chance, once and for all, to prove which was stronger: his phobia or himself. "I'd *like* to come along, believe

275

me—" He faltered then, because he realized only too well which was the stronger.

"Oh, I forgot," Colonel Kingsbury remarked casually. "That flying phobia of yours . . ."

The blood rushed to David's face and beat at his temples.

"Sorry!" the Colonel said. "I promised Winkler I wouldn't let on. But all this liquor—"

David burst out, "But he promised never to tell!"

"Don't hold it against him, Chaplain. Winkler was trying to do you a favor, telling me so I'd get the men to lay off pestering you to fly. At least, that's what Winkler likes to *think* was his reason. But I know human nature better than that. You see, after telling me about *your* problem, Chap, it wasn't so hard for Winkler to tell me about his *own*."

"How did you ever solve his problem? How did you get him to lose his fear of flying?" David asked anxiously.

Colonel Kingsbury snorted. "Who tried to get Winkler to lose his fear? You think I want to *kill* the boy!" he exclaimed. "Chap, you know what flying is? Let me tell you: It's hours and hours of boredom punctuated by seconds of stark terror. And until a flyer knows terror, he doesn't know flying. Because fear is a flyer's oldest companion in the air. So a flyer must make it his friend— have it make him always more wary, ever more skillful— because no flyer can afford to have fear as an enemy in the air. Yet even then, when they're as close as husband and wife are supposed to be, there isn't a flyer alive, including myself with eight thousand hours, who doesn't feel at times that he's not coming back from some mission." He allowed himself a smile. "But, as you can see, I've always made it back. I guess that's why I continue to fly—because planes have always been the kindest things to me in life. They lift me far above the earth to skies crowded with a beauty I can't even describe, and they always bring me back whole and refreshed—so far, anyway. And if one time my plane does *not* bring me back— well, I suppose that takes care of that too, doesn't

276

it?" He shrugged his massive shoulders. "Come on, Chap. Let's recess to the bar. The first toast is mine though." He lifted up his right arm and held it high. "To the death of TDY's!"

David nodded in sympathy. "I'll be happy to drink to that," he said. "I'll get Alex." He started away.

"You know, Chap, I was just thinking," the Colonel said, and David paused, only to receive a clout so hard on the back that both his knees buckled. "A chaplain doesn't *have* to be a bastard." He checked himself. "Sorry! What I meant to say was—"

David interrupted, smiling for the first time since his ears had been frostbitten. "That's all right," he said, then confessed: "I was just thinking the same thing about colonels." And swiftly he left the room.

Behind him he could hear Colonel Kingsbury exclaiming: "Sonofabitch!"

Chapter : 20

THE return trip to Fairfield proved to be David's least painful encounter with flying, possibly because this time he started gulping sleeping pills as soon as he awakened in his room on the morning of his departure from Labrador. As a result, he could not even recall seeing the plane he had presumably boarded in Goose Bay and was now about to leave at Fairfield after landing there, likewise presumably.

Alex and his wife Marge, a very young and rather blurred brunette, helped him into their car on the flight line and propped him up between them. "Xuif tyhsb grtyu jhsge hjuko v kplmer!" said Marge, whose soft speech seemed to David in his somnambulent state as blurred as her looks.

"Marge!" Alex responded indignantly. "Of course he isn't."

"Zsdc bnhu klibv sdfed xcvz sderw hj sdwaq?"

"He's just tired, that's all—tired and sleepy." Alex said. "Now if you'll close the door, we'll be on our way."

"Qlkjnb dftgvc j," Marge said and the door slammed, snuffing out what remained of David's consciousness.

He came to as he was being helped into his apartment at the B.O.Q. Alex was asking him, "All right, Chap, are you all right?"

He tried to be obliging. "All right, all right." He plopped down on his bed. "All right already."

"How do you like this wife of mine—saving the news for my homecoming present?" Alex was saying. "Imagine! I'm going to be a father! Me!"

"A father!" David sat up in bed. "That is wonderful. Mazel tov!"

"A baby—you can't beat that for a marital dividend, can you! Oh, I'm going to have to find you a girl now, Chap. I want you to be a father too. It's the only play. I mean, it's important, gives a fellow a purpose to his life. Gives the world a whole new dimension, meaning. Am I talking crazy, Chap?"

Wistfully David said, "I wish I had as good reason to talk crazy."

"All the mistakes that my parents made with me— I'm going to start rectifying them in exactly four months from now. Isn't that one big reason everyone wants to become a father or mother—to enjoy a perfect, happy childhood retroactively?" Alex was serious, David could tell from the intense expression in his voice and on his face. But to assure them that he was not, he added with a wink, "Now the first thing I'll do as soon as the baby's born is, of course, see to it that he isn't an only child."

Marge laughed. "Jkdme ntrhyu sd bvhyr s gtyhf nbe." She turned to David, and added, "Mhedft hefgd bv klijgh nbyetg xz gtrd a cvgetf vbhyef ghd vbytdl nhyfg vh."

Alex took David's hand and shook it warmly. "Marge

278

has said it for both of us, Chap. She knows how much you've meant to me." And the two of them left before David could cut through his sleep-fogged brain to find the words to express his happiness over their good fortune and, he could not deny it, his envy too.

Struggling to his feet, he undressed, showered, and returned to bed. Then he lay awake for the rest of the night because he was completely slept out. And so when the phone rang some six hours later, he was happy to answer it. After all, how long could he lie there talking to a girl some three thousand miles away who wasn't interested in listening to him?

"You're late!" a familiar voice said. "We had a date for January 27th at 7:00 P.M., and here it's 8:00 A.M. already and April 15th."

"Dena! It's been such a long time! How are you? What have you been doing with yourself? Why didn't you answer my letters?"

She laughed. "For the answer to those and other intriguing questions, meet me at the Officers Club tonight. And, my friend, prepare yourself for an S-H-O-C-K."

"Oh, no! No more shocks at the Club," said David. "How about the Penguin Club in town?"

"The Penguin is fine, but I don't want you to pick me up. I'll meet you there at seven. A jewel like me deserves to be seen first in a properly glamorous setting. Besides, I want to see if you'll recognize me. And if you can, David, please don't." And she hung up before he could make sense of her cryptic words.

Promptly at seven o'clock David arrived at the Penguin Club, Fair City's finest restaurant. He had just checked his hat when a familiarly sultry voice stopped him. "Well, hello there, big boy."

Standing beside him was a statuesque young girl with a carefully overly made-up face and wavy auburn hair falling to bare, meaty shoulders. She was wearing a tight black sheath that clung to her body like a sunburn, and she rested her hands on a pair of well-rounded, twitching hips. "Hello," he said politely and moved away.

The girl stalked him. "Lonely, honey?" she suggested, and again he felt there was something familiar about her.

"No," he said, then finally recognized the voice. Of course! It was Mae West's.

"Wanna come up and see me sometime, honey?"

"Suppose," said David, annoyed now, "you just leave me your card."

All of a sudden the undulating girl beside him broke into an adolescent giggle and clapped her hands. "You *didn't* recognize me, David, *did* you?"

"*Dena!*"

"You were expecting maybe Two-Ton Tillie Galento?"

Having heard that Dena was dieting, David had expected some change in her appearance. But *such* a change! "I just can't believe it!"

"Thanks," she said softly. "Your astonishment—that's my diploma."

He shook his head. "I still can't get over the transformation."

"Good! I don't want you to, not for a long time." She noticed his bandaged ears and asked with concern, "But what's happened to *you?* You look like Hear-No-Evil."

David, explaining that his ears had been frostbitten without revealing the circumstances, led her into the dining room, a place so intimate—with its candlelit tables, shadowy people, hushed voices, muted music—that it seemed suggestive. "I'm glad it's so dark in here," he said as they sat down at a table. "People would be shocked to see a chaplain out with such a sexy female."

Dena laughed happily. "When you lose seventy-three pounds, David, there's practically nothing left *but* sex. Isn't it wonderful! Eight months ago people had to look at me *twice* just to see me *once*—that's why I could never blame you for your swan dive that night, David. But that's the last reference tonight to the caterpillar I used to be or to the worm I was that last night with you. All that's allowed henceforth are testimonials to the butterfly I am now. David, are you proud of me? You should be, you know. Because I did exactly as you advised."

"But I never advised you to do anything," he protested.

Dena smiled. "Not much you didn't! I heard you, David, every time you winced when I disparaged myself, or turned color when someone passed a remark about my being so fat, or suggested circuitously that I go see the base psychiatrist."

"Then you did go to Dr. Evans? I *knew* he could help you."

She wagged a finger at him. "It's terrible the way you underestimate yourself, David. Maybe Dr. Evans could help *you*."

"What?"

"It wasn't any psychiatrist who did any of this. Oh, I went to him all right—for a month. But he never cured me, unless it was his yawn that did it. I was going to him steadily, unburdening myself of the usual things—a lonely only childhood, excruciating shyness, the frequent changes of Air Force stations before anyone at school had started calling me by my first name, mother's death, acne on my face, Dad's TDY's. And all of a sudden it struck me one afternoon how ordinary, how unusually usual my case history was, nothing to justify my converting myself into a mountainous gargoyle. So I turned around on the couch to ask Dr. Evans whether I wasn't wasting his time. And that's when I got cured: I saw him *yawning*. Clearly I was boring him to death, poor soul. What's the fun of being a psychiatrist if you can't extract at least one Tennessee Williamsish story from each patient? So I flew down to Mexico City the next day to start my treatment."

"Mexico City?" David was puzzled.

"It's beautiful there, and they have the most divine food. But best of all, you're almost guaranteed to get dysentery in Mexico City—that's what I had heard, and fortunately it's true. I ate a delicious meal in one of the best restaurants, insisting on unbottled water and a salad made with unpeeled and uncooked vegetables. Then I re-

281

turned to this swanky hotel I was stopping at and brushed my teeth with water from the tap, and I waited. In two hours I was good and sick, and in three days I had lost ten pounds."

"You're joking!"

"Do I *look* like I'm joking?" She patted her flat abdomen and smiled. "Well, I was sick for a week and lost six more pounds. The next week my stomach wouldn't tolerate anything other than rice and tea and toast, so I lost five pounds more. And by that time my stomach had shrunk, so I came back to Fairfield and didn't suffer too much sticking to a diet Dr. Evans had given me. Just the usual drying-out symptoms—salivating when I passed a bakery, following after airmen who were licking ice-cream cones. But other than that—"

David laughed happily. "I *knew* Dr. Evans would help."

Dena looked amused. "Haven't you been listening, David? Dr. Evans didn't help me. He never could have. Other people perhaps, but not me. Because it was his *job* to help and, greedy girl that I am, I have always craved more than a doctor-patient relationship. That's so impersonal, like the carryings-on between a plumber and a sewer. David, the one who worked this minor miracle is *you*. And don't look so amazed. You remember that it took a kiss to awaken Sleeping Beauty. Well, Sleeping Uglies are no different. They can be aroused too—I mean, they can be made to feel they have something to get up for in the morning by finding someone who cares, not professionally but *personally*. Cares enough for them to date them, suffer with them, even sacrifice for them."

"Suffer? Sacrifice? Me?" David protested. "I see your diet hasn't reduced your imagination any."

She laughed. "Oh, I'm not the one with the imagination, David. Why, I no longer even imagine that I'm the most repulsive girl in the world. What do *you* think?" She moved closer to the candlelight and her long auburn hair suddenly seemed to catch fire.

"Oh, you'll do," David said casually, then added with a grin, "And how!"

Dena picked up the menu from the table and pretended to study it. "Well enough to make you forget Barbara?"

He started, but before he could think of a reply, the waiter intruded. As Dena was ordering her dinner, he thought: Why not? Why not forget Barbara—that shouldn't be too difficult—and Ilona too? Dena was a fine girl, intelligent, attractive now. And since he would never again see Ilona anyway, why *not* Dena?

The incontrovertible reason immediately presented itself: It would take him more than his few remaining months at Fairfield to forget that Dena's eyes were not the color of wet violets. It wasn't fair!

"Sir?" the waiter was saying.

"Yes?"

"Your order, sir."

"Oh." He ordered his dinner, all the while trying to think of something to say about Barbara.

The waiter withdrew, and Dena held out her hand. "David, could I see your wallet?"

"Sure." He was happy to comply with the request. *Anything* to change the subject.

She opened the wallet to a folder of snapshots inside. "Now, which picture here is Barbara's? Surely you must carry at least one picture of your fiancée."

"Well," he faltered, "well, as a matter of fact—"

"David, you know something? I don't believe that there *is* such a girl back home as Barbara whom you left behind and whom you're going back to."

"Dena!" He flushed. "Are you calling me a liar?" He moved back out of the candle glow.

She nodded. "Uh-huh. What fiancée ever describes the love of his life as a nice kid, and not bad looking, and a good sport? Or calls the girl he's going to marry by six different names?"

"Only *two*."

"There!" Dena chortled. "I'm afraid you *are* a liar, David, and not a very good one at that. Only a *wonderful* one. Now, David, please don't feel bad about being found out. If I know that you lied to me, I can also

283

guess *why*. And that's the important thing, that you *cared* enough about me to lie, and that—David, am I wrong in believing that the fat slob of a girl you told me of who emerged from analysis worthy of your love, which is the reason I dared ask for it outright that evening, premature though it was—David, couldn't Barbara have still another name, a shorter one perhaps, like—Dena?"

David gritted his teeth and silently cursed himself for having misled Dena, unwittingly though it had been. How could he now avoid hurting the girl? When he had impulsively invented a fictitious fiancée, it had been for the express purpose of excluding himself from Dena's possible romantic imaginings. Yet now that he himself knew the pain of rejection, his sole concern was to spare her feelings. There was no other recourse, he now realized with shame, but for him to resort to the truth.

He leaned forward, digging his fingernails into the palms of his hands. "Dena, I hope you can forgive me. You're right—I did lie to you. Except for one thing. There was—rather, there is a Barbara. Only her name's Ilona, Ilona Lazarus."

The wallet slipped from Dena's hand and fell to the floor. "What a stupid butterfingers!" She bent over to retrieve the wallet. Straightening up, she glanced through its folder of snapshots which, he only now recalled, did contain several pictures of Ilona. "She's really very—" She checked herself, then asked in confusion, "Then what did you lie *about*, David? And why did you call your girl every name *but* Ilona?"

"Because—because Ilona's a girl I met at Goose Bay—"

"*Oh . . .*"

"—whom I proposed to three nights ago." He let out a sigh. "The only trouble is she didn't—"

Dena uttered a small cry. "Why was it *her*? You met *me* first!" She quickly recovered. "That was moronic—please forgive me, David. I must sound like all the losers at the sweepstakes. David, I hope you'll both be very—I hope—David, can we go now?" She started to rise.

He put a restraining hand on her arm. "You're wrong, Dena. I met *Ilona* first. I wish now that you had been first, but—"

"You said you just met this girl at Goose Bay—"

"Yes, but when I met Ilona, she was eligible—or at least I thought so. You never were, Dena, before. Before you had clearly stamped yourself ineligible and unavailable. Your size told everyone that."

Her chin quivered. "And I thought that you cared for me—"

"I do, Dena, I do," he said earnestly. "And if you can tell when I'm lying, surely you must also be able to feel when I'm telling the truth. I do care for you—a great deal. But it isn't love, not in the sense that you deserve."

She eyed him accusingly. "But, David, you were so *kind* to me!"

"Oh, Dena, Dena," he said. "Hasn't anyone ever been kind to you before?"

She bowed her head and her long auburn hair fell over her face. "I never let anyone get that close after Mother died. I always made people keep their distance." She laughed sarcastically, and her voice quavered. "Just look how successful I've been with you!"

"Why, Dena? Why wouldn't you let anyone near?"

"I was afraid they would find me out. You see, I'm just not—lovable." She was silent for a moment, then said mockingly, "Oh, you're wise not to be fooled by the new packaging, David, because inside is still the same old fat, ugly, neurotic, unlovable Dena Gordon. *She'll* never change!"

"That's not so!" He grabbed her hand. "Dena, you're one of the finest, one of the most intelligent, nicest, loveliest—"

She snatched her hand away. "Stop that! I don't want any more kindness treatments from—" She checked herself. "I'm sorry, David! I didn't mean to—it's just that someone going to a psychiatrist knows she's supposed to fall in love with him during the course of treatment, but who on earth ever expects to fall for a *rabbi*?" She

285

forced a smile. "My mistake was confusing *Pygmalion* with *My Fair Lady*. I reread the Shaw play while I was dieting. David, did you know that Liza Doolittle never ended up with Professor Higgins at all? That happens only in *My Fair Lady*. Wasn't that stupid of me? I'm a big girl now; I should have *known* that Life isn't a—a musical." She looked directly into his eyes. "But I'm very glad for you, David. I really am. Because you deserve a musical-comedy ending."

He smiled crookedly. "Do I?"

The waiter returned with two orders of tomato juice. She held up her glass. "A toast: To your forthcoming marriage to—her."

He winced and gulped down the drink. Dear Dena! Never for an instant had she doubted that Ilona had accepted his proposal.

At the door to her home, Dena held out her hand. "Friends, forever; forever—friends," she said. "For old times' sake, friend?" And she pressed her lips fleetingly to his.

Caught unawares, his response was instinctive. His emotions triggered by his frustrated yearning for the girl in Goose Bay whom he had never so much as embraced, he clamped Dena's face between his hands and kissed her so hard on the mouth that he felt the ridges of her teeth behind her softly yielding lips and tasted the warmth of her inside.

Her lips parted and her tongue darted out toward his, meeting it in a mucid caress. His arms reached out to gather her in, but abruptly she pulled away. "That didn't feel at all like good-bye, David! That was more like *hello*—"

"Well . . . ?" he burst out.

Dena caught her breath. "Oh, David! Do you mean—" She checked herself, grimacing. "I'll *never* learn! For a moment I actually thought you meant—"

"I *did* mean it!"

She eyed him curiously. "And Ilona?" she said, and he flinched.

Mortified, he released her. He had been trying to forget Ilona by using Dena as the anodyne, and that was a *sin*. "Forgive me!"

"Forgive you?" she exclaimed softly, her green eyes caressing his face with a lingering look. "Oh, David, I'll do more than that— I'll love you."

"You will?" Still feeling with every tingle of his frostbitten ears the pain of rejection, he opened his mouth to accept, then stopped short, conscience-stricken: Aware of his sin, he was continuing to sin *still!* "Dena! Dena! Dena!" he cried, intoning her name like the passage in the High Holy Day liturgy which said, Forgive! Pardon! Blot out my iniquity!

She uttered a sound that almost succeeded in sounding like a chuckle. "Don't look so unhappy, David. When I said I'd love you, I was speaking *figuratively*, of course." She hesitated for an instant, then said abruptly, "Good-bye, David." Her voice softened. "Be happy." Then she was gone.

And David was left alone, again.

Chapter : 21

THE ensuing days dragged David ahead with them while his thoughts remained anchored behind to the girl he had left in Goose Bay who was not awaiting him and to whom he would never return. For weeks he wrote to Ilona every night, but she never replied, not even to the letter in which he had enclosed photographs of Dena marked "Before" and "How About *This?*"

Disconsolate, he took thirty-days' leave, which he had never done before because the round trip to New York by train took several days. He had to get away from the Air Force—everything in it now reminded him painfully of Ilona—even if it meant incarcerating himself in a portable jail on rails.

Tiring as the long train trip was, the hour's subway ride from Grand Central Station to Brooklyn was worse. For David arrived in New York just in time to be caught up in the city's daily *Walpurgisnacht*, the evening rush hour. ("Compared to subway riders," Tante Dvorah had once remarked, "anchovies lounge around in their cans on love seats.") It wearied him still more to keep repeating to the scores of people who besieged him, "I am *not* the conductor. . . . Yes, I know we both wear uniforms."

The old neighborhood in Brooklyn, through which the el rumbled overhead as noisily as a jet fighter, was busier than ever when David arrived there. Men, women and children were racing in every direction except down, from kosher butcher store to appetizing store to bakery to tailor shop to delicatessen to candy store to drugstore to grocery to Jewish pizzeria.

Quickening his steps in anticipation, he neared Uncle Asher's fruit store. He could almost smell it now! Suddenly he caught his breath and stopped short.

The store was closed.

Not a single bushel of fruit or vegetables was spilling over onto the sidewalk, and here it was the height of the evening shopping hour. One of his foster parents must be sick, or worse. The store had never closed on any day other than an American holiday, a Jewish holy day, and the week Uncle Asher had sat *shiva*, mourning and saying *Kaddish* for David's parents.

He dropped his suitcase and ran to the store. "*Please,* God," he murmured.

On the door was tacked a familiar red sign heralding: SPECIAL TODAY. On it Uncle Asher had written in blue crayon:

> CLOSING EARLY TODAY
> ON ACCOUNT OF
> COMING HOME OF
> NEPHEW

(Below that, scribbled in pencil, was: "Tell him re-
ards from Mrs. Lipman (Helen's mother). She just
raduated from N.Y.U.—Cum Lauder.")

"Thank God!"

He went back for his suitcase and returned to the sign.
With his pen he crossed out the last word and wrote
bove it: SON. Then he went around the corner of the
tore, entered the vestibule of the building and hurried
o apartment 1-A. He kissed the mezuzah on the door-
ost, the small metal container encasing a Hebrew scroll
vhich proclaimed the Biblical words: "Hear, O Israel,
he Lord our God, the Lord is One. . . . Thou shalt love
he Lord thy God with all thy heart, with all thy soul,
nd with all thy might. . . ." He rang the bell and
apped impatiently on the door.

Pots banged inside the apartment. "It's him! It's
im!" he heard Tante Dvorah cry.

"Just look this time who's there," Uncle Asher said.
You don't want to kiss the exterminator again."

The door swung open. *"Duvid!"* Tante Dvorah rushed
orward and hugged him with the combined fierceness of
a mother bear defending her cub and a woman shopping
at a sale at S. Klein's. She pulled away quickly, not
permitting herself a lengthy embrace. "You must be
hungry. Come." And she pushed him into the foyer where
he aromas, drifting in from the adjoining kitchen,
started him salivating.

"Here, let me have the suitcase." She grabbed it from
his hand. "Your coat." She pulled it off his back. "Here's
a towel." She thrust one into his hand.

David was taken aback. "What's going on here? You
used to make me put away my own things, yell at me
for not hanging up my coat. And why did you close up
the store?" He was saddened by a sudden realization.
"You're treating me like a *guest!*"

Tante Dvorah looked wistful. "Duvid," she said,
"you're no longer ours any more." She turned away and
busied herself with hanging up his coat in the hall closet.
"Now hurry up and wash before all my cold things get
overheated and my sweet and sour turns."

Uncle Asher thumped David on the shoulder. "Don't mind your tante. She's only being her usual twenty years behind the times. You know how some mothers feel when their child starts his first day of school? Well, Tante is just beginning to feel that way now. But I guarantee she'll be all ready to let go of you altogether just as soon as you become a grandfather." He looked into his nephew's eyes. "*Nu, Duvid*, how are you?"

"Happy, *very* happy to be home!" He scrutinized his foster parents, looking for every familiar line on their lambent faces, fretting over the rough skin on their worn hands, warming to their goodness. They had not changed. They looked no older, no wearier, no less content with their lot—and he was grateful. And then he realized that, of course, they *couldn't* change—not to him. For he would always continue to see them, as he always had seen them, through the eyes of love.

"You look *beautiful*," he said. "*Both* of you look beautiful."

Uncle Asher grunted—sentiment embarrassed his foster parents—and Tante Dvorah tsk-tsked. "But you're so *thin*. All that gentile food—"

David protested, "I've gained *ten pounds* in the Air Force."

"Ten *Air Force* pounds," Tante Dvorah sniffed.

Excusing himself, David went to wash up. His aunt called to him through the bathroom door: "Before I forget—a Ben Harris called a while ago; he said he sang the *Kiddush* for you at a Pesach Seder. I invited him over for supper, of course, but he couldn't make it. He'll be by a little later on, though."

"Wonderful. I wrote him I was coming in. I've been wondering how he's made out in civilian life. He had hopes of getting into show business."

He joined his foster parents at the kitchen table, elongated now with two extra leaves and resplendent with the white Sabbath cloth, the good dishes and silverware, a centerpiece designed out of a red cabbage head, and napkins that clung like cloth. "What's all this?" Before him were heaping platters of chopped liver, pastrami, corned beef, sweet and sour stuffed cabbage, gefülte fish, smoked white fish, herring, lox, bagels, rolls, fruit, and three different kinds of cake. "The last time I saw so much food, a honeymoon followed the dessert!"

Tante Dvorah held herself in check until the blessing had been recited over the bread and everyone had filled his plate and started to eat. Then she began, "Speaking of honeymoons . . ."

"And when *weren't* you speaking of honeymoons?" Uncle Asher said wryly.

"Here," she said with the unperturbed aplomb of Queen Elizabeth, as she picked up a piece of paper from under a seltzer bottle, "here's the names and numbers of five very nice Jewish girls, all personally inspected by me. But, Duvid, you don't have to call a single one of them up if you don't want. You can wait till you're finished eating first."

David had no heart for any five girls so long as he was still mourning the one girl he had lost. "I'll be running you up quite a phone bill," he said with pretended lightness. "I have all these other people to call." He dug out a list from his breast pocket.

Tante Dvorah took the list from him and examined it. "Such funny names," she said, reading aloud, "Johnson, Adams, Morgan, De Carlo, Williams, Kennedy . . ."

"They're airmen," David explained, "from Fairfield. I'm calling up their families to say hello."

"They don't have a chaplain of their *own* to do that? I mean, what can a rabbi say to someone who doesn't know gefülte fish from a kashe knish?"

"Well, that's one nice thing about the Air Force," said David. "Things like that don't matter. After all, 'Have we all not one Father, hath not one God created us?'"

Tante Dvorah, whose chief contact with gentiles had been pogroms she and her family had fled the Old Country to escape, regarded her nephew with surprise. "America!" she exclaimed, mystified.

"No," David corrected her with a smile, "Malachi." Soberly he added, "Tante, it's only right, it's only

291

Jewish. The more people a person can bring into his 'we,' the more human he himself becomes. The more people you can establish community with, have concern for, the greater opportunity there is for you to serve God. Because, as Judaism teaches, the Divine is reflected in every single human being."

Tante Dvorah pondered his words for a moment. "Christians, too?" she asked.

Uncle Asher sighed.

David continued, more to clarify his thoughts to himself than to explain them to his aunt, "Embracing *all* men in their foreignness of backgrounds, strangeness of customs, peculiarity of outlooks—this is the only way to transcend self-preoccupation and self-limitation. This is how a human being approaches the universality of God—by universalizing his concern, by identifying with all men. *God* doesn't limit Himself to particular individuals—how, then, can *we?*"

Someone rapped at the front door.

Tante Dvorah, who was following David with difficulty, said, "Saved by the knock!" Apologetically she added, "An Albert Einstein I never was." She arose from the table and left the kitchen to open the door.

"I'm Ben Harris," the men heard a baritone voice say.

There was a moment's pause. "Yes?"

"I called before."

Another pause. "Yes?"

David and Uncle Asher looked at each other in wonder. Didn't Tante Dvorah remember who Harris was and that she herself had invited him over?

"Is Chaplain Cohen at home?"

"Yes, he is."

"Well, can I see him?"

"Of course, of course."

As soon as Harris entered the kitchen with a surprised Tante Dvorah, David understood her hesitancy. For he had forgotten to mention that the former airman was a Negro.

And that pleased him, he realized. What pleased him

292

even more was that there was no trace of self-righteousness in his pleasure. For his omission had not been deliberate. (Uncomfortably, he recalled how proud of himself he had been the time he had so consciously defended a Puerto Rican youngster at his Army physical, and the time when he had insisted on Harris' accompanying him to the Mississippi Seder.)

"I dropped by because I thought you might still need a tenth man for a *minyan*, Chaplain," Harris said.

David laughed and greeted him, and the former airman responded with warmth. He looked different: older, naturally, a little heavier, nattily dressed, smile less shy, manner self-assured.

"This is my Tante Dvorah and my Uncle Asher—Ben Harris."

Tante Dvorah, who had been scrutinizing Harris during the exchange of greetings and introductions, shook her head. "Funny," she said to him, "you don't *look* it."

"Jewish?"

"*Colored.* Jewish I know you are. You sang the *Kiddush* at the Seder."

Harris was taken aback, along with David and Uncle Asher. "But I *am* colored—as *well* as Jewish. Didn't Chaplain Cohen inform you? Can't you *tell?*"

There was a startled pause, then: "Have a fruit." And Tante Dvorah held up a plate of chopped liver.

"Thank you." Harris scooped up some liver on a cracker, swallowed it whole, broke into a spasm of coughing, and gasped politely, "You make it every bit as good as my own mother."

"Oh!"

Uncle Asher said, "We're finished eating already. Suppose we adjourn to the next room while the womenfolk clean up." To his wife, he added, "And settle down."

The men retired to the living room to talk. David inquired about Harris' wife, and the former airman said with pride that she was pregnant, "for *real,* this time." Uncle Asher asked Harris about his try at show business, and he told him, almost apologetically, that he was doing surprisingly well, then went on to explain that a fluke had established him as a promising young recording star. It seemed that since his separation from the Air Force, he had been trying to sell demonstration records of his own songs to various companies, but they had been rejected as too slow or too solemn or too square for the teen-age market. Finally, on the verge of abandoning show business, he had submitted two last songs, parodies of some sick rock 'n' roll ditties, and one company had bought them and, with Harris as the singer, had marketed them as serious rock 'n' roll love songs. Over five hundred thousand records had been sold.

"Marvelous!" said David, rejoicing that his judgment of Harris' chances for a career in show business had been wrong. "What are the names of the songs?"

Harris fidgeted. "I don't think it's your kind of chopped liver, Chaplain. It's not even *my* kind, God knows."

"I want to buy a copy myself," Uncle Asher said. "What did you say the name of the record is?"

"Now, remember, they were written as parodies." Harris hesitated.

"Yes?"

"Well, one side is 'I Loved You So Much, I Wish You'd Drop Dead.'" He shrugged, as if to disclaim all responsibility. "And the other side is 'That's Why I Killed You, My Darling.'"

"America!" said Uncle Asher.

Tante Dvorah entered and announced: "The womenfolk has finished in the kitchen. Can she rejoin the human race now?"

With *nachus*, David told his aunt of Harris's success, then commented to him, "That must account for all your new poise, your self-confidence. Why, anybody would take you now for at least a colonel, maybe even a sergeant."

"*Is* there a difference in me?" Harris looked pleased. "Well, if there is, I suppose money in the bank and a recording contract, not to mention a pregnant wife, have something to do with it. But I think Mississippi is what started it—that time I went to the Seder and sang.

I did it because you forced me, of course, and was I scared! But that night made me feel more like a man than I did even on my honeymoon." He paused. "Say, that reminds me! There's this girl at my recording company, a wonderful person. I'd like you to meet her and maybe—"

David groaned. "You, too?"

Quickly Tante Dvorah said, "Is she—?"

"White?" Harris asked tolerantly.

Tante Dvorah shook her head impatiently. "*Jewish.*"

"*N'vu den?*" said Harris, using Yiddish shorthand for: What else? Of course! How could you even *ask* such a question?

Tante Dvorah beamed. (She had voted regularly for La Guardia simply because he had once called someone a *goniff*, Yiddish for thief.) She went over to Harris and pulled him by the arm. "Come, eat."

"Thank you very much, but I just finished supper before coming here."

Tante Dvorah looked at him, perplexed. "What kind of excuse is that not to eat?" And she pushed him into the kitchen to ply him there with food.

When Harris left—with jars of chopped liver and gefülte fish for his wife and a pot of stuffed cabbage for his mother and some fruit for his unborn child, all of which Tante Dvorah forced upon him—she turned a reproving eye on her nephew. "Why didn't you tell me *beforehand* your friend was a Negro? So I wouldn't have acted in the beginning like such a dumb Dvorah. But who ever knew from colored Jews?"

"I'm sorry. I *should* have told you, I guess. But it just never occurred to me." He added, with sudden realization, "Any more than it would occur to me now to announce that someone's a Christian or a Moslem or a Republican."

"You're too accepting," Tante Dvorah commented. "What about all the *goyim* who wouldn't be so accepting of *you* just because you're a Jew?"

David shrugged. "Well, I'd say that's *their* problem

295

so long as I know I've done nothing to provoke any hostility."

Uncle Asher regarded his nephew thoughtfully. "Duvid, you've changed." He smiled.

"Have I?" said David, reflecting that whatever change he had undergone was in the direction of his becoming *more* Jewish, *truly* religious. For the *Sh'ma* directed Jews to be universal in their concern. This declaration of the oneness of God *forced* Jews to affirm the oneness of men.

(He recalled the beautiful *Midrash* wherein, according to the ancient rabbis, God had reproached His angels for breaking forth into songs of jubilation when the Egyptians were drowning in the Red Sea, saying, "How *dare* you celebrate when my children are lying dead upon the seashore!" And He had pointed to the drowned Egyptians. And then there was the traditional custom of spilling ten drops from each cup of wine at the Seder in memory of the ten plagues because, according to rabbinic proscription, no one's cup of joy should ever be full when anyone on earth had been harmed.)

Of course, no one could *begin* as a universalist; one came to a universal concern only by way of the particular. For no man lived in an abstraction; he had to start from a defined point: a particular home, a particular tradition, a particular religion. But his particularities should not limit him forever. (Thousands of years before the rabbis had posed the question: "Why did the Lord create only *one* man, Adam, when He created the world?" Their answer: "In order that no man afterwards should be able to say, 'My ancestors were better than yours.' As all human beings are traced back to one parent, all human beings must necessarily be brothers.") Just like with the Star of David, he thought. Its center remains constant, but its six arms, nourished by its source, radiate to the corners of the earth.

Aloud, he concluded, "I guess I *have* changed. In fact, you might even call it a conversion."

Tante Dvorah nodded. "Change, conversion. Conversion, change. *Something's* different, Duvid. You used to *ve my strudel. And tonight you only ate two pieces."

After three weeks of looking up old friends and professors, attending lectures and the theater and concerts, visiting airmen's families, dreaming of Ilona, and avoiding Tante Dvorah's five girl friends, David returned to airfield. There he found that in his absence Dena had left the base to live with relatives in Chicago, the Stratfords had been transferred to England, Colonel Kingsbury had been appointed the new Base Commander, and that the A.R.S.'s TDY to Thule was being postponed for six months.

He was pleased to discover also that his five-minute walk from the B.O.Q. to the chapel now took at least an hour. For people were always stopping him to ask for appointments, or to try to borrow some money, or to invite him to speak in Fair City, or to inquire whether he'd be going along on the next TDY, or to consult him on the advisability of going AWOL, or to wish him a happy Jewish New Year, or to reminisce about Goose Bay, or to thank him for his previous help, or to match him up with a wife's cousin's Jewish girl friend back home.

People soon began pressing him, as his separation date neared, to make a career of the Air Force. Sergeant Winters of Personnel, then Mitchell, and even Colonel Kingsbury tried to convince him to go Indefinite and extend his tour of duty. This David could not bring himself to do, not even when Alex broached the subject on the night of his newborn son's christening.

"Chap, it's the only play," Alex said as they were driving back from the chapel to his home. "You just *got* to re-up."

Marge, now no longer blurred in either her dark good looks or gentle voice, intervened. "What Alex means is that *he* re-upped the other day over my objections—maybe it's because I'm a mother now, but I think flying is too dangerous an occupation for any father—and now he's looking for reinforcements. You know how misery loves re-enlistments, Chap."

David could not conceal his surprise. "Alex, you actually re-enlisted?"

"Sure I did. Of course it doesn't mean that all of a sudden flying doesn't bother me any more—I was going to say 'terrify me'—but I guess I'm still too scared to use that word, although not *that* scared any longer that I haven't finally told Marge all about it. Nor does it mean that I've gone completely dry when I'm not high in the sky."

"What *does* it mean then, Alex?"

"I don't know. I guess it means I enjoy what I'm doing now—doesn't it?—and I want to keep on doing it. See, I look at it this way: Cows and milk and wheat and stuff like that, which is what's waiting for me back in Illinois, just don't stack up against flying, not in my book. Farming's so *stationary*, you know what I mean? And dull. And insignificant, compared with SAC. SAC is absolutely the biggest job in the world today—that's the way I feel, and being a father now with a baby to look out for has something to do with the way I feel, I'm sure—because if we fail to keep the peace and another war breaks out, nothing will be able to save us ever—not science, not religion, nothing."

Ruefully, David nodded. "I guess I have to agree with you there."

"Then why don't you re-up?" Alex insisted. "You know you're needed as much here as among all those sillyvilians."

David hesitated, reviewing in his mind his reasons for not staying on in the Air Force. First and foremost, how could he continue as a rabbi without ever having a congregation of his own? And how would he ever be able to get married while stationed at bases with no eligible Jewish girls nearby? And how could he, as a career Air Force chaplain, manage to avoid flying for twenty years? Finally, how long could someone like himself maintain his precarious balance on the tightrope before falling off for good? He felt certain that the only reason he wasn't dangling from it now—and by his neck—was that the opportunity had not as yet presented itself.

"For one thing," he said finally, nodding in Marge's [di]rection and offering the most understandable reason, "[I] want to make some lovely young girl a mother my-[sel]f. But there are no Jewish girls around here for me [to] date, let alone marry. Now I know you're going to [sa]y that my next station may be McGuire Air Force [Ba]se near New York's Jewish girls, or outside Los An-[ge]les or San Francisco, but what if I get assigned to [T]hule or Goose Bay or Morocco? Alex, gambling with [yo]ur life as you do when you fly is one thing, but I'm [su]re you'll agree that it takes a good deal more bravery [fo]r a man to gamble with his *love* life."

Marge laughed. "Give up, Alex."

But Alex was stubborn. "Oh, no. I still have almost [tw]o more months to work on him." He added myste-[ri]ously, "Besides, I have a plan." And he winked.

Chapter : 22

[I]t was eleven o'clock on a Tuesday morning and David [w]as in the middle of a lecture when the sirens sud-[d]enly broke out into an insistent wail.

For a moment the men in the theater sat immobilized —never before had sirens been employed to signal a day-[t]ime Practice Alert—then they dashed out of the theater, [D]avid with them.

Some of Stewart Alsop's words raced through his mind [a]s he ran toward the flight line. "For the real target [o]f the Soviet missiles is, of course, SAC."

All the available aircraft at Fairfield were now warm-[i]ng up in a deafening cacophony of engines. By the [t]ime he reached Wing Headquarters and reported to [M]itchell, who had preceded him there, B-47's and KC-[9]7's were already streaking down the runways.

Men from the Wing Command Staff were huddled together in the briefing room in a tight little cluster, conversing quietly. The Intelligence Officer raised his voice. "Well, we should know in ten minutes or so," he said, and the other men nodded.

David pulled Mitchell aside. "What's *happened?*" He pointed through a nearby window at planes rolling down the runways like cans off an assembly line. "All those planes! This isn't just a Practice Alert, *is* it?"

Gravely Mitchell shook his head. "No, it isn't. Some of our DEW-line radarscopes registered the appearance of foreign objects. All SAC bases have been alerted to move—"

"Foreign objects?" David's heart skipped a beat. "You mean—*planes? Missiles?* You mean—*Russian* planes? *Russian* missiles?"

"No one knows yet. Could be. I don't think so. But could be."

"Are our planes carrying nuclear bombs?" Mitchell nodded soberly, and David shuddered. "I was just thinking . . . This is sure to turn out to be a false alarm —I hope!—but what if one of our bombers doesn't get word to return to Fairfield?"

"The bombers don't continue on to Russia," Mitchell replied, "unless they get a second signal while in the air to proceed to their targets."

David looked through the window at the runways that seemed to stretch all the way to infinity and the silvery bombers streaking down them carrying eternity in their bomb-bays. "The thought just occurred to me, Mitchell. What if it were only some flocks of birds on our DEW-line radarscopes that triggered this Alert, and what if the Russians then send out their planes in reaction to *our* approaching aircraft? Neither of us would want to pull back her planes for fear the other was launching an attack—each would feel compelled to send that second signal continuing the bombers on to their targets. Or am I wrong?"

Mitchell shook his head. "No, you're not wrong, David," he said, facing the runways with bowed head, like a mourner at a funeral. "The *world* is wrong when

300

he merest accident can destroy millions of people and
ll of civilization. If only we had less men of science
nd more men of God! Our brains have outstripped our
ouls—" He paused as something like a thunderclap
ounded outside.

"What was that!"

David looked up at the sky in the direction of the
hunderclap as men crowded him against the window
rame. He saw four wings disentangling themselves from
one another in a shower of pieces.

"Good God in heaven!"

As he watched in dread, a bomber and a tanker, gushing flames, sprinkled bits of themselves over the ground
below them. In a moment the B-47, now without any
wings, dropped like a rock into a lake beneath as three
white mushrooms bloomed in the sky above it. The
KC-97, twirling on its one remaining wing like a brightly
colored pinwheel, nosed over and, with a crazy whine,
swirled lazily toward the earth.

"No!" several men exclaimed in horror. *"No—"*

But another officer cried, "Faster! Faster! Get the
damn thing over with!"

Gradually, almost reluctantly, the tanker disintegrated,
breaking up into a flaming junkshop in the sky. The
cockpit and left wing remained attached, dropping together in giant spirals, trailing fiery fragments in their
wake. The right wing followed close behind, but the tail
section was more leisurely in its descent. It glided earth-
ward like a plane and came down in one piece in an
open field.

There was a shattering blast, and a great ball of fire
leaped from the wreckage. It hovered over the crash as
if solicitously inspecting the havoc, then lazily drifted
upward into the gray sky, now smudged with billowing black smoke.

"Please, God, let it not be anyone I know!" David
prayed, then felt ashamed of himself.

The crush of bodies behind him eased abruptly as the
men raced out of the room. Fire-trucks and ambulances
were screeching all over the base.

"Chaplain! Come on!"

David wheeled around and ran to the door where the Wing Commander was standing.

"I meant Chaplain Wrightson," the officer said as Mitchell appeared beside him.

"The KC," David said, "those are my men aboard."

The Wing Commander hesitated for a moment. "All right. Maybe two chaplains will double their luck. God knows they need it. Let's go!"

The All-Clear signal sounded as the men ran out of the building, and the Wing Commander swore at it. "Damn siren! Where were you five minutes ago!"

They jumped into an empty car on the flight line. David took the wheel. Two more men got into the back seat and one told him to start.

He jabbed his foot down on the gas pedal and the car leaped forward past the flight line gate and through the streets of Fairfield. In minutes it was outside the base, hurtling in the direction of the crash.

A large, callused hand clamped down on his shoulder. "You drive any faster, Chap, and we'll never get there." It was Colonel Kingsbury in the back seat.

He slowed the car down to seventy miles per hour. That was still fast enough to force him to concentrate all his attention on the road and to stop him from thinking of the collision and guessing who had been on the tanker. Still he had to ask the question aloud: "Whose tanker was it? Was it Major Givney's?"

"We don't know yet," Colonel Kingsbury said. "All we know is some of the men escaped. We spotted their parachutes."

"That's the bomber crew," David said, wishing that he did not now know as much about the Air Force as he did. "They could eject themselves, but the tanker men —they never had a chance, did they?"

There was no reply.

Small fires were burning all over an open field alongside of the road, and soon the car was bumping over metal debris. Up ahead, spread out over a half a mile

302

area, were three major sections of the fallen aircraft, now flaming piles of rubbish. David brought the car to a stop. Everyone jumped out.

To the right was the only part of the plane that could be easily recognized, the tail section. Its fin had sliced a three-story barn in half. Four hundred yards away lay the fuselage mashed into the earth, a twenty-foot crater framing it. Three hundred yards beyond that was the front section of the plane, one propeller still turning, shooting out flames three stories high. Over all hung a charcoal pall of smoke, blacking out the landscape.

Firemen were hosing down the flames but crowds of civilians were clogging their way, trying to get closer looks at the wreckage. Air policemen were pushing the curious away and roping off the area while some people were busily collecting mementos from the debris. Nearby stood doctors and nurses with bottles of blood plasma.

"Any survivors yet?" Mitchell asked the doctors.

They shook their heads.

An Air Force tow truck attached a cable to the tail section and yanked away the side wall. The gaping hole revealed an airman inside mashed against the floor like hamburger meat.

David, recoiling, turned and ran away. A human being who was only a little lower than the angels had been reduced in a moment to dog food—it was *horrifying*. He stumbled over a smoking pile of debris. Looking down he saw an arm in a flying jacket sticking up out of the rubble. He shouted, almost sobbed, "Come quick! Come quick!" and reached down and seized the arm. Gently he lifted it.

A noiseless scream escaped him as the rubble yielded him the arm and nothing more. Gagging, he dropped the unattached arm, and suddenly he was throwing up.

"Chaplain! Over here!"

The doctors were yelling for him and, wiping his mouth on his sleeve, he dashed to them. Maybe a remnant had been saved—*halvai*. Nurses were beating at someone on the ground with blankets while two docto[rs] were rolling him, smoking like a wet log, over thi[ck] dampened mattresses. They stopped and peeled off th[e] remains of a uniform; some charred skin peeled off wit[h] it. One doctor began administering plasma while another wrapped the airman in blankets.

Most of his body and face, his hair and eyebrows were badly burned and his leg jutted out at a crazy angle, but the man struggled with the doctors and tried to get to his feet. "I have to jump! I have to jump! I have to jump!"

David laid a restraining hand upon his shoulder. "It's all right. You're on the ground now. You're safe."

The man went limp. "I'm on the ground now? I'm safe?"

"That's right. You're safe now."

The man sobbed, *Thank God!* The doctors picked him up and placed him on a stretcher. "Chap? Is that you? Chaplain Cohen?"

David started. The voice was the voice of Sergeant Cribbs, but the face was no face at all—only a scorched blister.

The doctors carried the stretcher to the ambulance. "Wait!" the sergeant exclaimed. He turned toward David. "Chaplain? God's here, isn't He? Isn't God here?"

David bit into his lower lip until he tasted blood. He reached out—the man's flesh was still smoking, he stank like a scorched chicken, he was repulsive to look at—and he took the boom operator gently in his arms. "Yes, Sergeant," he forced himself to say, "God's here."

The ambulance took Cribbs away, and David darted down the road to the place where firemen were trying to douse twenty-foot flames shooting out from the tanker's forward section. He hesitated for a moment, then plunged toward the wreckage, but he could not get closer than twenty-five feet to it; the heat and the flames drove him back, singeing his eyelashes.

"What are you doing!" Colonel Kingsbury was beside him, grabbing hold of his arm.

"Alex is in there, and Major Givney, Chuck Conte—"

The Colonel shook his head. "No, they're not," he said, "not any more."

Tears started to David's eyes, but the heat dried them as quickly as they fell. He looked again at the wreckage, Alex's funeral pyre, and a shudder gripped him. It was as if Alex had never been. *God!*

All at once David found himself thinking of leaving the rabbinate. All the misery, affliction, and suffering that were his daily portion as a chaplain were too much to bear. Ilona's tale of horror and Colonel Kingsbury's pitiable story were only two of the many pathetic confessions that he heard regularly—among accounts of beatings, deaths, alcoholism, adultery, bastardy, sadism, perversion, psychosis, even one case of incest. And now, the crash. It was difficult for him, though not even directly involved, to understand and to reconcile himself to some of the calamities, so how could he presume to comfort their victims? There were people who came to him to whom he could offer nothing but sympathy, and what good was that? Empathizing hardly improved others' misfortunes—it hadn't alleviated any of Ilona's torment, and how could he possibly console Marge Winkler now?—and it only left him desolate and despairing. What good was he as a rabbi if the real answers eluded him too?

"Colonel Kingsbury? Are you Colonel Kingsbury, the base commander?" An elderly, dapper civilian with a cane and a distraught look creasing his ruddy, rotund face was addressing the Colonel. "Colonel Kingsbury?"

The Colonel nodded.

"Is it true what your air police are telling people around here, or are they just trying to scare them away from the wreckage? I'm Richard Whitney, the Mayor of Fair City. Is it true that one of the planes that crashed carried nuclear bombs? Is that true?"

Colonel Kingsbury pointed to the civilians surging around the crash site. "If you want to help your people, keep them away from here and from the lake where the bomber fell."

The Mayor mopped his brow with a silk handkerchief.

305

"You haven't answered my question, Colonel." He paused, suddenly stricken. "Or *have* you? *Did* that bomber carry atomic or hydrogen bombs?"

"We can discuss this at another time, Mayor. Right now—"

"O my God!" The Mayor's ruddy face blanched. "It *is* true! Your planes—flying over Fair City day and night—carrying bombs capable of wiping out a thousand Fair Cities at one swoop. This cannot be allowed! Colonel, do you realize there are over a hundred thousand people less than two miles from here, all of whom would have been killed if just one of your bombs had been set off by this collision? And now, the radioactive fallout—this cannot be allowed! We must do something about it—move the base, petition the government, let people know—"

Colonel Kingsbury spoke up sharply. "Five men just died in this crash and one of them was burned beyond recognition, Mayor, and I've yet to hear you say you're sorry. And who do you suppose they died *for?*"

Mayor Whitney flushed. "Of course I'm sorry. Do I have to say so? But I have a responsibility to a hundred thousand people in Fair City who are still living."

If only both men weren't so right! thought David. That was the tragedy here—everyone was right and everyone was likely to end up in a literal hell. Alex had been the first to go, and now Marge was the second. Next would be he, for he had to go now to tell her. He started for the car.

Behind him Colonel Kingsbury was saying, "Suppose we discuss this after the funerals. You *were* planning to attend, weren't you, Mayor?"

Chapter : 23

FLOWERS were everywhere, a multicolored cancer running wild in the chapel: roses, carnations, lilies, mums,
gladioli, arranged in bouquets, wreaths, baskets, stands,
blankets. Spilling out from the sanctuary where they ob-
scured the altar, the flowers skirted the pulpit, covered
the Communion rail and buried the flag-draped casket.

For Fairfield personnel and their wives, filling every
part of the chapel where there were no flowers, nothing
could soften the tragedy of Tuesday's crash, except perhaps the thought—banished from mind yet its memory
still lingering—that if a plane *had* to crash, they were
glad it had not been theirs.

Yet there were some flyers who sat there, as organ
music washed over them, supremely confident that
neither of the two wrecked planes could possibly have
been their own; aircraft would continue to crash, of
course, but it would always be someone else's. What
person can envision his own death?

Their wives, however, felt equally certain that Alex
Winkler, who was being buried that morning, and Harry
Givney and Alan Banks, whose bodies had been shipped
to their respective home towns, and Charles Conte and
John Slevin, who would be buried after Friday's Mass,
had never expected to be killed either. What flyer's wife
cannot envision her husband's death?

And so, not all the tears that were falling in the
chapel that morning were for the dead. Some were being
shed for those still living.

At precisely 1100 hours, the side door at the front
of the chapel opened, and Mitchell appeared leading in
Marge, supported by her father. Her eyes framed with
black shadows, like twin death wreaths, she passed in

front of David in the first pew, and he averted his gaze. Who could look upon the face of anguish without feeling a vague sense of guilt for having been spared?

"Why? why? *why?*"

Marge had paused before him, her black-rimmed eyes imploring an answer which he did not possess. *"Why?"*

He bowed his head, mute.

The girl's father pulled her forward. "Come, Marge."

She shuffled to her seat and sank down, moaning. "They wouldn't even let me see Alex to say good-bye. They put him in the coffin and they nailed it up tight. They wouldn't even let me see him."

Mayor Whitney, in the pew behind her, mopped his brow.

Marge's father put an arm around her. "You've got to think of the baby now, Marge, you've got to."

"Why did he have to *burn?* God! Why did he have to *burn!*" She buried her face in her father's shoulder.

Mitchell, his gray face and black robe clashing with the festive flowers all around him, made his way to the lectern. Invoking the name of God, he began to pray aloud.

David clapped a hand to his mouth and chewed off a fingernail. He could not escape Marge's question for long. In a few minutes he would have to answer it, and publicly too. If only she hadn't asked him to deliver the eulogy for Alex! What could he possibly utter now by way of explanation for what had happened? How could he interpret the tragedy? What was there for him to say except that he too mourned Alex, his friend.

He leaned forward, putting his clammy head in his damp hands. *Why?* Who knew the answer? Certainly not he. But he *should* know; he was, after all, a rabbi. If only God would help him find the right words—now! For Marge's sake. That was all she had to grab hold of now: words. Please, God—the right words, words that would comfort, impose some semblance of order, impart some measure of meaning to Tuesday's tragedy.

All at once the chapel was still. Mitchell had stopped praying, disappearing behind a stand of pink and white carnations, the congregation was waiting expectantly. Please, God—the right words now, at least *that*.

David rose and stepped up to the lectern. He turned around and faced front without looking at anyone. He fixed his eyes upon a corner star in the flag covering the casket, then confessed:

"I don't know *why* Alex Winkler and four others died any more than his wife and baby do. I've thought about it, I've questioned, I've sought the answer. But there is no ready one—not for Marge Winkler, not for the baby, not for me, a chaplain as well as a friend of Alex's—and I can't pretend there is an ultimate answer that anyone can fathom."

He sighed. "And yet, saying that, I trust that I haven't said it all. For there *is* a reason why Alex died —as unsatisfying as any reason that cannot change what has happened, that does not bring back the departed. And that reason is: Alex died because he deliberately and continuously and purposefully risked his life every week of the year.

"Had Alex left the Air Force to return to a successful family farming enterprise in Illinois, it is safe to assume that he would still be alive today. Instead, after enlisting in the Air Force, he chose to remain after completing his initial hitch.

"Why?

"Since it is this decision, as much as a malfunctioning bomber that ultimately brought about Tuesday's collision, we must, in tracking down the why of Alex's death, examine his reason for remaining in the Air Force.

"That reason, I submit without exaggeration, even though Alex himself would have been the first to challenge me, that reason was a heroic one—heroic in the religious sense of choosing to assume risks for the sake of a noble cause.

"This noble cause, simply put, was: to buy time— time in which the nations of the world could work out an answer to peace." David searched out Mayor Whitney and addressed the next few words to him. "Or, to put it perhaps more concretely, to buy time in which

309

finally to see the junking of SAC and the rest of U.S. armed might as general world disarmament takes place.

"For it was obvious to Alex, as it is to the rest of us in SAC, that SAC is no permanent solution to world peace. At best, it is a temporary holding operation till peace is achieved not for our country alone but for the entire world. At best, SAC can be only the posthumous avenger of a nation's murder."

Mayor Whitney lowered his eyes.

"We in SAC must realize too that our holding operation cannot be expected to last out the next decade. SAC's finger may be in the dike, but the water level outside is steadily rising. For ever-faster means to deliver ever more destruction are beguiling the nations of the world, seducing them ever closer to atomic apocalypse with each new threatening crisis.

"This, in all likelihood, would already have been our lot were it not for men like Alex, and Harry Givney, Charles Conte, Alan Banks, John Slevin, Edward Cribbs —men who have been buying time for the world's leaders to arrive at a peaceful solution to our conflicts, paying with their sweat, anxiety, TDY's, terror, often strained family relationships.

"Yesterday, alas, another note fell due—notice not of God's failure, but of the world's—and this time five young men paid the supreme price with their lives.

"Were their deaths a waste?

"Yes, most certainly.

"Yet, also, *no*, in the sense that at least Alex and the others died *for something*, which is more than most men do. For surely next in importance to *why* a man dies and *when* is *what* he dies *for*.

"We do Alex a disservice if we think of him as a mere sheep, slaughtered by a bomber running wild. For he had some voice in his destiny, as much as anyone ever does: Deliberately, continuously and purposefully he endangered his life for the sake of the worthiest of goals, world peace.

"A visionary goal, you think? Not unless you think world survival is also visionary and impractical.

310

"And when this dream of world peace is finally realized—and realized it must be, or men will dream no more—Alex will be one of its architects.

"And if this dream is *not* realized, then *we* shall be the ones to die like sheep. But *our* deaths will not be caused by any mechanical malfunction. Mankind's death certificate will read: mind failure, spirit failure and nerve failure.

"May the Lord God grant that we do not fail, if only for the sake of Alex Winkler whose soul we commend to Him this morning."

David, his chin digging into his chest, returned to his seat, and a collective sigh rippled through the chapel.

Mitchell came forward again and prayed aloud, beseeching the Lord's mercy upon the fallen airmen and their families. Then, nodding to the pallbearers, he descended from the pulpit and started slowly down the center aisle. "The Lord is my shepherd . . ."

The pallbearers with their burden trailed behind, and Marge sobbed, *"God!* Why did he have to *burn!"*

David, reviewing the eulogy in his mind, joined the crowd filing out of the chapel. If only his words had been more comforting! He felt a slight pressure on his arm and turned sideways.

Colonel Kingsbury said, "I'll take you to the cemetery." And he led David outside. There Mayor Whitney stopped the Base Commander while David proceeded ahead to the car, still reviewing his eulogy. Why couldn't he have been more helpful!

"You know what the Mayor just told me?" the Colonel said when he joined him in the car and started after the procession. "After listening to that fine talk of yours, he's decided to abort his campaign to get Fairfield and Littlefield moved. That's what he said. Instead, he's going to educate his constituents to the importance of SAC. What do you think of that?"

David did not reply. His thoughts as well as his eyes were fixed upon the hearse up ahead, the remains of Alex inside and Marge behind it.

The Colonel allowed himself a smile. "Perhaps paying

311

all Fairfield personnel yesterday in two-dollar bills helped some too. Because when our men went around last night checking on what denominations were filling the tills of Fair City, eighty per cent of all the bills were deuces. In a year it amounts to something like ten million dollars. And when this simple fact was presented to the City Council this morning—Chap, I think we make a swell team: You appeal to the best in people and I take advantage of their worst."

The funeral procession wound to a halt at the edge of Fair City where a verdant cemetery with shrubs and vast lawns and tiny metal tablets substituting for tombstones sought to masquerade as a park. The casket was unloaded and Mitchell read over it from the Books of Psalms and Revelations. Then the coffin was lowered into an open grave and the chief pallbearer handed the American flag, now folded into a thick triangle, to Mitchell. He nodded to the firing squad, and a volley of shots rang out, splintering the silence.

A child in the crowd recoiled in fright, and David suddenly remembered the last military funeral he had attended, the mock ceremony at Landers. Only this time no one would rise up at the conclusion of the service; there was nothing in the coffin that was even capable of being resurrected.

The mournful echo of taps still hugged the air as Mitchell approached Marge with the flag. Presenting it to her, he said awkwardly, almost apologetically: "Mrs. Winkler, this flag is offered by a grateful nation in memory of your husband's faithful service."

Marge regarded the flag with horror, as if it were Alex's bones that were being handed her to pocket. *"I don't want no flags!"* she screamed. *"I don't want no gratefuls! I don't want no heroes! I only want Alex!"*

A red, white and blue triangle arched through the air and dropped into the grave. Marge, throwing herself after the flag, fell on top of the coffin. *"I only want my Alex!"*

Her father and Mitchell took hold of the hysterical

312

girl and half-carried, half-dragged her away to the car while all the time she kept screaming, *"Alex! Alex! Alex! Alex! Alex!"* like a litany.

David's teeth dug into his lower lip until he tasted blood. He turned on Colonel Kingsbury beside him as Marge's car drove off. "If only I had made you *ground* Alex—!"

The Colonel grabbed him roughly by the arm. "You'd *still* be attending a funeral today, Chap. Only difference is it would be someone else's, another lieutenant with a different name. *Hundreds* of Air Force men die in crashes every year—don't you *know* that?"

"Maybe so," David sighed. "But at least I wouldn't feel so guilty."

Colonel Kingsbury's thick fingers tightened around David's arm, bruising it. "It's like you intimated in your talk," he said in a hard voice. "In this filthy business of cold war and near war, there's enough guilt to go around for everyone, civilian and military, clergymen and lay people, Russia and even our own United States. So don't you go around assigning or appropriating more than your own rightful share, you hear?" He released David and strode away without another word.

Lingering behind as the crowd dispersed, David intoned the ancient words: "The Lord hath given, the Lord hath taken away; blessed be the name of the Lord." But for the first time in his life he could not drop his voice at the end of the verse, and the Biblical words remained suspended in air, as if in a question.

Still he continued, *"Yisgadal v'yiskadash sh'meh rabbo,"* sobbing the *Kaddish*, the prayer traditionally recited by a Jewish mourner for a blood relative, *"b'olmo di v'ro chiruseh v'yamlich malchuseh . . ."*

Chapter : 24

SUDDENLY less than a week separated David from civilian life. In five more days he would be boarding the train first to Roger's wedding, then back to Brooklyn and home and Tante Dvorah and Uncle Asher and a synagogue of his own and eventually a wife and his friends and one of the main centers of Jewish learning in the United States and New York's many cultural offerings and . . . so why was he beginning to miss Fairfield and its people even before he had bought his train ticket?

Only one last official act remained for David to perform as a United States Air Force chaplain, and that was to deliver his final lecture to the Food Service Squadron that evening in one of the dining halls. The following morning he would begin clearing the base, and four days later he would be on the train returning home. It had taken him two years to make that train, and now it all seemed too sudden.

David walked to the dining hall, glad that it was at the other end of the base. Now that he would be leaving Fairfield shortly, he frequently took walks about the base at all times of the day and night, taking mental pictures all the while of his—what did the men call it dryly?—home away from home, which in all probability he would never see again.

Fairfield was an extremely noisy place, he was now discovering after twenty-one months there. For the first time he was conscious of the continuous roar of airplanes warming up, taking off, landing.

It was dusk now as he walked up Fairfield's wide main boulevard, lined on both sides by redbud trees and encircling a verdant middle isle of St. Augustine grass, evergreens, shrubs and late-blooming bushes. Through the lighted windows he could see Fairfield families gathered together at home eating their evening meal, watching television, visiting with friends, or starting out for the Club. A stray dog barked at him, and a lawn sprinkler sprayed him too, and the omnipresent scooters streaked to and from the flight line.

Occasionally a passing car would honk its horn at him, outlined in the headlights, and the driver, faceless within the dark car, would call out a greeting, and David would wave. Three of the cars stopped to offer him a ride, and two others paused to invite him home for dinner before he left Fairfield.

A few airmen sitting outside on their barracks steps greeted him, and jokingly he invited them to come along to his lecture. Across the way from them, other airmen were dancing with Wafs to the refreshment stand's blaring jukebox.

Stopping at the library, David returned the last Great Book he would ever read in Mississippi, pleased that he had never had the time to complete the series. Down the street at the Officers Club, couples were already beginning to arrive for the Air Base Group Dance that night, while in front of the Service Club a few airmen were diligently painting in the letters of a sign which read: HELP STAMP OUT OFFICERS. Beyond the Club, a B-47 Strato-jet was coming in for a landing with its drag chute billowing behind, looking almost as if the entire plane had bailed out of the sky. No, Brooklyn would never be like this!

Yet, in another sense, *this* would never be like Brooklyn. No precarious tightrope there between the twin authorities of religion and the military. But he mustn't be unfair, he swiftly told himself. For civilian life had its own tightrope, as did the rabbinate itself—he realized now—and his value as a man and as a rabbi lay in how skillfully he negotiated them. (Besides, a Jew should be *accustomed* to tightropes anyhow, no?) For civilian life it was now the agonizing race between education and annihilation, and for him as a rabbi it was the everlasting attempt to reconcile what was (Ilona's tale of horror, the KC-97 crash, all the heartbreaking counseling cases) with what *ought* to be. Tightrope after tightrope, *forever* tightropes!

Finally he reached the dining hall. Sergeant Shuster, the rawboned mess sergeant who had served with the Air Refueling Squadron at Goose Bay, was waiting for him outside. He greeted David casually, then led him into the kitchen.

"Oh, yeah," the sergeant said. "I better tell you so you don't get surprised when you step into the hall, Chaplain. I fixed up a spotlight out there special for the lecture, to help keep the men's attention on you all the time."

"That was extremely thoughtful. Thank you."

"You bet." Sergeant Shuster stopped as they reached the door leading to the dining room. "Oh, and there's another thing, Chaplain. Somebody just gave me this DF to give you before you start the lecture. He said it was kind of important."

David took the unsigned sheet of paper and read:

SUBJECT: Dynamics of Moral Leadership Lecture

TO: Chaplain (1/Lt) David Cohen

1. Please note that the topic for this month's Moral Leadership Lecture has been changed.

2. The new topic is What Not To Call the Base Commander's Wife While Kibitzing at Bridge.

David started. "Who gave you this note!"

"He said he was the base chaplain," Sergeant Shuster said. "I suppose he was, but the only chaplains I know for sure are you and Father O'Neill." Before David had a chance to worry about the odd DF—Who could have sent it? And why? Obviously, it was a joke. Or was there still time for him to be court-martialed? Where was Mrs. Stratford tonight?—Sergeant Shuster pushed him through the swinging kitchen door, saying, "They're waiting for you, Chaplain."

David walked to the lectern, turned to face the audience sitting in the dark, and immediately regretted Sergeant Shuster's thoughtfulness. For the spotlight was so strong that David was blinded when he faced front. He moved away from the lectern to escape the spotlight but it doggedly followed him, continuing to blind him.

Out front the mass of breathing blurs began to chuckle.

David stopped playing tag with the spotlight and, addressing the audience that he could not see, began his talk. "Good evening. The topic for—"

For no conceivable reason, the men interrupted. "Good evening, Chaplain."

David, taken aback at first, smiled. "As I was saying, fellows, the topic for this month's lec—"

"Chaplain, oh Chaplain . . ." Sergeant Shuster, somewhere to the right, was calling.

David turned in the direction of the voice. "Later, Sergeant, later," he whispered. "I've begun the lecture."

Sergeant Shuster stepped out of the kitchen and came toward him. "I just found this letter," he explained, "and it looks important. So I thought you'd want to return it to its owner, now that you have everyone here."

There was little that David could do except exercise self-control because, as luck would have it, that was the topic of his lecture for that evening. "All right, Sergeant. Who does the letter belong to?"

"Well, there's no name on it," Sergeant Shuster said, "but I can read the first few lines, and the owner will recognize it." And without waiting for a reply, he opened the envelope and took out the letter. "It starts: 'Dear Ilona'—"

"I don't think it's proper to read a personal letter aloud!" David exclaimed, blushing. Hurriedly he grabbed the letter and its envelope from the sergeant and began to stuff them into his pocket.

A singular thing happened then. The envelope *broke*. And from its open end seeped a thick yellow liquid that was unmistakably egg yolk. David uttered an oath and the audience burst into laughter.

All of a sudden the spotlight vanished, and all the lights in the dining room were turned on. They revealed to the startled David not airmen in white mess outfits but women in cocktail dresses, men in Class A uniforms or civilian dress, Chinese lanterns, streamers, decorations, signs, platters of food, and even a band. *"Surprise!"* everyone was shouting. *"Surprise!"*

David grinned sheepishly. "I—I—I—" he began, beholding the hundreds of smiling faces out front—all his friends, fellow chaplains, Rabbi Garfield, dozens of acquaintances, counselees, the men from the A.R.S. and their wives, Marge Winkler with her father, Colonel Kingsbury and his son sitting in the back beside a girl who reminded David, as had all slender dark girls for months now, of Ilona.

It was all so astonishing, so wonderful, that his eyes searched the crowd expectantly, wildly confident that Ilona was there also to share his joy and crown it with her presence. She *had* to be there.

Yet search as he did, eyes flitting from face to face without ever alighting on *the* face, he could find Ilona nowhere in the hall, any more than he could spot Alex Winkler there. And at last he was forced to admit to himself that she was not nearby; nor would she ever be. As far as he was personally concerned, she was as dead, alas, as poor Alex. (Reconciliation between the *ought* and what *was* begins so painfully close to home!)

In his wallet he carried the proof: a brief note from Ilona finally acknowledging his score of letters and, though informing him that at last she had decided to come to the United States, carefully omitting mention even of the city where she would be living. He had read the letter a dozen times, vainly searching for some word of encouragement, then had torn it to bits. But in his wallet, between the snapshots of Ilona that he still carried, he had saved the pieces. (To himself he vowed now finally to dispose of them.)

David concluded, "I—I—I—"

The crowd laughed and applauded.

Mitchell materialized nearby, a smile lighting up the crannies of his face. "You see, David?" He pointed to the people out front. "You may never have had a *minyan* at Fairfield, but a *congregation* you do have here now."

David, shaking his head in wonder, looked out at the smiling faces before him. Thank God, he thought, at least no tightrope here in the Air Force between Jews and Christians, but an inviting thoroughfare for all those of mutual respect who sought entrance.

Mitchell addressed the crowd: "And this brings up the reason Chaplain Cohen gave for leaving us. He thinks he has to go all the way back to Jewish civilization to get himself a girl."

Wistfully David's eyes returned to the girl sitting beside Colonel Kingsbury. She did look something like Ilona although she was not nearly as beautiful.

Mitchell turned toward David. "Now a certain base commander here has decided to call your bluff, David. Aided and abetted by a chaplain from Goose Bay and a friend of yours named—"

Colonel Kingsbury pushed the dark girl beside him to her feet.

"Ilona!"

Prodded by Marge Winkler from behind, the girl came forward slowly, embarrassed. David dropped his lecture notes and ran to meet her.

"I hope this does not give you the wrong idea," Ilona told him swiftly as they met in the aisle. "Lieutenant Winkler wrote me several times inviting me to this party—"

"Alex?"

"Then his wife wrote too after the tragedy, and Chaplain Allerton came to see me, and Colonel Kingsbury offered me a flight here and— To tell the truth, I *still* do not know what I am doing here!"

David grasped her hands in his. "Ilona!" was all he could say. "Ilona!"

"These chaplains know from nothing," someone yelled. "*Kiss* her!" The crowd roared its approval.

Ilona exclaimed, "Do not misunderstand, David. For us together there is nothing. You have a future—a happy one, I trust. But I only have a past, a haunted one. For us together there is—"

He broke in: "—there is *hope!* Jews have survived on little more than that for thousands of years. And as long as I can hope, Ilona, I ask nothing more—for now."

And then his friends were surrounding the two of them, pushing them together, smiling, laughing, joking, saying good-bye. And David—how could he bring himself to leave such beautiful people!—suddenly knew that the return trip to New York would be a far longer one than he had envisioned only two short years before.